# DEATH CRUISE

# DEATH CRUISE

## CRIME STORIES ON THE OPEN SEAS

## Edited by LAWRENCE BLOCK

CUMBERLAND HOUSE
NASHVILLE, TENNESSEE

Published by Cumberland House Publishing, Inc.
431 Harding Industrial Drive, Nashville, TN 37211.

Jacket/cover design by Gore Studio, Inc.
Text design by Lisa Taylor

ISBN 1-58182-0070-0

Printed in the United States of America

# THE INTERNATIONAL ASSOCIATION OF CRIME WRITERS PRESENTS:

# Welcome Aboard ...

**W**ell I can't claim to be an old sea dog. I tend to say *upstairs* and *downstairs* when I should be saying *above* and *below*, and I go to the *john* instead of the *head*. And when I read Patrick O'Brian's smashing sea tales of the Napoleonic wars, I rarely know what the hell he's talking about. I get swept up in the action, but I'm never entirely certain what's going on.

I've been on only two cruises. A dozen years ago my wife, Lynne, and I sailed to Bermuda and back on the *QE 2*. It was a brief voyage, just five days, and by the time we'd begun to adjust to the pitch of the deck and the easy pace of life aboard ship, there we were, back in New York and looking around for a taxi.

Then in the fall of 1996 we sailed on the SS *Nordlys*, one of a fleet of coastal steamers that take mail and cargo to the fjord ports along the jagged coast of Norway. It took us twelve days to make the round trip across the Arctic Circle to the Russian border at Kirkenes and back. We enjoyed every minute of it—well, I probably enjoyed the rough water around North Cape more than Lynne did—and I even managed to make the whole enterprise cost-effective. Spending mornings in the ship's library, surrounded by the collected works of Knut Hamsun, I handwrote the short story "Keller on the Spot," which sold to *Playboy*, appears as a chapter in *Hit Man*, and has now been nominated for an Edgar Allan Poe award.

The story, I hasten to add, takes place on dry land—old *terra firma*. But Keller does jump into a swimming pool, so perhaps the aquatic environment was not entirely without influence.

But enough about me. (More than enough, I'd say.) Let's consider the book you've had the good sense to buy (or, for all I know, the bad manners to steal): *Death Cruise*. Could there be a better theme setting for crime stories than a ship on open seas? Step onto any vessel—even the Staten Island ferry or a garbage scow—and there's an aura of romance, of adventure, of mystery. You're no longer on dry land. Once you weigh anchor—whatever that means—you're under way.

The excellent stories contained herein—and they are indeed excellent stories, as you shall shortly find out for yourselves—are the works of members of the International Association of Crime Writers, and a few words about AIEP might not be out of place, either. (The acronym is for Asociación Internacional de Escritores Policiacos, the organizations designation in Spanish. AIEP is what the name implies, a global fraternity of mystery writers. Organized before the collapse of the Iron Curtain, it brought together writers on both sides of that rusty barricade.)

In some countries, where no crime writer's organization previously existed, it was the local AIEP branch that first united the nation's crime writers. In other countries, the existing national organization was incorporated en bloc into AIEP. And, in countries like the United States and the United Kingdom, where Mystery Writers of American and the Crime Writers Association were well established, AIEP has served a special role, with a small but ardent membership keenly committed to building bonds with fellow mystery writers around the world.

Under AIEP's auspices, members have gathered in Prague (Czech Republic), Gijón and Zaragoza (Spain), Varna (Bulgaria), Havana, Mérida (Mexico), and Vienna. I have met and become friends with dozens of writers from all over the world. I'm sure the travel and the interchange of ideas and experience have enriched my work. On a more mundane level, I've made foreign sales and availed myself of some promotional opportunities as a direct result of my AIEP experience.

One of the things that pleases me most about *Death Cruise* is the presence of some outstanding stories by writers who are almost certainly new to you because they are not published in the United States. It is a sore point with European and Latin American crime writers that so few of them appear in print here. This is beginning to change, but it's still indisputably true that while many English-language crime writers get translated into no end of foreign languages, it rarely happens the other way around.

We're missing a lot. We tend to think of crime fiction as a local invention, but in Norway I learned from Nils Nordberg of a Norwegian writer who wrote what was unmistakably a detective story, and did so some years before Poe. He got there first, and, according to Nils, acquitted himself quite creditably—but he wrote in Norwegian, was not translated, and consequently nobody's heard of him.

Here, for your reading pleasure, we've gathered stories from Belgium and Denmark and Cuba and the Netherlands. I think you'll enjoy them, and I think you'll begin to get an idea of how rich and varied is the worldwide realm of mystery fiction.

And, too, we've assembled some leading talents of American crime fiction, members of AIEP's North American branch who've found the notion of shipboard crime stories inspiring.

My own response to this collection may be instructive, or even cautionary. Shortly after I finished the happy task of reading the stories, I found myself poring over brochures, and just the other day I booked us onto a transpositional cruise of the *Star Flyer*. It's a genuine clipper ship, a modern sailing vessel that winters in the south seas and summers in the Mediterranean. Twice a year it has to get from one venue to the other, and we'll be on it for its return to the Med. We sail from Phuket, in Thailand, with stops in the Andaman Islands, Sri Lanka, India, Aden, and Egypt, a transit of the Suez Canal, then Rhodes and Mykonos and Athens. Thirty-five nights under sail . . .

Sound good? I hope I've whetted your appetites, if only to set sail on a reading of *Death Cruise*. "There is no frigate like a book," Emily Dickinson has assured us. Conversely, I suppose, there is no book like a frigate. In the absence of frigates, however, a book is surely the next best thing, and the cruise you're about to embark on promises to be a fine old trip.

Bon voyage!

Lawrence Block
Greenwich Village

# DEATH CRUISE

# Problem at Sea

### AGATHA CHRISTIE

"Colonel Clapperton!" said General Forbes. He said it with an effect midway between a snort and a sniff.

Miss Ellie Henderson leaned forward, a strand of her soft gray hair blowing across her face. Her eyes, dark and snapping, gleamed with a wicked pleasure.

"Such a *soldierly*-looking man!" she said with malicious intent, and smoothed back the lock of hair to await the result.

"Soldierly!" exploded General Forbes. He tugged at his military mustache and his face became bright red.

"In the Guards, wasn't he?" murmured Miss Henderson, completing her work.

"Guards? Guards? Pack of nonsense. Fellow was on the music hall stage! Fact! Joined up and was out in France counting tins of plum and apple. Huns dropped a stray bomb and he went home with a flesh wound in the arm. Somehow or other got into Lady Carrington's hospital."

"So that's how they met."

"Fact! Fellow played the wounded hero. Lady Carrington had no sense and oceans of money. Old Carrington had been in munitions. She'd been a widow only six months. This fellow snaps her up in no time. She wangled him a job at the War Office. *Colonel* Clapperton! Pah!" he snorted.

"And before the war he was on the music hall stage," mused Miss Henderson, trying to reconcile the distinguished gray-haired Colonel Clapperton with a red-nosed comedian singing mirth-provoking songs.

"Fact!" said General Forbes. "Heard it from old Bassington-ffrench. And he heard it from old Badger Cotterill who'd got it from Snooks Parker."

Miss Henderson nodded brightly. "That does seem to settle it!" she said.

A fleeting smile showed for a minute on the face of a small man sitting near them. Miss Henderson noticed the smile. She was observant. It had shown appreciation of the irony underlying her last remark—irony which the General never for a moment suspected.

The General himself did not notice the smiles. He glanced at his watch, rose and remarked: "Exercise. Got to keep oneself fit on a boat," and passed out through the open door onto the deck.

Miss Henderson glanced at the man who had smiled. It was a well-bred glance indicating that she was ready to enter into conversation with a fellow traveler.

"He is energetic—yes?" said the little man.

"He goes round the deck forty-eight times exactly," said Miss Henderson. "What an old gossip! And they say *we* are the scandal-loving sex."

"What an impoliteness!"

"Frenchmen are always polite," said Miss Henderson—there was the nuance of a question in her voice.

The little man responded promptly. "Belgian, Mademoiselle."

"Oh! Belgian."

"Hercule Poirot. At your service."

The name aroused some memory. Surely she had heard it before—? "Are you enjoying this trip, M. Poirot?"

"Frankly, no. It was an imbecility to allow myself to be persuaded to come. I detest *la mer*. Never does it remain tranquil—no, not for a little minute."

"Well, you admit it's quite calm now."

M. Poirot admitted this grudgingly. "À *ce moment*, yes. That is why I revive. I once more interest myself in what passes around me—your very adept handling of the General Forbes, for instance."

"You mean—" Miss Henderson paused.

Hercule Poirot bowed. "Your methods of extracting the scandalous matter. Admirable!"

Miss Henderson laughed in an unashamed manner. "That touch

about the Guards? I knew that would bring the old boy up spluttering and gasping." She leaned forward confidentially. "I admit I *like* scandal—the more ill-natured, the better!"

Poirot looked thoughtfully at her—her slim well-preserved figure, her keen dark eyes, her gray hair; a woman of forty-five who was content to look her age.

Ellie said abruptly: "I have it! Aren't you the great detective?"

Poirot bowed. "You are too amiable, Mademoiselle." But he made no disclaimer.

"How thrilling," said Miss Henderson. "Are you 'hot on the trail' as they say in books? Have we a criminal secretly in our midst? Or am I being indiscreet?"

"Not at all. Not at all. It pains me to disappoint your expectations, but I am simply here, like everyone else, to amuse myself."

He said it in such a gloomy voice that Miss Henderson laughed.

"Oh! Well, you will be able to get ashore tomorrow at Alexandria. You have been to Egypt before?"

"Never, Mademoiselle."

Miss Henderson rose somewhat abruptly.

"I think I shall join the General on his constitutional," she announced.

Poirot sprang politely to his feet.

She gave him a little nod and passed out onto the deck.

A faint puzzled look showed for a moment in Poirot's eyes, then, a little smile creasing his lips, he rose, put his head through the door and glanced down the deck. Miss Henderson was leaning against the rail talking to a tall, soldierly-looking man.

Poirot's smile deepened. He drew himself back into the smoking-room with the same exaggerated care with which a tortoise withdraws itself into its shell. For the moment he had the smoking-room to himself, though he rightly conjectured that that would not last long.

It did not. Mrs. Clapperton, her carefully waved platinum head protected with a net, her massaged and dieted form dressed in a smart sports suit, came through the door from the bar with the purposeful air of a woman who has always been able to pay top price for anything she needed.

She said: "John—? Oh! Good-morning, M. Poirot—have you seen John?"

"He's on the starboard deck, Madame. Shall I—?"

She arrested him with a gesture. "I'll sit here a minute." She sat down in a regal fashion in the chair opposite him. From the distance she had looked a possible twenty-eight. Now, in spite of her exquisitely made-up face, her delicately plucked eyebrows, she looked not her actual forty-nine years, but a possible fifty-five. Her eyes were a hard pale blue with tiny pupils.

"I was sorry not to have seen you at dinner last night," she said. "It was just a shade choppy, of course—"

"*Précisément*," said Poirot with feeling.

"Luckily, I am an excellent sailor," said Mrs. Clapperton. "I say luckily, because, with my weak heart, seasickness would probably be the death of me."

"You have the weak heart, Madame?"

"Yes, I have to be *most* careful. I must *not* overtire myself! All the specialists say so!" Mrs. Clapperton had embarked on the—to her—ever-fascinating topic of her health. "John, poor darling, wears himself out trying to prevent me from doing too much. I live so intensely, if you know what I mean, M. Poirot?"

"Yes, yes."

"He always says to me: 'Try to be more of a vegetable, Adeline.' But I can't. Life was meant to be *lived*, I feel. As a matter of fact I wore myself out as a girl in the war. My hospital—you've heard of my hospital? Of course I had nurses and matrons and all that—but *I* actually ran it." She sighed.

"Your vitality is marvelous, dear lady," said Poirot, with the slightly mechanical air of one responding to his cue.

Mrs. Clapperton gave a girlish laugh.

"Everyone tells me how young I am! It's absurd. I never try to pretend I'm a day less than forty-three," she continued with slightly mendacious candor, "but a lot of people find it hard to believe. 'You're so *alive*, Adeline,' they say to me. But really, M. Poirot, what would one *be* if one wasn't alive?"

"Dead," said Poirot.

Mrs. Clapperton frowned. The reply was not to her liking. The man, she decided, was trying to be funny. She got up and said coldly: "I must find John."

As she stepped through the door she dropped her handbag. It opened and the contents flew far and wide. Poirot rushed gallantly to the rescue. It was some few minutes before the lipsticks, vanity boxes, cigarette case and lighter and other odds and ends were collected. Mrs. Clapperton thanked him politely, then she swept down the deck and said, "John—"

Colonel Clapperton was still deep in conversation with Miss Henderson. He swung round and came quickly to meet his wife. He bent over her protectively. Her deck chair—was it in the right place? Wouldn't it be better—? His manner was courteous—full of gentle consideration. Clearly an adored wife spoilt by an adoring husband.

Miss Ellie Henderson looked out at the horizon as though something about it rather disgusted her.

Standing in the smoking-room door, Poirot looked on.

A hoarse quavering voice behind him said:

"I'd take a hatchet to that woman if I were her husband." The old gentleman known disrespectfully among the Younger Set on board as the Grandfather of All the Tea Planters had just shuffled in. "Boy!" he called. "Get me a whisky peg."

Poirot stooped to retrieve a torn scrap of notepaper, an overlooked item from the contents of Mrs. Clapperton's bag. Part of a prescription, he noted, containing digitalin. He put it in his pocket, meaning to restore it to Mrs. Clapperton later.

"Yes," went on the aged passenger. "Poisonous woman. I remember a woman like that in Poona. In '87 that was."

"Did anyone take a hatchet to her?" inquired Poirot.

The old gentleman shook his head sadly.

"Worried her husband into his grave within the year. Clapperton ought to assert himself. Gives his wife her head too much."

"She holds the purse strings," said Poirot gravely.

"Ha ha!" chuckled the old gentleman. "You've put the matter in a nutshell. Holds the purse strings. Ha ha!"

Two girls burst into the smoking-room. One had a round face with freckles and dark hair streaming out in a windswept confusion, the other had freckles and curly chestnut hair.

"A rescue—a rescue!" cried Kitty Mooney. "Pam and I are going to rescue Colonel Clapperton."

"From his wife," gasped Pamela Cregan.

"We think he's a *pet.* . . ."

"And she's just awful—she won't let him do *anything*," the two girls exclaimed.

"And if he isn't with her, he's usually grabbed by the Henderson woman. . . ."

"Who's quite nice. But terribly *old.* . . ."

They ran out, gasping in between giggles:

"A rescue—rescue . . ."

THAT THE RESCUE of Colonel Clapperton was no isolated sally, but a fixed project, was made clear that same evening when the eighteen-year-old Pam Cregan came up to Hercule Poirot, and murmured: "Watch us, M. Poirot. He's going to be cut out from under her nose and taken to walk in the moonlight on the boat deck."

It was just at that moment that Colonel Clapperton was saying: "I grant you the price of a Rolls Royce. But it's practically good for a lifetime. Now my car—"

"My car, I think, John." Mrs. Clapperton's voice was shrill and penetrating.

He showed no annoyance at her ungraciousness. Either he was used to it by this time, or else—

"Or else?" thought Poirot and let himself speculate.

"Certainly, my dear, *your* car," Clapperton bowed to his wife and finished what he had been saying, perfectly unruffled.

"*Voilà ce qu'on appelle le pukka sahib*," thought Poirot. "But the General Forbes says that Clapperton is no gentleman at all. I wonder now."

There was a suggestion of bridge. Mrs. Clapperton, General Forbes and a hawk-eyed couple sat down to it. Miss Henderson had excused herself and gone out on deck.

"What about your husband?" asked General Forbes, hesitating.

"John won't play," said Mrs. Clapperton. "Most tiresome of him."

The four bridge players began shuffling the cards.

Pam and Kitty advanced on Colonel Clapperton. Each one took an arm.

"You're coming with us!" said Pam. "To the boat deck. There's a moon."

"Don't be foolish, John," said Mrs. Clapperton. "You'll catch a chill."

"Not with us, he won't," said Kitty. "We're hot stuff!"

He went with them, laughing.

Poirot noticed that Mrs. Clapperton said No Bid to her initial bid of Two Clubs.

He strolled out onto the promenade deck. Miss Henderson was standing by the rail. She looked round expectantly as he came to stand beside her and he saw the drop in her expression.

They chatted for a while. Then presently as he fell silent she asked: "What are you thinking about?"

Poirot replied: "I am wondering about my knowledge of English. Mrs. Clapperton said: 'John won't play bridge.' Is not 'can't play' the usual term?"

"She takes it as a personal insult that he doesn't, I suppose," said Ellie drily. "The man was a fool ever to have married her."

In the darkness Poirot smiled. "You don't think it's just possible that the marriage may be a success?" he asked diffidently.

"With a woman like that?"

Poirot shrugged his shoulders. "Many odious women have devoted husbands. An enigma of Nature. You will admit that nothing she says or does appears to gall him."

Miss Henderson was considering her reply when Mrs. Clapperton's voice floated out through the smoking-room window.

"No—I don't think I will play another rubber. So stuffy. I think I'll go up and get some air on the boat deck."

"Good-night," said Miss Henderson. "I'm going to bed." She disappeared abruptly.

Poirot strolled forward to the lounge—deserted save for Colonel Clapperton and the two girls. He was doing card tricks for them, and noting the dexterity of his shuffling and handling of the cards, Poirot remembered the General's story of a career on the music hall stage.

"I see you enjoy the cards even though you do not play bridge," he remarked.

"I've my reasons for not playing bridge," said Clapperton, his charming smile breaking out. "I'll show you. We'll play one hand."

He dealt the cards rapidly. "Pick up your hands. Well, what about it?" He laughed at the bewildered expression on Kitty's face. He laid down his hand and the others followed suit. Kitty held the entire club suit, M. Poirot the hearts, Pam the diamonds and Colonel Clapperton the spades.

"You see?" he said. "A man who can deal his partner and his adversaries any hand he pleases had better stand aloof from a friendly game! If the luck goes too much his way, ill-natured things might be said."

"Oh!" gasped Kitty. "How *could* you do that? It all looked perfectly ordinary."

"The quickness of the hand deceives the eye," said Poirot sententiously—and caught the sudden change in the Colonel's expression.

It was as though he realized that he had been off his guard for a moment or two.

Poirot smiled. The conjuror had shown himself through the mask of the *pukka sahib*.

THE SHIP REACHED Alexandria at dawn the following morning.

As Poirot came up from breakfast he found the two girls all ready to go on shore. They were talking to Colonel Clapperton.

"We ought to get off now," urged Kitty. "The passport people will be going off the ship presently. You'll come with us, won't you? You wouldn't let us go ashore all by ourselves? Awful things might happen to us."

"I certainly don't think you ought to go by yourselves," said Clapperton, smiling. "But I'm not sure my wife feels up to it."

"That's too bad," said Pam. "But she can have a nice long rest."

Colonel Clapperton looked a little irresolute. Evidently the desire to play truant was strong upon him. He noticed Poirot.

"Hullo, M. Poirot—you going ashore?"

"No, I think not," M. Poirot replied.

"I'll—I'll—just have a word with Adeline," decided Colonel Clapperton.

"We'll come with you," said Pam. She flashed a wink at Poirot. "Perhaps we can persuade her to come too," she added gravely.

Colonel Clapperton seemed to welcome this suggestion. He looked decidedly relieved.

"Come along then, the pair of you," he said lightly. They all three went along the passage of B deck together.

Poirot, whose cabin was just opposite the Clappertons', followed them out of curiosity.

Colonel Clapperton rapped a little nervously at the cabin door.

"Adeline, my dear, are you up?"

The sleepy voice of Mrs. Clapperton from within replied: "Oh, bother—what is it?"

"It's John. What about going ashore?"

"Certainly not." The voice was shrill and decisive. "I've had a very bad night. I shall stay in bed most of the day."

Pam nipped in quickly, "Oh, Mrs. Clapperton, I'm so sorry. We did so want you to come with us. Are you sure you're not up to it?"

"I'm quite certain." Mrs. Clapperton's voice sounded even shriller.

The Colonel was turning the door-handle without result.

"What is it, John? The door's locked. I don't want to be disturbed by the stewards."

"Sorry, my dear, sorry. Just wanted my Baedeker."

"Well, you can't have it," snapped Mrs. Clapperton. "I'm not going to get out of bed. Do go away, John, and let me have a little peace."

"Certainly, certainly, my dear." The Colonel backed away from the door. Pam and Kitty closed in on him.

"Let's start at once. Thank goodness your hat's on your head. Oh! gracious—your passport isn't in the cabin, is it?"

"As a matter of fact it's in my pocket—" began the Colonel.

Kitty squeezed his arm. "Glory be!" she exclaimed. "Now, come on."

Leaning over the rail, Poirot watched the three of them leave the ship. He heard a faint intake of breath beside him and turned his head to see Miss Henderson. Her eyes were fastened on the three retreating figures.

"So they've gone ashore," she said flatly.

"Yes. Are you going?"

She had a shade hat, he noticed, and a smart bag and shoes. There was a shore-going appearance about her. Nevertheless, after the most infinitesimal of pauses, she shook her head.

"No," she said. "I think I'll stay on board. I have a lot of letters to write."

She turned and left him.

Puffing after his morning tour of forty-eight rounds of the deck, General Forbes took her place. "Aha!" he exclaimed as his eyes noted the retreating figures of the Colonel and the two girls. "So *that's* the game! Where's the Madam?"

Poirot explained that Mrs. Clapperton was having a quiet day in bed.

"Don't you believe it!" The old warrior closed one knowing eye.

"She'll be up for tiffin—and if the poor devil's found to be absent without leave, there'll be ructions."

But the General's prognostications were not fulfilled. Mrs. Clapperton did not appear at lunch and by the time the Colonel and his attendant damsels returned to the ship at four o'clock, she had not shown herself.

Poirot was in his cabin and heard the husband's slightly guilty knock on his cabin door. Heard the knock repeated, the cabin door tried, and finally heard the Colonel's call to a steward.

"Look here, I can't get an answer. Have you a key?"

Poirot rose quickly from his bunk and came out into the passage.

THE NEWS WENT like wildfire round the ship. With horrified incredulity people heard that Mrs. Clapperton had been found dead in her bunk—a native dagger driven through her heart. A string of amber beads was found on the floor of her cabin.

Rumor succeeded rumor. All bead sellers who had been allowed on board that day were being rounded up and questioned! A large sum in cash had disappeared from a drawer in the cabin! The notes had been traced! They had not been traced! Jewelry worth a fortune had been taken! No jewelry had been taken at all! A steward had been arrested and had confessed to the murder!

"What is the truth of it all?" demanded Miss Ellie Henderson, waylaying Poirot. Her face was pale and troubled.

"My dear lady, how should I know?"

"Of course you know," said Miss Henderson.

It was late in the evening. Most people had retired to their cabins. Miss Henderson led Poirot to a couple of deck chairs on the sheltered side of the ship. "Now tell me," she commanded.

Poirot surveyed her thoughtfully. "It's an interesting case," he said.

"Is it true that she had some very valuable jewelry stolen?"

Poirot shook his head. "No. No jewelry was taken. A small amount of loose cash that was in a drawer has disappeared, though."

"I'll never feel safe on a ship again," said Miss Henderson with a shiver. "Any clue as to which of those coffee-colored brutes did it?"

"No," said Hercule Poirot. "The whole thing is rather—strange."

"What do you mean?" asked Ellie sharply.

Poirot spread out his hands. "*Eh bien*—take the facts. Mrs. Clapperton had been dead at least five hours when she was found. Some money had disappeared. A string of beads was on the floor by her bed. The door was locked and the key was missing. The window—*window*, not port-hole—gives on the deck and was open."

"Well?" asked the woman impatiently.

"Do you not think it is curious for a murder to be committed under those particular circumstances? Remember that the postcard sellers, money changers and bead sellers who are allowed on board are all well known to the police."

"The stewards usually lock your cabin, all the same," Ellie pointed out.

"Yes, to prevent any chance of petty pilfering. But this—was murder."

"What exactly are you thinking of, M. Poirot?" Her voice sounded a little breathless.

"I am thinking of the *locked door*."

Miss Henderson considered this. "I don't see anything in that. The man left by the door, locked it and took the key with him so as to avoid having the murder discovered too soon. Quite intelligent of him, for it wasn't discovered until four o'clock in the afternoon."

"No, no, Mademoiselle, you don't appreciate the point I'm trying to make. I'm not worried as to how he got *out*, but as to how he got *in*."

"The window of course."

"*C'est possible*. But it would be a very narrow fit—and there were people passing up and down the deck all the time, remember."

"Then through the door," said Miss Henderson impatiently.

"But you forget, Mademoiselle. *Mrs. Clapperton had locked the door on the inside*. She had done so before Colonel Clapperton left the boat this morning. He actually tried it—so we *know* that is so."

"Nonsense. It probably stuck—or he didn't turn the handle properly."

"But it does not rest on his word. We actually heard *Mrs. Clapperton herself say so*."

"We?"

"Miss Mooney, Miss Cregan, Colonel Clapperton and myself."

Ellie Henderson tapped a neatly shod foot. She did not speak for a moment or two. Then she said in a slightly irritable tone:

"Well—what exactly do you deduce from that? If Mrs. Clapperton could lock the door she could unlock it too, I suppose."

"Precisely, precisely." Poirot turned a beaming face upon her. "And you see where that leads us. *Mrs. Clapperton unlocked the door and let the murderer in.* Now would she be likely to do that for a bead seller?"

Ellie objected: "She might not have known who it was. He may have knocked—she got up and opened the door—and he forced his way in and killed her."

Poirot shook his head. "*Au contraire.* She was lying peacefully in bed when she was stabbed."

Miss Henderson stared at him. "What's your idea?" she asked abruptly.

Poirot smiled. "Well, it looks, does it not, as though she *knew* the person she admitted. . . ."

"You mean," said Miss Henderson and her voice sounded a little harsh, "*that the murderer is a passenger on the ship?*"

Poirot nodded. "It seems indicated."

"And the string of beads left on the floor was a blind?"

"Precisely."

"The theft of the money also?"

"Exactly."

There was a pause, then Miss Henderson said slowly: "I thought Mrs. Clapperton a very unpleasant woman and I don't think anyone on board really liked her—but there wasn't anyone who had any reason to kill her."

"Except her husband, perhaps," said Poirot.

"You don't really think—" She stopped.

"It is the opinion of every person on this ship that Colonel Clapperton would have been quite justified in 'taking a hatchet to her.' That was, I think, the expression used."

Ellie Henderson looked at him—waiting.

"But I am bound to say," went on Poirot, "that I myself have not noted any signs of exasperation on the good Colonel's part. Also, what is more important, he had an alibi. He was with those two girls all day and did not return to the ship till four o'clock. By then, Mrs. Clapperton had been dead many hours."

There was another minute of silence. Ellie Henderson said softly: "But you still think—a passenger on the ship?"

Poirot bowed his head.

Ellie Henderson laughed suddenly—a reckless defiant laugh. "Your theory may be difficult to prove, M. Poirot. There are a good many passengers on this ship."

Poirot bowed to her. "I will use a phrase from one of your detective story writers. 'I have my methods, Watson.'"

The following evening, at dinner, every passenger found a typewritten slip by his plate requesting him to be in the main lounge at 8:30. When the company were assembled, the Captain stepped onto the raised platform where the orchestra usually played and addressed them.

"Ladies and Gentlemen, you all know of the tragedy which took place yesterday. I am sure you all wish to co-operate in bringing the perpetrator of that foul crime to justice." He paused and cleared his throat. "We have on board with us M. Hercule Poirot, who is probably known to you all as a man who has had wide experience in—er—such matters. I hope you will listen carefully to what he has to say."

It was at this minute that Colonel Clapperton, who had not been at dinner, came in and sat down next to General Forbes. He looked like a man bewildered by sorrow—not at all like a man conscious of great relief. Either he was a very good actor or else he had been genuinely fond of his disagreeable wife.

"M. Hercule Poirot," said the Captain and stepped down. Poirot took his place. He looked comically self-important as he beamed on his audience.

"*Messieurs, Mesdames,*" he began. "It is most kind of you to be so indulgent as to listen to me. M. *le Capitaine* has told you that I have had a certain experience in these matters. I have, it is true, a little idea of my own about how to get to the bottom of this particular case." He made a sign and a steward pushed forward and passed up to him a bulky, shapeless object wrapped in a sheet.

"What I am about to do may surprise you a little," Poirot warned them. "It may occur to you that I am eccentric, perhaps mad. Nevertheless I assure you that behind my madness there is—as you English say—a method."

His eyes met those of Miss Henderson for just a minute. He began unwrapping the bulky object.

"I have here, *Messieurs* and *Mesdames*, an important witness to the truth of who killed Mrs. Clapperton." With a deft hand he whisked away the last enveloping cloth, and the object it concealed was revealed—an almost life-sized wooden doll, dressed in a velvet suit and lace collar.

"Now, Arthur," said Poirot and his voice changed subtly—it was no longer foreign—it had instead a confident English, a slightly Cockney inflection. "Can you tell me—I repeat—can you tell me—anything at all about the death of Mrs. Clapperton?"

The doll's neck oscillated a little, its wooden lower jaw dropped and wavered and a shrill high-pitched woman's voice spoke:

*"What is it, John? The door's locked. I don't want to be disturbed by the stewards. . . ."*

There was a cry—an overturned chair—a man stood swaying, his hand to his throat—trying to speak—trying. . . . Then suddenly, his figure seemed to crumple up. He pitched headlong.

It was Colonel Clapperton.

POIROT AND THE ship's doctor rose from their knees by the prostrate figure.

"All over, I'm afraid. Heart," said the doctor briefly.

Poirot nodded. "The shock of having his trick seen through," he said.

He turned to General Forbes. "It was you, General, who gave me a valuable hint with your mention of the music hall stage. I puzzle—I think—and then it comes to me. Supposing that before the war Clapperton was a *ventriloquist*. In that case, it would be perfectly possible for three people to hear Mrs. Clapperton speak from inside her cabin *when she was already dead. . . .*"

Ellie Henderson was beside him. Her eyes were dark and full of pain. "Did you know his heart was weak?" she asked.

"I guessed it. . . . Mrs. Clapperton talked of her own heart being affected, but she struck me as the type of woman who likes to be thought ill. Then I picked up a torn prescription with a very strong dose of digitalin in it. Digitalin is a heart medicine but it couldn't be Mrs. Clapperton's because digitalin dilates the pupils of the eyes. I had never noticed such a phenomenon with her—but when I looked at his eyes I saw the signs at once."

Ellie murmured: "So you thought—it might end—this way?"

"The best way, don't you think, Mademoiselle?" he said gently.

He saw the tears rise in her eyes. She said: "You've known. You've known all along. . . . That I cared. . . . But he didn't do it for *me*. . . . It was those girls—youth—it made him feel his slavery. He wanted to be free before it was too late. . . . Yes, I'm sure that's how it was. . . . When did you guess—that it was he?"

"His self-control was too perfect," said Poirot simply. "No matter how galling his wife's conduct, it never seemed to touch him. That meant either that he was so used to it that it no longer stung him, or else—*eh bien*—I decided on the latter alternative. . . . And I was right. . . .

"And then there was his insistence on his conjuring ability—the evening before the crime. He pretended to give himself away. But a man like Clapperton doesn't give himself away. There must be a reason. So long as people thought he had been a *conjuror* they weren't likely to think of his having been a *ventriloquist*."

"And the voice we heard—Mrs. Clapperton's voice?"

"One of the stewardesses had a voice not unlike hers. I induced her to hide behind the stage and taught her the words to say."

"It was a trick—a cruel trick," cried out Ellie.

"I do not approve of murder," said Hercule Poirot.

# Nine Points for Murder

## NANCY PICKARD

Stewards who worked for the cruise line the longest were assigned to the luxury suites on the upper decks of the *American Princess*. Though they, themselves, bunked below the water line in crew quarters, these mature, experienced butlers to the rich and famous spent their work shifts in some of the most sumptuous surroundings in the world. It was, perhaps, only to be expected that some of them came to believe they belonged there, in the exalted realms of caviar and champagne, silk, sea views, and chaise lounges.

Robyn Kurth harbored no illusions about his place among the wealthy passengers whom he served on sun deck. They were rich; he was not. Many of them were famous; he was not. They were the employers; he was the employee. He was perfectly clear about those facts and he believed he did not resent or regret them. On the contrary, he believed that he would not willingly trade his own interesting and mostly satisfying life for any of their gilded, and often aimless, ones. It was an attitude—and a sincere one—which he was convinced was the secret which had always enabled him to serve them well, beginning with his apprentice days among the bargain cabins on deck five, on up through his past twenty years in the luxury suites. He did not wish to be one of them. Frankly, he didn't have a high enough opinion of them for that.

By now, Robyn thought he had seen everything.

And so, normally he would have been displeased but not shocked to walk into the middle of a domestic quarrel, even in the princess suite. What did shock him was the fact that it was this particular couple who had violently quarreled, that they did not appear to remember him, and that they had aged so dramatically from the last time they had been passengers on this ship.

Oddly, in spite of the other shocks to his psyche, the first one to register was: Did this mean he also had aged so visibly?

For the first time in his life, Robyn Kurth felt shaken by and acutely aware of the many years he had spent wringing other people's wet towels, cleaning up their morning-after messes, and plumping their deck pillows. And he asked himself a horrifying question: Whose life had he really lived for the past thirty years, theirs or his?

Numbly, like a well-programmed mechanical butler, he knelt on the plush blue carpet to sweep up the pieces of the costly crystal decanter the woman had thrown at her husband, missing him and hitting a wall. Robyn saw the spreading dark wine stain and automatically thought of the carpet cleaner he would need to ring up and of the $450 price of the burgundy she had destroyed.

For an awful moment, he felt it was his own blood spilled there, soaking into the wool pile.

"Are you all right?" the woman inquired, from behind him. She had the good grace, Robyn noted even in his distress, to sound embarrassed and solicitous. "I'm so sorry to trouble you." Her pleasant voice softened, and she added, as if to herself, "I'm an awful fool sometimes."

Robyn turned to smile politely, properly, self-effacingly, reassuringly up at her, and he responded from his repertoire of stock phrases. "It's quite all right, Madam. We'll have this patch of carpet cleaned or replaced before the day is out." He longed to say something quite different to her, but he saw that she was staring down at him with absolutely no sign of prior recognition. For all she appeared to care, Robyn thought, he might as well have been the generic servant she obviously considered him to be. He also saw that she was too tactful to say what they both knew: Considering the king's ransom the couple was paying for the privilege of traveling in one of the world's most luxurious and famous "cabins," the cruise line could damned well afford to replace a foot-square patch of stained carpet, and a whole wine cellar of French burgundy, to boot.

She was silver-haired, considerably older than Robyn, and quite beautiful in an elderly way. He wondered what could possibly have caused a woman of such natural dignity to behave in such a manner as to launch a decanter at her husband, like a fishwife throwing cod. And yet, he also knew there had been at least one other time in this handsome woman's long life when she had behaved in a way which belied the appearance she presented to the world. Robyn didn't look at her husband, who had remained silent so far, but he thought, *What did you say to her?* He had expected these two elegant, successful people to be happy together; it was unnerving to discover that apparently they were not; at least, not always.

It was painfully obvious to Robyn that neither of them remembered him. He knew that should have been reassuring to him, in a way, but instead, he found it deeply disturbing. As he picked up the tiniest slivers with his bare fingers, he wondered, with a kind of sudden and frantic anxiety: How could they forget him, who remembered them so well, and who had changed their lives completely for them?

By the time he was ready to leave their suite, his white gloves back on his hands, the telltale broken slivers tucked into the covered dustpan, he had to fight back a terrible urge to tell them his name again, as if he were a callow waiter in a cheap restaurant: *Hi, my name is Robyn, and I'll be your steward this trip.*

Instead, he shut the door with perfect quiet behind him, realizing they had hardly known he was there, much less that he had gone.

"WHAT'S HE LIKE?" the young stewardess whispered to Robyn back in the pantry. "Is he nice? I just love his books, especially that first one. It was so sad! I just can't believe he's actually here again! Did he say anything to you? Is his wife nice?"

He silenced her with a repressive glance.

"Never gossip about your passengers," he advised her, coldly, "not if you want to stay in service on this deck."

Thus rebuked, she reddened and ducked her head and went back to pouring out careful jiggers of whiskey, although now with trembling hands. She was helping out during the crush of launch parties, as their ship, with its full complement of 2,000 passengers and 1,000 crew, pulled away from the harbor in New York City. (Far below the sun deck pantry, nine diesel engines drove 42-ton propellers smoothly toward the ship's running speed of 28.5 knots. The 70-ton cruise liner would take six days to reach Southampton, England.) "I beg your pardon," she muttered, adding other syllables under her breath, of which he caught the intent, if not the actual words.

He wasn't popular with the crew, he knew, and had never been or tried to be. But he was popular with the most demanding passengers, for which fact the cruise line administration held him in lucratively high esteem.

He had been strikingly handsome in his youth; the girls had not liked him, but they had eagerly loved him. Now he couldn't bed them on his looks alone; now, at fifty and a bit too stout, he needed personality, warmth and charm, but those were skills he had never cultivated. His passengers had not required them. Other top stewards might succeed with the gift of an Irish lilt or a cunning smile, but his passengers had been satisfied by that which he could well offer them: the appearance of respect, impeccable service, his good looks, intelligence, and perfect discretion. "Charm would gild your lily," a woman had once told him, laughingly. She'd been naked at the time. "If you were sweet and nice on top of being gorgeous, no one could stand you! Oh, yes, do that again!"

It was much the same with men, he'd found.

As he gazed at the stiffened neck of the young stewardess whom he had offended, Robyn thought, "Once, I could have been rude to you and the next minute you might have kissed me anyway." Now, he would have to struggle even to get her to cooperate in the cocktail service.

It was the second unwelcome reminder of age in less than an hour's time. And in another hour, when she was back on her regularly assigned deck, this girl would forget him, too.

"Aren't you going to take them, Mr. Kurth?"

"What?"

She was holding out a tray of drinks and staring at him, her hurt and resentment still pulling down the corners of her mouth.

"You didn't put napkins on the tray," he pointed out.

When she turned around angrily to rectify her oversight, Robyn suddenly, urgently required fresh air. Before leaving, he said, "Don't ever wear that much perfume when you come up to serve on this deck."

"You don't like it?" she asked, boldly.

"The passengers don't like it," he corrected her. "I couldn't care less. You could wear sewer gas for all I care."

He fled to a door and then to an outside railing where he could breath the cold, salty November air while the skyline of New York City grew smaller. After so many years at sea, he now took for granted the receding raised arm of the Statue of Liberty; he didn't even see the twin towers of the World Trade Center shrinking to bumps on the horizon and then to nothing. The smaller boats that accompanied the *Princess* out to sea were as invisible and inconsequential to him as minnows trailing in the wake of the great ship.

"You've got to get yourself in hand," he commanded himself. "Forget them. Forget her. Forget all of them."

*Just as they had forgotten him.*

That thought made him feel so ill, he was afraid he might actually retch over the railing, like some over-excited passenger who had never sailed before.

FORGET THEM, he instructed himself.

But he found that he couldn't let go of it.

Upon entering the princess suite the next morning, pushing their room service order on a rolling table in front of him, Robyn broke his own cardinal law: Never speak to a passenger unless spoken to, except for the formulaic phrases such as, "Will that be all, Sir?" and "Do you wish to have the beds turned down, Madam?"

But on this first morning at sea, after removing the domed silver covers from the two plates of eggs Benedict, Robyn stood to one side and said to the husband, "I hope you will forgive me for saying so, sir, but may I congratulate you on your great success in the publishing world."

The elderly man looked startled, then he frowned, but replied mildly enough. "Why, thank you." When Robyn did not move or speak, the man seemed to feel some additional words were necessary. "I guess you know it all started here. On this boat. I suppose I have come a long way since then, haven't I?"

"Thirty years ago."

"What? Oh, you know that. I suppose everybody on board does, too. Well, I guess when a man's wife kills herself by jumping down a stairwell on a goddamned boat, and then the man makes a bloody fortune off of telling the story of it, well, I guess people will know about it."

As if he hadn't heard the man's bitter tirade, Robyn told a diplomatic lie. "I read the book."

"Did you." It was said with heavy irony. The man sighed. "You and seven million other voyeurs who made me the rich and happy man I am today."

In his starched white coat and white gloves, Robyn stiffened.

"More coffee, Mr. Wainright?"

"No. Yes. Hell!" Terence Wainright, author of more than twenty best-selling books, threw his napkin onto the carpet like a petulant child. "The dammed eggs are for Mrs. Wainright. I don't want them. I don't even want—" He broke off suddenly, as if he sensed that he had said too much. Wordlessly, he got up from the portable table, went into the bathroom and closed the door. Shortly, Robyn heard a toilet flushing, then water running.

He straightened the tray a bit, put the lids back on, and refolded the napkin. Then he, too, left silently, feeling even more disturbed than he had the day before.

Only when he was standing back in the pantry again did he recall that he had failed to put the eggs Benedict back into the warming section of the portable table.

Their eggs would get cold.

"It's not to be borne!" he whispered, feeling desperate as he clung to the edge of the pantry sink with the tips of his fingers.


THE FAMOUS AUTHOR, as the crew were calling Terence Wainright behind his back, was scheduled to give a reading in the ship's theater that afternoon. Breaking every rule pertaining to such things, Robyn removed his starched white jacket and his gloves, abandoned his pantry, and slipped into the darkened wings of the stage to observe the much-anticipated performance.

It was extraordinary really, everybody was saying, that this man whose first wife had actually committed suicide on this very ship was returning to the scene of that tragedy exactly thirty years later. Not only that, but he had come with his second wife and they were staying in a suite that was just a few feet down the corridor from where the first Mrs. Wainright had jumped to her horrible death. He had told that story movingly in My Lost

*Love*, in which he had laid out the brutal truth of his first wife's struggle with depression and alcoholism, and of the steadiness with which he had loved her, of his loneliness while married to her, and of the guilt he felt at having failed her. It had been the first real-life account of chronic depression—told decades before Prozac—and it had hit an international nerve. Robyn had never read it, knowing it to be merely a partial account of the whole truth.

"That book made his reputation," one of the ship's bakers had said in Robyn's hearing. "But his books aren't selling so well now. Do you think this is just a publicity stunt, to boost his sales?" It was true that the return of the renowned author to the ship had occasioned great publicity, with photographers and journalists pursuing him right up to the gangplank. Everyone assumed there were journalists aboard who were masquerading as regular passengers, in hopes of achieving an on-the-scene story of this bittersweet cruise.

The ship's doctor, who was known for having a macabre sense of humor, had said, "Maybe he's hoping this wife will kill herself, too." Everybody around him had snickered, although they acknowledged it was a terrible thing to say. The doctor had then turned to the aloof steward who was hovering on the edge of the conversation. "Mr. Kurth, were you here then? What really happened? Was it like the way he told it in his book?"

Robyn hadn't dignified that with a response.

He knew they all called him "Mr. Kurth" as a way of mocking him, but he knew it was tinged with respect and fear, too. He'd been there longer than any of them. He had pull with the management. He could get people fired, and had done so. He made bigger tips than any of them. They had more fun, but he wasn't interested in fun, only in efficiency and respect. By providing the former, he received the latter. Because they did not meet his standards of the former, he did not give them the latter. He didn't care what they thought of him, but he knew they did care about his opinion of them. A negative appraisal from "Mr. Kurth" could ruin a steward's or stewardess's career. There were times he had done it, just to test his own strength.

Now, from where he stood hidden in the wings of the theater, Robyn could see the Famous Author's back, as the man stood at a podium, center stage. He could see the rapt faces of the nearly 400 people in the audience, all of them turned up toward the stage, except for the face of the beautiful, silver-haired woman seated on the inner aisle on the front row: Wainright's second wife. Robyn remembered when her hair was abundantly long, full and dark, and when her lovely face was turned up in seductive laughter. He remembered when the shoulders of the man at the podium did not stoop, and when the hands that grasped the lectern were not knotted with arthritis.

The lights in the theater were dimmed by an unseen hand and a spotlight focused on the man at center stage.

Without any introduction or preamble, he began to read aloud into a microphone. Robyn, who had seen the movie, recognized the passage at once. It was from *My Lost Love*, the book which had, just as the ship's baker had said, made Wainright's reputation and his fortune.

*"It was the perfect place on the ship to kill oneself, without causing undue and prolonged concern to other people,"* Wainright read to the suddenly hushed auditorium. It was the first sentence of his most well-known paragraph, of all the thousands of paragraphs he had written in his long, best-selling and prize-winning career. *"One might accomplish a suicide by leaping from any deck into the ocean, but then there would be the fuss of going 'missing.' One's husband would endure a long agony of worry, the ship's staff and passengers might be inconvenienced by the ensuing futile search for one. The ship's captain might even command the huge, famous ocean liner to turn around and to steam back to the approximate co-ordinates at which one was last seen alive."*

He looked up from the pages of his book, and spoke directly to his audience.

"She really talked like that, my late wife, and she thought like that, too. The worse Maudie felt, the more English she got, with even her most casual conversation pinned to the fabric of our days with dainty 'ones.' One might. One thought. One must. One did, and one did not. She was the most exquisitely kind, most torturously thoughtful woman I've ever known."

Robyn saw the beautiful elderly woman in the front row raise her face slightly, enough for him to see her grimace at the phrase, "pinned to the fabric of our days." He didn't blame her. It sounded rehearsed, sentimental and what was worse, badly written.

Wainright began to read from his book again.

*"Thoughtful to the end, she must have weighed the relative rudeness of the bloody mess she would cause by splattering herself onto a surface five decks below, against the attenuated inconvenience of a search at sea."*

The Famous Author closed his brief reading to his hushed audience, by completing the passage. *"In the end, she chose to give me, her husband, merely the instant and confirmed shock of the news of her death, and to limit the staff involvement to those unlucky few who were assigned to clean up after her.*

*"There is a spectacular view from the top of the A-staircase on sun deck. It is without doubt the last beautiful thing my wife ever saw."*

After a moment of awed, respectful silence, there was a burst of applause in which his wife did not join. After giving the ovation a full opportunity to swell, and before it entirely faded away, he spoke directly to his audience again.

"That was thirty years ago this week. It has taken me this long to get up the courage to come onto this ship and to make the very same voyage again. And, irony of ironies, when she and I traveled on this ship thirty years ago, we bunked down at the bottom, in the cheap beds, an inside cabin. She jumped to her death from the luxury deck, where my second wife and I are staying on this trip, thanks to the fortune I made off her suicide."

More than one person in the audience gasped at his frankness.

With a dramatically extended right arm and forefinger, he pointed up to the balcony. "Up there, on sun deck, that's where she jumped from the top of staircase A, which is right down the corridor from where we will be sleeping tonight."

The audience stirred; what was he trying to do?

Wainright bowed his head, folded the book to his vested chest, and walked off the stage without taking any questions. He'd left the impression of a melodramatic, haunted and guilty man, in a presentation that was notable not only for its brevity, but also for the glaring omission of any courteous mention of his wife of nearly thirty years who had sat frozen on the front row throughout. There'd been no credit given her, no mention of her help and succor in his time of sorrow, no testimony to her role in his recovery from grief, or any mention of a happy life with her afterward.

*Ungrateful bastard*, thought Robyn, as the great man brushed past him, without any sign of recognition. When he looked out into the audience again, Mrs. Wainright was walking up the center aisle toward the exits, along with everyone else, as if she were nobody special. Robyn, who had not often experienced empathy, was sure he understood exactly how she felt.

ROBYN FELT PULLED toward A stairwell, to look again at where it had happened so many years ago. Unfortunately, it seemed most of the other 400 people who had heard Wainright's reading had the same idea, afterward. They were already lined up four deep at the railing by the time Robyn looked out, after slipping back into his jacket and gloves in the pantry.

"Ghoulish," remarked a passing steward. "And them just two doors down the hall from it, too."

Robyn thought, *What did Wainright expect, if not this, after he had reminded everyone of exactly where it happened?*

Disgusted, Robyn hurried to make up for his time away from duty. It appeared that nobody had called for his services; no one had missed him. Instead of feeling relieved, he felt insulted and depressed. Earlier in the day, a journalist had attempted to bribe him to let the man into the Wainrights' suite while the couple was occupied elsewhere. Now Robyn felt tempted to go and find the man again, to take the money, and do it. But he valued his own position, and so he restrained himself, in spite of everything.

He'd had a fantasy about meeting the Wainrights again.

When at a staff pre-cruise meeting it had been announced they would be on board, he had felt a frisson of excitement go through him, and a fantasy had instantly begun to work its way into his imagination, until it seemed as real as a script from which they would all read when finally they met again.

The script of his fantasy said they would remember him, and that after a mutually graceful greeting, he would graciously explain to them how he had once, secretly and anonymously, assisted them. He even had proof, which he would show them, a piece of jewelry belonging to the dead woman. When they heard his story and saw the proof, at first they would be afraid, but then they would be deeply grateful that he had not attempted to extort money from them in exchange for his silence. They would fearfully, hesitantly, ask him why he was telling them now, and what he wanted from them. And he would, in a half-offended, completely dignified way, assure them he wanted nothing from them. And then they would give him what he did profoundly want and need: their humble appreciation.

In his fantasy, Mrs. Wainright cried in front of him, and her husband grabbed Robyn's hand and shook it in wordless, heartfelt respect. When he left their suite, Mrs. Wainright ran ahead of him to open the door for him, and to insist on giving him a kiss of gratitude.

There was more to his fantasy:

The gratuity they pressed on him in Southampton was enormous, but not so grossly overdone as to be construed as a payoff. They knew it was appreciation, not blackmail. He knew it, too. And for that reason alone—for the sake of their self-respect—he allowed himself to accept it. And never another word was spoken about it among them again, although they became annual passengers in the princess suite, and his most generous patrons and, eventually, they introduced him to other passengers as, "our old friend, our dearest friend, Rob."

For days, he had gone to sleep on that fantasy, awakened on that fantasy, and kept himself constant company with its telling.

But now, going off duty the second evening on board, he was afraid he was getting ill. He felt feverish, and he couldn't shake the idea that his fantasy was real, that it had come true, instead of being ridiculously dashed along with crystal against the wall. He considered going to see the ship's doctor, but knew the oaf would only ply him with sensationalist questions about Maude Wainright's suicide, and about Terence Wainright and his marriage to the second Mrs. Wainright.

Instead, Robyn medicated himself and went to bed, where he slept as if dead until his eyes flew open hours later.

He looked at his bedside clock: three a.m.

It was now the third day of the six-day voyage. On the evening of this day thirty years ago, he had seen one of his male, married passengers—a big, good-looking, struggling writer by the name of Terry Wainright—slip into the nearby cabin of another one of his passengers—a beautiful, effervescent, dark-haired single woman. They hadn't known they had been caught; he'd never told the secret of catching them together the night before Maude Wainright died, nor did he gossip about it after the book came out, a book without any mention of an adulterous shipboard romance which led to marriage.

Stimulated by the memory, and with other recollections crowding in on him, Robyn got up and got dressed in casual clothes. He made his way out of the crew quarters onto the first deck of passenger cabins, deck three, and down its long quiet nighttime corridor, past all the closed doors, to the bottom of A staircase. He climbed it, five decks to the top, to sun deck, his domain for twenty years, and the spot from where her body had tumbled five decks down to the floor of deck three.

Like the curious passengers before him, Robyn hung onto the railing and peered over the edge. It was dizzying, surely terrifying to someone afraid of heights. Even he, who had never suffered from vertigo, felt the uncanny pull that people talked about, the urge to go over, to fall, to fly, perhaps to die.

Robyn stood like that at the top of stairwell-A until the pantry door opened and a soft voice called down to him, "Mr. Kurth? Is that you? What are you doing up so early?"

Instead of answering, Robyn fled back down to his cabin, running down all the winding steps of the stairwell, circling the central vacuum through which her body had fallen like an anchor to the bottom.

HE USED TO relax by playing competitive games: Scrabble and bridge were his specialties. But he'd given up the card game years ago, because there were never at least two other crew members who played it seriously enough to play it well, much less at his level. As for the famous word game, Scrabble, which was a favorite with passengers, along with Trivial Pursuit (which Robyn had never played, having little memory for cultural trivia), the crew had long ago eliminated him as a player. He was too good, they complained, and he often did the impossible by forming seven-letter words, usually on top of double and triple word scores. He could only get the new employees to play with him, and they never lasted more than a few games. It was no fun to play with him. He never lost. A masseuse had once tossed the board in the air in a loser's fury, sending the letter "tiles" flying. Robyn had smiled and pointed to the accidental spellings which had landed face up on the floor: boy, advent, dog. "Or, god," he had remarked, "depending on where you're standing."

Serving the Wainrights the third day at sea was excruciating for Robyn. The weather being cold and gloomy, the passengers were cooped up together inside, and the crew along with them. Several times, the Wainrights called for service in their suite, and each time Robyn responded with an efficiency and rote courtesy that was increasingly difficult for him to maintain. The fact that neither of them appeared to have any idea who he was, the fact of his apparent invisibility to them, drove him from resentment to despair.

When he wheeled a tea service into the princess suite at three p.m., he felt close to bursting with things unsaid.

He found her alone in the sitting room, staring unhappily at a Scrabble board. It appeared that she had been playing the game with her husband, who had abandoned it before it was finished.

Without asking her permission, Robyn poured a cup of Oolong tea and took it to her.

"Oh, thank you."

She accepted it and set it on the game table.

"Cream or sugar?" he asked her, in the gentle, intimate tones of an old friend.

"No." Her voice caught on the word, and when she glanced up at him he saw that her beautiful eyes were brimming again. Maybe it was the effect of his tender question, perhaps it was due to her acute misery, but to his gratified surprise he heard her ask, "I don't suppose you'd like to sit down and finish this game with me?"

"I'd be delighted."

Robyn took the seat across from her and began to study the board. Right away, he saw that she was a more clever player than her husband, with a readier access to a more interesting vocabulary. Perhaps the Great Author had been bored by the game, but he had settled for the most simple and obvious of three- and four-letter words, wasting S's on words with the lowest of scores. Robyn noticed with a quickening of eagerness that her word choices depicted a state of mind: "Pain," she had spelled and crossed it with "enmity," a word he had never seen used in the game before. Still, he also spied at once her weakness: She had the vocabulary, but she lacked the patience to wait for the big kill of playing the words at positions on the board which ensured huge scores. She settled for single-letter word counts, when a better, more strategically-minded player would have endured the suspense of waiting for the chance at a triple word score.

He smiled as he pointed at the back of an envelope on which her husband had been keeping their scores. "You're way ahead. I'll have to climb out of a hole."

"He can't stand to lose."

"No?" Robyn asked, sympathetically.

She laughed bitterly, and Robyn suddenly realized she was drunk. "And he also can't stand to win."

"Difficult," Robyn said, as he laid out a word worth forty-five points, enough to catapult him into the lead with his first move.

"Years ago, he wanted to win me, and he did. And he wanted to become a best-seller, and he did, and he wanted to be rich, and now he is. But now our marriage is dead, and he can't stand that, even though he also can't stand me. And his sales are slipping, and he can't bear that, even though he'll always be famous and wealthy."

Robyn shook his head, and waited for her to play.

"If his first wife, the sainted Maudie, hadn't died, he would never have married me. Or had any of those other things he wanted so much."

Robyn flushed with the pleasure of hearing those words actually said, at last. The acknowledgment of his importance to their lives felt wonderful to him, and he basked in it. Finally, things were going according to the script of his fantasy!

"Now he blames me," she complained. "I'm supposed to feel guilty all the time, for everything. I'm supposed to feel guilty because she died, and because deep down inside he wanted her to, and because he got everything he ever wanted because of it. She has become the perfect woman, it was the perfect marriage, she was the perfect wife. This trip is all about rubbing my nose in it, as if she hadn't already been miserable before he met me, as if she wouldn't have killed herself anyway."

"She was no saint."

There was a moment of silence, before she reacted. "What?"

"The first Mrs. Wainright," he said, pleasantly, "she was no saint. He wasn't the only one playing around on this ship, you know." He had the proof in his pocket, on a gold chain.

She frowned, looking befuddled in a way that warmly amused him. Again, she said, "What?"

"She was coming around to my cabin before he went around to yours."

There! He'd said it, and now he could tell her the rest of it.

He reached toward his pocket, to show her.

Mrs. Wainright pushed back her chair and stood up. He fully understood the look of disgust and shock on her face; he had felt exactly the same way about pushy, drunk, weepy Maude, whom he had cruelly nick-named "Maudlin." He rushed to explain things more fully to the second Mrs. Wainright, in order to expiate her quite unnecessary sense of guilt.

"She wanted what she wanted, too," he told her. "When I got tired of her, which only took about two nights, believe me—" Robyn laughed. "She threatened to go to the captain and report me! Tell your husband that, and he won't be so likely to idolize her anymore."

"You have told him," she said, slowly.

Robyn turned around and saw that Terence Wainright had come out of the bedroom and was staring at him. For an instant, Robyn felt so relieved that his hand relaxed on the proof it held. He wouldn't even need to show it to them, because they would believe him without it. He was just as glad of that, since the proof in his hand did hint at a violence that might pain them. Perhaps he could spare them that, and save one secret for himself. Now the truth was coming out, and they would know how much they owed to him.

"Get out." Terence Wainright's voice sounded tight, choked. "If you want to see how fast somebody can report you to your captain, you watch me, you pompous, lying little shit. Get out of here, before I stuff that game down your fat throat."

Robyn looked toward Mrs. Wainwright for understanding and support, but she was staring at him as if he were a cockroach on the carpet.

He fled, without even having the chance to tell or show them the rest of it: how he had secured their golden lives for them by pushing Maude Wainright over the railing of A staircase thirty years ago, to protect his future and, inadvertently, theirs.

WHEN THE CAPTAIN sent for Robyn Kurth the next morning, the head steward for sun deck could not be found. Robyn, who hadn't given a damn how many other people he inconvenienced, had elected to fall unseen into the ocean in the middle of the night, rather than make a bloody spectacle of himself. He left no note, because there was no one to leave it to. Among his effects which went to charity there was a broken, golden chain-link necklace with the letter "M" upon it.

\* \* \*

THE STEWARD became a footnote to Terence Wainright's next book, *Ship of Ghosts*.

"*Fame lures the oddest creatures out of the darkness,*" the author wrote in his new best-seller. "*There are persons who would attach themselves to the dead, for strange purposes of their own. One of those was the steward on our cruise, a man who evidently so identified with my dead wife that he made the preposterous claim of a shipboard romance with her, and then a few hours later took his own life. He left behind a message of sorts, spelled out on a Scrabble board: "Cryptic," a triple word score, for forty-five points. Thus did one anonymous, unhappy man define his own death and my wife's, for surely there is nothing so little understood as suicide.*"

# Hodegetria

## JEREMIAH HEALY

The woman who had knocked on JOHN FRANCIS CUDDY, CONFIDENTIAL INVESTIGATIONS opened the pebbled-glass door and entered my office tentatively. "You are Mr. Cuddy?"

*An accent, Italian maybe.* "I am."

"My name is Carmen Viola. There was a telephone call made to you about me, yes?"

*Just after lunch, by an old friend from my days as an insurance investigator.* "I've been expecting you. Please, come in."

Viola was a slim five-three, walking toward me in conservative, two-inch heels. Thirtyish and pretty, she wore a black blazer and matching skirt, a leather attaché case hung from her right shoulder by a strap. Her dark hair was short, kind of a mushroom shape on top, nearly shaved around the ears and neck. Up close, her eyes were bright blue behind wire-rimmed glasses, and a slight pong of tobacco came off her clothes as we shook hands.

I said, "Take a seat."

Viola chose the left-hand client chair, turning her face slightly against the September sun streaming across the Boston Common and into the office from the window behind me.

Settled, she said, "My superior was met with your friend from a prior claim against one of our ships, but I do not know how much he tells you about our current situation."

I brought a legal pad and pen to the center of my desk. "Just that an employee had died under suspicious circumstances, and your cruise line felt it might need a Boston-based investigator for some reason."

"Some reason, yes." Viola looked as though she needed a cigarette.

I said, "If you'd like to smoke, I don't mind."

"Thank you. Truly, but I am trying not to use the cigarettes when I am in America. As practice for quitting them when I return home."

"And home is?"

"Italy. Rome. Our company is headquartered there, but of course the ships go here and everywhere."

Viola might mangle an idiom, but her voice was musical even if her manner was all business. "How can I help you?"

"One of our employees, Mr. Daniel Boyle, died on his ship, the *Star of Genoa*. You know of it?"

"No."

"The *Star* is in the middle of our fleet. Not too big, not too small, not too old, not too new. Mr. Boyle, age thirty-four years, was an entertainment specialist."

"Entertainment . . . ?"

" . . . Specialist, yes? The player of a piano in the lounge of our casino."

"I think I can picture that."

"Well, he embarked on this last cruise of the *Star* to the Caribbean. One day before its first stop in the islands, he is found dead. . . ." Viola swiped an index finger under both eyes.

"You knew Mr. Boyle?"

"I hear him play once, on a cruise I took with the ship for its inspection of the year."

"As part of your job?"

"Yes."

"Which is?"

"My job?"

I nodded.

Viola pursed her lips. "I was trained in the university as a lawyer, but I am used by our company as—how you say it, 'a troubleshootist?'"

"Shoot-*er*."

"Ah, thank you so much."

"And Mr. Boyle's death is the current trouble."

"Yes." Another swipe under the eyes. "I have seen the pictures of him dead on his bed. Not a good thing."

"What did he die from?"

"When he was found, next to him was a hypodermic needle. After the *Star* reaches its first port, there is an autopsy and analysis by laboratory of the needle holder." Viola paused. "Heroin."

"Mr. Boyle died of an overdose?"

"Of too much, too pure, yes. When his body is examined, the island doctor there found evidence of drug injection on the feet between the . . . ?"

Viola wiggled her fingers at me.

"Toes?" I said.

"Ah, of course. His toes."

I turned things over. "Long-term?"

"Long . . . ?"

"Had Mr. Boyle used drugs for a long time?"

"From the doctor's report, yes."

In Boston, heroin had gotten swept away by the avalanche of another white powder and its smokable alter-ego. But I'd heard horse was making a comeback against cocaine and crack in some circles. Even so, a long-term addict—especially one controlled enough to be regularly employed—ought to be pretty in tune with his dosage limits.

"Mr. Cuddy?"

"Sorry. Was your company aware of Mr. Boyle's condition?"

"That he was addict to the drug? No. We never hire him if we know, we fire him if we find out."

"And he would have known that was your policy."

"Our rule," Viola said firmly.

I gave it a beat. "I don't quite see why you need me."

She drew in a breath. "Because Mr. Boyle breaks our rule, my company must be sure now the problem is with him only. We do not wish to prosecute any person officially, but we do wish to know what happened so we can prevent the same thing in the future."

"And where do I come in?"

"Mr. Boyle when he is not on the ship lives here in Boston. The house of his mother in a neighborhood that is not so good. My superior thinks it better for me to work with an investigator who knows this city."

I focused on the dead man's name. "And maybe one that is Irish-American also?"

"I believe that was for my superior a consideration, yes."

*Direct, anyway.* After I quoted my retainer and fee schedule, Viola accepted it, taking a leather case from her attaché and writing a check I was pleased to see drawn on a Boston bank. "You have offices in the city as well?"

"Not as such, 'offices.' But the *Star* is sometime in port here for minor repairs, so it is helpful for our company to have a relationship with a local bank. In fact, I am seeing you today because the ship lies now at dock in your East Boston."

"And her crew?"

A brightness came into Viola's eyes. "So you can talk first with those who knew Mr. Boyle?"

"Yes."

"I have arranged them to be available."

As troubleshooters go, I thought Carmen Viola might do nicely.

"THE STAR OF GENOA," said Viola as she paid the cab driver who'd brought us to the waterfront in East Boston.

I'm not sure what the thing would look like next to a battleship, but standing dwarfed on the wharf, I thought of one. Painted white instead of gun-metal gray, though, with portholes like large pixels dotting her hull and the red "trim" halfway north turning out to be a deck level lined by lifeboats.

As we began walking toward the gangplank, I said, "How long is she?"

"Almost two hundred meters."

"And how tall?"

"The height of your Statue of Liberty less one floor."

Viola showed some kind of ID to a security guard near the base of the gangplank, then led me up a succession of metal treads like construction crews use to cover trenches in roads. At the top, a second guard admitted us onto a deck, deserted except for a dozen men and women in green maintenance jumpsuits.

I said, "Anybody entering or leaving the *Star* gets checked like that?"

"You mean by the guards?"

"Yes."

"We try always, but no system is perfect."

Viola opened a hatch door, and I thought we'd entered a tower branded with the name "Trump." A three-floored, escalatored atrium of brass and glass sporting see-through elevators and strategically placed observation balconies; not to mention arrowed signs or visible fixtures for a jewelry store, beauty salon, library, theater, ice cream parlor, tennis—

"So you will understand the investment our company has to protect, yes?"

I returned Viola's gaze. "Yes."

She pressed a button for one of the elevators. "Because it is his ship, we must see first the captain."

"GOOD DAY TO YOU. I'm Captain Sjeng Rippen. And you, sir?"

*That almost-German accent, but with a little hoot-owl on the vowels that I thought signified Dutch.*

Viola said, "May I present Mr. John Francis Cuddy, who will investigate for us the death of Daniel Boyle."

Rippen nodded gravely, shaking hands with fingers nearly half-again as long as mine. About an inch shorter than my six-two-plus, his fringe of hair and mustache were as white as his uniform, the latter with black epaulets and buttons on the short-sleeved tunic. The hair made judging age difficult, but I'd have said somewhere between fifty and sixty, with the body of a tri-athlete if the forearms were any indication of overall fitness.

After seating us in—appropriately—captain's chairs across from his chrome desk, Rippen looked once around the chart-walled and book-shelved room before focusing on me. "I must tell you, I never cared for this man."

"Mr. Boyle?"

"Yes. Oh, not for any offense, mind you. More the way he exploited his disability."

I turned to Viola. "Didn't you tell me the company was unaware of Mr. Boyle's addiction?"

Rippen answered for her. "Oh, I do not refer to that . . . poison, Mr. Cuddy. I mean the man's use of his cane."

"Mr. Boyle had an injury?"

"Indeed he did. And while I recognize that the days are long past when I could insist that only able-bodied seamen be among my crew, I still do not have affection for ones who take advantage of their circumstance."

I could sense more than see Viola cringe, both at "able-bodied" and I thought "seamen" as well. "How did the injury happen?"

"Not on my ship," said Rippen. "It was from his schoolboy days, the reason he took up the instrument in the first place."

"The piano."

"Or so he said, *frequently*. That's what I mean, Mr. Cuddy. The man traded on his infirmity instead of dismissing it and surmounting it."

A great vocabulary in an at-least second language for Rippen, but while the words might have impressed the V.I.P. passengers seated at his table for dinner, I wondered how well he was able to mask the arrogance behind them.

Viola said, "Captain, we would like for Mr. Cuddy to tour your ship and interview the crew who knew Mr. Boyle the best, yes?"

A coolness pervaded the room. "If that's what the company thinks appropriate."

"It was my superior's specific suggestion," replied Viola.

"Well, then, Carmen," said Rippen, a degree or two chillier despite addressing her by first name. "Since we're not at sea, I suppose that is what will happen. However, even in port, I am quite busy. May I suggest you start Mr. Cuddy with the room where our 'entertainment specialist' met his coward's end?"

"Not the easiest man to spend time with," I said.

"No, the captain is not that."

We'd reached what Viola had advised me was called "B deck." The shopping-mall spaciousness above had given way to dimensions more like those you'd see in a submarine movie. "This is the level where the crew is quartered?"

"Yes. The next door here was the berth of Mr. Daniel Boyle."

Viola produced a key and used it to open a metal hatchway that revealed a small stateroom with twin beds along each of the long walls. "Long" might be deceptive, as even those were only ten feet against the eight-foot width. Just room enough for a night table under a window—hibiscus-print curtains drawn—and a single lowboy bureau before the door to a closet-size bathroom.

"Cozy," I said.

"I am sorry?"

"Never mind. Mr. Boyle was found where?"

"The one there." Viola pointed to a bedspread in the same pattern as the curtains, but stained brown and yellow, probably from the release of Boyle's control muscles after death. "We have changed nothing. Except, of course, to take away the body and the hypodermic needle."

Even so, there wasn't much in the way of evidence that someone had lived in the room. I saw the cane Captain Rippen had mentioned, resting upright against the nightstand separating the two beds. It had the usual curved handle, a brass ring like a cigar band where the handle joined the shaft.

I pointed to the closed curtains. "Was that window open?"

"I would be surprised." Viola crossed to the night table, then pulled back the curtains to reveal just an additional expanse of wall. Smiling at me, she said, "This is an 'inside' stateroom. Our passengers who can afford more money prefer the 'outside' ones."

*Afford more . . .* "Meaning, some passengers might stay in the rooms on this deck?"

"In the season, yes, when the bookings are like so." Viola raised her palm above her head. "But in the hurricane time, we have discount specials for the better berths, so these lesser ones are not sold."

As I turned that over in my mind a color photo on the nightstand caught my eye. "In the high season, then, the crew often sleeps two to a room."

"I am sorry?" said Viola, more cautious than confused, I thought, as she let me slide past her.

"Sometimes two crew members must share the same room?"

"Ah, 'share.' Of course."

I picked up the photo, an old five-by-seven in a horizontal, Lucite frame. It showed a young, red-haired woman and a baby boy with even redder, curly hair, the tail-lights of a '63 Ford visible behind them. The infant was cradled in the crook of his mother's left arm, her right arm gesturing outward. The expression on the baby's face was serene, almost maturely resigned, but the woman's features were etched with worry as she seemed not to quite make eye contact with the lens.

Behind me, Viola said, "*Hodegetria.*"

I turned to her. "What did you say?"

"It is from the Greek, I believe. *Hodegetria* describes the pose and the . . . look the Byzantines showed in their painted icons of the Madonna and Child. We are to think that Mary and the tiny Jesus can see into the future, the suffering the Savior will endure for us all."

"Is this a photo of Mr. Boyle and his mother?"

*Cautious again.* "I assume so, yes."

*Not the best omen for him, as things turned out.* "May I go through the drawers?"

She canted her head, and I pointed to the night table and bureau.

"Ah, of course."

From top to bottom: underwear, socks, shirts, a Polaroid, Ace bandages, back issues of Playboy and Penthouse. Nothing unusual in the bathroom, either. Just a stall shower and wash basin next to the hopper, a Dopp kit with typical male toiletries in it.

I said, "How about the roommate?"

"The roommate?"

"Can I speak to the person who shared Mr. Boyle's room during the high season?"

"Ah, yes. I bring you to him."


"ARNE, THIS IS Mr. John Francis Cuddy. Please, you will answer any questions he has?"

I thought, Carmen Viola knows the crew on a first-name basis, then remembered she'd cruised once on her inspection trip.

As Viola moved off to one of the coral-colored barrel chairs in the empty cocktail lounge, Arne turned to me. He was in a tee-shirt and canvas shorts, standing on a stool as he held a clipboard near some liquor bottles on the secured shelves over the perimeter of the bar. Maybe five-eight when he hopped down off the stool, Arne had sandy hair, green eyes, and no facial hair, though his sideburns were worn a little long and flared toward the nose like miniature mutton chops.

"Mr. Cuddy," he said, extending a hand to shake. "I am Arne Nyquist."

*An engaging, sing-song accent.* "From Sweden?"

"Stockholm, before I choose the sea and the *Star of Genoa* choose me." *A practiced smile.*

"Doing inventory?"

He looked back at the clipboard. "Inventory, yah. We must be full up with liquor for our next cruise. Food we can run out. Liquor, never."

I nodded. "The company has asked me to look into the death of Daniel Boyle."

Nyquist's face fell. "Danny, Danny, Danny. 'Tragedy' is what you call it."

"How long had you known Mr. Boyle?"

"Almost two years? Yah, he come aboard with us three years after me."

"And you roomed with him during those two years?"

"In the high season, when we are full up with passengers. Danny is no trouble, however. He sleeps like the dead, and . . ."

Nyquist closed his eyes. "I did not—"

"Don't worry about it. But you shared the room he died in?"

"Yah, yah."

"Why did you move out?"

The eyes opened. "Why? Because in the low season, we are not so full up with passengers."

"Yes, but you were the more senior employee. Why didn't he move to another room while you stayed in that one?"

"Oh, yah. Yah, now I see you. It was his leg."

"Because he had a disability."

"Not so much 'disability.' But with the . . . with his leg, it was harder for him to move his stuff than me."

"So you moved instead."

"To have my own berth."

"When you roomed with Mr. Boyle, did you ever see him use any drugs?"

"No." Then a little louder, I thought to reach Viola in her chair. "No, against company rule. Never."

*A bit hard to swallow.* "You roomed with him. Saw him undress or come out of that shower, yet you never saw any track marks?"

"'Track marks?'"

I used myself as an example. "Marks of a needle, on his arms or his legs."

"No. No, never."

I motioned toward my shoes. "How about between his toes?"

"I not look at Danny's feet. Why would I?"

*A fair question.* "Tell me, when you moved to a different room, what did you do with your key to the shared room?"

"Do? I keep it." Nyquist dug into the front pocket of his shorts, came up with a ring of keys. "This one it is."

"Anyone else Mr. Boyle was . . . friendly with on board?"

Nyquist looked away, at first I thought toward Viola in the barrel chair. Then he pointed past her to the baby grand on a tiered stage. "Danny played the piano. Friendly with everybody."

"Anybody in particular?"

Nyquist came back to me, then stole a definite glance at Viola this time, lowering his voice to say, "Genna Drake."


"SHE IS ANOTHER specialist, in our Ship-Shape Spa."

"Your what?"

Carmen Viola led me toward a staircase, the sign next to it reading SPORTS DECK under an upward arrow. "The Spa is our exercise lounge on the *Star*."

We climbed to the next level, Viola showed me a glass-walled room maybe twenty-five feet square. It was crammed with Nautilus and Cybex exercise machines, some treadmills and StairMasters sprinkled in. Off to the side was a reception counter, a blonde woman with a gymnast's body stretching her neon-chartreuse Spandex sheath as she did toe-touches.

"Genna Drake," said Viola as we entered the room. "This is Mr. John Francis Cuddy."

Drake straightened, hands going to hips. "Can you spell that for me?"

*Midwestern inflection.* Approaching her, I said, "C-U-D-D-Y."

She huffed out a breath. "For some reason, I can remember names better when the person spells it."

Drake had a nice blush to her cheeks, with maybe a little more facial hair than she'd like creeping over them near her ears. The hands and arms gleamed with a sheen of perspiration that had already drenched the Spandex.

Plucking a hand towel from a stack of them on the counter, Drake began to mop her brow. "I'd ask you to sit, but there's no real comfortable machine."

"Genna," said Viola, "Mr. Cuddy is investigating for our company about the death of Mr. Daniel Boyle."

Drake blinked at her, then at me. "The poor piano guy?"

*Awfully casual.* "Somebody said you knew him pretty well."

Drake looked back to Viola, who said, "I must do a small errand. Mr. Cuddy, I will meet you here after fifteen minutes, yes?"

"Fine."

Drake waited for Viola to close the glass door on her way out. "Arne, right?"

"Arne?"

"Okay, you don't have to tell me. But if I were you, I'd have talked with Danny's roommate before the one he wanted to room with."

*Sharp lady.* "Mr. Boyle was interested in you romantically?"

A huffed laugh now. "Romance wasn't Danny's strong suit, believe me. Aside from that piano of his. You've heard the expression, 'He talked a good game'?"

"Yes."

"Well, Danny 'played' a good one." Drake seemed to go inside herself. "He could make the damned piano cry till it nearly broke your heart." Then she looked at me again. "But that was his only talent. The musician was fine, the man left a lot to be desired."

"How well did you two know each other?"

More mopping with the towel, up and down the arms. "You mean, how far did Danny get with me? Some hand-holding, a little ass-grabbing. I could have fended him off, but hey, with that leg he couldn't dance, so I figured, cut him some slack, right? Only thing, with Danny it was give him an inch, and he'd take a mile."

"So you never became . . . intimate?"

"No. No way." Now she used the towel on her neck and chest. "I worked hard for this body. I wasn't about to risk its future."

"I'm not sure I understand."

Drake tossed the towel into an open hamper behind the counter. "After a particularly good set he played in the lounge, I brought him a drink, and we ended up in his room. But Danny made the mistake of taking off his socks before he turned off the light."

"And . . . ?"

"And I saw the needle marks. The pig shot up down there with whatever it was made him happy."

"To your knowledge, did he use drugs with anyone else?"

"No. Never even talked about it, the way some will."

"Some?"

"Some druggies I've had the bad luck to hook up with."

I thought about what Arne Nyquist had told me. "The track marks on Mr. Boyle's feet. Visible enough for anybody to see?"

Genna Drake went inside herself again. "Well, with his leg and that pale Irish skin, he never hung around the pool, but if somebody saw him undressed, I suppose, yeah." She glanced at the clock over the counter. "Hey, I've got to shower, and I'd like to do it here instead of my room so I don't steam everything up."

"I'll wait for Ms. Viola outside."

A different look in Drake's eyes now. "Or you could wait for me?"

"Thanks, but no."

"How come?"

"I'm sort of spoken for."

Genna Drake huffed out a final breath. "These days, show me a good one who isn't."

I WAS ON THE other side of the Spa's glass wall for only a couple of minutes before Carmen Viola came up to me.

"Mr. Cuddy, I am sorry to be late."

"I was early."

"There is no other person on the *Star* I know for you to speak to."

"No problem. I think I'd like to try Mr. Boyle's Boston connection next."

"His 'connection'?"

"Do you have his mother's address?"

"Ah, of course." Viola dipped into her attaché case for a slip of paper. "Here it is. You would like me to come with you, yes?"

I looked down at the number and street. South Boston, where I'd grown up.

Which would let me make a little visit afterward.

"Mr. Cuddy?"

"I think I can find it on my own."

THE ADDRESS belonged to a single-family matchbox, the runt of the litter on a block of three-deckers off West Broadway. Even with the Massachusetts bottle-deposit law, the remains of quart-sized Bud and Schaefer beers lay in shards all over the sidewalk in front of the house. Its ocher paint was peeling like an onion; its cement stoop crumbling at the edges and corners. After ringing the doorbell three times, I got no answer to the bumble-bee buzz inside.

I went around to the side entrance. The screened door was closed, but the inner, wooden one stood ajar. I knocked on the aluminum jamb and heard a tired voice say, "It's open."

The doors gave onto an empty kitchen, the kitchen onto a small dining room and then a proportionately sized living room. Dust motes floated through stale air, the worn rug supporting a scarred coffee table centered before an old sofa against the wall.

A woman sat on the sofa. Or sagged on it.

She raised her eyes to me, but not her face. The eyes were veined, the cheeks and nose as well. Her reddish hair had sprigs of gray, no attempt at style that I could see. A house dress was as shapeless as the body it covered, the flesh puffy at wrists and elbows. Her mouth hung open, less like she wanted to speak and more that she couldn't quite muster the strength to shut it. You'd have to look very hard to see even the troubled young woman in the shot from the stateroom's nightstand. She held another photo in her lap, though, hands clutching the sides of the frame.

"Mrs. Boyle?"

The mouth stayed open, the lips flaccid. "Yes."

"Mrs. Boyle, my name is John Cuddy." I unfolded the leather identification holder, moving it to eye level for her. She glanced at my license, but not long enough to have read much of the printing on it.

I put the holder away. "I'm a private investigator."

No response.

"I've been asked to look into your son's death."

"Danny."

"Yes. Your son, Danny."

"My only child. First I lose his father to the drink, and now him to . . ."

Her face went back to the photo in her lap. This wasn't going to be easy.

"Mrs. Boyle, I'd like to ask you a few questions."

No response again.

"Could I maybe see Danny's room here?"

"Upstairs."

"Thank you."

"The one that isn't mine," said her mouth without using its lips.

THERE WERE ONLY two bedrooms on the second floor, and not much doubt which was whose. Danny Boyle hadn't taken down his boyhood posters of sports stars from the seventies: Havlicek shooting a jumper, Yaz looping a home-run swing, Esposito scooping a puck past an opposing goalie. Some trophies, apparently from musical competitions, decorated the top of the oak dresser, "Daniel X. Boyle" engraved on flaky bronze captions.

Thinking of the bureau on the ship, I started with Boyle's dresser. Top drawers of socks and underwear, though not much of either. Same quantities of shirts and sweaters in the next two. His bottom drawer functioned as a memento box, with more back issues of men's magazines, some old newspaper clippings, and three photo albums. I skimmed the clippings, mostly short articles paralleling and expanding upon the music trophies. Then I flipped through one of the photo albums, finding an empty space where I thought the "mother-and-child" shot might once have been mounted before going on board with the son depicted in it.

As I went to return the album, some loose Polaroids tumbled out the back. Gathering them up, I noticed the first showed an apparently surprised Asian woman, shying off from head-on while she pulled a bed sheet up to her chin. I caught the hibiscus print of the curtain in Boyle's stateroom behind her pillow, so I thumbed through the rest of the photos. The array included two white women and one black, all similar candids in the same setting, all anonymous until I reached number five.

Carmen Viola—her wire-rimmed glasses visible on a corner of the stateroom nightstand—apparently was not quite as quick with the sheet as the others.

Putting the album back in the bottom drawer, I pocketed the Polaroids.

"MRS. BOYLE?"

Same position on the sofa, and nearly the same posture, staring down at the photo in her lap. I moved over to where I could see it, too.

Another shot of her son, but an eight-by-ten head-and-shoulders portrait. Probably high school yearbook, given the shaggy hairstyle and the sepia texture of the print.

"Mrs. Boyle, I need to show you some other photographs, okay?"

"Others?"

"I need you to tell me if you recognize any of the people in them."

She looked up at me.

I shuffled the photos to make Viola's next to last, then cropped each with my fingers so only the face was visible. Holding up the Asian woman first, I said, "Do you know her?"

"Know her? No."

Same for the next two, and then Carmen Viola as well. When I showed Boyle the black woman, though, she said, "Colored."

"You recognize this one?"

"No, but they're what did Danny in."

I returned the photos to my pocket. "How do you mean?"

Boyle spoke to the yearbook portrait in her lap. "The liberals with their busing, they brought the colored."

Boston had barely survived a terrible time in the seventies over forced integration of its public schools. Black kids were bussed into Southie. Unapproving white parents not only protested but actually threw rocks and bottles at school bus windows as terrified children from other parts of the city supposedly rode toward a more equal education.

"My Danny never knew about drugs till then. And he swore to me that he never used them himself. Swore it on his father's grave."

I didn't say anything, hoping she'd just keep going, when Boyle looked back up. "Danny couldn't play sports because of his leg. Car accident when his father was . . ." Back to the portrait again. "During the busing, Danny got friendly with this colored football player. He's the one got my son started."

"Started on what?"

Boyle's face actually snapped up at me, impatience the first emotion crossing her features. "Smuggling the drugs on his ship, what do you think? If my Danny had never met that Tuggle boy, none of this would've happened."

She looked down at the photo of her son.

"Mrs. Boyle, do you know Mr. Tuggle's first name?"

"Of course I do. He had one of those names the colored give their kids. 'Vardell.' Vardell Tuggle. Danny would say, 'Ma, they're people, too.' But I knew better."

I couldn't see moving Boyle off her fixation, but she'd helped me, so. . . . "Do you have somebody checking on you?"

Her face stayed fixed on the photo. "What?"

"Is anybody coming to see you. A neighbor, a priest?"

"Just my son."

"Your son?"

Her eyes never left the frame in her lap. "My Danny. He visits with me every hour of every day."

I made sure the wooden side door closed and locked on my way out.

GIVEN IT'S a poor neighborhood, I think the cemetery people do a pretty fair job of maintaining appearances. The grass gets mowed regularly, and once a month somebody whacks the hard-to-reach weeds with one of those portable machines spinning stiff fishing line. But a little gardening can't do much to disguise a place you'd never mistake for any other. And it can't do anything for the freeze-thaw effect of Boston winters, reducing the lettering on a headstone while different forces of nature reduce what lies beneath.

Arriving at the granite reading ELIZABETH MARY DEVLIN CUDDY, I paused for a moment before speaking. "I picked up a tough one today, Beth."

*Tough how, John?*

I told her about Daniel Boyle. Then the people on his big ship, and the woman in her little house.

*So, what are you going to do?*

I looked off, down the slope and toward the twilit harbor. A couple of crows were playing keep-away with a much larger gull. The scrap of unidentifiable food would dangle from one black bird's mouth as the gull wheeled and dived. When the larger bird got too close, the carrying crow would drop its treasure, the other snatching the scrap up again before the gull could react.

*John?*

"Sorry, kid. Kind of winking out on you. Your question?"

*What are you going to do about the new case?*

"Wait till tomorrow, then make a call and pay a visit."

*To whom?*

I told her.

*John, I don't think that's such a good idea.*

"Frankly, neither do I."

*At least, be careful.*

I caught myself before offering the same advice back.


THE NEXT MORNING, my call went to a police detective in the Narcotics Unit who owed me a favor. His computer popped out several addresses, and I got lucky—in some sense of the word—with the first.

It was in the African-American neighborhood called Roxbury, on a main drag displaying a lot of plywood windows. Stencilled above the entrance in place of a street number were the words PRIVATE CLUB, a Boston euphemism for any place that could serve alcohol to its "members," a group that in turn would be loosely defined regardless of the dominant ethnicity of the men drinking there. Coming through the door, I was the only white I saw.

The room was humid despite the brisk fall air outside, some aftermath of liquor spilled making the atmosphere heavier than it had to be. The chairs and tables were mismatched, mostly cast-off dinette sets salvaged from alleys on trash day. All talk stopped the moment people looked up at me, a guy going six-five in a Chicago Bulls singlet and dungarees coming over right away.

He said, "Use your eyes over the door, you see 'Private Club.'"

"And I'm not a member."

"And ain't never gonna be."

"I'm looking for somebody who might sponsor me, though."

Almost a laugh. "Sponsor you for what?"

"Kind of a guest pass." I took out a twenty-dollar bill from my pants pocket. "Just for the day."

I hadn't exactly extended the bill, and the Bulls fan didn't exactly reach for it.

He said, "You smell like the Man, but don't no cop be flashing money at the get-go."

From one of the dinette tables, a man in his early thirties with good shoulders called over to us. "Dude buys me a round, he can sit for a while."

My tall greeter half turned to him. "Vardell, ain't you got enough whitey friends?"

The words that came back were just, "Man can't have too many friends, Kenneth," but the tone was, "step aside," and Kenneth did just that, shrugging in a face-saving way as he ambled loose-jointedly toward the makeshift bar on the other side of the room.

I walked toward the man who'd interceded for me. He ran somewhere over six feet himself, close to two-thirty with a developing beer belly. His hair was cut short, sharp furrows razored down to the scalp in a V-pattern. The green polo shirt had a teddy bear logo on the breast and a stain from dark tea or dried blood below that. The eyes were the color of chocolate, but the look in them made you wonder if all God's killer whales stayed in the sea.

I said, "What are you drinking?"

"Establishment don't serve but one kind." Light, bantering tone now. With a pump-sneakered foot, he pushed a chair away from the table for me. "Only somehow I get the feeling you ain't here to drink anyways."

I sat down, then laid the twenty on the table. "Still happy to stand treat, Mr. Tuggle."

He reached over, slid the twenty toward him under the middle finger of his right hand. "Way you dealt with Kenneth up there at the door, I figured you for the real thing. Hell, you just walk in here all by your lonesome, there got to be some cards in your hand besides that Southie accent of yours." The twenty slipped under the table, the bantering tone disappearing with it. "You know my last name, you come here for me. Why?"

"I've been hired to find out about Daniel Boyle."

"Danny Boy?"

"He died from an overdose of heroin. I'm not talking prosecution, not even a lawsuit. I just want to know what happened to him and why."

"What and why, huh?" Bantering again. "You find me before I hear somebody looking, that mean you got connections on the police. Private eye?"

I showed him my ID, and he nodded once.

As I put it away, he said, "Also means you know about my principal means of support."

"Probably, but enlighten me."

A little rumble noise from his chest that didn't make it past his teeth. "Now you sound like old Danny Boy. First day I met that carrothead—was during the busing time?"

"I'd moved on before that."

"Yeah, well, lots of folks in your neighborhood, they still there then. The shit we had to face . . ." Tuggle's eyes left me for a moment, a little fear flickering in them. Then he seemed to come back. "First time I met Danny was the first day we in that South Boston school. Nobody except a couple of the girls talk to us, but old Danny Boy, he read the newspapers, knew about me and the football."

"Which he couldn't play on account of his leg."

"Which his father fucked up for him in a car accident, drove his clunker straightways into a lightpole when he dead drunk behind the wheel. Well, I guess Danny figure he could use a bodyguard, even a homeboy nobody else'd hang with." The rumbling sound again. "Shit, Danny Boy was all right, but that momma of his? He actually apologize to me one day, account of he saw her throw this brick at my window in the school bus." The eyes went funny again. "Imagine that, the carrothead figure we tight enough he can actually admit his momma like to take my face off."

"You were friends with him."

"I suppose."

"So, what was the story?"

"The story?"

"About why Danny Boyle was shooting up on that ship."

The hard tone again. "Why the fuck should I tell you?"

"Because I've been hired to find out, and if you tell me, then maybe I won't have to ask a whole lot of other people the sort of questions that might bounce back on you."

Tuggle thought about it. "Cop-type people, you mean."

"Probably."

He looked casually around the room, as though checking to see if another guest had finally arrived for the party. Then Tuggle leaned forward in his chair, voice low. "My man, I hear from folks that what I'm about to tell got around, you be having to find yourself a new town. You know what I'm saying?"

I nodded once.

Tuggle stayed forward, voice still low. "Okay. Your connections on the police must of already told you about me and the smack."

*Heroin.* "Just a little."

"Well, they's kind of a 'boutique' market for the junk now, and I kind of fill it. Danny Boy, he know this, account of him and me talked about it over drinks one time he back in town off that big boat of his. Well, next time Danny on dry land, he want to know can I give him a little product."

"A piece of your action?"

"Right, right. So I say to the man, 'Shit, why you want to get into the smack for?' And he tell me, 'Vardell, you would not believe the coke and shit come north from Colombia, but the beauty is, the Customs people and all only watching for the nose candy coming north, not anything going south.' And Danny got some friends on the islands, they pay plenty for just an itty-bitty taste of the Old White Horse."

"So Mr. Boyle wanted you to give him some heroin to smuggle down there aboard the ship?"

"Yeah, yeah. Chump change for me, man. But to Danny Boy, it like twice his salary, you hear what I'm saying to you? And with that cane of his, ain't no real risk, neither."

"His cane?"

"What he use to hide the smack in. Danny hollow out the wood, then he take these little plastic bags, and he slide them down inside. That Danny Boy limp the product right past everybody, account of they know he play the piano on the boat."

I thought about it. "You know he was using, too?"

"Uh-uh. Man showed no signs of it. Besides, anybody dealing smack know better than to use it. Pretty soon, you shooting the money oughta be in your wallet up your arms instead."

"I was told Mr. Boyle injected between his toes."

Tuggle looked at me carefully. "Danny, he really shooting up regular?"

"According to the autopsy report."

A shake of the head. "Well, then, that explains it for you."

"How do you mean?"

Tuggle lowered his voice some more. "Say you dealing with these buyers in the islands, but you know they ain't real familiar with the product itself. So, before you give it to them, what you gonna do?"

"Step on the heroin a few times, make it go further."

"Right, right. And once the product down there, these customers step on it some more. Shit, they probably step on it so many times, you get a better hit from orange juice. But say these buyers, they ain't completely dumb, neither. So, before they give you the cash, what they gonna do?"

"Test the heroin somehow."

"Right on. So what Danny Boy told me he did, he keep this near-pure bag at the top of his cane, the first one in by the handle. That way, the island customers want to do a test, he give them that one."

"Bait and switch."

"Say what?"

"Show the buyers the pure, but sell them mostly the diluted stuff."

"Right, right. So, that's what must of happened on the boat."

"I don't get you."

"Listen what I'm saying to you." Tuggle slowed down, as though tutoring a poor student. "If Danny Boy on the shit like you telling me, can't be he was real heavy into it, account of I'da noticed the signs in him. So he just a dilly-tant, probably use the stepped-on product he selling on the way down there for his own recreation purposes. What happen must of been he got confused."

"Confused?"

"Yeah. Danny cook up some shit from the wrong bag—the pure one—and shoot it into himself."

It made more sense than anything else I'd been told. "Thanks for the . . . enlightenment."

Vardell Tuggle smiled, but the eyes were as hard as his earlier tone. "Just don't be expecting no more."


I'D ASKED FOR her at the gangplank. Five minutes later, she walked down it.

"You wish to come back on the *Star?*" said Carmen Viola.

"Yes."

She got me past both security guards. As we started toward the atrium elevators, I said, "Let's sit a minute first."

Adjusting her glasses, Viola looked at me oddly, but led the way to a cushioned bench like a hotel lobby might provide. We sat side by side, and I took out the Polaroids, showing them to her in the same order I'd shown Boyle's mother.

Viola didn't jump at the fourth one quite as much as I expected. "Why do you show me this thing?"

"I found these at Mr. Boyle's house. In his bedroom bureau. Why didn't you tell me you'd been intimate with him?"

She glared now. "It was not your business."

"That the company's troubleshooter and the man whose death she's hired me to—"

"It was the 'shipboard romance,' yes? Only the one time last year on my cruise to inspect. And I know before Danny Boyle takes this picture that I will not see him again."

"Why?"

A self-possessed shrug. "He was better at his piano than he was in his bed."

*Direct again.* "You were that close to him, yet you didn't realize Mr. Boyle was using drugs?"

"Never while I am with him."

"And the track marks on his feet?"

Another shrug. "I do not see them."

"His feet?"

"The marks." Viola removed her glasses. "Before the plastic lenses, these were very thick. I am nearsighted, I do not see things without my glasses unless they are close to me, like so." She held her palm six inches from her eyes. "And Danny Boyle's feet never so very close."

"How about his cane?"

Now just a confused look.


WE WERE INSIDE Boyle's stateroom, me unscrewing the handle of his cane at the brass cigar band. When the handle came off, I held the open ends up to the light, then turned both shaft and handle upside down before shaking them.

Nothing.

Viola said, "Why do you do this?"

"I have reason to believe Mr. Boyle smuggled heroin in the hollow of his cane."

"*Narcotraffico?* On the *Star of Genoa?*"

A *little disingenuous*, I thought. "You said when Mr. Boyle's body was found, the syringe was still there."

"Yes. He died from the overdose."

"Were there any bags or packages of drugs as well?"

"Not in the report."

"Whose report?"


GENNA DRAKE looked from Carmen Viola to me. "What's the big deal?"

"The big deal," I said, "is that you found Daniel Boyle dead."

She leaned her elbows on the Spa's counter near the hand towels. "I thought you already knew that when you came to see me yesterday."

"I didn't."

"Yeah, well, maybe you should have."

I found myself conceding Drake the point. "You told me then you wanted nothing more to do with Mr. Boyle."

"Nothing sexual. He could still play the piano, though."

Viola said, "You went to his stateroom to ask for him to play for you?"

"Not for me. I was off-shift, just sitting there in the casino bar, and Arne said, 'Hey, Genna, Danny's late. Can you go get him up here?'"

I waited for Drake to finish.

"And when I got down to B deck, the stateroom wasn't even locked, so I pushed in the door, and—yuck, was I glad I never slept with that jerk."

I didn't look at Carmen Viola, and she didn't look at me.


"THERE'S A REASON I asked Ms. Viola not to come up here with me."

Arne Nyquist busied himself rearranging glassware that looked fine where it had been. "Yah, and I should be interested?"

"Probably. You knew Daniel Boyle pretty well."

"Just because I share a room with—"

"Probably some sense of his . . . love life?"

Nyquist wouldn't meet my eyes. "Some."

"That he was fairly successful with women?"

A pause before another, "Some."

"Well, that says to me that you wouldn't send Genna Drake down to

Mr. Boyle's stateroom to check on him when he was a little late." I beckoned Nyquist closer across the bar top. "What I think you'd do is go down yourself, give your friend a break in case he was bedding the lady du jour."

Now Nyquist didn't know where to look. "All right. I go down there first, yah."

"And when Boyle didn't answer your knock, you used your key to open the stateroom door."

A nod.

"And found him."

Another nod. "It was . . . horrible. His face, and . . ." A violent shudder.

"But most important of all, you took away the heroin."

Nyquist decided it was time to look at me. "I see his cane open at the top, and I do not understand. Then I look inside, and shake out the . . . I do not know what the powder was. Just that it . . . must be drugs, and Danny . . ."

"And Danny what?"

"The company fires him for such if he is still alive, so I take the drugs and throw them into the sea."

I wasn't sure I bought that, but I said, "And you left the stateroom door unlocked, and then in the bar asked Ms. Drake to go down and 'get' Danny."

"Yah, yah. I did not know what else to do. Danny was always telling me about his mother, how hard the life is for her. . . ." Arne Nyquist ran out of steam. "I thought so much drugs lie there with his body, it can be worse for her. And maybe this way, the company pays her something, yah?"

It sounded so stupid, I found myself believing him.


I LEFT THE *Star of Genoa* and went back to my office. Looked across the Common at the gold dome of the State House. Watched the tourists flocking like swallows for our foliage season. And thought about how I'd spent my last two days.

The piano player, with his job and his friends, his cane and his smuggling. And, most of all, his death. Such a bizarre mistake for—

Then I thought of a question I hadn't asked. And though I wasn't sure I wanted the answer, I owed it to myself to find out for sure.

\* \* \*

THE SCREENED DOOR at the side of the house was still just clicked shut, but the inner, wooden one that I'd closed and locked remained that way. When knocking didn't work, I mentally devoted some of my fee from Carmen Viola's company to fixing any damage I might cause.

The third time I put my shoulder to the inner door, the lock cracked out of the jamb, and I was inside the kitchen. No lights, no sound. I moved very slowly to the dining room and through it into the living room beyond.

Mrs. Boyle was still in the same place on the sofa, but now the year-book photo was on the coffee table instead of her lap, as though she must have gotten up at some point since I'd left her. The room was mostly in shadows, some slats of half-light dimly striping her features.

I took a threadbare chair across from the sofa. "Mrs. Boyle, I'll pay for your door."

"My door?" Her mouth stayed open, the lips still not contributing much.

"When I was here yesterday, we talked about your son, remember?"

She spoke to the photo. "Danny's my only child."

"You told me. You also told me about how Vardell Tuggle got Danny involved with drugs."

"Colored. Colored did that to him."

*The question I hadn't asked.* "When your son talked with you about the drugs, did he describe how the deals were done down in the islands?"

Boyle looked at me now, the head swaying stolidly, like a cow watching a car go by on the road outside its pasture. "Danny thought he was so smart. He knew how to fool those people he sold the drugs to, fool them with that one pure bag he'd show them. 'My calling card, Ma,' he'd say to me."

"And you were afraid for him?"

"Afraid?" She looked back down at the photo of her son. "No, I wasn't afraid. I just didn't want my only child doing that colored thing there."

"I'm sorry?"

Back up to me again, but now with the impatience in her voice. "Selling drugs, the way the colored do." Then a softening. "But I was smart, too. Smarter than Danny. I figured out a way to get him out of it."

*Jesus.* "To get him out of dealing drugs?"

"Right. I waited till the day before he was going back to his ship again. When he was asleep—Danny was always a sound sleeper. Slept through the night from the time he was seven months old."

"Mrs. Boyle?"

"Yes?"

"The night before your son went back on the ship . . ."

". . . he'd already packed and everything. So, I went into his room upstairs, and I took that cane of his, with the colored drugs already in it. Then I opened the handle part and switched the first two bags around."

What Vardell Tuggle had suggested to me. "So the pure bag wasn't on top anymore."

A nod. "The people on the islands—Danny's customers, they wouldn't want to buy from him anymore." The head went back to her coffee table before a sigh like a skyscraper collapsing on itself. "Danny swore to me . . ."

"That he didn't use drugs himself."

"Swore on his father's grave." She reached down with her right hand, picked up the yearbook shot and cradled it, face out, in the crook of her other arm. "This is Danny. He's my only child."

Recalling Carmen Viola's explanation of *hodegetria*, I left Boyle on the sofa with her son.

# Under My Skin

CHRIS RIPPEN

After running eight laps around the jogging track he'd had enough. The narrow, dark green track was supposed to suggest that you were running on moss. But it was still just a ship's deck, tartan on wood. He could feel it in his muscles. Breathing hard, he leaned over the railing. His fitness level was never going to be any good anyway.

That dark mass in the Southeast, *could that be Corsica already?* It was only a quarter to seven, the sun hung low and red over the metal-colored sea. It was still too early, they wouldn't go ashore at Bonifacio until one o'clock. Below him a member of the crew was hosing down the promenade deck. The deck chairs were already back in their usual line-up, but it would be a while before anyone appeared on deck—the lively nightlife kept most of the passengers up pretty late. He was certainly not expecting to see Stella yet.

The time, when he had heard her come in behind the partition of their suite, had been three-thirty a.m. He had woken an hour and a half earlier, startled by an anxiety dream of which he could only remember that it had something to do with sunglasses. Afterwards he hadn't been able to go back to sleep and had picked up his book, as usual. He read volumes at night. Stella didn't. Shortly after midnight he had left her in the Piano Bar, where she had settled in for the night with the Jensens and the couple from Ghent. Nice people, even after three days of social talk, but he'd been exhausted from dancing and his head was throbbing with the music. Stella had looked at him for a minute, head cocked, a quizzical expression on her face, but she hadn't said anything. After all, *isn't that what they had agreed on?* She had set the terms herself: They would each go their own way. But then when he went to kiss her goodnight on the cheek, he'd suddenly felt her lips on his, full and warm; he'd almost sat back down.

Carrying his bathrobe he walked to the Jacuzzi, hoping to soothe his aching muscles. When he shifted the cover, the scalding steam took his breath away. Cautiously he lowered himself into the hot water, and when his body had acclimatized he opened the filter halfway. Air bubbled up from hidden places. Bubbles wriggled past his legs, tickled his scrotum, climbed up his back to his neck making him shiver almost nauseously. He slid down and closed his eyes. A decadent, pamper pool like this one fitted in perfectly with a cruise, he thought. An empty kind of luxury, which you surrendered to simply because it was there. Just like all those other entertainments on board. That it wasn't his idea of a vacation was the first thing he'd told Stella when returning her call, but he already knew he would have gone with her, even if she had wanted to go to Disneyland.

Resting his neck on the edge of the basin he floated on the columns of air. He felt his eyelids getting heavy. He didn't want to go to Corsica. Or rather, he didn't want to go on the obligatory outing that would accompany the stop—sauntering around the umpteenth little port town with its touristy ambience, all the while keeping one eye on his watch as they closed in on the departure time. Always the same. More galleries. But staying on board was an even less attractive prospect. The program booklet said *Ile de Beauté*, they'd listed all the cliches in italics, and just by chance this one was true. But how much of it could you see in five hours?

He remembered Bonifacio mainly as being high and hot, and if the shuttle busses were full they would have to walk, an hour there and back. *How many galleries could Stella do in four hours?*

There would, however, be one difference from previous days. He was sure that that man wouldn't be waiting for him anymore. Now that they had left the mainland behind, he no longer feared seeing the tinted glasses in unexpected places, turning away from him after a brief moment. The feeling of being spied on. Pursued.

Water was seeping into his mouth. He coughed and spat it out as he jerked into an upright position. He could fall asleep if he wasn't careful.

He'd read somewhere that people had drowned that way, in the tub. *Wouldn't that be ironic. Man drowns in hot tub at sea.*

Feet were pounding the jogging track behind him and he looked around. Two women in high-cut shiny suits ran past. He waited until they were out of sight and quickly grabbed his bathrobe. The water in the shower next to the gym was just cold enough to wash away the spongy feeling. While he was drying himself he saw the contours of mountains on the horizon, their misty flanks flecked with yellow. It was Corsica after all.

He wouldn't have to wake Stella for a while yet. It had occurred to him that, in contrast to the vast majority of the passengers, she always stayed below deck during arrival or departure. She had answered his passing remark on the subject with a provocative look.

"That's right, it's more enjoyable that way. I don't like all this hanging around. Any objections, Vincent?"

"Suit yourself, but it does mean we're always last to go ashore."

"Go ahead then, you really don't have to wait for me, you know."

But he always did, because he knew she was counting on it. He had come to the conclusion that she hated gradual changes and their accompanying rituals. Stella preferred to jump quickly and suddenly from one situation into the next. That was how she had disappeared from his life five years ago and that was how she had come back into it a month ago.

"Hi, Vince. We really should get together again and talk. What would you say to a Mediterranean cruise? I have an extra ticket," said the voice on his answering machine. It had been a change from her brief scribbles on the postcards she sent him from time to time. The woman friend she had booked a suite with had gotten sick and she had been looking for another traveling companion. He wouldn't have to contribute much to the fare.

At the door to the enclosed deck he turned and looked at the island where, in a few hours, they would go ashore. In the distance, the rocky coastline was interspersed with houses stacked on the hillsides. Behind them he saw angular high rises looking like flat-topped towers. *Ajaccio?* They were moving fast. In the cabin he listened at the partition, but didn't hear her yet. Even after he'd dropped his bottle of aftershave in the porcelain sink of their communal bathroom, the other half of the suite remained silent. *Time enough,* he thought.

The contractor's family from London they'd shared a taxi with in

Portofino was already having a noisy breakfast. He pretended not to see their inviting gesture to share their table and carried his tray to a table for one. That's what made a cruise so tiresome. After three days you knew just about every face and a kind of mandatory bond developed that made it virtually impossible to ignore people. You could hardly ever have a moment to yourself. In every port, at every stop, there they were. You exchanged greetings and smiles, you accepted drinks from each other, you heard the same stories over and over. It was a small world on a cruise ship. That's why, at first, he'd thought that the man with the tinted glasses had been one of the passengers, even though he had always been on his own.

The first time Vince had been aware of him was in San Remo, at a gallery, the third or fourth on their walk through the center of town. Stella had been having a conversation with the owner as usual, and Vince was staring at some prints by a local celebrity. Something made him look aside, a group of people that had been looking in at the window display moved away, which is why his eyes fell on the man standing across the street. In his cream-colored summer suit and his elegant cane, he seemed lost among the colorfully clad tourists who were passing him on all sides. Stella had asked him a question from the back of the gallery and he had gone to her. Sauntering back, he saw the man standing in front of the window and Vince got the impression that his eyes, hardly visible behind the tinted glasses, were looking at him rather than at the painting on display. The moment their eyes met, the other man turned and walked away. When Vincent saw his profile he knew he'd seen him before, and even remembered where: on the dockside beside a newsstand just off the gangway. A tall, slim figure with thin hair combed slickly back. A gaze that seemed to skim just over everyone's head. At first sight, to use shipping terms, he looked more like a ship owner than a cruise passenger. But there were over seven hundred passengers on board and in the day and a half they had been under way, Vince hadn't seen nearly all of them yet.

Once back on the street, after the ritual exchange of business cards, Stella had put her arm through his. "I'm not boring you, am I Vince? Me and my art mania. Promise you'll tell me when you've had enough."

He'd looked into her radiant eyes. "If you're happy, I'm happy. If it gets to be too much for me, I'll take in a cathedral," he'd said, in just the light ironic tone such an answer needed.

It wasn't even a lie, for Stella's sunny mood had compensated for everything so far. Even his disappointment over her choice of this particular cruise. Although San Remo still had the picturesqueness of faded glory, it was hardly distinguishable from other Mediterranean seaside towns. Saint Tropez, their next port of call, would undoubtedly still be the same flashy, overcrowded place it had always been. And of Le Lavandou, the only place he didn't know from earlier vacations, the worst could be feared if the travel brochure was to be believed. For a popular entertainment tour, they were skipping the best bits. To him, the only special thing about the trip was the fact that they approached everything from the sea, but the novelty of this, too, had worn off.

The only thing he was looking forward to was Naples, the next port after Bonifacio. Given her monomaniacal interest in art galleries though, Stella would have done better to take the train rather than this floating fairground. Still, he'd been happy.

Deep in thought, he spooned up his yogurt. It didn't taste of anything. *Should he go and get something more substantial at the buffet?* "You haven't gotten any thinner Vince," Stella had said when he rubbed suntan lotion on himself, on that first day in the marina park. "Are you eating right?" She had rolled onto her side and prodded his mid-section teasingly. "A bit chubby suits you, by the way. But at our age you should be careful."

She was thirty-eight, six years his junior. Somehow it made him feel good to see that her slender shoulders had fleshed out a bit. Her skin was flabbier, especially in her neck and above her full breasts, and thin blue lines were showing on her long muscular legs, just like on his. He felt it brought them closer together. Men still looked at her, as they always had, especially down here in the South, but not with the customary horniness; more with something like respect. She wasn't lacking in attention in the onboard bars either. Gallery owners always asked her whether she was a painter herself. It was her expressive face, which was striking rather than pretty, and her nonchalant, graceful way of walking.

When they had entered the Piano Bar on their first night on board, for a moment he had caught himself feeling what he detested so much in other men: pride. Although, in his case, there was nothing to be proud of. In the softly murmuring salon jazz the trio was playing, he'd recognized a song from years back: "I've Got You Under My Skin." The pianist was watching them as they walked past. It was true, he'd thought, she was an essential part of his existence, even though he wasn't fooling himself about her, even now. This was better than five years of solitude. He suddenly wondered if the man with the tinted glasses been at the dock then? On the night they had started out on the cruise?

As the tender had taken them to the dock of St. Tropez he hadn't been alert. On their way to the town center, where, according to Stella, a new, promising gallery had recently opened, they sauntered past the long row of yachts preening themselves in the harbor. With a mixture of envy and disgust, they'd commented on the groups of people posing on the aft decks with studied carelessness. "What else can you do with an object like that?" Stella had remarked. "If you sail off you lose your audience."

He had stopped to watch a street artist shadowing a tourist in silent mimicry and caught a glimpse of a pair of tinted glasses among the spectators' heads, focused on him rather than on the mime.

"Corny," Stella had said, pulling him along. He'd turned and looked around, and for a minute he thought he'd been mistaken. After all, it was impossible. But when they turned the corner at the end of the dock, there he was, sitting on a corner terrace. A waitress was cleaning the table and the man was looking past her, his glance following him.

"Do you want to keep walking along the harbor some more?" Stella asked, observing his indecision.

He had taken her arm. "No, I've seen all there is to see. Onward to art."

Vince hadn't been able to shake off the feeling of being watched the whole time they were in St. Tropez, although he didn't actually see the man anywhere. Not until after lunch, as they waited in line for the tender, did he see him standing by the harbor office. A slim, distinguished figure—almost foppish. There could just as easily be a Mafioso hiding behind those shades as a shipping tycoon. One thing he was sure of, the man had not boarded any of the tenders, so he wasn't a cruise passenger. *How then, did he manage to arrive at every port at the same time they did? What's more, why was he targeting him?*

At night they'd gone dancing, another thing he hadn't done in years, and afterwards, when they'd settled themselves in the Piano Bar, the pianist had again woven the theme of "I've Got You Under My Skin" into his improvisations. "Hear that?" Stella said. "He's playing our song." She hummed along, something about "a warning voice that comes in the night." She hadn't noticed that he was even quieter than usual. The pianist had a young-looking serious face; he wasn't one of those slick entertainers they had in the other onboard bars. He played well, as far as Vincent was able to judge. He'd made a general remark about playing the same tunes night after night on a ship that went round the same ports week in and week out, and how that had to be lethal to one's talents.

"It's not as bad as it sounds," Jensen had said. "More often than not, they're seasonal gigs, and the performers change ships regularly. The pay isn't bad and they even get to see something of the world." Jensen was from Copenhagen, not even fifty years old but already a retired business-man. He and his wife were crazy about cruises; this was their second one this year.

THE DINING ROOM was slowly filling up. Vince went back to his cabin. The partition was still closed. He got some stuff together for the sun deck and slowly, indecisively changed his clothes. Almost eight-thirty. *Shouldn't he wake Stella up?* She was usually up by now. Besides, he remembered she wanted to enter some kind of competition. *Would she consider it a breach of their agreement not to commit each other to anything?* Just by coincidence, they had done almost everything together over the past few days, not just in the ports but on board as well. She had dragged him along to shows, promotional lectures, wine parties, the electronic golf course, all sorts of things, up to and including the Captain's Dinner. She had worn a sophisticated evening gown, brought along for the occa-sion, and he had rented a tux that was a little too small for him. All things considered, he had done as she suggested the whole time, and in most cases, things he detested. She knew, and teased him with it. "You will enjoy yourself!" He wasn't even sure she liked it. It really didn't suit her. When they lived in The Hague and were seeing each other on a reg-ular basis, they sometimes agreed to meet at the municipal museum or at a lunch concert. Had she changed that much since she had moved to Germany or had she simply adapted to her surroundings? Luckily, she left him to himself now and then so he could go away and read a book. What she did in the meantime, he didn't know. They spent the nights on either side of the partition. He would happily have broken that part of the agreement, but he knew she trusted him.

In the corridor, the crooning Muzac from the intercom was interrupted for a morning greeting and the first of today's announcements. He only half listened to the hostess's melodious voice. The debarkation time at Bonifacio had been moved forward by half an hour, and with it the rest of the day's program. He knocked on the partition. "Stella?" There was no reply.

He settled in a quiet corner of the sun deck with a cappuccino. The sea was green with white crests and there was a northwesterly breeze. The light was sharp and clear. He held his book so that the pages were in the shade. "There's finally time to read that book; it's been waiting for years," Stella always said when she found him reading—a quote from the cruise brochure—and every time she said it, she turned it into a performance that she herself laughed at most.

Yesterday he had suddenly blurted out: "You're that book to me." A heavy statement which he'd regretted immediately. Stella had been a bit giggly afterwards, then she had put her hand on his arm. "Vincent, my good and faithful friend. What would I do without you?" He hadn't known whether to be happy with that reaction or not.

He was startled by a loud jovial voice. "Well, Mr. Hofman, you're hitting the books very early again. The shuffleboard competition is already under way, you know. Shouldn't you be watching?" *Jensen, of course.* From the looks of him he'd already finished his first game of tennis and was now undoubtedly on his way to his morning sherry. The robust Dane used the facilities on board to the fullest.

"What time did it start?" Vince asked, more out of politeness than interest. Jensen was better at small talk than he was. All he really had to do was listen.

"About fifteen minutes ago. I haven't seen Stella, either. She was supposed to compete, wasn't she?" He peeked at the book cover. "Just between you and me, Hofman, you've a charming wife. Just as well I'm happily married, otherwise . . . !" He moved away, laughing.

Vincent checked his watch. Ten past nine. In just over three hours they would be going ashore at Bonifacio. In spite of everything, he felt restless.

Yesterday, in Le Lavandou, he'd seen the man even before they had set foot on the dock. Was it because he had gradually become fixated on him, or was the man managing to show himself for a moment, only to disappear again? He'd been standing on something, facing the dock; a light figure shown clearly against the terra gable of the building behind him, as if he were posing. The sunglasses and his stillness made him look like a blind man. Although Vincent had gone ashore amid a large group of people, he knew the look was meant for him. There was somebody following him from port to port, waiting for him, checking his movements, registering his departures. *Why?* He had searched his memory the night before, for something that could link him to that man's presence. There was nothing in his past, in that bourgeois, dreary life of his that could possibly make him fear retribution, vengeance, or retaliation. There was even less in his future. There was still a chance that his imagination had run away with him. That an accidental meeting had caught his attention, that this observation had grown into something resembling an obsession. He'd read books in which this happened. There was also a possibility that the man had mistaken him for someone else. He'd read books in which that happened, too. He read a lot. There was only one way to make sure.

"Is something wrong, Vince?" Stella had been beside him.

"No," he'd replied. "Wait here for me."

He had pushed his way to the front of the throng, to the surprise of the others, Jensen had been yelling something. When he reached the place where he'd seen the man, he had disappeared. He looked at the marble balcony. In the middle there was a bed of roses with a bust on a pedestal, a well-fed autocratic head, looking sternly out over the sea.

"What got into you, all of a sudden?" Stella asked when he had rejoined her. He didn't want to spoil her relaxed mood, and knew that he would make a fool of himself if he told her, so he made up some excuse. On their walk through town he had hardly dared to look around. Even as they waited for the tender, he had not allowed himself to look at the dockside. What purpose would it serve? he'd thought. That night they would make the crossing to Corsica and it would all be over.

At night, as he watched the lights of the Côte d'Azur disappear beyond the horizon, he felt liberated, relieved, to the point of recklessness. Stella seemed to be affected by his mood. They'd danced with gay abandon, first on deck and later in the Piano Bar, where the outer wall was slid back so the clear starry sky could form a high and endless ceiling. Of course, they played the Cole Porter song again, and even though the melody was now droning in his ears, the improvisations went further than ever. The pianist and bass player stretched the melody and dissected it into minute particles that seemed to be floating free in space, on the compelling rhythm of the drums. They tossed it back and forth in a virtuoso dialogue. People stopped dancing and gathered around the piano. Jensen was there, along with Stella and that Norwegian that was always tipsy, their bodies moving in place to the music. The young pianist—eyes closed and face relaxed—concentrated on what his hands met, touched, and left out. Vincent felt a shiver running down his spine, a resonance which released him and swept him along. He heard himself singing along with the others when the song was repeated in the finale. He remembered fragments of text. "Don't you know little fool, you never can win . . ."

Suddenly there was champagne. Stella pushed a glass into the musician's hands and everybody drank their health. For a minute it had reminded him of the past, the last day of the vacation when all its beauty had almost gone, and the wish that it would never end. He'd sat down, a little numbed, somewhat surprised at himself. He hadn't known he was still capable of sentimentality. But then, when the easy listening came back on, the chattering and excitement died down. Shortly after, he'd gone to the suite. There, he'd picked up his book, which she had taken with her earlier that day, from Stella's bed. When he opened it, a picture that she had obviously used as a bookmark fell out: her daughter Esmée at a garden party. In the background groups of people were standing around on a sunny lawn, underneath the tangle of festoons and garlands. He put the photo back with a feeling that he was missing something. He took another look. Obliquely behind the girl stood a man wearing sunglasses. Vince was looking at his profile and the image was out of focus, the face was no more than a blur. Now he was really seeing things. In order to get a grip on himself, he counted the number of people wearing sunglasses: three of the seven people in the picture, two of whom were women. He shook his head and went into the bathroom.

Stella didn't appear on the afterdeck until ten o'clock.

"You've already had your swim I guess?" she asked. Her face looked pale behind the big sunglasses and her voice sounded husky.

"No, but I've done a lot of other things. Did you just get up?"

"What if I have?"

"Wasn't there something you wanted to do this morning? Some competition or other?"

"I didn't feel like it." She was leaning over the railing and watching the waves.

"Shouldn't you cancel?"

"Oh Christ, Vincent, just leave it to me, will you." She pushed herself up off the railing with a tired movement and walked away. Fifteen minutes later she returned and shook out her wet hair above him. "Sorry about before, Vince. I've had a rough night."

At twelve-thirty he was on the gangway looking at the citadel of Bonifacio. Behind him, passengers were jostling for a place on the first tender. While he was still trying to decide whether to go ahead without her, Stella was suddenly standing beside him.

"Well," he remarked. "You're very early by your standards." She still looked a bit peaked; the hangover lingered.

He felt tense when they sailed into the harbor, scanning the dock with his eyes. It wasn't busy at this hour, everyone preferred the shade of the upper part of town, and the cruise passengers hurried over to the little busses that were lined up along the waterfront. But only after he'd walked round, camera in hand as an excuse, was he sure. The man wasn't there.

"Vince, you're so restless," Stella said. "Just like a school kid on a field trip. You've been here before, haven't you?"

The line for the bus moved and he took her arm. "Come on, it's almost unbearable here." The bus was like an oven, his shirt was sticking to him, but he wasn't bothered. There were flags everywhere and banners were hanging between the houses displaying the Corsican Moor's head. Music penetrated the bus from several sources. Not until they got off did he realize. "It's the fourteenth of July," he said. "*Quatorze Juillet*. I completely forgot."

Stella wasn't on form. Slowly she climbed the loping streets, as close as possible to the houses stopping now and then to fan herself.

"What do we do?" he said. "There's every chance all the galleries are closed today. Do you want to see anything, shall we walk around the citadel? A great view, but probably boiling hot."

"Let's just walk around a bit," she said. "We'll see what we can find." When he looked around he saw their ship lying far below. The marina park was extended, and surfboards and jet skis were fanning out across the sea.

On one of the little squares, they had to wait for a passing marching band. The out-of-tune brass blared against the houses, the very young majorettes and the red-faced standard bearer were being photographed from all sides. Stella was leaning against the wall of a house.

"Shall we go for a drink somewhere?" he yelled over the noise.

She shook her head. "I'm going back." She'd taken off her sunglasses and he saw that her eyes were bloodshot; it looked like she had been crying.

"You're not feeling very well, are you?"

She got a tissue from her purse and dabbed her face with it. "I hardly got a wink last night. Do you mind?"

He only understood half of what she was saying and pulled her into an alley. "Shall I go with you?"

Her eyes shot back and forth across the square and she grimaced. *Was she in pain?*

"Come on," he said.

"No, no, there's no need. You just stay here, I'll be all right. A couple of hours sleep and I'll be fine." She looked at him smiling faintly and tapped him on the cheek. "Really, Vince, I'll be fine. You're in luck, no galleries today."

He watched her until she disappeared around a corner and then walked back to the square. To the sound of a drum roll the band marched on, and the drum majorettes marked time with their batons. "A la Bastille," somebody in front of him said, a corpulent man he knew from the ship. He grinned and scanned the square that was now being overrun by tourists again.

On the other side, not sixty yards away, stood a slim figure wearing a light suit, sunlight reflecting off his tinted glasses. The man turned away and walked off. For an instant Vincent couldn't move. Then he crossed the square, hesitant at first, as though something was restraining him, then hurried. *This couldn't be.* He reached the other side, walked into the small street on the corner, the direction in which the man had disappeared. From the narrow passages between the houses people were flooding into the square. He wrestled his way through, close to the walls, avoiding the inhabitants standing in their doorways. Running was useless. He slowed his pace while trying to see over the heads of the crowd. Colorful beaded curtains fanned out, and among the houses smells of herbs and roasting meat hung in the air. Suddenly the surge stopped. He was on an enclosed square with a small fountain at its center and an arcade on the other side, with shuttered shops. The walls of the citadel towered over the houses, he'd almost walked a full circle. Somewhere behind the building to the right should be the busses.

The heat was beating down on him. At the fountain, he let the water run over his hands for several minutes. It couldn't be true, he thought. They had sailed for nine hours, hundreds of miles from the mainland. Impossible. Past the corner beside the cloister wall there was an alley, sloping downwards and after a curve it opened onto the parking space where they had left the bus. Along the houses there was a small terrace under the overhanging trees. A man in a summer suit was sitting at a table, with his back towards him, facing the bus stop.

Vincent walked slowly past the terrace, turned back and stopped in front of the small table. The man looked up. The tinted glasses gave his cheeks a yellowish tinge.

"Who are you?" Vincent asked.

The man didn't answer.

"Why are you following me?" Realizing he'd asked his question in French, he repeated it in English.

A hint of a smile crossed the smooth, narrow face that looked up at him. The man was older than he'd expected, sixty at least. "Why am I following you? I'm not following you." He spoke with a heavy accent. *German?*

"In San Remo, St. Tropez, Le Lavandou. Everywhere we dock, you're waiting for us." He was searching for words. "You follow me into town, everywhere. And now you're on Bonifacio."

"You're overestimating yourself."

The other's calm made him furious. "I want to know why you're doing this. What do you want from me? You look at me and when you know I've spotted you, you walk away. Then, in another place, there you are again." Feeling powerless, he was muddling his sentences. He couldn't utter what he felt. He started over. "It's annoying, cowardly. You stay at a distance and watch, you disappear. Cowardly."

The man's face tightened. "Sir, as I've told you, you are overestimating yourself. You're not important. I'll reverse that. You are in places I am, and whether by coincidence or not, you happen to be in my line of vision. Do you follow? This isn't about you. Sit down for a minute, it's pretty tiring to have to look up all the time."

Vincent remained standing. "I'm not interested in your opinion of me. I want an explanation. . . ."

The man shrugged his shoulders. "You're being used but seem to be unaware of it. That is to your credit, but such naïvetè does make you vulnerable. And now you want an explanation from me. . . ."

His hand went up in a weary gesture, he sighed.

Vincent felt a chill running down his spine. "I have no idea what you're talking about. Used? How am I being used? By whom?"

"Please sit down." Pushing himself up with both hands on his cane, the man sat up in his chair. Suddenly he's old, Vincent thought, it's an act, he's playing the role of superior old man. He's even got a tremor. But he can walk perfectly.

"Did you know," said the voice, the languid speech making the German accent heavy and more pronounced, "did you know that Estella also took a cruise two months ago? With me. A fascinating journey in a different part of the world, northern, icy. The exact opposite to this one, with a ship belonging to the same company though. Do you have any idea why she chose this banal trip? And at the peak of the season too, something she's always hated?"

Vincent pulled up a chair and sat down. *He'd called her Estella.*

"You are company for her. You're filling a void, you're an excuse. On paper, you're taking my place, she'd booked for two but when I found out what she was up to I cancelled."

Contradictory thoughts were whirling through Vince's head. "Stella doesn't need an excuse for a cruise, for visiting galleries where she . . ."

The man didn't let him finish. "Those galleries are another part of the excuse. She has a warehouse full of daubs by some cute young artists swarming around her and she tries to peddle the stuff. She thinks she can achieve something in this business and I don't stop her, even if it means her coming to these kinds of places. But they weren't her choice either, the cruise itineraries are fixed. Legitimizing something pleasurable with what's useful."

"All part of the excuse, just like you."

He was silent for a moment, then said, "Can I get you anything?"

Vincent shook his head.

"Please understand, I mean no offense. I have nothing against you. You're an old friend of Estella's and you should, therefore, be my friend as well. But her circle of friends is rather big. . . . It's just . . . for an old friend, I must say you don't know very much about her. You didn't know that she has been married to me for five years now, nor that she left me a month ago, am I right? You also don't know why she's taking this cruise, and to what purpose you, an old friend, were invited. That you were part of a diversion, a legitimization." He paused, "You therefore also don't know that she's leaving the ship tonight before it sails."

"Tonight?"

He reached for the glass in front of him. "Yes, tonight she's flying back to Munich with me. Bonifacio is her last port of call. At least . . . I know her well enough to predict what her choice will be."

Vincent looked at the calm face across the table from him, at the lips which were pursed in an expression of careful contemplation. He's crazy, he thought, crazy and blind. But doubt crept slowly into his mind. There was something going on that he'd been completely unaware of.

"What am I legitimizing?" he asked.

The man appeared not to have heard. "In the end she'll realize what she's losing if she doesn't: everything. It's more of a choice between a romantic flight of fancy and the return to a—be it one-sided—secure relationship. It's a choice between all or nothing. Life or death. It won't be a difficult choice for Estella to make. She loves herself, therefore she loves life. Loves it very much indeed."

The eyes behind the tinted glasses stared into the distance over his head. "Whatever happens, she won't finish this cruise. There was a plane ticket waiting for her in every port, she knew that. At every port I reminded her of it by my presence. Every new port brought her nearer to the end. Every departure seemed to be challenging me, but only *seemed* to. She knows where the line is drawn. Bonifacio is her final chance. The last chance for her to escape."

"What happens after that?"

He looked at Vincent. "You know what the next port is."

"Naples."

He nodded. "Fifteen hours sailing. A long night on board. There'll be dancing, the Piano Bar will be open until sun-up. Intoxicating music for those who are sensitive to it. A web of sweet dreams. Oh well, all cruises are the same. Ready-to-wear romance, which is the same the world over. Tempting but banal. The longest night on board. Estella will have to choose right now.

Seeing Naples will mean death. I have contacts there. . . ."

He took off his glasses and rubbed his eyes with his fingertips. "Would you like something to drink now, perhaps?"

AT THE DOCK he found the owner of a small boat with an outboard motor who was prepared to take him to the ship for two hundred francs. He remained standing during the crossing, his hands clasped around the windshield. The spray was soaking his clothes but he didn't feel anything. Stella's husband would keep his word, he was convinced of that. *He had to be obsessed with her. Or was his vanity hurt. Couldn't he deal with the thought of being left? A suffocating, selfish love.*

You're being used, the man had said. He didn't feel used. He had been in close proximity to her for four days and that was enough. Desire was enough. All possession was an illusion anyway. But something was wrong. If Stella had really met someone on that first cruise, surely she didn't need to hide that she was travelling with him? She had broken with her husband, there was nothing holding her back.

At the top of the gangway, he was hailed by Jensen. "Hofman, you're back as well? Far too hot, of course. What about Stella? Did you lose her?"

He looked at the Dane's smiling, sunburnt face. "Later," he said.

The partition was closed. He waited until he had his breathing under control and then knocked. Cautiously opening the door to the bathroom, he saw that there was water in the tub with a few bubbles on it. The floor was awash and the door to Stella's room was ajar. He pushed it open. A man was sitting on the bed. Stella was standing in front of him holding his head against her naked stomach and gently rocking him to and fro. Vincent saw the tan lines her bikini had left on her back. Slowly she turned her head towards him. Her eyes were red.

"Vincent," she said. "You're back. Are we sailing? Good."

She loosened the towel around her head and held it up to her chest as she turned around. The man sat hunched over. His brown shoulders were as skinny as a boy's and when he rose from the bed and looked up, Vincent saw that he was a boy, with a confused, worried expression on his face, very different from the concentrated profile at the piano last night but just as young and vulnerable. He stood between them as though he wanted to protect Stella.

"Naples." Her husky voice sounded dreamy. "We'll sail to Naples."

"No," Vincent said. He pushed the pianist aside. His outstretched hand didn't touch Stella, he spread his fingers in an imploring gesture. "No, you have to get off the ship. There's still time. Bonifacio is . . ."

"That's what they say isn't it? Once in your life . . . Nothing can stop me from going to Naples. Nobody."

Vincent felt the pianist's hands on his shoulders and pushed them away. "*I'm* stopping you. You can't . . ."

"Get out of the cabin," the boy said. Vincent saw his hands coming towards him, powerful hands. He felt them against his chest, they pushed him into the bathroom. *What a ridiculous situation*, he thought. He braced himself but his feet slipped on the wet floor. "This is your life we're talking about," he yelled. "Surely it isn't worth that." He saw her eyes behind the pianist's back and knew he had to give her up. He lowered his hands. The pianist lost his footing and fell full against his chest. Vincent staggered back and lost his balance. He crashed backwards against the sink, groped wildly around him for support and then cracked his head against the wall above the tub. The water was oily and dark. It flowed into his mouth, his throat, slowly filling him up, and there was nothing he could do about it.

*What a ridiculous situation*, he thought. *I'm drowning at sea.*

# S.O.S.

## JOHN LUTZ

**D**r. Mona Pilsing was frowning.

Across from her sat station manager Harvey Wellstone, staring at her with concern from behind his wide desk. He said, "You must take some time off, Mona."

Dr. Mona—as she was known to the many listeners of her radio call-in psychological aid show *Dr. Mona Cares*—merely glared at him. She was a waspishly thin woman with a lean, lined face that had endured three cosmetic surgery procedures that had improved the firmness and symmetry of her features yet had somehow made her appear older than her forty-five years. Her flesh was like parchment, and her wise blue eyes looked as if they might emit rays that would etch glass. Right now, they were making Harvey Wellstone squirm.

"I am *not* responsible for that man's death," she said.

"Of course not, Mona. But you are the one who advised him to leave his wife and move in with his mistress."

"Only to save his marriage," Dr. Mona said. "His wife was out of control with her credit cards and refused to communicate with him about their expanding debt."

Wellstone sighed. "She used one of her cards to buy a shotgun, Mona."

"*I* didn't pull the trigger," Dr. Mona said. She breathed deeply and centered herself. "This is a classic example of responsibility displacement."

"The station's worried about a lawsuit."

"And ratings that mean big advertising revenue," Dr. Mona pointed out.

"Of course, Mona. This is a business and I don't deny we're looking at the bottom line. But there are those who say instant psychological advice over the radio on the basis of a phone call can be harmful, even dangerous. Now they have an example. It would be best if you went on vacation for a month. We'll rerun Frank Lee Speeking programs in your time slot."

Mona grimaced. Frank Lee Speeking was the radio name of the station's youth movement, a pimply-faced redheaded boy who had an unimaginative opinion about everything. "My audience won't stick around to listen to cockeyed theories voiced by a child who doesn't remember the Reagan era."

"Still," Wellstone said, shifting in his leather chair as if he might avoid Dr. Mona's fierce stare and prevent burns in his clothes, "we think it would do you good to rest for a while and get in touch—"

"I *am* in touch with my feelings!" Dr. Mona snapped.

"—with the station now and then to see what's happening," Wellstone finished.

Dr. Mona leaned forward in her chair, her brow furrowed, her eyes angry. Wellstone was such a fool to even suggest she was losing control. "Let's be clear on this, Harvey. I am not responsible if some weak-willed wife, who finds it easier to shoot her problem than to solve it, lacks a psychological trigger lock and stirs herself from her pathetic zeitgeist of her own making long enough to fall victim to her id and react negatively to her husband's rational act by acting irrationally."

"That's clear enough, Mona," Wellstone said, "to convince me of the rightness of my decision. You don't think you're under a strain and need rest, but I've thought so for a long time. Even before this shooting incident. You're out of control. And that's dangerous for the station. While our attorneys iron out this problem, you're going to be safely out of reach of the media, with a lot of other stressed-out people finding relaxation and renewal—on a cruise."

DR. MONA had never been on an ocean-going vessel. As the bus from the airport approached the docked ship, the immensity of the *Sea Frolic* surprised her. The cruise ship's pristine white hull loomed like a building wall over its berth in San Juan, Puerto Rico. Passengers who'd already boarded and white-uniformed crew members swarmed on the upper decks. Flags with champagne glass emblems or the bright gold Benington Cruise Line logo snapped in the breeze.

No sooner had Dr. Mona boarded than a smiling steward directed her to her outside cabin on B deck. Her suitcases were already on board and lined side by side at the foot of the bed, so she wasted no time in unpacking and hanging her clothes in the tiny closet.

The cabin itself was larger than she'd anticipated, with a suitable bathroom and plenty of built-in drawer space. There was a comfortable looking bed with a royal blue spread embossed with the insignia of the Benington Cruise Line that had appeared on the flags and travel brochures. The drapes were a matching blue with gold flecks. Dr. Mona stepped around the small writing desk and opened the drapes to find herself taking in a view of San Juan as if she were observing it from a fourth-story window. The city looked more peaceful than it had when the travel agency bus transported her to the docks. And a light haze hung over it—not pollution, she was sure, but a faint fog caught by the sun and made magical.

Two hours later, Dr. Mona watched the dock and city recede into a low ribbon of land before gradually disappearing into the bright horizon line of the ocean. The *Sea Frolic* had left port and set course for its first stop in the Caribbean, the sunny island of Curacao.

Dr. Mona experienced apprehension as she felt the great power of the ship's engines throb through the floor beneath her feet. Panic disorder threatened. But she sought and found her calm center, then left her cabin to explore the ship.

She was surprised by the luxury of the *Sea Frolic*. Everywhere she looked were thick drapes and carpets, tasteful decor, much rich wood paneling, and strategically placed mirrors to make large areas appear even larger. There were elevators to carry passengers between decks, and softly upholstered chairs to lounge in air-conditioned contentment while the sea slid past outside tinted windows. Were it not for a nautical touch here and there, Dr. Mona could have imagined herself in a luxury hotel.

She'd signed for early seating at dinner, so after a nap in her cabin, she went up to the cavernous plush dining room and was led to a table by an unctuous maitre d'. Several other passengers were already seated and introducing themselves. There were three elderly women from Seattle, traveling together; Dr. Mona didn't quite catch their names over the background noise in the dining room. Next to her sat a mustached man and his frumpy wife; Evers or Nevers, she thought their names were. A detestable couple from Indianapolis with two teenage girls sat across from her. Dr. Mona didn't bother to try to understand their names. When she introduced herself as Dr. Mona Pilsing, one of the Seattle women opened her mouth and stared. Then she squealed that she listened to *Dr. Mona Cares* on the radio as often as she could.

Not often enough, Dr. Mona thought behind her polite smile.

The waiter arrived to take their orders, interrupting all adulation. As he pointed out items on the menu to the teenage beasts from Indiana, the three Seattle women gossiped and stared at Dr. Mona. She was sure they were talking about that foolish man being shot at the hands of his more foolish wife after reacting foolishly—

"I recommend the cold banana soup as an appetizer," a waiter was saying to her.

Dr. Mona stared up at him. "Yes, I'll have that. And the trout amandine."

*Fish?* She seldom ate fish. Why had she ordered fish? Was she really not herself lately, as the idiot Wellstone assumed?

She wondered less about the question as the appetizers were placed on the table. By the time her soup bowl was empty, she had rediscovered her sense of self.

Dinner went smoothly enough, though the conversation was banal. As she excused herself and rose from her chair, Dr. Mona was glad no one had asked for a free consultation. But as she walked away, she was sure the obnoxious couple with the beastly daughters would ask her advice before the end of the voyage. Maybe she'd recommend that they file for divorce and fight over who wouldn't get custody of the children.

Dr. Mona stopped walking and gripped a brass handrail. Why had she thought such a thing? Maybe Wellstone was right and she did need a rest, a long sea voyage to get her own psyche straightened out.

Then she centered herself and shook off the thought. She was the same Dr. Mona she'd always been. That was the bottom line. No one could convince her otherwise because no one knew her better than she knew herself.

Having found her comfort level, she continued toward the casino to kill time until the scheduled evening floor show in the lounge, a dance troop of some sort.

She was impressed by the size of the ship's casino. There were blackjack and crap tables, keno, roulette, and over a hundred slot machines. The place was alive with voices, bright colors, the clinking of coins, and the tinkling music of machines rewarding small, selfish dreams. The voices and laughter further cheered Dr. Mona. She got a roll of quarters from the cashier's cage and sat before one of the gleaming slot machines.

She wasn't normally a gambler, and it took her a while to figure out what this was all about. The idea seemed to be to match rows of number sevens with images of various kinds of fruit.

"I'm sorry, but I was playing that machine," said a voice on her left.

Dr. Mona turned and saw a short, plump man in a skimpy white dinner jacket. He had a porcine face, oily skin, and tiny, nasty dark eyes. She had never seen anyone who reminded her so much of a pig.

"There was no one here when I arrived," Dr. Mona said.

"That doesn't matter," the man said impatiently. His flesh-padded eyes fairly glittered, as if he were regarding warm mud after a meal. "I only left for a moment to get change."

Dr. Mona looked around at the rows of slot machines, several of which weren't being played, and decided it was a time for constructive assertiveness. "There are plenty of other—"

"I was working on this one," the porcine man said. "I have money invested in it and it's about to pay off."

"How could you possibly know that, Porky?"

"What'd you say?"

"I said how could you know when a machine is about to pay?"

He stared at her for a moment, his shoulders bunched and tense. Then he said, "I got a system. I'd explain, but it'd be too hard for you to understand." He was throbbing in his eagerness to return to the machine.

"Gambling is compulsive," she told him. "It can easily become an addiction. Often it's linked with a sense of loss stemming from a deprived childhood. There are psychological techniques for breaking the bonds of—"

He glared at her. "Get lost, lady!"

As he gripped her shoulder to try to remove her from the stool in front of the machine, Dr. Mona stood up and ground the spike heel of her shoe into his instep. He squealed precisely like a pig and jumped back.

"I can hurt you worse than that," she told him in a hoarse voice that frightened even her.

Porky started to challenge her until he saw what was in her eyes.

"There are plenty of other machines for me anyway," he mumbled after a few seconds.

She stepped close to him, her face hard, the flesh beneath her right eye dancing. I am *not* out of control, she told herself. She locked gazes with the man and whispered, "Get in touch with yourself, who you really are."

"Huh?"

"Be your own best friend," she hissed fiercely.

He stared at her in confusion as he backed away, then walked hurriedly toward the blackjack tables.

He was wrong about the slot machine with the sevens and fruit. Dr. Mona played it for more than an hour and lost twenty dollars.


THE FLOOR SHOW in the lounge later that evening was awkward and mistook energy for talent. The dancers were followed by a stand-up comedian who joked about how all the honeymooners on board were rocking the boat so hard he was seasick before it left port. That made Dr. Mona glance around the dim lounge. The comedian seemed to be right about the number of honeymooners. There certainly were a large percentage of moon-eyed men with adoring females at their sides. Some of the lovesick fools looked too young to drive cars, much less marry. Unfulfilled lifestyles seemed inevitable.

The comedian, Bucky something or other, was telling a joke about honeymooners, sex, and a psychoanalyst as Dr. Mona finished her drink and left the lounge.


THE NEXT MORNING she decided to work harder at relaxing.

It wasn't easy. She had no desire to take part in a limbo competition, watch a short film on how to treat sunstroke, or observe the contest in the pool to see which honeymoon couple could stuff the most ping-pong balls into each other's swimsuits.

When she returned to her cabin in disgust, she saw a large envelope on her bed. It contained an invitation to dine at the captain's table that evening. The dinner would be in a private room, and she and other "notable personalities" on board would be present.

At lunch a few hours later, the women from Seattle jabbered enviously when Dr. Mona told them why she wouldn't be joining them that evening for dinner. Dr. Mona watched them with contempt from behind her polite mask. Celebrity really threw the idiots' switches.

Then she silently reprimanded herself for entertaining such a thought. It was celebrity that made troubled souls tune to her radio program and enabled her to help them and her other listeners. She was a good person, not someone who deliberately did harm. Helping people was what she was about. It was her identity and the currency of her self-worth. She centered herself and smiled across the table at the giggling Seattle women. They weren't really so terrible. Why had she been thinking such dreadful thoughts about people lately? Was there a disconnection in her emotional mechanism? Or was it the feng shui of her cabin? Whatever the reason, she didn't feel good about herself, and that was something she could hardly bear.

As soon as she returned to her cabin, she switched the covers and pillow on the bed so that now she would lie facing the door. She removed her shoes, stretched out on the bed, and let her eyes take in the cabin from this new perspective.

Much better, she thought. The feng shui. She decided to take a nap so she'd be at her best for dinner with the captain.

THIS WAS AN improvement over her company in the dining room.

Captain Waveschmidt was a tall, bearded man with a barrel chest who looked as if he could command a ship with physical presence alone. He and his crew all wore neat white uniforms resplendent with gold braid and insignia. The other honored guests besides Dr. Mona were a young actress who had appeared in rental car commercials, a Hollywood producer with a compulsion to name drop, and two women who worked at the cruise line's European office. After drinks and strained but polite small talk, everyone enjoyed a delicious dinner. Dr. Mona sat on the captain's right.

"I must confess," he said, "that I hadn't heard of you until my purser raved about you this morning, Doctor. That is due to my busy schedule in other parts of the world where American radio seldom reaches."

"Don't be embarrassed, Captain," Dr. Mona said around a mouthful of asparagus spear. "I've never been on an ocean liner until this one. It's beautiful, and the size of a small city."

"We're very much like a city, even with our own onboard radio station. Which brings me to my invitation: would you consider letting some of our passengers phone in to your own commercial-free shipboard program some mornings? You would, of course, have complete freedom. I realize you're on holiday, but we thought it might be fun for you as well as for your fellow travelers."

Dr. Mona didn't hesitate. She was *not* out of control. She did not need a rest. What had happened to the fool's husband had not been her fault. She smiled warmly at the captain and said yes.

DR. MONA'S first program was the next morning, before the *Sea Frolic* docked at Curacao. She sat in the ship's wonderfully intricate communications room, wearing earphones and a headset microphone. After the last announcement enumerating island attractions, she was introduced by the communications officer, talked for about five minutes, then began taking calls. She was pleased to see a dozen lights winking immediately on the switchboard, indicating calls from cabins about the ship.

"I didn't have the money to buy new clothes and I feel underdressed at the ship's dinners," said a woman named Louella.

"It's not what you wear but how you wear it," Dr. Mona said. "If you carry yourself with self-esteem and pride, others will think your clothes outshine their own. It's human nature, Louella. And it wouldn't hurt to pick up a few colorful shells on the beach and glue them onto some of your clothes. People will think you're clever."

Louella thanked her, and a man named Bing from Oklahoma was on the line.

"My wife's spending too much money and I don't know how to control her," he said.

Another numb-headed woman with too many credit cards, Dr. Mona thought angrily, wishing she had a frequent-flyer mile for every call like this one she'd received. "Talk to her reasonably, Bing, and point out that you two have another life at home. Then be specific about some things she might have to give up later if she continues to overspend on your vacation. Sometimes specificity is what you need to make your point. And always remember: communicate and your relationship will flourish."

"Hmm. Well, thanks, Dr. Mona."

"And if she won't listen, Bing, point out that it's an awful big ocean and she'd have to do a lot of swimming to find her credit cards if you toss them over. Be proactive, Bing."

"Hmm. Well, yeah . . ."

Nincompoop! Dr. Mona thought. She could tell by his voice he wouldn't have the nerve to threaten his wife, who was probably an expert in passive resistance.

Ginny from Iowa was on the line:

"I'm sure my husband's having an affair with another passenger he knows from high school, Dr. Mona. We're all going to be together for two weeks on this ship, and I don't know what to do. I'm at my wit's end."

Easy to believe, Dr. Mona thought. "You have to do *something*, Ginny. That's key. Take control of your life. Talk to your husband, then to the other woman if you must."

"We're on our honeymoon," Ginny sniffled, "and he spends most of his time with her in the pool. They're doing things under water, I know!"

"Buy goggles, Ginny! Find out what they're doing. Don't be a willing victim. Problem solve. Getting this all out in the open would be so life-affirming for you. Believe me, when things are exposed to the light, the shadows disappear. So might your problem."

Ginny thanked her profusely before hanging up.

Several men called asking how they might increase their chances of a shipboard romance. Women called wondering how they might extend a shipboard romance into a long-term commitment. A man complained that his fellow diners wouldn't talk to him. A woman called protesting the tradition of women being first, like children, into the lifeboats if the ship was going to sink.

"I'll tell you how I feel about that if the ship starts to sink," Dr. Mona joked. She used humor sometimes to make herself more human and accessible.

Bing from Oklahoma again: "You sure about throwing those credit cards overboard, Dr. Mona?"

"Of course, Bing. Take control of your life."

"Of my wife?"

"Of your *life*, Bing. Don't be manipulated by evil passive resistance and people whose own lives are running wild with surrender to impulse and foolishness. Do you deserve a lifetime of debt?"

"Nope."

"Remember then, be proactive. It's essential not just for you, but it's a step toward your wife's self-actualization. Then she'll take control of her own life and you two can be happy. Right now, she's standing squarely in the way of your happiness, Bing, and she holds a credit card in each hand. If you expect to harvest the fruits of life, you have to shake life like a tree."

"The wife'd kill me if I shook her," Bing said with a chuckle.

"You only *think* that, Bing. And it's what she wants you to think. But it's up to you. If you don't have a sail and a rudder, you'll drift toward the rocks. Do you understand?"

"This is a steamship, Dr. Mona."

"Don't try to hide your anguish with humor. It's time to dip your oars into the water and give yourself direction."

"Yes'm."

After Bing hung up, Mona took a few more calls then saw that her allotted half hour was at an end. She was smiling when she left the communications room. It felt good to be on the air again, and she'd done just fine, despite what that pea-brain Wellstone thought about her mental state. And what was nice about doing this little daily program was that she could enjoy her celebrity, but still most of the passengers didn't know what she looked like. She would have enough anonymity to have time by herself and relax on the cruise.

Dr. Mona went on shore and enjoyed herself touring the picturesque island and having a lunch of shrimp and fruit and a tropical drink with rum in it. Before going back aboard the *Sea Frolic*, she bought a wide-brimmed straw hat with a bright yellow ribbon to tie beneath her chin when the breeze kicked up. She was napping peacefully in her cabin when the ship set sail for their next stop, the island of Tortola.

During Dr. Mona's half hour radio show the next morning, Ginny called again: "I bought goggles, like you suggested, Dr. Mona, and took a good look when we snorkeled on the island. That woman and my husband *are* doing things underwater!"

"Then you must confront them, Ginny."

"I don't think I can," Ginny said, beginning to sob. "I'm afraid. And I'm so miserable!"

"They're not making you miserable, Ginny. You are."

"But the situation—"

"You can change the situation if you'll be proactive and take control. This is your husband, Ginny, not hers. You have a confrontational issue here and you must communicate and deal with it if you're looking to save your relationship. The woman is a threat that must be removed."

"But he's cooperating."

"Then get everything out in the open, tell him to make his choice. And if he chooses her, make sure he knows that as far as you're concerned, he's history."

"I always hated history. I failed it in third grade."

"That's your inner child talking."

"But we didn't get married because I was—"

"Ginny, you're using oblique subconscious avoidance techniques."

"I guess I am, Dr. Mona."

"Don't be an enabler. Talk about these things, the two of you. Or better still, the three of you."

"Me, my husband and my inner child?"

"I mean the other woman. Let her know she's breaking up your marriage before it has time to get started, and you won't stand for it. You might be surprised to find she backs down. It's human nature, Ginny."

"I guess it is."

After Ginny, a woman from Rockport, Illinois, called and said she couldn't stand her traveling companion and didn't think she could bear being stuck in the same small cabin with her for the next two weeks. She'd asked to be moved but was told there were no more cabins available.

"Then there's nothing you can do short of shooting her," Dr. Mona said.

"Yes," said the woman. "I know that now. Thank you, Dr. Mona."

Dr. Mona signed off and went to the dining room for breakfast before going ashore.

Unlike at lunch and dinner, there was open seating at breakfasts. Dr. Mona sat at a table with two elderly couples and a young family from Miami. The talk was of a man and his wife who'd been too late to get back on board when the ship had left Curacao. Dr. Mona thought it served them right. They could shop until they were sun-struck on the island while they tried to arrange other transportation. It might teach them how cause and effect played a role in their life experiences.

But while Dr. Mona was sipping a second cup of coffee, a woman sat down near her and asked if she'd heard the news. A man named Bingham Bradford had thrown his credit cards and then his wife into the sea and was under arrest for murder on Curacao.

"Did he go by the name Bing?" Dr. Mona asked.

"I think so," the woman said. "He told some of the other passengers he thought his wife married him because his name sounded like a cash register."

Dr. Mona couldn't help but believe the wife had gotten exactly what she deserved. There was also no doubt in her mind that she hadn't been instrumental in the woman's death. She certainly hadn't instructed Bing to murder his wife, whatever the man's interpretation of what she'd told him. He was the one who'd killed his wife, and that was the bottom line.

After lunch, Dr. Mona went on shore and shopped for some duty-free perfume. She wore her straw hat with the yellow ribbon, which made her even more unrecognizable. But a few people from the *Sea Frolic* stared at her strangely in the streets and tourist shops.

After lunch at a charming combination shell shop and restaurant, she returned to the ship for an afternoon nap. That numbskull Wellstone had been right about one thing: a cruise was undeniably relaxing.

She'd awoken and was propped up in bed, fully dressed except for shoes, reading a copy of *I Feel Good About Myself and You*, when the lamp flickered as a resounding *whump* traveled through the ship.

Dr. Mona looked about, then continued to read, until several minutes later when she heard activity in the passageway outside her cabin. Curious, she got up and went to the door.

Half a dozen people were standing in the passageway, yammering excitedly about something.

"What happened?" Dr. Mona asked.

A woman with wild blond curls and even wilder eyes stared at her. "Didn't you hear? Someone cut an electrical line that ran near the swimming pool so that it fell in the water. Six people were killed."

"It was the line that supplied power to the Limbo Lounge," a man in a flowered silk shirt added. He was holding a yellow drink with a paper umbrella in it and appeared inebriated.

"Honeymooners were in the pool having the ping-pong ball competition," Wild Woman said. "You know the contest where they stuff as many ping-pong balls as possible into their swimsuits."

"I believe those are table tennis balls," the man with the drink said.

Wild Woman ignored him. "I heard it was a jilted woman who caused all the trouble, hacked through the line with a hatchet from one of those fire-control boxes. Odd part was, her husband wasn't even in the pool. He'd just climbed out and he's okay."

"They already got the bar in the Limbo up and running again," the man said, raising his drink. "Service is amazing on these cruise ships."

Dr. Mona stood dumbfounded.

Ginny! The woman who'd electrocuted everyone in the ship's pool had to be Ginny, trying to wreak vengeance on her new husband and his lover.

Dr. Mona walked to the end of the passageway and found that power hadn't yet been restored to the elevator, so she climbed the stairs to the pool deck.

Alongside the pool lay several still forms beneath beach towels. Crewmen were loading another onto a stretcher. A knot of onlookers were standing about talking to the ship's officers. The men looked grim and many of the women were sobbing.

Dr. Mona saw Captain Waveschmidt talking to half a dozen passengers and went to him.

"Is there any way I can help?" she asked. "I mean professionally, to make it easier for the passengers to cope."

Everyone was silent. The captain drew a deep breath and stared at her.

"It would be better if you went to your cabin," he said, stroking his beard. "I'll be in touch with you when we finish sorting out things."

Dr. Mona nodded and withdrew, though she didn't agree with the captain's assessment. Some of these people needed counseling, even if they were uninjured. But she could understand why he was upset. He was the ship's captain and was ultimately responsible for what had happened. Maybe when he came to her she could help him to distinguish between professional and personal responsibility and counsel him in his anguish.

She'd been in her cabin about fifteen minutes when there was a light knock on the door. Obviously, Captain Waveschmidt had come to enlist her help.

But when she opened the door, Porky from the casino pushed inside.

He was wearing swimming trunks and was fatter than he'd appeared with clothes on. And hairier. His stomach bulged over the elastic waist-band of his wildly colored trunks. He raised a bulky arm and leaned against the wall, blocking Dr. Mona's path to the door. Her attention was caught by something white attached to the seat of his trunks. At first she thought it was a fake bunny tail. Then she realized it was a half-melted ping-pong, or maybe table tennis, ball stuck to the material.

His mouth grinned at her but his little pig eyes were malicious. "You've been talking to my wife Ginny on the radio," he said.

Dr. Mona knew what he wanted and her mind whirled, seeking words that might save her. "You're both still alive," she said. "You can save your marriage and each other with a life-affirming approach. However you felt about the woman in the pool—"

"I'm not concerned about either one of them," Porky said. "After you left the casino another woman sat down and won six thousand dollars on the slot machine I'd been feeding quarters to for hours. I was going to keep working that machine until it paid off. It was my machine, but you stole it from me, and someone else got the triple sevens and the banana and my six thousand dollars."

"No, no," Dr. Mona said, backing away.

"It won't do you any good to scream," Porky said. "Everybody just rushed to C deck where some stupid woman shot her cabin mate."

"I wasn't going to scream. I want to help you. You're acting out. This is a classic case of grief transference. You're not responsible for the other woman's death. It was Ginny who electrified the pool."

"Six thousand dollars," Porky said, lowering his arm and moving toward her. "That's the bottom line."

Dr. Mona backed farther away until she felt the bed against the backs of her legs. She summoned all her confidence. She knew better than any-one how to deal with distressed people, understood how to reach them. "Please calm down and try to center yourself. Despite what's happened, you can still achieve self-actualization and contentment if you listen to me and be pro—"

But Porky's hands were at her throat, his thick thumbs digging into her larynx. Dr. Mona's confidence level plunged. She tried to scream but no sound emerged, save the muted crunching of cartilage.

As gathering dimness carried Dr. Mona from pain into death, she was aware of Porky's flushed, contorted face close to hers, the laser-like gleam in his eyes, his voice hoarse with madness chanting, "Closure, closure, closure . . ."

# Honeymoon Cruise

## RICHARD DEMING

**W**hen the employment office sent me down to the Miami Yacht Club to be interviewed by the owner of the *Princess II*, I had no idea she was tin heiress Peggy Matthews. I was told to ask for a Mrs. Arden Trader.

The *Princess II* was moored in the third slip. It was only about a thirty-five footer, but it was a sleek, sturdy-looking craft which appeared as though it could weather any kind of seas. No one was on deck or in the wheelhouse.

I climbed on deck, stuck my head down the single hatch behind the wheelhouse, and yelled, "Anyone aboard?"

A feminine voice from below called, "Be right up."

A moment later, a slim brunette of about twenty-five came up the ladder. She wore white Capris and a clinging white blouse that showed off a lithe, extremely feminine figure, thong sandals that exposed shapely feet with carmine toenails, and a white sailor hat. Her features were slightly irregular, her nose being a trifle aquiline and her chin line being a little short, but her face was so full of vitality and there was such an aura of femininity about her that she was beautiful, anyway. Lovely dark eyes, a suggestion of sensuality about her mouth, and a creamy suntan probably helped the general effect.

I recognized her at once from news photos I had seen. Only a few months before, on her birthday, she had come into full control of an estimated fortune of twenty million dollars, which had been left to her in trust until she was twenty-five by her widower father, tin magnate Abel

Matthews. Matthews had been dead about ten years, but until Peggy's last birthday the terms of the trust fund had required her to struggle along on the piddling sum of about a hundred thousand a year. Now she was one of the richest women in the world.

"Aren't you Peggy Matthews?" I asked.

"I was," she said with a smile which exposed perfect white teeth. "I've been Mrs. Arden Trader for the last couple of days. Are you from the employment agency?"

"Yes, ma'am. My name's Dan Jackson."

She looked me up and down, and suddenly a peculiar expression formed on her face. Even now I can't quite describe it, but if you can imagine a mixture of surprise and gladness and apprehension, that comes close.

I think there must have been a similar expression on my face, except for the apprehension, because I was having an odd emotional reaction, too. Just like that, on first meeting, static electricity passed between us so strongly, it seemed to crackle like twin bolts of lightning.

I still don't believe there can be such a thing as love at first sight, but I learned at that instant that there can be an almost overpowering physical attraction between a man and a woman the first moment they look at each other. I had experienced it a few times in much milder form but never with this sort of thunderous impact.

We stood staring at each other in mutual dismay, hers probably from guilt, mine because she was already married. It was incredible that this should happen with a bride of only two days, but it was happening. There was no question in my mind that my impact on her was as strong as hers on me.

We gazed at each other for a long time without speaking. Finally, she said in a shaken voice, "Did the employment agency explain the job, Mr. Jackson?"

I took my eyes from her face so that I could untangle my tongue. "I understand you need someone with navigational and marine engine experience to pilot the *Princess II* on a Caribbean cruise and also double as a cook."

She turned and looked out over the water. "Yes," she said in a low voice. "It's to be a honeymoon cruise. My husband can pilot the boat all right, but he's not a navigator and knows nothing about engines. Neither of us is a very good cook, either. Incidentally, our marriage is to remain a secret until after the honeymoon because we don't want to be met by reporters at every port."

"All right," I agreed, still not looking at her.

I did risk a glance at her left hand, however. She was wearing both a diamond and a wedding band. I wondered how she expected to keep it a secret when people were bound to recognize her at every port of call. But that was none of my business.

She suddenly became brisk and businesslike. "May I have your qualifications and vital statistics, Mr. Jackson?"

"In that order?"

"As you please."

"I'll give you the vital statistics first," I said. "Age thirty, height six-one, weight one ninety; single. Two years at Miami U. in liberal arts with a B average, then I ran out of money. My hobbies are all connected with water: swimming, boating, fishing, and as a chaser for rye whiskey. No current romantic entanglements."

"I'm surprised at the last," she said. "You're a very handsome man."

I decided to ignore that. It didn't seem a good idea to involve myself as a third party on a honeymoon cruise if the situation were going to become explosive. I wanted to know right now if we were going to be able to suppress whatever it was that had sparked between us at the instant of meeting and keep our relationship on a strictly employer–employee basis.

"Now for qualifications," I said. "I did two years in the navy, the second one as chief engineer on a destroyer. I took an extension course in navigation and chart reading, intending to buck for a reserve commission, but changed my mind before my hitch was up. I finished the course, though, and am a pretty good navigator. I'm also an excellent marine mechanic. I had my own charter boat out of Miami Beach for two years. I lost it in moorage when Betsy hit, and there was only enough insurance to cover my debts, so I've been unable to finance another. Since then I've been odd-jobbing at any sea job I could get."

I looked directly into her face as I spoke, and she gazed back at me levelly. Whatever had caused the lightning to crackle between us was gone now, I was both disappointed and relieved to find. Her manner remained the brisk, almost brittle one of a business-woman conducting a personnel interview. She still held an immense physical attraction for me, but now that she wasn't sending out rays of static electricity, I wasn't responding by sending them back.

She asked, "How about your cooking ability?"

"I'm no chef, but I've been cooking for myself for some years and have managed to remain healthy."

"That's not too important so long as you're adequate," she said. "We'll probably dine either with friends or in restaurants at our ports of call. You can furnish references, I presume?"

"They're on file at the employment office, which has already checked them. All you have to do is phone."

"Very well," she said. "I think you'll do, Mr. Jackson. The salary is five hundred dollars plus your keep for a one-month voyage. Is that satisfactory?"

"Yes, ma'am."

"We'll leave tomorrow morning about ten. Our first port will be Southwest Point in the Bahamas, which should only take about four hours because the *Princess II* cruises at twenty-one knots. I'll outline the rest of the voyage after we're under way. Now, would you like to look over the boat?"

"Sure. Where's Mr. Trader?"

"Shopping for some last-minute supplies. We'll start below with the engine."

I judged the boat to be a couple of years old, but it was in excellent shape. I started the engine and listened to it for a time, and it seemed to be in top condition. There was a separate generator engine for the lights when we were in port, and the main engine was idle.

The galley was clean and shipshape, with an electric range and electric refrigerator, the latter well stocked with food. The food cabinet was well stocked with canned goods, also. There was a bunk room that slept four, and off it was a small head and a salt-water shower.

Just she and her husband would occupy the bunk room, Peggy Trader explained. There was a leather-covered bench in the pilothouse which folded out into a fifth bunk, and I would sleep there.

Her manner was entirely impersonal as she conducted the tour. Once, as we were moving from the bunk room into the galley, she accidentally crowded against me in the close quarters, but I sensed no reaction from her at the physical contact.

She merely said politely, "Excuse me," and continued through the hatch.

I knew the instantaneous physical attraction between us hadn't been just my imagination, but apparently she had decided, after her one brief lapse, to bring the matter to a screeching halt. I couldn't help feeling a bit rueful, but at the same time I was relieved. I needed the money badly enough so that I probably would have risked taking the job even if she had thrown herself into my arms, but I preferred not to break up a marriage before it was even fairly under way. If she could restrain herself, I knew I could.

I reported aboard at nine the next morning. Peggy's husband was present this time. Arden Trader was a lean, handsome man of thirty-five with dark, curly hair and a thin mustache. He had an Oxford accent and treated his bride with the fawning indulgence of a gigolo.

Later, I learned he had been the penniless younger son of an equally penniless English duke and had been existing as one of those curious parasites of the international set who move from villa to villa of the rich as perennial house guests.

I knew he was a fortune hunter the moment he flashed his white teeth and gave me a man-to-man handshake. I wondered why Peggy had allowed herself to be suckered into marrying him. I learned that afternoon.

The plan for the cruise was to sail east to Southwest Point the first day, a distance of about a hundred miles. After a two-day layover, we would head for Nassau, and after a similar layover there, we would cruise to Governor's Harbor. From there we would island hop to Puerto Rico, then hit the Dominican Republic, Haiti, Point Morant on the east tip of Jamaica, then head back northeast through Windward Passage to Port-de-Paix on the northern coast of Haiti.

The last would be our longest single jump, a distance of about two hundred and fifty miles. With a cruising speed of twenty-one knots, we could make it in about ten hours, however, so no night sailing would be required during the whole voyage.

After Port-de-Paix, we would touch at the island of Great Inagua, island hop from there back to Governor's Harbor, then cruise nonstop back to Miami. With all our scheduled stops, ranging from one-day layovers to two or three days, we would spend more time in port than at sea during the one-month voyage.

At noon the first day out, I called Arden Trader to take over the wheel while I went below to prepare lunch. When it was ready, as we were in no hurry, we cut the engine, threw out the sea anchor, and all lunched together.

After lunch, I pulled in the sea anchor and got under way again. The sea was rolling a little, but it wasn't rough, and the sun was shining brightly. We were clipping along at cruising speed when Peggy came into the wheelhouse wearing a red bikini swimsuit.

"Arden wants to try a little fishing," she said. "Will you cut to trolling speed for a while?"

Obediently, I throttled down until we were barely moving. Glancing aft, I saw Arden Trader seated at the stern rail with a sea rod in his hands. Peggy made no move to go back and join him after delivering the message.

"He probably won't troll more than fifteen minutes if he doesn't get a strike," she said. "He bores rather easily."

I didn't say anything.

She moved over next to me in order to look at the chart book lying open on the little ledge between the wheel and the pilothouse window. The nearness of her scantily clad body made my pulse start to hammer so hard I was afraid she could hear it.

"Where are we?" she asked.

I pointed silently to a spot a little more than halfway between Miami and Southwest Point.

She said, "We should be in by cocktail time, then, even if Arden decides to fish as long as an hour, shouldn't we?"

"Oh, yes."

There was no reason for her to remain where she was, now that she had seen the chart, but she continued to stand so close that our arms nearly touched. I didn't have on a shirt. In fact, I was wearing nothing but a pair of my old navy dungarees and a visored yachting cap, not even shoes. She was so close I could feel the warmth of her body on my bare arm.

Although the sea was fairly calm, our decreased headway caused the boat to roll slightly. One swell a little larger than the rest caused a heavier roll to port. Instinctively, I leaned into it, and at the same moment she lost her balance.

She half turned as she fell against me. My right arm went around her waist to steady her as she grabbed for my shoulders. Her full bosom, covered only by the thin strip of the bikini halter, crushed against my bare chest. The bolts of lightning that crackled between us made that of yesterday morning seem like summer lightning. We remained rigid for several seconds, staring into each other's faces. Her lips parted, and her eyes reflected the same mixture of surprise and gladness and dismay I had caught when we first glimpsed each other. Then she straightened away from me and glanced out the aft pilothouse window. I looked over my shoulder, too. Her husband was fishing with his back to us.

"I shouldn't have hired you," she said quietly.

I faced forward and gripped the wheel with both hands.

"I knew I shouldn't have when I did it," she said. "Don't pretend you don't know what I'm talking about."

"We'll head back for Miami tomorrow," I said. "You can have the employment agency send you another man."

"No, I don't want to. It's too late."

With her gaze still on her husband, she reached out and gently squeezed my bicep. I tingled clear to my toes.

"It's ridiculous," I said tightly. "You're a bride of three days. You must be in love with him."

Her hand continued to caress my bicep. "I'm not going to try to explain it, Dan. I was in love with him until you came aboard yesterday. I took one look at you, and everything turned topsy-turvy. It did for you, too. I could see it in your eyes. I can feel it in your muscles right now."

"Stop it," I said, keeping my gaze rigidly fixed ahead. "It's impossible. Why did you marry him?"

"Because I hadn't met you," she said simply.

"That's no answer. You must have been in love."

Her hand left my arm and dropped to her side. "I went into it with my eyes wide open," she said. "I've had a hundred offers of marriage—women with money always do—but I'd given up ever finding the man I dreamed of. The rich ones were all fearfully dull, the charmers all fortune hunters. I'm twenty-five and tired of being single. I hardly needed a rich husband, so I decided to settle for a charmer. Arden has been pursuing me for a year. Last week at a house party in Mexico City, I gave in. We were married there, then flew to Miami to pick up my boat for a honeymoon cruise. On my second day as a new bride, I had, finally, to meet the man I've been looking for all my life."

I continued to grip the wheel and stare straight ahead. The whole situation was incredible. A series of wild thoughts ran through my mind.

I'd always considered myself a confirmed bachelor, but suddenly the thought of having Peggy for a wife was so appealing, I've never wanted anything more. Her money had nothing to do with it, either. I would never marry for money because it had been my observation that men who do usually earn it. It had never occurred to me that I might fall in love with a rich woman.

I wasn't sure this was love, but no woman had ever held as strong a physical attraction for me, and I was sure I wanted to marry her. And it was hardly a disadvantage that she was one of the richest women in the world. Would it be sensible to turn her down merely because a few villas scattered around the world, a few yachts and foreign cars went with the deal?

Then the bubble popped. She already had a husband.

"Aren't you going to say anything?" she asked.

"Uh-huh. Do you plan an annulment?"

"From Arden? Impossible. He would hold me up for a half million dollars."

"Can't you afford it?"

From the periphery of my vision, I could see her frown. "Nobody can afford to throw half a million dollars down a hole. My father spent too many years building his fortune for any of it to be tossed away capriciously. It's not a matter of being able to afford it; it's a matter of principle."

"Then I guess you'll just have to stay married to him," I said.

There was a yell from the stern. "Strike!"

I cut the engine and looked over my shoulder. Trader was straining back in his seat, and a hundred yards behind the boat a sailfish broke water.

Peggy said, "We'll postpone discussion until later," and hurried aft to stand by with the gaff.

There was no opportunity to resume discussion that day, however. Trader lost his fish, and it discouraged him from further fishing. He devoted his attention to his bride for the rest of the day.

About five p.m. we berthed at Southwest Point. Trader and Peggy dressed and decided to go into the settlement for dinner. Trader invited me to go along but I knew the invitation was only politeness, so I refused.

I had a lonely meal and afterward sat on the stern rail smoking a cigarette. The night was warm enough so that I didn't bother to put on any more than I had worn during the day. I had finished my cigarette but was still seated there bare-chested and barefooted when they returned about nine.

Arden Trader had donned a white linen suit to go to dinner. Peggy had put on a dress but hadn't bothered with stockings. She wore thong sandals on her bare feet.

There were two inflated rubber mats with removable canvas back rests on the stern deck. Without the back rests you could lie full length on them for sunbathing. With the back rests in place, they made deck-level lounging chairs. Peggy sank onto the one right in front of me, leaned against the back rest, and kicked off her sandals.

"Let's enjoy the moonlight for a while," she said to her husband. "How about a cigarette?"

He knelt beside her with his back to me, placed a cigarette in her mouth, and lit it. After taking one draw, she took it from her mouth, put her arms about his neck, and drew him to her.

Ever since she had left the wheelhouse that afternoon, I had been stewing about what transpired there. I had finally decided that if she wasn't going to leave her husband, we were not going to have just an affair. I still wanted her as a wife more than I've ever wanted anything, and maybe if she had been married ten years, I might have settled for having her just as a mistress. But I wasn't quite rat enough to cuckold a groom on his honeymoon.

Apparently, my soul-searching had been for nothing. I could think of no reason for her deliberate show of affection in front of me other than that she had decided to let me know in definite terms that the scene in the wheelhouse had been a mistake. I looked away, not wanting to see her kissed by Trader.

I felt something touch my left foot and glanced down. My pulse started to pound when I saw her right foot rubbing against my instep. Her carmine-tipped toes wiggled in urgent demand for some response.

With her arms wrapped around her husband, the gesture seemed more likely to be an invitation for a clandestine affair than a signal that she wanted a more permanent relationship. Since I had already decided against settling for that, my conscience told me to withdraw my foot.

My desire for her was stronger than my conscience. I raised my foot and pressed its sole against hers. Her toes worked against mine and along the sole of my foot in a lascivious caress, all the time her arms tightening around her husband's neck until finally it was he who broke the kiss.

As he started to rise, her foot drew away from mine, and I dropped mine back flat on the deck. Trader sank onto the other mat and lit a cigarette.

"I'm beginning to like this married life," he said to me with a grin. "You ought to try it, Dan."

"I may if I ever meet the right girl," I said, getting to my feet. "Think I'll turn in. It's been a long day."

"Good night, Dan," Peggy said softly.

"Night," I said without looking at her, and headed for the wheelhouse.

The following morning when I climbed down on deck, Arden Trader was screwing some kind of bracket to the timber immediately right of the hatchway which led below.

"Morning," I said. "What's that?"

"Morning, Dan," he said affably. "I'm installing an outside shaving mirror I picked up in town last night. The head's too small and too poorly lighted to get a decent shave."

He lifted a round shaving mirror from a paper bag and slipped the two small vertical shafts at its back into holes in the top of the bracket. Then he moved the bottom of the mirror in and out to demonstrate that it could be adjusted to suit the height of anyone using it.

"Now all I need is a basin of hot water and my shaving equipment," he said as he started below. "You can use it when I'm finished if you want."

I did use it from then on.

I had no opportunity to be alone with Peggy during the two days we were in port because Trader was playing the attentive groom. By the second day, I couldn't stand his constant little attentions to her and, since I wasn't needed aboard because they were taking their meals in town, took the day off and spent it on the beach by myself.

On the third day, we pulled out for Nassau. As the trip would take six hours, we got under way at eight a.m. About ten, Peggy came into the pilothouse, again wearing a bikini.

"He's taking a nap," she said, and with no more preamble moved into my arms.

I spiked the wheel so as to have both arms free. Hers went about my neck, and her body pressed against mine as our lips met. We were both trembling when she finally struggled from my arms and stepped back. It was none too soon.

She backed clear to the pilothouse door. We were both so out of control, if her husband had walked in at that moment, neither of us could have concealed our naked emotion from him.

"What are we going to do?" she whispered.

My good resolutions lay in shreds. I didn't care what we did so long as it meant being together in some way. If she wanted to shed Trader and marry me, I would be happiest. But now I was willing to settle for just an affair if she wanted that. If she had suggested solving our problem by holding hands and jumping over the rail, I would have at least considered it.

I jerked out the spike and gripped the wheel with both hands in an effort to control my trembling. "What do you want to do?"

"Do you love me?"

"Do you have to ask?" I demanded.

"I want to hear you say it."

I took a deep breath. "I love you. I'm absolutely nuts about you."

She closed her eyes. "I love you, too," she said almost inaudibly. "I've never felt such overwhelming love. Do you want to marry me? Answer me truly, Dan."

"There's nothing I want more," I said in a husky voice.

Her eyes opened, and she seemed to get a little control of herself. In a more normal tone, she said, "I couldn't just have an affair, Dan. Despite my behavior, I'm really a quite moral person. I'm not a prude. If I were single, and we were alone out here and planned to get married when we reached port, I wouldn't insist we wait until the proper words were spoken. But there's some Puritan strain deep within me that makes it impossible for me to violate my marriage vows."

"We aren't going to have an affair," I told her. "I've already told you I want you for my wife."

"But I have a husband."

"You shouldn't have any trouble getting an annulment after this short a marriage. Why do you think it would cost you a half million?"

"Because I know Arden. I know him so well, I made him sign a premarital agreement waiving all claim to my estate except whatever I decided to leave him in my will. I didn't think it wise to put him in a position where he could become rich if I died."

I turned to stare at her. "If you thought him capable of murdering you, why in the devil did you marry him? What possessed you?"

"Oh, I really didn't think he might try to kill me. But he's a fortune hunter, and you don't place temptation in the hands of men such as Arden. Because he is a fortune hunter, I know he'll hold me up if I ask for an annulment. My guess that his price for cooperating will be a half million is based on sound experience. That's exactly what it cost each of two women friends of mine to shed fortune-hunting husbands."

"Wouldn't your premarital agreement cover that?"

"That only applies in case of my death," she said. "Actually, I could get out of paying him a red cent if I wanted a legal battle. No court would grant him any kind of settlement. But there's a pattern of blackmail men such as Arden use. If I refuse to pay him off, Arden will fight me in court with every dirty tactic he knows. He'll drag my reputation through the mud by filing countersuit for divorce and accusing me of infidelity with a dozen men. The tabloids will have a field day."

I said sourly, "You knew all this in advance of marrying him. How the hell did you bring yourself to do it?"

"I assumed it was going to last, Dan. How was I to know you would come along?"

I took my gaze from her and looked ahead again. "If you don't get rid of him, how are we going to marry?"

"Oh, I intend to get rid of him," she said softly.

"By paying him off?"

"There's a much simpler way, Dan. Who would suspect anything if a brand-new groom fell overboard and was lost at sea on his honeymoon? The wife might be suspected after a ten-year marriage or even after a year—but not after just a week, Dan."

A sudden chill doused the warmth I still felt from having her in my arms. "Murder?" I said shakily.

"There wouldn't be a chance of suspicion. Who could suspect a love triangle when I'm on my honeymoon and you and I have only known each other a few days? It's even incredible to me that we're in love. How could the thought ever enter the heads of the police?"

The logic of what she said was penetrating my mind even as I was rejecting the thought. Under the circumstances, who could possibly suspect? My throat was suddenly so dry I had to clear it.

"There would be some suspicion after we announced our marriage."

"Why? No one knows you're only a temporary employee. I'll simply keep you on in some permanent capacity—say as my social secretary. I'm the only woman in my set who has never had one, and it's about time I acquired one. You'll show sympathy for my bereavement, and I'll show appreciation for your sympathy. Gradually, your sympathy and my appreciation can ripen into love. It won't be the first time a sympathetic male friend has ended up marrying a grieving widow. I think it would be safe at the end of as little as two months."

Again her argument was so logical I had no answer, except that it takes more than mere certainty that you won't be caught to condition your mind to murder.

"It has to be that way or not at all," she said in a suddenly definite tone. "I'll leave you to think it over." She turned and left the pilothouse.

I was still thinking it over when it came time for the noon mess. By then, we were passing through Northwest Providence Channel. I had deliberately kept to the center of the channel, and land was barely visible on the horizon on both sides. The water was calm, with only a slight roll, and the sun was shining brightly. There wasn't another vessel in sight.

Arden Trader had emerged from below in swim trunks about eleven o'clock, and both he and Peggy were lying on the inflated mats at the stern, deepening their already rich tans. I yelled for Trader to come take the wheel while I prepared mess. He rolled off his mat, leaned over Peggy, and gave her a long kiss. Jealousy raged through me so hotly I had to turn my back to get control of myself. When he came into the wheelhouse, it was an effort to keep my voice calm while I gave him his bearing.

The sight of his kissing Peggy had brought me to a decision. Peggy came into the galley only a moment after I got there and stood looking at me expressionlessly. "All right," I said.

Her nostrils flared. "When?"

"Right now if you want."

"How?"

"Why don't you go out and suggest a swim before lunch? The water's calm enough. I'll do the rest."

Without a word, she turned and left the galley. I waited a moment, then followed, pausing astern while she climbed to the pilothouse. A moment after she entered, Trader cut the engine, then they both emerged.

"Okay, Dan," Peggy called. "You can throw out the sea anchor."

I was already standing next to it. I tossed it overboard and let down the wooden-runged ladder strung with rope so that swimmers could more easily get back aboard ship. "Think I'll have a dip with you," I said. "I'll put on my trunks."

When I came back out on deck, Trader and Peggy were already in the water. Trader was floating on his back about four feet from the boat, his arms outstretched and his eyes closed. Peggy was treading water near the rope ladder. I motioned her aboard. Quietly, she climbed up on deck. Trader opened his eyes and looked up at her.

"Be right back, honey," she said, and ran below.

Trader closed his eyes again.

It had been my intention to swim up behind him and give him a judo chop, but his outstretched position made him vulnerable to a safer form of attack. Taking a running jump, I launched myself feet first at his stomach, bringing my knees to my chest and snapping them straight again with terrific force just as I landed. The air whooshed out of him, and he was driven deeply under water in a doubled-up position.

I must have caught him in the solar plexus with one heel, temporarily paralyzing him, because when I reversed myself and dove after him to grab his shoulders and push him even deeper, he barely struggled. I forced him down and down until my own lungs were nearly bursting, then reversed again, got my feet against him, and gave a final shove which drove him deeper and shot me toward the surface.

I made it only a microsecond before I would have had to breathe in water myself. Starting under with no air in him, I was sure Trader couldn't possibly survive. But when I recovered my breath and had climbed aboard, I crouched at the rail and studied the water for a good ten minutes just to make absolutely certain. Then I called Peggy from below.

When she came up, her face pale beneath its tan, I said tonelessly, "There's been an accident. I think he had a cramp. I was on deck with my back turned and didn't see him struggling until I happened to glance around. I tried to reach him, but he went under before I got there. I kept diving for nearly an hour in an attempt to spot him, but he must have sunk straight to the bottom. That's my story for the record. Yours is simply that you were below when it happened."

She stared at the gentle swell of water in fascination. "Will he come up?" she whispered.

"Eventually, if something doesn't eat him first, which is more likely.

Not for days, probably."

She gave a little shudder. "Let's get away from here."

"We have to stick around for at least an hour," I said. "I spent an hour futilely diving for him, remember? If we head straight on, somebody just might check to see when we left Southwest Point and when we arrived at Nassau. It would look fishy if there weren't enough of a time gap to allow for our hour of waiting around."

"Why say we waited an hour?" she asked. "We'd know after ten minutes he wasn't coming up."

"You're a brand-new bride," I said. "You wouldn't give up hope after ten minutes. We'll do it my way."

"Do we have to kill the time right here?" she asked nervously. "There's no mark on the water where he went down. Run a few miles and throw out the sea anchor again."

With a shrug, I hauled in the sea anchor, pulled up the rope-strung ladder, and went tops to start the engine. Peggy went along with me and stood right next to me, with our arms touching, as I drove the boat through the water at full throttle for about five miles. Then I reduced speed until we were barely making headway, scanned the horizon in all directions to make sure no other vessel was in sight, and finally cut the engine altogether. I went aft, tossed out the sea anchor, and lowered the ladder again, just in case another vessel came along during the next hour and I actually had to start diving.

Peggy had followed me from the pilothouse. She emitted a deep breath of relief and threw herself into my arms, clinging shakily.

We were only about two hours out of Nassau. We arrived about three-thirty p.m.

No one showed the slightest suspicion of our story. As Peggy had surmised, it didn't even occur to the police that it might be a love-triangle murder when they learned she had been a bride for less than a week and she had never seen me until two days after her marriage. Their only reaction was sympathy.

Since we said we had waited in the area for a full hour after Trader went down, they didn't even bother to send ships to look for the missing man. A couple of helicopters scanned the general area for a couple of days in the hope of spotting the floating body, but it was never spotted, and Arden Trader was finally listed as missing at sea, presumed dead.

Since Peggy's secret marriage wasn't revealed to the press until the drowning of the groom was simultaneously announced, both got wide news coverage. But again there wasn't the slightest intimation that it could have been anything but a tragic accident.

Peggy owned a half-dozen villas in various parts of the world, and one of them was at San Juan. When the police at Nassau released us, we continued on to Puerto Rico, where the grieving widow went into seclusion. News reports said that the only people accompanying her to the villa were a female companion and her personal secretary, neither of whose names were reported.

The "female companion" was a middle-aged housekeeper who spoke nothing but Spanish. I, of course, was the personal secretary.

The villa had its own private beach, and we spent an idyllic two months on a sort of premarital honeymoon. Long before it was over, there was no question in my mind about being in love. The physical attraction was just as strong, but that wasn't Peggy's only attraction anymore. I was as ludicrously in love as the hero of some mid-Victorian love novel.

At the end of two months, Peggy thought it safe to emerge back into the world and for us to be quietly married. She had been in correspondence with one of her several lawyers meantime, and the day before the ceremony was to be performed, she presented me with a legal document to sign, a waiver of all rights to her estate except what she voluntarily left me in her will.

"You think I might murder you for your money?" I growled after examining it.

"It's my lawyer's idea," she said apologetically. "While I'm not legally bound to follow my father's request, it was his expressed wish in his will that if I had no heirs, I leave most of my estate to set up a research foundation. If we have children, naturally the bulk of the estate will go to them, and of course I'll see that you're well taken care of. But just suppose I died the day after we married? I have no other living relatives, so you would inherit everything. Would it be fair for my father's dream of a Matthews Foundation to go down the drain?"

"I'm not marrying you for your money," I told her. "If you died the day after we married, I'd probably kill myself, too. But it's not worth arguing about." I signed the document.

The ceremony was performed before a civil judge in San Juan, with our housekeeper and the court clerk as witnesses. Peggy wanted only a plain gold band, and it cost me only twenty-five dollars. The diamond she wore, I discovered, had not been given her by Arden Trader but had been her mother's engagement ring. She said she preferred to continue to wear it instead of having me pick out another.

As in the case of her previous marriage, Peggy didn't want the news released to the press until we had completed a honeymoon cruise so we wouldn't be besieged by reporters at every port of call. I pointed out that she was too well known to escape all publicity, and unless she wanted to pretend deep gloom at each stop, people were bound to guess we were on a honeymoon. She said she didn't plan to withhold the news from friends and acquaintances but was going to request them not to relay it to any reporters, so there was a good chance we could keep the secret from the general public until we completed the cruise.

"It won't be a tragedy if reporters find out," she said. "I just want a chance for us to be alone as long as possible."

For our cruise we decided to complete the circuit of the Caribbean we had already started. This time there would be only two of us aboard, however.

We got as far as the island of Great Inagua when we ran over a floating log in the harbor, broke a propeller shaft, and lost the prop. The spare parts weren't available anywhere on the island, but I knew I wouldn't have any trouble finding them back at our previous stop, Port-de-Paix.

A packet ship plied every other day from Great Inagua to Haiti, then on to the Dominican Republic and finally to Puerto Rico. I checked the schedule and discovered that if I caught the one on Friday, I could catch the return ship from Port-de-Paix to Great Inagua on Saturday.

Peggy knew some people named Jordan on the small island where we were laid up, and as they were having a house party on Friday night, she decided not to accompany me.

I got back with the new propeller shaft and propeller about four o'clock Saturday afternoon. The private boat slips were only about fifty yards from the main dock, and I could see the *Princess II* as we pulled in. A slim feminine figure in a red bikini was on the bow waving to the ship. I doubted that she could make me out at that distance from among the other passengers lining the rail, but I waved back, anyway.

When I lugged my packages aboard the *Princess II*, Peggy was no longer on the bow. She was leaning back into the canvas back rest on one of the air-inflated mats on the afterdeck. A tanned and muscular young man of about twenty-five, wearing white swim trunks, was seated on the stern rail.

As I set down my packages, Peggy said, "Honey, this is Bob Colvin, one of Max and Susie Jordan's house guests. My husband Dan, Bob."

The young man rose, and we shook hands. He inquired how I was, and I said I was glad to meet him.

"Bob was planning to take the Monday packet ship up to Governor's Harbor, then fly from there to Miami," Peggy said. "I told him if he wasn't in a hurry, he might as well leave with us tomorrow and sail all the way home. He can sleep in the pilothouse."

Counting our two months in seclusion at San Juan, our honeymoon had now lasted long enough so that the urgency to be completely alone had abated somewhat for both of us. I don't mean that my love for Peggy had abated. It was just that both of us were ready to emerge from our pink cloud back into the world of people. My only reaction was that it would be nice to have someone to spell me at the wheel from time to time.

"Sure," I said, and knelt beside my wife to give her a kiss.

She kissed me soundly, then forced me to a seated position next to her and pressed my head onto her shoulder. Smiling down into my face, she began to stroke my hair.

With my face in its upturned position, I could look right over her shoulder into the shaving mirror attached to the timber alongside the hatch leading below. By pure accident it was slanted slightly downward to reflect the deck area immediately in front of the inflated mat.

In the mirror I could see Bob Colvin's raised bare foot. Peggy's bare toes were working lasciviously against his and along the sole of his foot.

# Rhine Ablaze

## JACQUES TOES

### TRANSLATED BY HANS VAN DEN BERG

The *Rhinestar* was about to sail when I reported for duty. The vessel was tied up along the quay of the Rhine in Arnhem; from the smokestack, greasy smoke curled skywards. The passengers were gathered on the top deck, waiting in a relaxed atmosphere. The chief stood waiting for the cables to be hauled in. The moment I set foot on board, he spun toward me and enjoined, "Hurry up, son, first meet the boss, then on with the job."

The chief walked ahead of me to the bridge, where the captain was seated at a small table. The captain was a rather short man who had developed around his waist what he missed in length. He offered me a weak handshake and turned to the chief.

"Is he going to be with us for the rest of the season?" he inquired.

The chief looked at me with an obvious question in his expression. I briefly answered that I did not have much choice.

Musing, the captain knit his eyebrows but did not inquire any further. It saved me the embarrassment of having to admit that I just recently had concluded one of the least successful episodes of my life.

The day before, I had just enjoyed a brief, but obtrusive, chat with Mr. Bonner, the manager of the accounting firm where I was engaged as a junior clerk. In discreet terms he informed me that he had not been able to detect any form of the exactness, the perseverance, the team-spirit and a number of other characteristics, which in a firm such as this—he made a gesture like the Pope blessing a multitude in the Square—were indispensable.

He was right, of course. Actually, I knew better than he did, that numbers, calculations and graphs had bored me to tears from the moment I opened the first ledger. However, to save face, I admitted that I might have been a bit too flexible with the working hours, but that the rest was utter nonsense; figments of his imagination. Indeed, malicious lies. The result was that the interview was transferred to the main office where I was requested to clear my desk. Mr. Bonner watched carefully to ensure that I left with nothing belonging to the firm, not even a paper-clip. Meanwhile, my colleagues watched me in stony silence and merely nodded as I left the office.

On my way home I happened to pass the office of a shipping company, where I spotted a HELP WANTED sign stuck in the window. In a surge of rebellion I decided then and there to start a completely new career and applied for the position of junior sailor enginehand—whatever that might mean—and was accepted on the spot. This should have made me immediately suspicious. However, the next morning found me unpacking a suitcase filled with clean underwear, a pair of overalls, and my passport. I was on my way. My three-piece pinstripe suit stayed behind in my wardrobe.

The captain looked me up and down once more and said to the chief: "Oh well, we'll have to put up with what the head office sends us. Just hand him over to the boson."

The chief smirked and took me via a labyrinth of ladders and narrow corridors to the engine room, where a short muscular man was stretched out under one of the pipes, cursing continuously.

"Those fucking seals are going bust one after the other," he shouted when he spotted the chief. "Fucking rubbish and bloody dangerous in the bargain!"

The chief shrugged his shoulders.

"This is the new bloke," he said. "The replacement for Hazelnut."

The boson let out another stream of curses as the wrench slipped from his hand and hit the steel floor with a clang. He sat up and wiped his hands on a dirty rag. He looked at me as if he were being confronted with a newly discovered, sub-human species.

"What am I going to do with that?" he snorted.

The chief stepped back a few paces.

"Give the man a chance to fix his cabin and show him his way around the ship," he ordered as he wiped some dust from his white slacks. "There is plenty of polishing up to be done around here," he continued, showing his displeasure as he left the engine room.

Shaking his head the boson got up on his feet and indicated that I was to follow him.

"Your name?" he asked, as we were walking farther aft.

"Andrew Petterso—"

"Right, Andy," he interrupted. "We're sailing in fifteen minutes. Get changed and report to the poop deck."

"Aye-aye, sir," I answered smartly.

He spun around abruptly and I nearly collided with him.

"Boson!" he snapped. "You address me as 'boson.' Got that?"

He did not bother waiting for a reply and disappeared through a low steel door that more closely resembled a hatch than a door. I dragged my suitcase with me until we got to a small compartment, where it was impossible to stand at full height. A faint, yellowish light shown from one miserly lightbulb, sitting among the overhead pipes. A narrow board fit against the far wall.

"This is your cabin," the boson explained. "This here is your bunk and over here . . ." He kicked against a rusty trunk and was about to say something else, when the ship's engines came to life and started to produce an earsplitting racket. The entire cabin started to shake, even the lightbulb began to quiver.

The boson tapped his watch, raised five fingers and then pointed upstairs. He left the cabin, slamming the door behind him. He gave me the distinct impression he would have gladly locked me in my cabin for the duration of our journey.

Five minutes later I stood on the poop deck, attempting to coil a dripping steel cable. I scored my first cuts in the palms of my hands as I was without work gloves. Peals of laughter from my fellow sailors followed. I was hardly aware of the fact that the ship had moved away from the quay and had started to disturb the smooth surface of the river.

Far above me, on the top deck, I caught a glimpse of passengers lining the railing, waving enthusiastically at passers-by on the quay. They acted as though they were undertaking a world cruise instead of a short trip up the Rhine.

On a passenger ship sailors and ship rats share more or less the same place in the pecking order. However, as the *Rhinestar* did not have ship rats, I was left in the undesirable position of being the only candidate for that position. But after three days I had reconciled with my fate, more out of fatigue than out of conviction.

So far, there had been two occasions in which I worked my guts out hauling in the cables which are used to moor the vessel. The *Rhinestar* had tied up in Düsseldorf and in Cologne, but my sight-seeing amounted to four straight days in my ugly, gray cabin.

Apart from those two interruptions, I had spent three days in the stern, behind the engine room. The space, covered with a pool of oil and water, was surrounded by four walls, thick with grime and rust. The boson had given me the task of chipping away at the rust with the help of a chisel, a hammer and a worn-out steelbrush. Balancing on wooden crates that floated like small rafts on top of the grime, I tried to clean up the stubborn mess.

Every two hours I got a visit from the boson. I could never hear him approach the area, as the racket of the engines silenced all sounds from the outside, but he always announced his arrival by banging on the door with a heavy steel rod, and then materialized right behind me.

He looked critically at the piece of wall I had already cleaned, and then yelled out at the top of his voice that there was a *bucket of slop* waiting for me in the galley. Once there, a kitchenhand put a mug of coffee in front of me, along with a plate of macaroni.

I sat with the rest of the crew: a couple of stewardesses, cabin boys and fellow sailors, who looked every bit as filthy as I. They cursed their prospective cabin supervisor, the purser, and other staff members when no one else was listening, but when the chief cook stuck his head around the door, they all got up meekly and went out to resume their various duties.

Two of the members were wearing white short-sleeved shirts, sporting tattoos on their suntanned, muscle-bound upper arms. Their names, I discovered, were Victor and Harold. They had worked for two years already on the *Rhinestar* and they told me that the vessel originally had carried freight only. The *Rhinestar* had fallen into the hands of a tour-operator, who converted the holds into forty luxury cabins. On top of that, a superstructure with two decks had been constructed. The bridge was brought forward to the fo'c'sle and the *Rhinestar* was now fit to provide seventy-two guests an unforgettable holiday, for trips up to ten days in length. The majority of the paying passengers were single females. However, war veterans, especially Americans, would often book tours that took them near old WW II battlefields. The seaman named Victor did not think much of the women passengers, whom he regarded as 'red meat,' the packing-date having expired a long time ago.

I inquired of the two sailors as to what their tasks were.

"A bit of everything," was their reply. "And what about you?"

I confessed that all I had done so far was chip rust down below. They looked at me with a mixture of loathing and commiseration.

"A filthy job," commented Harold.

"The boson wouldn't have been game to nail Hazelnut for something like that," remarked Victor.

"Who the hell is Hazelnut?" I asked.

"Ah, that poor sucker Hazelnut," Victor mused. "That was the bloke before you."

"Was he promoted?" I asked. "Or was he transferred to another ship?" Harold smirked.

"Hazelnut got promoted to minced meat," he said with a grin.

"He finished up in the grinder."

"The propellers," clarified Victor.

"How did that happen?" I asked.

"Nobody knows and Hazelnut is not here anymore to tell the story. Most likely he skidded on the railing and *woosh!* They found his upper arm—or what was left of it—the next day, washed up in Remagen, in the vicinity of the old Lüdendorff bridge. It was identified by his tattoo. Have you got a tattoo?"

I shook my head.

"Would you like one?"

I hesitated. Somehow I realized that a tattoo would be very useful as some sort of identification mark. Harold looked at my upper arms, still virginal white. I had cut the sleeves of my expensive shirts in an effort to looked more muscular, but I still looked like a pen-pusher.

"I know a good address in Cologne," he promised.

"Do they use anesthetic there?" I asked.

Roaring with laughter they both almost fell out of their chairs.

I shrugged and found myself yearning for my old job, for my old, dull routine, and even for my former manager.

* * *

THE NEXT DAY I asked the boson what the job of enginehand actually entailed. He looked at me with a sneer on his face and said, "Well, I'll show you, Andy."

Something which I never had thought possible turned out to be the unfortunate reality. I had been under the misguided assumption that no dirtier work existed on the ship than that which I had so far engaged in. This afternoon proved me wrong. The boson opened a hatch in the wall and shone his torch down a narrow, slick corridor. The overpowering stench of dead fish and used diesel oil hit me in the face. But it is was the smell that I couldn't quite discern that made my stomach turn.

"Watch it, it's slippery," he warned and indicated for me to follow him, walking over a number of loose-laying boards between two large pipes on the floor. There were pools of water everywhere.

"In here are the propeller shafts," he said.

I could feel the vibrations under my hands.

"Now this is the task of an enginehand. He has to keep every moving part greased," he yelled out over the noise. About a meter and a half away from us two large propellers churned in the water, pushing the *Rhinestar* at a speed of thirty kilometers per hour.

Halfway down the tubes, two cylinders had been fixed with a crank on top. The boson opened them and showed me the inside.

"These are the grease pots."

I looked down into a dark evil-smelling lump of grease, which nearly made me heave.

"Fill it up!" ordered the boson, but I did not stir.

He laughed cynically and flipped the lid of a container. With both hands he scooped up some dirty-yellow mess and jammed it into the grease pots. When they were filled, he replaced the lids and turned the handles, forcing the grease into the tubes. He wiped his hands on a dirty rag. When we got back in my rusty cabin, he yelled, "That's the first thing you do every morning!"

AFTER THREE JOURNEYS I got pretty well used to the way of life on board, although the stench of the grease first thing in the morning robbed me of my appetite for breakfast. My language became just as coarse as that of the other crew members and in the galley I even managed to attract the attention of one of the stewardesses. Her name was Wendy. She had red hair and half of what she said was accompanied by a nervous giggle. But the moment she donned her hostess uniform, something maternal came over her. Most likely that was just what I needed, a bit of mothering. However, the question whether I had acted too impulsively in quitting my job with the accounting firm kept nagging at me.

One early morning I had what could be called a 'fortuitous' accident. It occurred after I had filled the grease pots. As usual, the stench was nauseating, and I could not get out of the compartment quick enough, walking over the slippery boards. Halfway down I lost my footing; the torch slipped from my fingers and disappeared in the murky water. I blindly snatched at the walls. Luckily, my hand caught some sort of handle that allowed me to steady myself and continue on down the corridor.

As I eased the sore spots on my shins, I wondered what it was that I had grabbed when my feet went out from under me. I recovered the torch and had a look at the handle. A bolt was fitted to a hatch, and when I at last had managed to wrench it open, I looked into an enormous space with a height of no more than half a meter, where odd strips of light could be seen. I shone my torch inside the cavity. The floor was dry and I decided to climb inside. As far as I could see, there was a forest of pieces of timber supporting wooden beams, and over those, steel plates. Above that should be the passengers' cabins.

I directed the beam towards the rear of the space, but about halfway down the length of the area, darkness took over again. I shut the hatch behind me and shuffled some ten meters through the low-ceiling compartment, until I got to the first cabin. I pressed my ear to the steel sheeting and could catch some indistinct noises, the murmur of a male voice, the sound of water running in a washbasin.

"Hoi, Andy!"

The coarse voice of the boson sounded from a distance. Quickly I switched off my torch. The hatch! Thank goodness, I had closed that behind me. I was sure that I would be in serious trouble if was caught snooping.

I listened intently. Was he going back? I could hear the sound of a steel door being shut and a few moments later the ship's engines started up, followed by the now familiar whistle of departure. That should mean the boson would be in the engine room. I scrambled back like a full-blown infantryman and hurried to the poop deck to haul in the cables.

"You were still having a kip?" the boson called as I ran passed. "Am I supposed to personally kick you out of your bunk from now on?"

THAT NIGHT I waited until I saw the boson climbed up to the bridge, a daily routine to report the activities down below, where he would be rewarded with a few shots of Schnapps. I sneaked via the engine room aft and slid through the newly discovered hatch.

On my back I crawled underneath the cabins and checked the floors, which were all firmly fixed. Only a faint sound of murmuring voices, creaking floorboards or at times cabin doors being opened or closed could be heard. Now and then small puffs of dust wafted down, which made me sneeze. The first few minutes I could still see the outline of the hatch, but as I progressed, winding my way around the numerous uprights, I lost sight of it. When at last I reached a steel wall, I realized that I had reconnoitered the hold sufficiently. I wriggled towards port and noticed to my amazement, that I had enough room to almost stand erect. As a matter of fact, the cabins—more or less like containers—had been lowered into the hold, each one fixed with a sizable window, allowing the occupants to look out over the river. These rested on the ribs of the ship, which left some twenty centimeters of space between the hull and the side panels of the cabins. I squeezed my head and shoulders upwards which gave me about half a meter extra height. Through the cracks in the panels I was able to observe the inside of the cabins up to knee-height of the occupants, therefore all I noticed were ankles and trouser legs. Sound-wise this position was much better.

I could hear the women complain about the meal they just had, the food being too salty, or too tasteless, or too fatty. They were also busy criticizing fellow passengers, judging them either too dull or too noisy. Most of all they were nagging their spouses, who were making nuisances of themselves, getting into the women's way in the confined space of their cabins.

I couldn't help smiling. None of these people had the slightest idea that I could clearly listen in on their most intimate conversations.

I paused at the last twin-berth cabin in the row. From my vantage-point, I could see a pair of well-shaped feminine ankles. Barely three feet away she started putting on a pair of nylon stockings. I wormed my head a bit more upwards to gain a better look through a crack in the paneling, paying for it with a nasty scratch to the back of the head. The woman was unclothed, standing in front of the wardrobe selecting something suitable. She asked whoever was in the room with her what he thought of her selection. A male voice answered, "No darling, there's no need to be trying on anything, we're not going anywhere tonight. In fact that goes for tomorrow night too and the night after that as well. Don't forget our arrangement. You'll just have to be patient for a few more days."

That voice, oh, that voice! That nasal, chagrined tone! So lazy, almost indifferent. I felt myself getting hot and cold at the same time, my forehead started to tingle and my fingers gripped the bottom edge of the cabin. I pressed my eye against the crack, hoping to catch a glimpse, but the man was on his bunk, outside my field of vision.

I listened intently, waiting to hear some more. The woman bent over and busied herself looking for something in the bottom part of the wardrobe. She made a pouty face as she complained bitterly, "I have absolutely had it! Being stuck in here all the time. Would it really matter so much if we went out with the rest of them for once? Nobody would notice us."

The man sighed and for a moment I thought he was going to remain silent. But then I heard a book close and the voice said, "Sweetheart, just have a little more patience; just be patient. For heaven's sake, let's not take any unnecessary risks, something we'll regret later. Look, Karen, when all this is over, we can go out every night, stay out all night for that matter, whatever you want. . . . How about doing some reading?"

The woman straightened up and turned her back toward me. She was wearing only a pair of sheer panties—a sight that would normally have excited me, but I was too scared and nervous to get caught up in it.

That voice . . . that was Vadas! No mistake about that! Vadas, one of the senior partners from the firm where I had worked previously, was a tall, gangly sort of bloke. You could take him for a junior clerk, if it was not for the wrinkles in his face, which showed the fact that he was well past his forties. He had his office on the top floor of the building and he was in the top tier of management in the organization. He carried the responsibility for the administration of the bigger clients, and his signature gave an aura of trustworthiness and stability.

Derek Vadas. How many times had I been called up to his office to do all sorts of calculations! And how often had he corrected my work, always in that lazy, arrogant tone, the same prissy, slimy tone he now used with that woman.

I sat there, riveted to that crack in the floor. It made me jump when I heard him get up, and he then appeared into my field of vision. He patted the woman consolingly on her backside and whispered something in her ear. She shook her head unwillingly.

No two ways about it, that was Vadas! What was he doing here? I was determined to find out.

Vadas took the woman gently by the arm and they both moved behind the wardrobe. A little while later I could clearly hear the juicy sounds of their love play, but frankly, it did not excite me in the least. I was confused. I carefully let myself down again and crawled out of the confined space. What the hell was Vadas doing here on one of those ordinary, common river cruises? Vadas, who would never go anywhere, unless in a limousine . . .

Was this the same Vadas, who now took part in the beer swillings from dripping Steiners in Weinstubes while scantily clad dancing girls in their Tirolian short dresses threw their pale thighs up in the air? The same Vadas, who was always boasting that twice a year he would go on an exotic world trip, and that he had seen all the art treasures of every continent!

And then this Karen . . . I was sure he was not married to her. On the annual Bonner-fête he turned up with a different woman, just as pale, just as tall and just as dull as he was. They had danced together, with bored expressions, without any sign of enjoying themselves, and they had left to go home around eleven. The ideal match!

I locked myself in my cabin to gather my wits.


THE NEXT MORNING during breakfast I asked Wendy if she cared to join me for a drink that night. "We tie up in Koblenz."

Giggling a little, she nodded.

Wendy did not need any encouragement that evening to tell me what I wanted to find out. I was seated next to her in a wooden mock-up of a mediaeval tavern, built on the quay side. Patiently I listened to her bitter complaints about the long working hours, the bothersome passengers, and the lousy wages, until I finally got a chance to get on to the subject of Vadas. At first she did not seem to understand who I was talking about, but when I described the tall, pale man and the young woman, she burst out laughing.

"Oh, you mean Mr. and Mrs. Jonkers," she said and added that so far this couple had spent the entire journey in their cabin.

"They must be on their honeymoon," she assured me. "They hardly take the time to have a decent meal. She arrives in the dining room first, gobbles up her breakfast and can't get back to the cabin quick enough. After that, he turns up. He is always finished in ten minutes or so, and then he's off like a shot. The same thing goes for lunch and dinner. And neither of them has taken part in any of the excursions.

"Wouldn't you like to know what they are doing all day?" she mused with an ambiguous tone in her voice. I replied that I did not have the foggiest idea. But just the same I decided then and there that I was going to find out.

"Even when the cabins are being serviced, he won't go outside," she prattled on. "He stays inside no matter what."

"By the way, which is their cabin?"

"Number eighteen. Do you think they could be ill?"

I shrugged my shoulders; the presence of Vadas puzzled me more and more. For a start, the fact that Vadas never left his cabin but for half an hour per day could indicate shyness. But I had never seen any evidence of that when I knew him at work. Was this cruise just a present to entertain his mistress? If so, it was backfiring. His mistress didn't seem at all pleased with the way things were going. Was that the reason he had boarded under the name *Jonkers*?

I called to the waitress and motioned for two fresh beers. Wendy moved a little closer to me.

"And what about you," she asked. "What brings you to the *Rhinestar*?"

"Oh, nothing in particular," I said. She did not seem to mind such a vague answer. She began to giggle again as I put my arm around her shoulder as we made our way back to the ship. She giggled all the way, and even more when I suggested a guided tour of my cabin.

Not until a few hours later when she darted back to her room did she finally stop giggling.

* * *

THE NEXT MORNING I was up very early. It was always quiet this time of morning. First, I carried out my evil-smelling chores at the grease pots. Having finished that, I disappeared through the hatch and worked out the position of Vadas's cabin. It was rather dark inside their cabin with the curtains closed. Vadas was snoring softly and Karen uttered quaint smacking noises. I assumed they were both sleeping. I spotted a low table that had a couple of drinking glasses and an ashtray, which was filled to the brim with cigarette butts. Throughout the cabin, clothing was either hung or draped, as if a few rounds of strip poker had been played the night before. I tried to find a better viewing position, but collided with an air conditioning duct. I fiddled around with the screws and found out I could undo them by hand. Carefully, I worked the pipe loose and moved it aside a few inches. Now I had a clear view of the whole cabin through the grill. Vadas was lying on one side of the bed; the heap of blankets on the other side had to be Karen.

As if an invisible alarm clock had gone off, Vadas suddenly jumped up from the bed and stumbled to the window. He opened the curtains and I nearly had a laughing fit. Here was Vadas, sporting Donald Duck pajamas!

He mumbled something I could not catch. Then said, "Wake up."

Sleepy sounds came from the bed. The mountain of blankets came to life and Karen appeared. In contrast to Vadas, she was not wearing anything at all. I followed her movements breathlessly while Vadas stared out of the window.

"You'd better go first," he said and sank into one of the chairs. Karen disappeared behind the shower screen and started to wash up. Vadas yawned and picked up a book. An icy silence filled the room. After she had dried and dressed herself, he threw her a vague hand kiss.

"Enjoy your breakfast," he said in a bored voice.

"Let's hope the coffee is not as weak as it was yesterday," she replied and left the cabin.

Vadas rose and sauntered over to the shower. I felt a bit disappointed. Apart from Karen's body I had not seen anything interesting, and I decided to withdraw from my observation tower, while Vadas was busy putting on a track suit. I changed my mind when he suddenly closed the curtains. Next he switched on the lights, locked the cabin door and with a firm tug pulled the blankets off the bed. I recognized his sturdy briefcase at once—the expensive snakeskin and those extra heavy-duty security locks. He cleared the table, put the case in front of him and tapped out the security code. He stretched his fingers in front of him and undid the locks.

I had to force myself not to let out a whistle.

Instead of the usual files and documents, bundles of banknotes appeared, nearly spilling out all sides of the opened briefcase. And in all sorts of currencies! I recognized German marks, Swiss francs and stacks of Dutch thousand guilder notes.

I stood there fascinated. Our senior partner was traveling around with a fortune!

Quickly, I tried to make an estimate of how much he must be carting around, while Vadas took out one of the bundles and gently checked the number of notes. He let them spin through his hands. He evidently liked the sound very much. He put the bundle back with such gentleness, you'd think he was putting a baby back in its crib.

Next, he took Karen's beautycase and opened it: no such thing as lipsticks or mascara, but here also were stacks of bank notes!

Had Vadas sprung the casino? Flabbergasted, I watched how he let the bank notes slide over his thumb as if he was counting the money once more. Why not deposit all that money in the bank? No wonder he never wanted to leave his cabin.

He was startled by a knock on the door. Quickly he shut everything and put it away, only to discover it was just Karen at the door. Right then I heard the ship's horns giving the departure signal, so I carefully retreated and went to my station. As I released the hawsers and hauled them in, I kept thinking about the huge sum of money Vadas had been hiding in his cabin. He could easily afford to buy the *Rhinestar* and most likely a few sister ships as well!

FOR THE REST of the day I did my work like a robot. I made sure to stay away from the passengers as much as possible. There was something suspicious about Vadas and Karen. All sorts of questions raced through my mind and I hardly noticed Wendy's sweet smiles during the break. Disappointed, she got up even before the cook came to hand out the bowls of custard.

After the evening meal, I was determined to find out what was going on in cabin eighteen. Near the engine room I hid myself behind a stack of deck chairs and waited until the boson emerged. I slipped inside and a few moments later I had taken up my position behind the grill. I was prepared to stick it out for the rest of the night, if necessary.

A gloomy atmosphere lingered in the cabin. Karen sat there bored, smoking one cigarette after the other, while she was doing a crossword puzzle. Vadas was reading a book. Now and then Karen asked for help with a clue. It was not until eleven that there was some movement, when Vadas filled glasses out of a bottle containing dark-brown liquor.

At long last Karen stretched and commented that the place was getting stuffy. Vadas closed his book.

"Christ, I'll happy when we can get off this ship," he said. "When exactly do we get to Basel?"

"The first officer has announced that the travel schedule has been altered," Karen answered in a lazy fashion. "There are supposed to be fireworks somewhere around here. We'll have to wait for that, but after that it is straight to Basel and our Monday afternoon appointment."

" . . .We'll say good-bye to this dump," he added. "And then we can finally deposit our precious cargo in the bank."

They raised their glasses and Vadas continued: "I'd love to see old Fritz Bonner's face when he finds out that Derek Vadas not only looked after the firm, but looked after number one at the same time."

"You're absolutely right," Karen said. "Why should you have to work your guts out just to get fat dividends for the shareholders? And you did not steal anything! They can't hold that against you, all you did was sell your signature. . . ."

Vadas smiled.

"Just the same, that prim and proper Bonner will fall over backwards when he finds out that a few of his largest customers are not as respectable as he always thought!"

"What a shame that the Internal Revenue smelled a rat," Karen said in an animated tone. "Do you think they were tipped off?"

Vadas shrugged his shoulders. Karen had a teasing look in her eyes.

"All right, I'll level with you," she began. "I put them wise. I was fed up seeing you only once a week in some little hotel room. . . ."

"You lying bitch!" Vadas grabbed a towel and tossed it at her playfully, something that was completely uncharacteristic of the Vadas I knew. She dodged and asked innocently, "Who did then?"

"In our circles one is only too keen to rat on the other," Vadas said coolly. "But it is going to take old Fritz Bonner and his staff a hell of a long time to sort out who was responsible for this."

"And by that time Mr. and Mrs. Jonkers will be sitting high and dry in a Brazilian bungalow!"

"Knowing Bonner, I'm quite sure that he'll do anything to thwart an investigation," Vadas continued. "The bigger the scandal, the bigger the damage for the firm. Poor old Fritz, a partner in spite of . . ."

Contentedly Vadas lit a cigar and blew the smoke in the direction of the grill.

"I wonder if that damned thing works," he remarked and fiddled with the switch. He disappeared from my vision and I heard him dragging some furniture.

All of a sudden his face was right in front of me, less than twenty centimeters away! I pulled backwards and banged my head against the hull. Vadas did not seem to hear. He looked at the grill and tried to determine why there was no fresh air coming into the cabin.

I was scared stiff. It seemed almost impossible that he did not spot me. I could even smell his smoker's breath, but he did not seem to notice anything. He knocked a few times with his knuckles on the grill and tried to work it loose. His face disappeared again.

"I'm going to ring the purser," he said and picked up the phone next to the bed. I let myself down and crawled back as quickly as I could.

Back on my bunk the excitement had been too much to make me fall asleep straightaway.

Vadas an embezzler! That dull, weaselly character a first-class fraud!

It did not take me long to work out what he had done. Vadas had put his signature under the yearly balance sheets of enterprises who did not mind coughing up a decent amount, if certain earnings could be hidden from the Prosecution and the Internal Revenue. In exchange for payment, Vadas had maneuvered the money in such devious ways that it was as good as untraceable in the bookkeeping. After all, his signature was the official approval of a respectable firm such as Bonner & Associates, which was a guarantee for the fiscal investigators.

And now Vadas was on his way to put his gathered fortune into some discreet bank in Switzerland and after that migrate to some distant country with his mistress, where life would be one big party.

Most likely, an arrest warrant had been issued against him, and to avoid all possible risks he had very cleverly selected the *Rhinestar* to transport himself and his loot across the borders. The customs officers would only come aboard to scrounge a decent cup of coffee or a good Dutch cigar.

My conclusion was that Vadas had arranged it very cleverly, indeed.

But by dawn, when I finally fell asleep, I had also concluded that it would be worth a very decent price to Vadas if I promised to keep my mouth shut. In fact, I had already worked out in my mind how I could get a piece of that fortune.

"Hoi, ANDY!"

The boson woke me up. It was six o'clock and I had been sound asleep.

"We're about to tie up in St. Goarshausen. We'll be there for the day. After dinner, we steam farther upstream and drop anchor near the Loreley. A big show there tonight, *Rhine Ablaze* they call it. Great fireworks, a laser show and all the trimmings. When they are finished, a pilot comes aboard. We'll be sailing all night as well as tomorrow. You'll be on stand-by during that period. Make sure you're ready aft when the last shots have been fired. The captain wants to leave immediately."

"Aye-aye, boson!"

"Just see that you get some shut-eye this afternoon. There won't be much sleeping for the coming thirty-six hours."

I saluted, which sent the boson on his way, shaking his head in despair.

Inside I was jubilant. What he had just told me was enough for me to organize the last details.

That afternoon I jumped back in my bunk, like the boson had ordered, and this time I did not need any rocking.

AFTER DINNER we slowly moved upstream towards the center of the river, a good vantage point for viewing Rhine Ablaze. Victor and I dropped both anchors, while above us on the upper deck the passengers, all carrying drinks, had gathered to make sure not to miss the spectacle. As I had expected, Karen was amongst them, minus Vadas. No doubt he had stayed in his cabin like a watchdog.

I waited until the first explosions echoed between the rock walls. The gigantic rockets brought a fairy-tale atmosphere over the ancient castles on both sides of the riverbanks. Everybody was gazing skywards, even the captain and the chief were using their binoculars to watch the display.

After about a quarter of an hour, I eased away from the gathered crew on the fore deck and got a very loving look from Wendy, who most likely was looking forward to a romantic evening. I winked back at her warmly.

I hastened to the passengers' quarters. I sneaked into the purser's office, where the telephone-exchange was situated and punched in the numbers of cabin eighteen. Vadas answered at once.

"Jonkers speaking."

I spoke in a deep voice. "Good evening, sir, this is the captain speaking. Sorry that I have to disturb you, but could you come up to bridge at once? Your wife has met . . . ah . . . with a slight accident. We don't think it is very serious, but I think it would be better if you came."

I could hear Vadas hesitate.

"A physician has been called for," I added.

"I'm on my way," he growled and put the receiver down.

I waited until Vadas had locked his cabin and I heard his hasty footsteps. I dashed over to the engine room, where I grabbed a crowbar from the boson's toolbox.

I collected my kitbag from my cabin and got down to the bottom of the ship. Outside, the sounds of the explosions kept bouncing back and forth between the high rock walls of the Rhine valley. I didn't have to worry about making any noise.

I jammed the crowbar in the crack, which I had used before as a peephole and started to force the paneling open. The wall did not give that easily, particularly as I had only twenty centimeters of space to get some leverage. Cursing and sweating, I banged away with the crowbar until something gave and an opening was formed. I bent over further until finally the entire panel shattered with a lot of noise and I stumbled inside the cabin. I made straight for Vadas's bed and tore away the blankets.

Empty!

There was nothing in the bed! Shit, did Vadas take his briefcase upstairs?

Quickly I went through all the drawers and wardrobes. Still nothing . . .

I looked around, something red under the washbasin caught my eye. Karen's beautycase! That would have to do!

I only had about a few more minutes to get back aft. Quickly, I stuck the safety chain of the night lock in its groove. Most likely Vadas was now on his way back and a locked door would keep him occupied for a while. . . . I jammed the beautycase in my kitbag and crawled back through the hole, panting.

Looking as relaxed as possible, I walked back aft and gazed over the river. Was the pilot launch already on its way? As the fireworks reached their climax, I calmed down a bit. It would be at least ten minutes before Vadas had forced the door of his cabin open. In the meantime the pilot would have come aboard, and the next thing I knew I would be safely tucked away in the pilot's launch. From earlier occasions I had learned that it was easy to bribe the young chaps who piloted the fast-moving motor launches.

A massive burst of rockets threw a bright glow over the Rhine. Veterans stood there cheering like they were back in the trenches and the long-awaited artillery support had come at last. I peered over at the river again. Finally, here came the pilot's launch. Right on time, or *Pünktlichkeit*, as the Germans would say!

I gave a wave and the pilot answered with a light flash. Another two minutes and a whole new life was ahead of me. From sailor to millionaire. How's that for a career change!

Vadas would not be able to get off the ship for at least twenty-four hours and would no doubt think twice before he would report the theft. I was wondering how he was going to explain the damage in his cabin!

"Hoi, Andrew!"

I turned around and looked into Wendy's radiant, smiling face. Bewildered, I stared at her. She had followed me, obviously taking my wink as an invitation.

The moment she spotted my kitbag, her eyes fell on the approaching pilot's launch. She put two and two together.

"So, you're thinking of jumping ship?" she asked haughtily. "Without saying good-bye? So it was a one-night stand after all?"

I opened my mouth to answer, but a deafening clap of rockets exploding, prevented me from being heard. I looked at the launch, which was then only about five meters away from the *Rhinestar*. The pilot was about to climb on board.

"You bastard!" she yelled in a high-pitched voice. Undeterred, I turned my attention to the pilot. I assisted him on board and said that the captain was anxious to leave as soon as possible.

"Hang on, I'm coming with you!" I called out to the young kid in the steering launch.

He nodded and maneuvered the bow of his launch against the poop.

As I turned around, Wendy got hold of my kitbag. I extended my hand, but Wendy moved back. Spitefully, she held the bag over the railing.

"You scum!" A hateful expression came over her face.

"Wendy, come with me!" I tried desperately.

"Isn't that a bit late?" she asked in an ironic tone. "Or were you perhaps too shy to ask? I never noticed any shyness last night. . . ."

I could hear the ship's engines being started up and the water around the propellers was whirling.

"What have you got in here?" she asked. "Your dirty laundry? Going to take this back to mammy?"

"Hand it over!" I yelled and gestured to the pilot's assistant that I was on my way.

The propellers stirred the water even more.

At that very moment the grand finale of Rhine Ablaze lit up the river and turned it into a sea of bright light.

Wendy was stunned for a second and I made a dash for my kitbag. She parried and I felt her sharp nails clawing my face. Through my momentum she lost her balance and fell backwards. Her arms were flying through the air, the kitbag right in front of me within reaching distance! But Wendy's eyes were terrified with a death fear and she let out a scream of anguish as she stumbled backwards.

Reflexively I grabbed her and pulled her back, saving her from the same dreadful fate that met Hazelnut. She clutched me, preventing me from grabbing at the bag. I was forced to watch my ill-gotten fortune disappear over the side and plunge into the river via the poop deck. I shut my eyes. I thought I could hear the crunch as the propellers split the beautycase wide open and began churning the precious contents into pulp.

I shoved Wendy, who had started to cry softly, aside, and gazed in stunned silence at the churning water behind the ship. An impatient cry from the kid brought me back to my senses. I jumped into the launch, waving goodbye to Wendy.


AS THE *RHINESTAR* disappeared from sight, I touched the scratches on my face. The kid offered me a cigarette.

"Holy Christ, what a bitch!" he commented. "She wasn't letting you go easy, was she? That never happens to me. What is it that you've got that I haven't?"

With an effort I swallowed.

"How about money," I said as I watched the churning waters of the Rhine light up one last time behind me in the wake of our boat.

# The Merry Ghosts of the Grampus

## ARNALDO CORREA

The sergeant opened the cell with keys he had lifted from the police officer snoring twenty feet away. Then he pulled out his revolver and pointed it at the head of the prisoner who stood inside the cell watching him, fearing the worst.

"Listen carefully. I am going to let you escape. Now I will wake that policeman, and bring him up here for you to strangle him."

"Strangle him! So I will give you an excuse to kill me?"

"You are a dead man already. If I wanted that, I would have let the mob lynch you yesterday."

"It was a fair fight and I won."

"I know, I was there watching. That is the problem, you won the fight with Antoine Canalet."

"I had no choice. If I had not killed him, he would have butchered me."

"You are right on that. He butchered all his adversaries before you. That is the reason natives blindly bet all they had on him every time he fought. Yesterday, they lost a lot of money. Those people are very poor; they cannot stand such heavy loses. It was a big mistake to win your fight. Now I am supposed to take you to the city's prison. Three of Antoine's brothers and five cousins are locked up there. All three hundred inmates are Antoine's dear friends. Every time he won a fight, he sent them a big chocolate cake. You will never get out of prison alive. Each one there would love to fight to the death the man who killed Antoine Canalet."

Convinced by the persuasive talk of the sergeant that he had no salvation, the prisoner seemed to melt. He let himself down on the cement floor.

"Go ahead and shoot me!"

"Like most people, you hear but you don't listen. Do you remember what I said when I came in? Once you kill the guard, you have to run to the pier. A rowboat is waiting for you there. Take it and row as fast as you can to a ship standing about two hundred yards away. As soon as you are on board, the ship will weigh anchor and leave the island."

"Why do I have to strangle the guard?"

"No witnesses, that's why. Besides, I will have to have a reasonable explanation as to how you escaped. If anyone suspects that I let the man who killed Antoine Canalet go free, I will be a dead man myself."

The police officer with the missing keys stirred. He saw the sergeant pointing his gun at the prisoner. He hurried to the side of his superior, drew his gun with his left hand, and pointed it at the head of the young man in the cell.

The sergeant looked down to the guard and wrinkled his nose at the smell of cheap rum. The difference in height between the two men was more than a foot.

"How many times do I have to tell you not to drink while you are on duty? On top of that, you were sleeping like a starving dog when you were supposed to be guarding a dangerous criminal. Go inside the cell and handcuff the prisoner! It is past four o'clock; already it's high tide and I have to be past the channel at sunrise."

The guard put the revolver into his holster and stepped inside the cell. The young man sitting at a corner of the room got up, volunteering his two hands to the police officer ready to handcuff him. However, with a quick movement the prisoner grabbed the guard's left hand and twisted the arm at his back. Then, he clenched his right arm around the neck of the astonished guard, pressing the two carotid arteries dry. The thin old man put up a short struggle, gasping for air twice before quivering for the last time.

The prisoner took the big .45 caliber Colt revolver out of the dead man's holster and walked in a daze to the door of the town's jail. As soon as he stepped outside there was a big bang—a bullet went through the wooden door, just six inches above his head. He ran towards a pier that was just a block away. He heard a second blast after he had run about two hundred feet; a bullet smashed against a telephone pole less than a yard from him. A third shot hummed past him just at the moment he jumped from the pier into the rowboat, the fresh salty air filling his lungs. He saw for the first time the dark silhouette of a lonely ship stationed not far away.

The lights of the ship went on and the roar of an engine sounded louder. The forth and fifth shots hit the bay's quiet moonlit water while the escapee rowed for his life towards the big boat. The persecution ended when the now free man jumped out of the small boat to the plank on the side of the big vessel and climbed up to the lifeboat deck in a hurry. Once there, he hid inside a boat while the craft moved away from a little island lost in the southeastern rim of the Caribbean Sea.

AT NOON the next day, the former prisoner calculated the ship was far enough from the jail from which he had escaped that he decided to see the captain to try to make a deal with him. After thinking carefully on what happened, he concluded that those who organized his escape must have some sort of understanding with the captain. Maybe the merchants of the island who made very good money betting on him paid the sergeant and the captain for his freedom. Besides that, he was thirsty, hot and hungry. Under the canvas covering the lifeboat, the temperature had been steadily rising since sunrise. It was now up to about 120°.

It was a beautiful passenger ship. Everything smelled and looked brand-new. He loved ships, all sorts of ships, and this one was very easy to love, but he had no time for that now. No one was on the main deck. He decided to explore the ship, searching for a sailor or an officer before attempting to reach the captain's quarters. He went down to the engine room thinking surely he would find somebody there, but the place was locked up and there was nobody in sight. He climbed up to the command bridge only to find the pilot's cabin empty and locked. The ship was easily doing twenty knots with no pilot or anybody in charge! Bewildered by this strange situation, and nearly in a panic, he desperately looked around and started yelling.

"Looking for someone?" He heard a voice at his back.

He turned around, trying to look innocent. A well-dressed gentleman stood before him, about fifty, medium height, dark curly hair beginning to gray at the sideburns, with a triangular, funny-looking mustache. Nevertheless, his most impressive feature was his dark brown eyes, full of intelligence and understanding such as he had never before seen. The man, with his right hand, had a tight grip on the leash of a big dog that was surveying the stranger with suspicion and animosity.

"Easy, Tiger!" The dog relaxed. "I am the Master of the ship. Let's go into my cabin to have something to drink and to eat."

"Sir, my name is Arthur Gordon. Does anyone pilot this ship?"

"It is fully automated. Just set the coordinates where you want to go, the ship does the rest. A computer calculates the best route, taking into account the weather forecast, water depth, trade winds, sea currents, movement of the tide, and so on. The same computer with sensors and other peripheral equipment does all the navigator's and pilot's work. And just in case you suddenly decide to change your course, you have this."

The Master showed him something black with buttons, like a TV remote. Demonstrating, he pushed one button and the ship began to turn to starboard. He let the button go and the ship corrected its course by itself.

"What about sea traffic and other obstacles along the way?"

"All natural accidents are signaled on the marine charts in the computer's memory. The position of the vessel is determined constantly with the aid of satellites and other means, with an accuracy of plus or minus ten feet. The radar and sonar systems detect everything on top and under the surface. The computer has the finest expert programs to make whatever decision is best to keep its course, avoid collision, and cope with natural disasters, including hurricanes and tidal waves."

The Master pushed a big red button and the ship trembled, letting out the sound of a siren.

"I love that sound," he said softly.

The Master let the dog loose as they entered a large cabin. The upper half of the walls were covered with television monitors showing different sections of the ship. The lower half had a lot of electronic meters that gauged everything measurable on the ship. The Master's cabin resembled the cockpit of a gigantic spacecraft. Arthur understood he was seeing the first of a new ship's generation. On a table, there was lunch for two. The Master opened a bottle of champagne, already cold.

"Mister Gordon, your freedom deserves a toast."

"Thanks very much. I would like to explain to you everything that happened to me. I have had the most horrible luck. . . ."

"You owe me no explanations. I am well acquainted with your story. I watched your fight with Antoine yesterday. It is a savage custom of that island dating back from piracy days; a local character challenging an outsider. The merchants are to blame; they used to pay Antoine to pick a fight with whomever they thought fit. The unwritten rule of that sordid game is that merchants always have to bet on foreigners. Over the last ten years, Antoine Canalet made them lose a lot of money, but gave them good fights to enjoy. Yesterday, the merchants cleaned all the natives' pockets, but saw a lousy fight. Antoine Canalet was slow and clumsy, as if he had been drugged."

Arthur was startled to hear that. He kept silent for a few minutes, then remarked, "It was a nightmare!"

"Now, Mr. Gordon, you have to decide on your next move."

"I was thinking maybe I could buy a lifeboat from you. I can pay triple its worth. Back in the U.S. I have some money in the bank."

"If you want a boat, I can give it to you. Do not make a final decision until you see the warrant released by the Interpol High Commissioner for the Caribbean early this morning. I copied a tape for you."

The Master turned on a television and video set. The first image to appear was Arthur's photo with the heading "Vicious Killer at Large." An announcer came on and said, "Yesterday, this man murdered the well-known wrestler Antoine Canalet and the guard of a local jail. Interpol is making inquires to see if this man is 'Hyena,' the most wanted killer in the Caribbean." A long forensic description of the two homicides followed. The information was first announced in English, repeated in Spanish, French, and Portuguese. It was intended for all police garrisons in the Caribbean.

"What do you suggest I do? The sergeant mentioned the name of your ship. I do not want to cause you any trouble."

"You must not worry about that. Among the many features I had installed in this craft is the ability to change the ship's name and flags— all at the mere touch of a button. As soon as we were out of sight, the name *Ariel* changed to *Penguin*, the Panamanian flag to the Liberian banner. All the names this ship uses are registered in different countries.

Many nations offer that service at a competitive price. It comes in handy in situations like this one. You also asked me what you should do. I provided you with the information for you to decide. I never give advice."

"Sir, I beg you to let me stay on board at least for a few months. I will be captured as soon as I set foot on any shore. I am sure you can use an extra hand. I am from Nantucket, and I am very well acquainted with marine life. You do not have to pay me any salary, just room and board. I swear I am not Hyena."

The Master stood silent for some time, weighing the petition of the youngster.

"It is not a fair arrangement because you do not have any alternative. You are condemned to be on board this ship. On top of that, I know your real identity, and if I so choose, I can send you to prison and even to death. As time passes by, you will become increasingly resentful of this situation and eventually against me. Some day you will be tempted to change your luck, and the easier way will be to get rid of me with the skills you recently developed, thus solving half your problems."

"No, no, I became a killer only by accident; by destiny. I swear on the Holy Cross that I shall be grateful to you until I die. Please, help me, sir!"

The Master looked into the watery eyes of the young man kneeling in front of him as though he was attempting to read Arthur's true thoughts and feelings, those written very deep inside his mind. Arthur passed the test.

"Sure, I can use an extra hand, but what I need is somebody that I can trust completely. In the present situation you could never be that person. How can I put you in a position to be that man? It is something that I need to think on. Maybe later I can come up with another solution. Anyway, you can remain on board as long as you want. Now, let's eat."

THE NEXT DAY the ship anchored about twelve miles south of Les Saintes and Marie Galante islands. At mid-morning, a yacht brought in five men hired as sailors. Arthur, who already knew his way around, instructed the men, showing them to their quarters. The same day, in the afternoon, there was another stop close to Carlisle Bay in Antigua Island to pick up three cooks, two men and a woman. The voyage continued north, bordering the great chain of the Minor Antilles, with no other incidents.

That night they saw the lights from Saint Martin and Basseterre islands, and at dawn entered the Virgin Islands' waters. The whole next day they kept in sight of Puerto Rico and early on the following day they anchored close to La Romana in the Dominican Republic. At noon, a tugboat came towing a barge full of musicians. The band, once it was close to the ship, started playing salsa music, and the help already on board received the band with dancing and singing. Arthur was instructed by the Master to open a few bottles of rum and to keep the music, which was amplified by the powerful sound system of the ship, going all night long. It made the swimmers at Playa Real and Hamaca beaches dance, while the ship cruised by. Next stop was close to Les Caves, Haiti. Men hired as deck stewards and two waiters boarded the ship. The last stop in the Caribbean was near Montego Bay, Jamaica, where a barman and a small band of calypso players boarded.

Once the crew started coming on the ship, the Master remained in his cabin, watching everything they did on the closed-circuit television system. He instructed Arthur on a cellular telephone about the details of the work needed to be done by each one. After the day's work, Arthur visited the Master's cabin and had dinner with him. To the young man, the conversations with the Master were among the most enlightening events in his whole life. Day after day the man revealed himself as an incredible mixture of a bright entrepreneur with his feet solidly set on economic facts and earthy logic, and a dreamer with great vision. All of that, wrapped into the loneliness of a pessimistic personality, made the Master a man who was firmly convinced of each man's inescapable fate.

On their way northwestward, they bordered the island of Cuba far off its coasts, crossed the Yucatan Channel and entered the Florida Straight. Arthur worked as hard as he could to team up with the crew before the men who were to take over the ship came on board. He had let his beard grow and the sun had tanned his skin and bleached his hair. He had lost fifteen pounds since he left his native Nantucket three months earlier, still being a boy. Now he was a hard-core outlaw, a murderer wanted by Interpol. He thought his best chance for the moment was to stay on board until he found a way to change his identity and rebuild his life in a remote place where nobody knew who he was; maybe he would travel up the Amazon River with the ship and live forever among the Indians. The first conversation he had with the Master came to his mind. In less than a week he was already planning how to change his fate, and the Master did not fit into any of his plans.

The rest of the crew was picked up in the United States. The captain, three main officers, the first engine man, and two more mechanics boarded the ship in Key West, Florida. None of them had met before. The captain and the officers were lodged in cabins reserved for the passengers, something they did not find suitable. Later, they were amazed to discover that they did not have to take care of the ship. Their work was to be well-dressed in uniforms, all the time entertaining the passengers. The captain reviewed for quite some time the pilot's cabin, watching how everything worked by itself, then went to the Master's cabin to complain only to find a world of equipment he was not acquainted with.

"Are you capable of taking over?" asked the Master, showing the captain his cabin.

The captain took one look around, saw that he and his skills were not needed, and made up his mind to just enjoy the cruise. He adapted to his new "work" quickly; he drank a bottle of whisky a day without showing the slightest sign of drunkenness.

In the New York harbor, the ship took on all sorts of provisions. One hundred fifty passengers, all winners of some sort of contest, came on board. They were eager to enjoy a two-week trip to the Caribbean Islands on the maiden voyage of the *Grampus*.

The night the ship left New York's harbor, the Master was more animated than usual. He said to Arthur, "This whole idea comes from a child's nightmare. This trip will tell me how close my imagination has been able to foretell reality. Rather, how reality can match my imagination."

For several days afterward, Arthur wondered about the real meaning of these words, but like many other times the Master's thoughts remained obscure and hard to grasp, cloaked in a mysticism impossible for Arthur to understand.

<u>August 1</u>

I have decided to keep a diary. Many ominous thoughts crowd my mind. My mother always told me that if you write down what is troubling you and study it carefully, that things would become clearer. If I die some horrible death, as I often obscurely fear, this diary may also be of help for someone trying to seek the truth. I haven't started it earlier because I've been devising a way to keep *him* from knowing about it. It would be disastrous if he ever read these notes. I know he has ways of spying on all angles of every cabin, even inside the closets. There must be hundreds of tiny television cameras, some of them with infrared vision, installed in all places, making him capable of seeing every part of the ship on his monitors. I know he has the means to listen to all conversations on board no matter where and how they occur. Here is the way I am writing in my diary so he doesn't see me doing it: I set the cabin temperature very low with the air condition control so I may use a thick blanket on top of the linen sheet when I go to sleep. With the aid of a small flashlight, I write every night in the diary beneath the blanket, keeping the notebook on me at all times.

Soon after I settled myself in the ship, I began to reflect on the tragic events that had changed my life so completely. I wondered how it was that Antoine picked on me for a fight until death. Who arranged my escape and why? Later, I began to wonder why I had ended up in that godforsaken tiny island in the first place, with a population of less than ten thousand people.

The first event I can link in some way with all of these was a booklet I received by mail with wonderful color pictures and a description of a place like a heaven. The advertisement caught my imagination because it undoubtedly was written by a good poet, and I like poetry very much. Three months later, just when I was about to finish my BS degree at the university, I received an unexpected invitation from a cousin to visit him in Guadeloupe, a French colony in the Antilles. The man was a son of my father's elder brother who went to Europe during World War II, married in France, and never came back to the U.S. Tempted, but not persuaded, I wrote back thanking him for the invitation and the opportunity to know a close relative. At the same time, I gave him some vague economic reasons for not being able to accept his invitation. A week later, I received a round trip plane ticket to Guadeloupe with a letter saying I would have little, if any, expenses on my visit. I could stay in his house in Guadeloupe as long as I pleased. Also, whenever I wanted, I could use a cottage at a beach on a nearby island which remained unknown to tourists because of its poor communication and transportation facilities. *A single word could describe the place: Paradise* was the exact wording in the letter.

When I arrived in Guadeloupe, my cousin met me at the airport and told me he had to leave on short notice for France. We both decided it was a good opportunity for me to go to the beach and live in his cottage during his absence (about two weeks). He arranged the trip and everything else from the airport. When I arrived by a small seaplane, I discovered it was the same place in the advertisement I had received. At this point, I wondered if this ad was sent to me by chance or if there was an obscure linkage with everything that occurred later. How to explain the ad if the place was not opened to tourists? A letter I received from my mother just before I went to the airport struck me now as most disturbing. She recalled my father's brother had had only girls. I was to question my cousin on that matter and send her the explanation. She, like all women of her generation, wanted to know if my cousin was born out of wedlock.

I decided to start questioning the Master in a subtle way, at the right moments, because every day I convinced myself that "chance" had little to do with what had happened to me since I left Nantucket. The evening we left New York, the Master and I had an especially nice meal. He was happy and drank more than usual; it seemed like the right time.

"Master, why do you think Antoine provoked me to fight him?"

He answered with his usual frankness, "My dear Arthur, everything in nature is based on facts. If you keep that in mind with the facts in hand, you can figure out everything. Your handsome figure and the way you flaunt yourself, running around in bright-colored sports clothes, wearing dark glasses nobody else wore, with a plug in your ear and a cord hanging to a black box on your belt. Your provocative swimming outfit at the beach and your weightlifting demonstrations . . . All of that aroused the curiosity of the prettiest girls on the island, and later it stirred their sexual desire and created infatuation among many. Everybody knows the best looking girls on the island are the fat merchants' mistresses, and they are very observant to their dames' moods and interests. With those facts in hand, it is easy to conclude that the merchants decided to put an end to all your fooling around. That's why they hired Antoine to fight you."

## August 2

Yesterday we left New York with a total of 186 people on board, counting the physician who arrived late to Key West and then flew to New

York to meet us there. Things are going much better than expected with a first-time crew. Why didn't the Master get at least part of the help already experienced in this sort of voyage? The captain and the officers told me they had no experience in this business. The captain used to command a cargo ship, the only thing the first officer knew about was oil tankers, and the second officer had his experience fishing. Relieved of their regular duties, they developed quickly into wonderful hosts for the passengers. They appointed me head steward and left the detailed work to me.

## August 3

Today is my twenty-second birthday. Since yesterday, I have been home-sick, wanting to talk on the telephone, or at least send messages, to all my relatives, especially my mother. However, nobody must ever know I am hiding here. Besides, there was so much work to do that soon I forgot about my birthday. To my surprise, when I went that evening to the Master's cabin, he had ordered for me a special dinner and a cake with my age written in chocolate. I asked him how he knew, and he said my birthday was on the information released by Interpol. He was in a very good humor. He told me the most fantastic story about the origin of his wealth. At the age of twenty he decided to become rich because poor people are very limited on what they can do. He went to Spain to study old Spanish records on the galleons that left Mexico and Peru and never reached Spain. Then he studied all the shipwrecks and pirate attacks against the galleons. All of that took him four years. For the next two, he looked for the records of the treasures that had been found and the techniques used to recover them. He ended up with a plan to search for some of the most amazing treasures ever put together in history. He went to see the richest man on earth at that time, the Greek Aristotle Onasiss, who agreed to provide a ship at his disposal and foot all expenses for 50 percent of the findings. Six months later, the partnership was dissolved with around 100 million dollars in profit being the outcome for each partner. The Master invested part of his money in buying his own outfit, and for the next five years he made no new finding of importance, spending much of his fortune, until he made his greatest discovery, a galleon with the fortune of Aztec Emperor Montezuma.

"The worth of that treasure is incalculable," the Master said, then got up and walked about the place adding, as if he was thinking aloud, *"but the ghosts in the mind don't go away regardless of the size of your fortune."*

<u>August 4</u>

I can't wait to write down the transcendental conversation I just had with the Master. He was most agitated. Today he made me look at his eyes—I don't know for how long. Then he asked me what was I hiding from him. I couldn't resist his sight. I ended up telling him about the diary! He took the notebook when I showed it to him, read all of it in a minute, then smiled at me and again was the gentle friend he is most of the time.

"Poor Arthur," he said, "maybe I owe you an explanation. Yes, of course, I was the one who wanted to save you. I was there at the park. Like everybody else in town, I witnessed how Antoine ridiculed you in front of a crowd. I saw your fight with Antoine, and I knew what was going to happen next, so I bribed the sergeant. A few thousand francs changed owners that night, and I only had to weigh anchor two hours earlier than I'd planned. Is that what you wanted to know?"

I felt as ashamed, like a child caught doing something forbidden. He read again all the foolish things I'd written down about my cousin. Then he went to a closet where he keeps his liquor and selected a bottle of very old Spanish brandy. He opened, tasted, and approved it, before serving two cups and proposing a toast.

He said, "Arthur, I know how you feel. In your present condition, it is natural that all sorts of ideas come to your mind about me. It is your subconscious mind grinding and grinding to find me guilty of any shady scheme against you. Once you find it, the next step is clear. Do you remember what I told you when you asked me to remain on board? I've been thinking hard and I found a way to straighten up our mutual relationship. Since it is impossible to erase your killings, I am going to do my own. So, we both will be at the same level, then mutual trust and, eventually true friendship can grow. Let's drink to that."

I drank with him, not quite grasping the meaning of his words or the consequences that toast might later have. Now, when I read again what I wrote, I realize that he gave no explanation why Antoine was drugged.

Did he pay for that too? The implications of a positive answer to that question are overwhelming for me.


August 12

The last entry I wrote on August 4 was meant to be the end of the diary because its purpose had been fulfilled in some way. But the thoughts that assaulted me in the last minute I wrote it justify keeping it open. The nature of the matter certainly kept my subconscious mind "grinding, grinding, at all times," to use the Master's own words. Since I have proven myself so vulnerable to the inquisitiveness of his sight, I hesitated for many days to write down anything in the diary. On the other hand, the strenuous work of feeding, entertaining, and keeping 150 people from doing foolish things left me little free time. I even missed most of the dinners with the Master because of work that could not be delayed.

Our first stop was Havana, on the fourth day of the voyage. The passengers and part of the crew went on a short tour to Old Havana, and a dinner and show at the famous Tropicana nightclub. The captain and the officers had a difficult time bringing back some of the single males. Three days later, the ship anchored in Montego Bay, Jamaica. From there on, most of the travel was done at night. Each day the ship stayed anchored at a different place in the Caribbean: Haiti, Dominican Republic, Saint Martin, Antigua, Guadeloupe, Martinique and Santa Lucia. On those stops, most of the passengers went on shore after breakfast for sightseeing and came back late in the afternoon.


August 13

After twelve days of voyage, we started last night to return to the United States, taking a northern route through the Bahamas to reach Key West as a final destination on August 14. Late in the afternoon, the Master called me on the telephone and asked me to come at once to his cabin. I found him in a gloomy mood.

"This is preposterous, Arthur. What sort of animals are we herding from place to place? I have selected for you some of the most atrocious and flagrant distortions of human conduct you've ever seen."

He turned on ten monitors. On each one appeared images of passengers and crewmembers doing immoral things. The Master moved excitedly from one monitor to the next.

"Look at this woman. She has had an average of five men each day. Almost all the men on board have been to bed with her, except her husband. Look at the piano player. He had women in pairs and trios. No wonder he shows up to work only half of the time. What about the cooks, the deck steward and all the sailors? They are the most voracious thieves I've ever seen. Watch how many different ways they steal. Look how and where they stashed a ton of silverware. Do you see that fat ugly man? He had anal intercourse with all the Negro sailors, paying up to 300 dollars each. As disgusting as seeing him is to listen to the negotiations to arrange itemized prices. Look at that woman with the body of a gladiator. She has been pestering most of the women on board with some success. Do you want to see all the people who use drugs? Look there . . ."

"I don't like to see those things, Master," I lied to him.

He replied, "I know my dear friend." We are the only pure souls on this condemned voyage. Tell me what are we going to do about all of this evilness?"

Startled, I looked at him. He insisted, "Answer me, Arthur. Do you think we ought to let this pass unchecked?"

"No, of course not, sir," I replied, not knowing what else to say. He shook my hand.

"I knew I could count on you. Let's strike back right now."

"Right now?" I asked, suddenly becoming aware that something dreadful was about to happen.

"Yes. Within a few hours we'll be landing in Key West and they will escape. We have to act quickly. Call the captain and tell him to gather all the people in the theater. He must tell everybody that the Master of the ship has a very important announcement to make. The band must keep on playing. Order the leader that all the musicians including him must be seated and playing soft music."

The captain told me it was going to be difficult to gather all the people. Drinking had been heavy since very early, this being the last day on board, but he'd try his best. For the first time, I noticed the captain's tongue was sticky. I told him the Master would be in the theater at ten o'clock sharp.

He dressed up in a black tuxedo. At five minutes before ten we made a toast with the old Spanish brandy and left the cabin. To my dismay, the captain had not been able to cage most of the passengers in the theater yet. Master and I went through a crowd still dancing, drinking, swimming and necking. Until that moment I had avoided all contact with the passengers, fearing someone may recognize me. Going through them, most of whom I'd just seen in their most intimate relationships, produced in me the strangest feelings. A head counting at ten after ten showed there were about a quarter of the people missing. The captain made a last effort, calling all passengers and crewmembers as if it was for a boat drill. Still, eleven passengers didn't show up at twenty after, when the Master decided to walk in the theater. All this time he had been waiting in a room close by.

When the Master came in, all dressed up in his tuxedo with Tiger on a leash, a passenger half yelled.

"Good God, Charlie Chaplain is here!"

A lot of the public started to clap and yell. Everybody was in a merry mood. The Master, very disturbed, picked from one of his pockets ship controls and blew the siren several times. This unexpected sound made miracles. Suddenly everybody stayed quiet The missing people appeared—some of them half-dressed—wondering if the ship had hit an iceberg.

"Ladies and gentlemen. I am the Master of this ship. Each one of the passengers and members of the crew were selected by me to participate in this voyage for a particular reason. It will not be fair if I do not warn you on what is going to happen in a few minutes. I'll give you a demonstration first. The collar around the neck and chest of this dog has twelve needles that will inject into the animal's lungs two chemical substances: one that will paralyze the animal instantly but not kill it. Spiders use the same substance with the insects they catch in their webs to keep them alive and fresh until they are ready to eat them. The other substance is a silicon compound that combines readily with the blood and is carried through the bloodstream to every cell of the body that little by little becomes plastic. Death will come after several days when the heart stops pumping after the muscle slowly loses its elasticity.

People were amused and startled by the strange accent of the Master's voice, trying to understand the meaning of it all. The captain, completely drunk, rose from his seat and asked for applause. The public clapped and laughed.

The Master told me to hold Tiger's leash with my two hands, while he pulled from the other pocket of his tuxedo a red control set.

"Attack, Tiger!" he ordered signaling to the crowd.

The animal made a ferocious roar, showing its teeth. Some of the people in the first row backed up. The dog tried to jump forward, but I was holding the leash with all my strength and weight. The Master pushed a button in this new control set and Tiger froze instantly, standing on two legs with a fierce expression on its face. The change was so sudden that the people, marveled by the trick, gave the Master a great ovation.

"Now it's your turn!" he said, pointing his red control set toward the crowd. Many people laughed. The Master once again pushed, and from the back of the seats, two metal arms held everyone firmly to the high-back chairs covered with red velvet. There was a wave of admiration for what appeared to them to be a comedian ready to produce his most outstanding trick. The arms tickled a fat man who began to laugh loudly, apparently unable to stop. The crowd started to laugh because of the contagious laughing of the fat man. Suddenly the Master pushed a button in his red control set. A strange cry came out of the crowd; a mixture of surprise, pain, laughter, and terror.

The band stopped playing. Silence invaded the ship until all that was heard was the rumor of the black waters of the Caribbean Sea being cut by the sharp keel of the vessel on a moonless night and the permanent moan of the engine.

The Master sat down on the floor, looking at all the paralyzed people in the theater.

"This is a masterpiece, my friend. We did it!"

"Are they all dead?" I asked.

"No, not yet. Like I told them, they are still alive for another three to five days. Although they are all paralyzed, they can hear everything we say; feel cold, heat and pain . . . We must hurry with all the work we have to do in the next twelve hours. After that, they become too stiff to shape up."

"What work?" I asked.

"Arthur, you look at me as if you're terrified. You shouldn't be. Now we are both killers, there are no barriers between us. Your destiny no longer depends on the will of my tongue. We're both bound by this feat."

Instinctively, I backed away. For a few seconds, I stood speechless.

Then, with an audacity I did not know I had, I spoke my mind. "You said everyone here was carefully selected by you. What I have feared for so long is true. You set me up! You trapped me! You lured me to that island full of women so fond of sex that altered all my senses and my hormones glands, making me do things I never dreamed of doing, until I became a killer and a fugitive ready to be your slave. Why me?"

The Master got up and walked among the entranced audience to tell his story. He talked loud enough for them to hear, because he felt he owed them an explanation, too.

"When I was seven years old I read a book that has haunted me forever, *The Adventures of Arthur Gordon Pym*, by Edgar Allan Poe. In the story, a youngster named Augustus and his friend Arthur Gordon Pym sailed in the whaler *Grampus*. The ship wrecked and the two friends on top of the overturned hull saw a ship coming apparently to rescue them. There were many people on the deck of the ship dressed like Dutch people. As the ship passed by, they realized that all the people on board were dead. A tall man that seemed to smile at them and nod 'yes' in answer to their plea for help was dead, too. His teeth shown: his lips had been eaten away by a carnivorous bird. The affirmative nods of his head were caused by the bird eating away at the corpse behind his head.

You must realize that reading that story at so tender an age caused me the same trauma as if it had happened in real life. It was even worse, because my name is Augustus, a very uncommon name, and in the story Augustus died of gangrene, while his friend, Arthur Gordon Pym, lived to the end to tell the story. Every night of my life since then, I have seen that ship with its dead cargo, I have watched the Dutchman and his carnivorous bird pass just a few yards from me. Every night I've awakened with the horror of gangrene eating away at my members.

The Master pointed at me.

"That is why an Arthur Gordon Pym your age from Nantucket had to participate in this voyage."

"I am not Pym."

The Master did not pay attention to me. Instead, he faced the people frozen in their seats.

"All of your passengers deserve death. All of you are criminals. You have been judged by your fellow men and your guilt has been proven, but on account of the misuse of money and power you have been acquitted.

Technical flaws in the judiciary process, bribery and threats, and even committing other crimes in order to erase witnesses. As you may see, I have used the same money and power to punish all of you. That evens the score and makes my actions against you morally right."

The Master turned to me and said, "Arthur, we have to properly dress these people to place them where they are supposed to be. I want to replace the image of the ship that I carry in my mind with this new one. This action will be a catharsis for me. I know it will work because, since we left New York, just the feeling of having the prey in my hands has made me sleep well."

After a horrible night dressing and arranging the bodies of the passengers and the crewmembers the way the Master thought they should be—laying around the swimming pool, propped up at the bar, chaffing idly at the promenade deck, making love here and there . . . . Thank God the whole band was sitting in chairs while playing their instruments. The needles that came out of the chairs and sprayed the toxins into their bodies fixed them to the seats, and the only thing to do was bolt the seats to the floor. I must admit it was a beautiful arrangement.

The Master had selected, from all the recordings taped during the voyage, a twenty-four-hour tape to be played back, representing all the sounds of the ship: the best music played by the band, lively conversations here and there, contagious laughter coming from a corridor or the dance floor, the splash of bodies as they dived into the pool, the voices of people cheering a good play at a volleyball game. . . .

When we entered the waters of the Bahamas, full of small vessels of all kinds, many people greeted and probably even envied the merry "passengers" of the *Jane Guy*, the new name of the ship, under Togo's flag.

THE HISSING SOUND of the helicopter was clear. In less than a minute, the metal hummingbird sat on the main deck in the middle of the brightness of a glorious morning tinted of all shades of blue.

"This is where we depart, my dear Arthur. You don't have to worry about a thing. During the voyage I tuned up all the electronic equipment and software, and this ship will need no care whatsoever. Just apply yourself to the work of bolting bodies and chairs to the deck. I programmed the ship to tour all seven seas, so you will not be bored. You don't have to worry about fuel; the main engine of this ship works with enriched uranium and will not need refueling for the next twenty years. I'll see that you get whatever else you need by helicopter.

The Master boarded the helicopter and Arthur followed him without saying a word. He was pale and shaky and the Master made a signal to the pilot not to take off, yet.

"Arthur, I have to confess that on one important point I have to make a change in my original plan. As always happens, life is stronger than any idea, no matter how elaborate it may be. In my initial project, Arthur Gordon Pym had to die. I had to see him dead while Augustus remained alive. Therefore, I had to procure for myself a dispensable Arthur Gordon Pym from Nantucket that at the same time worked alongside me as a partner. I remembered a place I visited when searching for treasures. For many years on the little island you were 'lured' to, to use your exact words, there was a standard prank used with foreigners. For some money, Antoine Canalet would put under his elastic wrestler's outfit a plastic bag with the guts and blood of a recently butchered pig. Then at the park, when all the town's people gathered to walk, sit in the benches, and listen to the music played by a local band, he would pick a knife fight with the man selected. He'd cut his adversary once or twice to make him feel he was really fighting for his life. Then Antoine carelessly exposed his belly. As soon as the swine's guts came out, the sergeant stopped the fight while Antoine 'agonized' and all the people there got ready to 'lynch' the winner, who was 'saved' from the crowd and put into jail. At dawn next day, the townspeople would gather again, this time around the jail for another show: the sergeant chasing and shooting the escaped prisoner.

"I arranged everything very carefully, as I always do. This has happened so many times in the town that I didn't think I had to see about it closely. I arrived on the island the day of your fight. When I saw Antoine Canalet without his false belly and really trying to cut you, but at the same time acting as if he had been drugged, I instantly knew something had gone wrong I told the sergeant to stop the fight and put you in jail. He was going to do so when the real guts of Antoine were spilled on the grass at the park.

"That night when I was in my ship, a man who worked for me a long time ago came to ask a favor. He wanted me to smuggle his daughter off the island, because she had killed Antoine Canalet. When she came on board, a beautiful brunette only fifteen years old, she told me she had poisoned Antoine when she learned the zealous merchant she was to wed at the age of sixteen had paid Antoine a large amount of money for your death.

"I have tempted the girl every day, offering to take her with me, describing what sort of life she would have. But she has always refused to leave you on this ship of ghosts. Just a minute ago, I asked her for the last time if she'd rather go with me in the helicopter, and she refused again. My test with her was to learn about love, because I have never been in love. Now I have to correct my favorite theory: that given the facts, everything in society can be explained and forecast in terms of a power and money struggle. It seems that in love matters, given the facts, you can never tell what is going to happen.

"Take my cabin key, she is waiting for you there. Take the control set of the ship. I never intended to give it to anybody. Just hand me your diary. I am the one to write about these adventures, not you."

# Lost and Found

## BENJAMIN M. SCHUTZ

Acknowledgements
I'd like to thank the following people for the gracious donation of their expertise. Any errors are entirely my responsibility. Chanda Kinsey, defense attorney; Johnny Ringo of Carefree Jeep Tours; Paula Edgin, JoAnne Reiss and Arllys Filmer–Ennett, concierges at The Boulders; Sherry Mehalic of Travel Partners; and Rhoda K. Schutz.

"So, how would you like another shot at Derek Marshall?"

Inside, you learned to speak once and listen twice. I listened.

"Not interested?"

"Not saying. What does a 'second shot' mean?"

"He's come out of hiding. He left San Francisco, drove to San Diego and jumped on a cruise ship to Mexico. He has a woman with him."

"You think he plans to kill her?"

"I don't know. That's one of the things I want you to find out."

I looked at the old man. I hadn't seen Enzo Scolari in six, maybe seven years. Time had leached a lot of life out of him. He was frail and bony. Waiting for my reply, he massaged the swollen arthritic knuckles of his hands. His wispy, white eyebrows were now as unruly as smoke.

Six years ago he had hired me to prevent his niece's marriage to Derek Marshall. I wasn't able to do that. She married Marshall, and in short order he murdered her and became a millionaire. For two years after that I kept tabs on him, hoping that he'd step wrong and I'd be there to drop a net over him. It didn't happen.

"Why me?"

"I can't think of anyone better qualified, Mr. Haggerty. You know Marshall. You know how he works. You have a personal stake in this, or at least you did. And you're available. You can follow him wherever he goes."

"Marshall knows me, too. I can't get near him. He'll make me and that's the end of that."

"I don't think so, Mr. Haggerty. I knew you then and I would never recognize you now. You've changed quite a bit. How much weight have you put on?"

I shrugged. "Thirty-six pounds."

"It looks good on you. All muscle. How did you do that? I hear the food is not fit for animals."

"I lifted weights four hours a day, seven days a week. That and good genes. I can turn shit into muscle."

"That seems to be the case. With your shaved head and goatee, sunglasses and a hat, he'll never recognize you."

I let it pass. "I lost my license. I can't carry a gun. I have no contacts anymore. I don't know how I could be of any use to you."

Scolari waved my words away with a swat of his bony hand. "You didn't get stupid, did you? You were a bright man. I'm betting you still are. You don't need a license or a gun, just your wits. As for contacts, I know all you'll ever need to about Derek Marshall. I maintained my own surveillance on Mr. Marshall after he left Virginia."

Scolari touched the switch on his wheelchair, spun towards the desk and poured himself a glass of water. His hand shook so badly that he had to stop two inches from his mouth and let his head close the distance. He drained the glass and put it on the desk.

Scolari turned back to me.

"What was prison like, Mr. Haggerty?"

"Just like any gated community, Mr. Scolari. Too many rules."

"How does it feel to be back in the world?"

"I wouldn't know. I'm just out. I'm not back."

"Yes, well let me tell you about Derek Marshall. After he settled in San Francisco, I had our local office keep track of all the women he dated. After the first date, we sent them a press kit, so to speak. All the clippings about Gina's death, the inquest, the unanswered questions. Most of them never went out with him again. There were a few that we could not dissuade. However, Derek Marshall spent many, many nights alone. I also tried to recover the money he got when Gina died. I was not quite as successful there. I have many business contacts all over the country. Those that I could influence in San Francisco made it hard for him to get loans, or closed mutual funds to him. I ruined a couple of his investments; cost him and some other people quite a bit of money. All of this forced Mr. Marshall into a very low profile lifestyle. He wasn't enjoying the spoils of his crime.

"I'm worried about this trip to Mexico. It's his first attempt to shake my surveillance. I want to know what he's up to. Is he planning to disappear? Who is the woman with him? Is she an accomplice to his plans? Is she in danger from him? That's where you come in, Mr. Haggerty. As I said, you know Derek, how he thinks. You have no ties to this area anymore, am I correct?"

I just listened.

"I kept track of you, too. You have no license, no job, and no career. No family. Your friends in the police department can't help you because you're a felon. Same with your friends at other agencies. No one can use you. You have no home, no money. Your lawyer got all that.

"I however, have a plane ticket for you, a car waiting at the airport in Tucson, and a cabin on the ship where he's staying. Right now they are wet-docked at Puerto Penasco for repairs. They'll be there for three days. I also have a company credit card for you. While you're on the job, all your living expenses will be covered."

"What do you want from me?"

"Find out what he's up to. I don't want to lose him. That's the first thing. Find out who the girl is. If she's in danger, warn her off. I don't want anyone else to go through what I've gone through."

"That's it?"

"That's it. Report to me as soon as you find out anything. I don't care what time it is. I sleep badly when I sleep at all. That's your 'second shot.' Are you interested?"

Scolari's offer beat everything else I had going. I was too old to be starting over from scratch.

"When's the next plane out?"

\* \* \*

IN THE AIR over Tucson, I thought about my talk with old man Scolari. He was awfully eager to get me out here with Marshall. Why? Maybe he blamed me for Gina's death. Maybe he'd decided to have us both killed? No. I went to prison two years after Derek left. He never tried it then and he had plenty of time. Maybe he wants to set me up for Derek's death, do it that way. Why now? He can maneuver me into position a lot easier than before. Five years ago a lot more people would have cared about what happened to me, not now. Maybe he was tired of waiting and decided to make something happen. How sick was he?

Maybe what I should do is milk this for all it's worth. File dummy reports, stay away from Marshall in case it's a frame and see how long I can ride this until he catches on. They say living well is the best revenge. Besides, what's the worst that he could do, fire me? Why am I not scared?

We began to descend over Tucson. I looked out the window at the ground rushing up at us. Most crashes occur on takeoffs and landings. I watched all the way down. We bounced once on the runway, then settled down and began to slow.

Scolari had asked me how it felt to be back. I really didn't know. I remember thinking about Humpty Dumpty when I was sentenced. How some men shattered when they hit bottom, while others armored themselves all the way down and they didn't feel a thing. Not then, not ever.

My rental car was in a lot across the street from the airport. I threw my bag in the passenger seat, got in and turned on the air conditioner. The airport information board said it was 110 degrees today. The rental agent had given me a courtesy map of the area. I unfolded it and decided on a route. I pulled out of the lot and entered the freeway traffic that ran by the airport.

I drove south out of America into Mexico. My last case had started in Mexico. It ended in the Maryland State Penitentiary Maximum Security Facility at Jessup. There was only one thing I knew for certain. I was not going into a Mexican prison.

I crossed the border at Nogales and headed towards Hermosillo. Halfway there I turned west towards Mexicali, then south again to the Gulf of California.

God must have had only a few crayons left in his box when he got to the desert. Everything was one shade of brown or another. Scraggly plants sprouted up on the hills that flanked the road. Each group had its own shepherd; a tall cactus watching over it. Some were as straight and narrow as Giacometti's men. Others had arms: some up; some down; some both, signalling each other like giant green semaphores.

An hour or so later I saw the sign for the docks, pulled off the road and stopped at the guard's station. Razor wire ringed the area.

"Name sir?"

"Haggerty, Leo Haggerty."

"Yes sir. You are registered on the *Calypso Moonbeam*. Drive straight ahead to the parking lot. Check in with security at the gangway."

I surrendered my passport, got my security pass, room key, and directions to my cabin. It was clean. It was bigger than I was used to, it was all mine, and I had the key to the door.

I dropped my bag on the floor and lay down on the bed. I took off my sunglasses and stared at the ceiling fan. Its blades seemed to move as slowly as the hands of a prison clock. It wasn't long before I was asleep.

I awoke lying on my back and looked at my watch. It was after four o'clock. I checked the ship's map and found the lounge. I left the room and went there.

I sat in a soft chair and ordered a gin and tonic from the waitress. My seat allowed me to watch the entrance to the bar and the dining room. At the very least, I ought to see what Derek looked like these days. No use letting him surprise me. I sipped my drink and watched the people come and go. It was almost eight when Marshall showed up. The last seven years had not hurt him any. He'd put on a few pounds and erased his jawline along the way. His hair was still fine and brown, but he parted it on the left now. The glasses were gone, so I guessed he wore contacts.

He had his arm around a tall blonde, whose pale blue eyes and bright smile stood out against her tan face like turquoise and ivory in the sandy desert. Derek laughed at something the maitre d' said, squeezed his friend to him and kissed her ear. I took a long slow pull on my drink and thought of Gina Dalesandro. I could still see her wiping tears off her cheek on her wedding day and asking me, "What's so wrong with me? Can you tell me that?"

I whispered what I hadn't said then. "Nothing Gina, not one single thing. I'm sorry I've darkened your day. I'm sorry I didn't do better." I hadn't been able to save her back then and I'd tried my best. This grinning bastard had murdered her and gotten rich doing it. I raised that drink to Gina's memory and asked her to "wish me better luck this time." I raised the rest to forget.

I nursed a port until Marshall and the girl were done eating and then followed them out of the dining room. They walked back to the cabins and entered room 116, a deck below me.

Still haunted by Gina Dalesandro, I went back to my room and called Scolari. It was 1:30 a.m. back east, and, good as his word, he picked up on the second ring.

"Yes."

"Mr. Scolari, this is Leo Haggerty. I've located Derek Marshall. I saw him at dinner this evening. He has a woman with him. A blonde, tall and very tanned. Do you know anything about her?"

"No, we're still working on it. What else have you found out?"

"Not much. I'll follow him tomorrow, see if I can get a line on what he's doing here. If I have to, I'll try to get closer to the woman, see if she's in any danger and warn her off."

"Careful, Mr. Haggarty. I don't want Marshall spooked. He hasn't recognized you, I presume?"

"No."

"We'll try to find out who she is and if she's in any danger."

"Call me here anytime with any information you get. Especially on the girl."

"Of course, Mr. Haggarty. You'll be the first to know. Goodnight."

I hadn't lifted or run today, so I did seven hundred sit-ups as penance, showered and lay naked on the cool, clean sheets of the bed. I listened hard into the darkness. No one was crying, or cursing. No one was praying or screaming. No one was begging for the mercy that never came. In the middle of the night, I got up and left my room, just because I could.

I awoke around seven, slipped into a T-shirt, shorts and running shoes, and trotted down the gangway. I showed the security guy my pass and headed for the guard's station. I passed him and turned right down the road and ran off into the desert. I came back an hour later.

I trudged back up the gangway. At the top, a woman was putting up a notice on the bulletin board. I stopped to read it.

She looked at me. "How far did you go?"

I shrugged. "Six miles."

"You take any water with you?"

"Nah, it wasn't that far."

"Provided you don't turn an ankle, step on a rattler, and you stay on the road. But if things go wrong, you'll need that water because you're sweating quite a bit. Heatstroke and dehydration can drop anyone. You ever been out in the desert before?"

"No, I haven't. Maybe my ignorance has led to disrespect."

"Why don't you come on my hike this morning." She tapped the notice. "You'll learn more about the desert than you ever wanted to know."

Her chestnut hair was pulled back under a beige baseball cap and flowed out the back, thick and smooth as a thoroughbred's well-curried tail. Silvered sunglasses shielded her eyes like a beetle's shiny shell. I found that strangely reassuring.

"When is it?"

"Nine."

"Okay," I said, and walked away. I went into my room, stripped down and took a shower, ending it with the icy needle spray I knew so well was only one mistake away.

I had a light breakfast, then went outside to find my guide. She was standing out by the notice board alternately staring at her clipboard and looking all around to see who was missing. I'd once heard a camp counselor call it "urchin searchin."

I pulled up in front of her.

"Looks like you're it."

"Hike still on?"

"Sure. Here, take this." She gave me a water bottle on a belt. I saw she had one on her hip, so I strapped mine on.

"We may as well start with the rules of the desert. They're real simple. This is God's country not man's. We're not welcome here. It's not user friendly. If you don't respect that, it will kill you. There are three absolutes: Never travel without water; never go out in the desert alone; always tell someone where you are going. Got that?"

"Got it."

"You ought to wear a hat. That shiny scalp of yours is a solar collector."

"I'll get one after the hike."

"Here, put this on your head, like a do-rag." She handed me a bandanna from her back pocket. "You look like you're in pretty good shape.

Why don't we go out to those mountains over there." She pointed into the distance. "It's probably a couple of hours out. We can see a number of things on the way."

"Sounds good."

She held out her hand. "My name's Kiki. Kiki Davenport."

"Leo Haggerty." I shook it, and then tied the bandanna around my head.

"Where are you from?" she asked and turned to lead the way. She had on a small fanny pack.

"Back east."

We left the road and walked out into the desert. After about twenty minutes she stopped by a twisted tree decorated with a fuzzy necklace.

"This is a chain fruit cholla. It's a kind of cactus. I like to start with them to show people the enormous variety of the cactus family."

"The big ones with the arms. They look like they're guarding the others. What are they?"

"Those are Saguaro. The largest of all the cacti. It's funny you should describe them like that. Saguaro means *sentinel* in Spanish.

"I find cacti fascinating. This is a very harsh environment. Great heat and light, very little water. The parameters for survival are very narrow, not only do they survive, they thrive. And they do so in many, many ways. They remind me of how creative the will to live can be."

She looked out across the desert. "Here, let's look at this one." She walked off the path into the bush. I followed.

She looked like the land itself. All variations of brown, from her beige hiking boots, white socks and tanned skin, to her khaki shorts and cream shirt. She'd be hard to see at a distance. I made a note of that.

"This is a jumping cholla. Very, very nasty."

The cactus was covered with very fine spines so thick that they looked like a soft yellow fur. "Why?"

"This plant reproduces asexually. These last segments of the stalks get carried off by animals that brush up against them. The spines are hooked and so fine that they're almost impossible to get out. When the animal finally gets it off them it falls to the ground, roots and starts to grow."

"Why jumping cholla?"

"When it breaks off, it looks like it jumped onto you. The slightest contact leaves you covered in these spines. Bend down and take a closer look."

She squatted down and I got down next to her and looked at the tiny barbs on the spines. Six inches away, they were invisible.

I avoided looking at her but I could smell her; sweet and clean, flowers and spice.

"You go out into the desert, you should always carry a comb. That way you can get the cholla off if you have to. You slide the teeth down into the spines and flip it off. You can't use your other hand. They'll both wind up full of spines."

"I'll bet falling into one of these is a real mess."

"Oh yeah," she said, nodding in sincere agreement.

"Let's head for those rocks over there. It's a mile or so. We'll climb them, check out the valley beyond, and then head back." I followed her extended arm. She wore a large ring on her right hand, an oval, rose colored stone in a heavy silver and gold setting.

I followed her back to the path and we set off in silence. For twenty minutes I walked in her footsteps up a gradual incline on a narrow, winding path. Eyes down, I watched her legs move, each step a precise placement on a flat rock surface. The steeper the incline, the closer the attention I paid. We stopped on a plateau.

"Look there," she said. I saw a paddle-shaped cactus with several of its paddles half chewed off.

"Javelinas."

"What's that?"

"Javelinas, peccaries, wild pigs. They eat prickly pears—spines and all. They travel in packs. Nasty customers if you're hunting them."

"Are they interested in hunting us?" I asked.

"No. I suppose if you got between a mother and her young they'd charge and drive you off.

"They've got very sharp tusks, and they'd give you a bad bite. I had an old boyfriend who used to hunt them with a bow and arrow. When they were cornered, they'd charge. Then they were real dangerous. They were really fast and they'd be on you before you could get a shot off."

"You go hunting with him?"

"Yeah."

"Ever get one?"

"No. Too fast. One of them opened my leg up, though."

She pointed down to her thigh. I saw a long white scar on the inside.

"Up near the artery. I left the javelinas alone after that. You ever hunt?"

I waited too long to answer. It was a simple question. "No."

"Funny, I'd have thought you did. You have that look."

"And what look is that?"

"Patient, watchful. A stalker. You don't say much. Most people talk my ear off on these hikes. They tell me all about themselves, ask me all about myself. You take information in but you don't offer any. That's hunter behavior. Plus, you don't look like a businessman."

"Really? Now why is that?"

"Your muscles. Getting those is a full time job. You wouldn't have time for an office."

"Maybe muscles are my business, like Arnold Schwarzenegger."

"Sorry. I've never seen you in any muscle magazines."

"You read that many of them?"

She nodded her head. "For years. The boyfriend with the bow and arrows, he was a body builder. Mister Southwest 1990."

"I like the way your mind works, but I'm not a hunter. I'm just out here to relax and enjoy the scenery. So tell me, are there any animals to be worried about out here?"

She smiled, chuckled softly and shook her head. "Okay. Let's see. Everyone will tell you about the rattlesnakes, the Gila Monsters, the scorpions, and the tarantulas. They're all here, they're all dangerous, but you need to be stupid and unlucky to get bit. Simple rules for the biters: Look where you put your hands and feet; shake out your shoes before you put them on; don't reach into dark places, and watch where you step. That's about it, for them.

"Then there's cougars and bears. Bears aren't a big problem in the desert. Much more so up in the mountains. We do get cougars down here. They like javelina. They're pretty shy of humans, and attacks are rare but not unheard of. If you meet one, stop, then back away slowly. Don't turn your back to them. Don't run. If they attack, protect your neck. Cats kill by asphyxiation. They'll try to bite your throat and cut off your air. Keep your hands up, protect your eyes and throat, and try to stay on your feet. If you can find something to hit them with, a thick stick or a heavy rock, so much the better. Keep backing away. We're not on their regular diet, so unless they're starving to death or protecting their young they're not likely to keep up the attack in the face of resistance."

She turned and headed up the path. As the grade steepened, we slowed as the footing got worse. I gave her more of a lead. No reason if she fell to take us both down the hill. We went into a cave made of fallen boulders and climbed up through an opening between the stones to the top of a giant boulder. Two rocks were on top of it in the center like the crown of a hat.

She walked over near the edge, squatted down, took the water bottle off her belt, and squeezed out a long drink. I walked over next to her and did the same.

"Beautiful out here," I said.

"Sure is. I just love it. I don't ever want to leave."

"What brought you out here?"

She turned and looked at me. I saw my sunglasses in hers.

"An '85 Chevy with a black interior, a busted tape player and no A/C."

I laughed. She smiled. She sipped her water, then leaned back onto her butt and crossed her legs Indian-style. I stayed squatting. One time the warden wanted to talk to me about an accident in the laundry. He wanted to talk to me so badly that I was listed as escaped for two days. Turned out to be a mistake of course. I had fallen into a box in the power plant. It was only thirty inches deep but I couldn't get out. Not until the warden and I had that talk. Every day after that, I practiced being folded up like a shirt in case I ever escaped again. I can squat a good long while.

"What do you like about it?" I said.

"It's empty out here. I like empty. You don't have to work to keep your distance. It's big and it's old out here. Not human time or human efforts. It helps me keep a good perspective on things, not take them too seriously. How about you? Do you like it out here?"

"Yeah, I like it out here. Like you said, it's empty. Empty is good. I don't ever want to be crowded again."

I looked around. You could see for miles in any direction. Dark clouds were forming to the south, and the wind said they were headed this way.

I closed my eyes and tilted my face against the breeze.

"There's a storm coming. Summer storms are filled with lightning. We don't want to be up on the heights. Let's start down."

"I think I'll tempt fate a little longer. I haven't felt rain in a long time."

"Not smart. The storm isn't that far away. You'll get all the rain you want if we don't start back now. Monsoons can fill up these arroyos in a minute."

When I didn't move right away, she stood up and headed back down.

I sat on the hill and waited for the rain to come. The breeze picked up and caressed my face. A bolt of lightning flashed a jagged path to the ground. A thunderclap boomed almost immediately afterward. Time to go.

I caught up with her at the base of the rocks. "Uh, Mr. Southwest 1990 . . . you still with him?"

She shook her head. "No, he left me for Mister Southwest 1993."

I hadn't said this much to a woman in years. I decided to press my luck. Prison, like the desert, helps you with perspective. "Could I buy you dinner tonight?"

She thought about that for a minute. "Okay."

"What time should I come by?"

"Oh," she tilted her head, "you wanted to eat it with me, too."

I must have made a face.

"I'm kidding. I'm kidding," she said.

"Staff isn't supposed to fraternize with the guests. Why don't we meet off the ship. There's a little place in town called the Aztec Café. How about I meet you there, say, eight o'clock?"

"Great."

She checked the sky. The clouds were rolling on while we stood still. "We really ought to head back."

"Sure." I followed her back into the desert. All the way back I wondered what color her eyes were.

At the ship's store I purchased a water bottle, some sunscreen and a soft, wide-brimmed hat.

I found Derek by the pool, reading a book about moneyless investing. He had a drink on the table next to him. His soft white body was starting to get a little pink: medium-rare. His legs were crossed at the ankles, and the upper foot tapped the lower one incessantly.

I walked around the pool and into the spa area. The weight room was beyond a pair of doors in the far wall. The blonde stood in line behind an enormously fat man. I brought up the rear.

The whale wanted a massage. He looked like he'd have to be stirred. I checked the blonde out head to toe, looking for any distinguishing marks. She had on a pair of clogs. They looked like hooves back in the '70s and they still did today. She adjusted her cover-up, and I saw a nice bruise on her right thigh. I glanced down into her bag, but it was fastened. She had a tennis bracelet on. It could have been diamonds, could have been rock candy for all I knew. No rings, but long hot pink nails.

"The couples massage, how long does that last?"

"It's about an hour," the attendant said.

"Okay. We'd like to schedule one this afternoon. Cabin 116. How late do you do them?"

"We schedule the last ones of the day at five p.m."

"Okay, let's do it then. We'd also like room service at seven thirty."

"Do you want to order now?"

"No. We'll call it in later."

"Very good. Your masseurs will be Carl and Rita."

"Where is the Jacuzzi?"

"Through the doors and into the ladies' locker room."

She picked up a towel from a woven basket next to the counter and glided off towards the locker room.

I took a quick glance at the schedule book to see what was entered. Just cabin numbers, no names. That made sense. Everything was automatically billed to the cabin to be settled up at departure.

"May I help you, sir?" asked a stocky girl with short dark hair wearing a green and beige uniform that made her look like a park ranger.

"Weights?"

"Through those doors."

"Anybody inside to spot?"

"No sir, we don't have free weights, just machines."

I nodded. I picked up a towel and walked into the weight room. It was empty and silent. I walked around the circuit of machines, looking at their maximum settings. No work here. I sat on a bench, pulled out my gloves and belt, and tossed my bag into the corner.

I saw Marshall through the glass. He was having a nice vacation. I was having a nice vacation. He didn't have the jumpy, worried look of a man on the run. No furtive glances of the frightened schemer trying to lose a shadow. Maybe he's up here having a nice time with some bimbo. They go back to San Francisco, I go to San Francisco. This is a good gig. I'm paid to live the good life watching someone else live the good life. Don't fuck this up, Derek, I thought to myself. I could get used to this. A life sentence of pointless luxury. Guilty, your honor. Show me no mercy.

I did the circuit slowly, drawing out the negatives on each rep, squeezing the most work out of the machines. The weights slid smoothly, silently, up and down their spines like a steel bellows I inflated with each effort.

In the yard, you set your load by hand, hoisting each plate onto the bar, slamming it against the others, metal on metal, clanging like a cell door. When I finished my workout, I rubbed my face and scalp with my towel and draped it around my neck.

I looked around the empty room. Here the weight meant nothing. There, you were watched by everyone. Sheer physical strength was important.

Early on I met all the animals. The spiders who run the joint; the great apes who did their bidding; the zombies; and the bunk bunnies. The great apes don't do the same time as everyone else, so I became a great ape and things got better.

The fact that I was in for killing a cop didn't hurt my status any. I didn't correct anyone who thought it was murder, but I also didn't claim it. Inside, you don't say anything you can't back up.

One thousand eight hundred and twenty-five days later they opened a door and returned me to the world. Bigger. Stronger. Harder.

You go to the property room before you leave in your shiny black state suit. They hand you a bus ticket and then give you your belongings in a brown manila envelope. They open it up and dump it out; your wallet, watch, some coins, a ring, keys, and a pen. Then they slide a form over for you to sign. I remember reading: "CHECK YOUR BELONGINGS. YOUR SIGNATURE CONFIRMS THAT EVERYTHING TAKEN FROM YOU HAS BEEN RETURNED IN ITS ORIGINAL CONDITION."

I looked into the bag. I turned it over and shook it. I tapped it with my hand. The guard asked me what I was looking for.

"Somehow, I don't think this is quite everything you took when I came in here."

"We didn't take anything you didn't deserve to lose," was his reply.

I stopped in front of the mirror and looked at myself. A bullet head, a mask for a face, empty eyes, and a miser's mouth. My shirt was soaked in sweat and hugged my wedge-shaped torso, armor-plated in muscle. Kiki was right. Everything that survives adapts to its environment. Well, I've changed environments again. Can I change myself again?

The blonde must have come out of the sauna by another door because I never saw her pass me but there she was sitting next to Derek.

Derek's hand stroked lazy figure eights on her thigh with the tip of his index finger like a tiny figure skater.

I went back to my room, showered and lay down for a nap. At six, I got up and dressed for dinner. I knew where Derek and his friend would be for the evening.

I sat by the pool and ordered a Salty Dog. I sat sipping it in the fading daylight and stared at the jagged peaks of the distant mountains. It looked like someone had torn off the edge of the sky.

I finished my drink and waved the waitress over for a second. She was dark skinned with thick, black hair, held in place by a bright multicolored ribbon. Her hair was stiff and wiry like a cord of very fine kindling. Her eyes were as dark as her hair, without discernible pupils. I imagined her hair ablaze with gold and crimson flames.

"Another one, please."

She nodded, took the glass and left.

I drank steadily until the sun flattened itself on the horizon like the yolk of a dropped egg. My day now had a wavy, shimmery edge to it, like the air on a hot, still day.

I got directions to the cafe from the excursion desk and arrived a little before eight. Inside, the big room was divided into three separate areas. To the left was a small dance floor. Something Spanish with pedal steel was playing on the sound system—Country-Mexican, I guess. A long bar ran across the back wall of the middle area. A couple of the men at the bar spotted me in the mirror and watched me walk across the room. I stared into their broad, flat Indian faces. They didn't like what they saw and returned to their conversation. A waitress in a white shirt with a string tie showed me to one of the tables in the dining section and handed me a menu. I glanced at it. Mostly Mexican, with some steaks, chili, and barbeque.

Kiki showed up a little after eight. She wore tooled mid-calf boots, the leather a brown and white patchwork and a short, clingy white sleeveless dress, cut low in the back. Her white Stetson had a turquoise ornament on the crown.

I stood up and pulled out a chair for her. She scooped her dress underneath herself and sat down.

"May I get you something to drink?" the waitress asked.

"I'm fine," I said. "I got an early start."

"Iced tea will be fine," she said.

"You look great." I nodded in agreement with myself.

Easy boy, you're just passing through. What would a good-looking young woman want with a beat-up old man like you? Nothing. Don't go thinking about it or wishing for it. Just do what you said you would. Enjoy some pleasant company, for a change. If you wanted to get laid, you should have lined up a pro.

"Thank you," she said and smiled. Her eyes were green.

"So what's good here?" I asked.

"Everything. I usually get the Carne Asada."

I sipped my water and just looked at her. Her face was a narrow oval with a thin straight nose and mouth. With her thick red hair, I thought of a fox. I could do this for hours, I thought. Not say a word. Just look. Prisons are the tower of Babel. Everyone scrambling over each other to be heard, to make their point, to tell it like it ain't. Silence reminds you what a sloth time is.

"Did you hear what I said?"

"I'm sorry. I wasn't paying attention."

"I could tell."

"I was, but not to what you were saying, just how you look."

"There was a time that would have pleased me, but I know I'm not that good looking. You looked at me like you'd never seen a woman before."

She drank her iced tea. "Let's see. How bad is this? You haven't felt rain in years, you hardly say a word about yourself, and you look at me like I'm a Martian." She paused then clapped her hands. "Hospital. You've been in a hospital. In a coma and now you have amnesia."

She shook her head. "No, not a coma. Where'd you get the muscles? I've got it. A monastery. Lot's of time on your hands. You pump iron for Jesus. You're some kind of ninja monk."

"Why is this so important to you? I don't like to talk about myself. That's all. You're like a starfish on a clam. The harder you pull the harder I'm gonna pull."

"No. You aren't a monk. Not now, not ever. I got it wrong again. When will I learn?" She took another drink, picked up her purse and pulled out her wallet. "I'll pay for the tea, thank you very much, don't bother to get up."

"What are you doing?"

"I'm leaving is what I'm doing."

"Why? What did I do?"

She put her elbows on the table and leaned forward to speak. "Just do me this, answer one question, okay?"

She didn't say tell the truth. "Okay, what is it?"

"You're a con, aren't you? You're just out of prison. That would explain things. Am I right?"

I weighed the effort in constructing and carrying off a good lie against her green eyes, the wisp of hair that had eluded her French braid, and her fragrance riding across the table at me.

"That's it, I'm outta here." She started to get up.

I reached out and grabbed her wrist. She stared down at my hand. She was shackled to me, unable to move.

"Don't go," I said, and released her. "Please. I'm sorry I touched you, that was wrong. Yes, I'm an ex-con, and yes, I'm just out of prison."

She sat down, rubbing her wrist.

"Did I hurt you?"

"No. You just scared me."

I shook my head amazed at my stupidity. Maybe I did want to go back inside. "I'll pay for the tea. I'm sorry I scared you. You're the first woman I've spent any time with in five years. Just looking at you is enough for me. I can imagine that's not as much fun for you."

She stared at me, considering what I had just said. "What did you do?"

"Does it matter?"

"Yes. It does."

"What makes you think I'd tell you the truth?"

"I think you will. Let's leave it at that."

I exhaled long and slow, and closed my eyes to gather my thoughts.

"I was charged with felony murder of a police officer, a capitol offense. I was found guilty of involuntary manslaughter, and sentenced to and served the maximum, five years. Any questions?"

"Did you do it?"

I nodded yes. "Sure did. He was trying to kill me and a witness I was protecting. There was a gunfight in the street. I was chasing him. He got hit by a car."

"You say you were protecting a witness. Were you a police officer?"

"No. I was a private investigator. She was a witness who could expose the involvement of the police and the district attorney in a pornography ring. He was sent out to kill her. He bought it instead."

"If that's true, why were you found guilty?"

"I couldn't prove the conspiracy part. By the time it went to trial, all the other witnesses had had fatal accidents. All that was left to see was that he was a police officer pursuing a legitimate warrant on a fugitive. I was assisting her in escaping. That's a felony. Chanda—that's my lawyer—she did a good job in getting it knocked down from murder to man two. For felony murder I'd have gotten the chair. Considering what could have happened, five years was a bargain. But then again, I don't often look at it that way."

She sat staring at me, her mouth pursed in thought.

"So," I said. "It's been nice having this talk. I'm glad we got that all cleared up. I won't try to stop you if you want to leave." I hoisted up a dead smile.

"I'll stay," she said.

"I'm glad. Why don't we order something."

She ordered the Carne Asada and I followed her lead.

"You said you got it wrong again? What did you mean?"

"I can't say 'nothing' can I?"

"Not a chance."

"Thought so. My track record with guys isn't so great. There's a line out there between exciting and dangerous that always confuses me. My compass goes haywire and I always wind up on the wrong side of that line. That's what I meant. That's why I was being such a pain. I had all these questions about you. I figured let's just go straight to the bottom, avoid the whole disappointment part. That's really gotten old."

"If you had all those questions, why did you say 'yes' to dinner?"

"How else was I going to get them answered? Besides, you look like no two days with you would be the same. That's exciting."

Her food arrived, and she ordered a beer to go with it. I stayed with water.

"You know an awful lot about cactus. Are you a botanist?"

"No. I mean, I read a lot about them, but I don't have a degree or anything."

"You could have fooled me."

"Good. You see, I invented my job. So, if I sound like I know what I'm talking about they won't replace me with a trained botanist."

"What do you mean 'invented' it?"

"Well, I was living up in the desert with Ricky. Ricky Mendoza—Mr. Switch-hitter 1990. We both worked in gyms in Tucson. Anyway, after we split I didn't want to be part of that crowd anymore so I got a job as a trainer for the cruises. It was okay but I hated being indoors all the time and around all those pampered bitches, waiting on them hand and foot. I started going for hikes on my own whenever we pulled into port. People started going with me, and they liked them. It got back to the cruise director, and I made a pitch to make it my full-time job. And now it is. I'm always afraid I'll screw up and they'll replace me, so I read all the time: botany, zoology, geology."

"What about you? What are you really doing out here?" she asked.

"I'm working—following a guy who's on board. He murdered his first wife and got away with it. He even inherited her estate. I'm here to see that he doesn't do it again."

"What do you feel when you see a guy like that? Someone who got away with murder."

"What do I feel? I feel like picking up a steak knife and burying it up to the hilt in his chest and then breaking off the blade. That's what I feel. Then I try not to feel anything. That's the way back inside. I don't want to go back inside."

"Are you working as a private investigator?"

"No. I can't do that anymore. I can't ever do that again. This is just something I'm doing until I can find a permanent job."

"Do you have any offers?"

"Oh yeah, I've got a permanent job waiting for me in Fresno."

"That's good."

"No, it's not. How shall I put this? Chief of Security for a west coast pharmaceutical distributor. How's that? The head of a biker gang liked my work in prison so much that they want me to handle security for all of their west coast runs. In return, I get the pick of the litter for my woman, a company chopper and all the product my body can process. What's not to like?"

"You aren't going to do that are you?"

"I don't know. Most of the time I think 'no.' Then there are some days I get up and think 'why not'? I was one of the good guys once. What did it get me? Maybe it's my way of getting to the bottom in a hurry, avoid all that pointless wishing and hoping that things will be different.

"The only thing I know for sure is that I'm not the man I once was. The man I am now is not an improvement. I'd like to get back the good things I lost, but it hasn't happened yet."

We finished eating and lingered over our coffee. I paid the check and escorted Kiki out of the café.

"How'd you get here?"

"Over there," she pointed to a white jeep in a corner of the lot.

"I'll walk you over."

"That's okay. I had a nice time. I hope you find those pieces that you're looking for."

"Thanks. Maybe your compass is starting to work a little better. You're still on the right side of things."

"Maybe," she said, smiling.

"Goodnight." I turned and walked away. Three steps later, I felt a hand on my arm. I turned. She was already backing away.

"Don't go to Fresno, Leo. That's not you. Keep looking. You'll find something better."

I started to speak, but she was already too far away, so I told myself, "I'll try. I really will."

The next day I saw Kiki after my run. She was taking two couples horseback riding. We exchanged smiles but nothing else. I was following Derek and his lady on a guided tour to some local ruins.

Throughout the tour, I kept my distance. I asked no questions and did nothing to draw attention to myself.

After lunch we went back to the ship. I was able to eavesdrop on Derek's plans to go soaring in the afternoon and got my own directions to the airfield. I spent the afternoon in the weight room and then just sitting in the lounge.

At four, I got into my car and headed for the airfield. Five miles from the dock there were no signs of human life, except the dirt road running towards the distant mountains. Up ahead, I saw the dust of Derek's cab and kept my distance. I knew where he was going, and a car in the desert gives itself away.

I turned into the lot off the road and parked on the far side of the office, away from their car. A bi-plane idled on the runway by the office. A white glider was descending out of the still, blue sky. It bounced twice on its tiny wheels and then rolled to a halt when one wing tilted over to touch the ground. A young man, tanned and muscular with silvered sunglasses jumped out of the cockpit and began to talk excitedly with an older couple sitting on a bench under some trees. He shook the hand of the man who exited the cockpit, walked over to the couple, and all three went to their car.

I watched Derek and the blonde talk to the glider pilot and then to the pilot in the tow plane. The woman shook her head 'no,' and Derek pointed to the bench under the trees. He helped the pilot roll the glider over to the cable and attach it to the tow plane. Derek and the pilot got inside, and the blonde helped keep the wing level until the tow plane began to taxi down the runway. Then she walked over to the bench.

How long would Derek be up, I wondered? How far could one of these gliders go? They couldn't go too far. Not with Blondie on the ground. She wouldn't want to spend her afternoon sitting out here in the middle of nowhere. But suppose Derek wasn't coming back? No way to follow him. Can't ride with him. There's only one tow plane. By the time it gets back he could be anywhere. I began to manufacture possibilities in my mind. You take a parachute with you. You don't need a big landing strip. You can bail out in the desert. With a four-wheel drive vehicle you don't need to be near a road. These planes don't file flight plans. Nobody would know where you were going until you're up in the air.

I got out of the car and walked over to the office. The man behind the counter squinted up at me.

"Can I help you?"

"Yes. These flights—how long do they last?"

"Thirty minutes to an hour, depending on whether you want to do any fancy maneuvers."

"Is that the maximum?"

"Oh, hell no. Depends on how high up you want to go. I've ridden the thermals here for almost four hours."

"How far would a trip like that take you?"

"Two hundred, two hundred and fifty miles. Why? Would you like a trip like that?"

"I don't know. How much is it?"

"A hundred dollars an hour."

"You got any scheduled like that now? Before I put out that kind of money, I think I'd like to talk to someone who's done it, see how they liked it."

"Nah. Nothing on the books right now."

"Okay, thanks."

I turned to walk away but saw the blonde at the other end of the porch by the soda machine. She bent over to pick up her drink, looked at me for an instant without recognition, and walked back to her seat.

I got into my car, left the parking lot and drove back toward the ship. A half-mile away I found a flat, open space, turned off and drove into the desert. I turned around so that I could see the road and waited for a dust plume leaving the airfield. A half-hour later one appeared. I pulled back onto the road, followed it to the paved road and then back to the ship.

I sat in the bar and watched for them in its mirror. A half-hour later they walked in. I watched the blonde pull him close to her and whisper in his ear. I bowed my head and reached for some nuts. They walked past me towards the pool. Time to go before my cover gets blown. Once is nothing; twice a coincidence; three times is a pattern. I'd give them a day or so without me in their space. I waved to the bartender for the check.

"You've been following me all day. What is this? I told them I'd make . . ." Derek, in full umbrage, had pulled up next to me.

I watched him in the mirror and spoke to his image, giving him only my profile to stare at.

"I have no idea what you're talking about." I picked up my drink and hid my face behind it.

He stared at the mirror. "No . . . Wait a minute. It's you. You can't fool me. Haggerty, Leo Haggerty. You son of a bitch. Old man Scolari sent you out after me." He pointed a finger at me.

I looked past him to see if heads were turning. They were. The blonde was standing at the far wall near the door. Her arms across her chest, she was worrying a nail.

"I won't be hounded like this. You have no right to harass me. This is stalking."

I focused on his soft, pale face, the color of outrage in his cheeks, his quivering lips, and his thin brown hair.

"I'm not stalking you, Derek. I'm not doing anything to you. I'm just out here on vacation, relaxing. It's nice to see a familiar face in a strange place." I smiled at him and began to raise my voice. "Old man Scolari didn't send me, Derek, Gina did. She can't rest, Derek. She wants to know why you killed her? Was it the money?" He stumbled, backing away from me, as my voice grew louder.

"What am I supposed to tell her? She loved you. Why did you kill her?" I smiled at everyone in the lounge.

Marshall disappeared into the hall. I returned to my drink. No sense in going anywhere. They'd just come to my cabin. I gobbled a few more nuts and held up my drink for a refill. No need to be parched when they arrived.

Ten minutes later, a gentleman in a suit came up next to me. I turned towards him and made my face a wall. I kept my hands in plain sight.

"My name is Munson. I'm chief of security here. We have a little problem. I'd like you to follow me to the captain's office."

"And if I don't?"

Munson stepped back so he'd have room to swing or draw. He had a high, square forehead and a flat nose dividing his broad, flat face. He looked like a mallet to me. A mallet that needed swinging, that cried out for John Henry to slam it against a steel spike. I grimaced as I suppressed that impulse.

"Then I'd have to call for backup and have you thrown into the brig."

"Really? You think so?" I started rocking, then stopped. "Let's do it the easy way," I said, and followed Munson to the captain's office.

He opened the door and motioned me inside. I sat in the chair facing the desk. The captain, a Nils Lennartson, had a phone to his ear nodding at what he heard. He put the phone down and spoke to Munson.

"No need for you to be here, Tom. I can handle this."

Lennartson's hair was cut short and waxed stiff like a blonde bristle brush. Ruddy-cheeked and fair, he had the penetrating gaze of a man who had no doubts.

"Mr. Marshall says you are here to harass him. That you are an agent for his ex-wife's family and that there's a long history of that sort of thing."

I laughed. "Ex-wife? Oh she's ex all right; ex as in dead. Derek Marshall murdered her. I know because he confessed to me." I held up my hands. "Don't ask why he's not in jail. He was very clever. He killed her in a way that left no evidence. I'm out here at the insistence of his "ex"wife's guardian. Whenever Mr. Marshall shows an interest in a young woman, Mr. Scolari gets very concerned. He doesn't want another family to know the misery he's gone through."

Lennartson put his elbows on the desk and leaned forward.

"Let me make myself perfectly clear, Mr. Haggerty. I have no idea what went on before. Frankly, I don't care. There's nothing I can do about that. What I do care about is the ship's reputation and the comfort of its guests. I've informed Mr. Marshall that you are forbidden from coming within one hundred yards of him. If you disobey me, Mr. Haggerty, I'll either clap you in irons or turn you over to the local authorities. Gringos fare very poorly in Mexican jails. As for your concern for the young lady who is with him, I think your tantrum created so much attention that she's probably the safest person here. I know security will keep an eye on her from now on. You should be able to go about the rest of your stay without that on your mind. So there's no reason for you to be near Derek Marshall. Are we clear?"

"Yes sir, warden, we are clear." I stood up and left.

I went back to my room, showered, ordered room service, and put in a call to Enzo Scolari. It was after eight when he returned my call.

"Mr. Haggerty?"

"Mr. Scolari. We've got some problems here."

"Oh?"

"Marshall made me this afternoon, and now the captain has made it clear I'm not to be any where near Marshall or he'll arrest me. I can't even be an open shadow. I also think you're right about why he came up here. He's found a beautiful way to lose a tail. Soaring. You go up alone, and aren't subject to the same rules as engined aircraft, so you can't be followed. You parachute out in the middle of the desert to a waiting car, and you've got at least a half-day lead on anyone following you."

"Mr. Haggerty, it seems your usefulness has ended. You're to leave the ship tomorrow morning and return the car to the airport. If you don't want to return to this area, feel free to convert your ticket to any other destination you'd like."

"Are you going to be able to get someone else out here that soon?"

"Don't worry, Mr. Haggerty, that's all been taken care of."

"Okay, when are they going to get here? I'll brief them on everything I've learned."

"That won't be necessary, Mr. Haggerty."

"What about the girl? Have you found out anything about her? What is she? Accomplice? Victim?"

"Mr. Haggerty, that is no longer your business."

"Wait a minute, that is my business. You don't want me out here because my cover's been blown, fine. You don't care if Derek Marshall disappears, lives the good life without ever paying for what he did, fine. I thought that was why you sent me out here, but I must have been mistaken. But don't tell me it's none of my business that *that* woman could still be a target. That's why I came out here."

"You're right, Mr. Haggerty, I'm sorry. You can rest assured that we've determined she's in no danger."

"That's nice, Mr. Scolari. Tell you what, though; I'm not convinced. How about a name and address? How is it she's here with Marshall? Give me that and then I'll rest assured."

"Mr. Haggerty, I don't have those details here with me. I'm at home. I'll call you with them tomorrow morning. How is that? Then you can leave without any concerns."

"Fine. I'll be waiting."

I hung up the phone, sat there and stared at it. Fuck him. Fuck Derek Marshall. Why was I getting all churned up? Because my easy ride was over? Sure. This was sweet. All expenses paid. Did I really think this would last forever? If old man Scolari didn't care what happened to Derek Marshall, why should I? It wasn't my niece he murdered. I wasn't the law. He'd gotten away with that one. Once upon a time I'd hoped to catch him at something, anything, and to help put him away, for him to pay even a little bit for what he'd done, but I'd lost my chance at that when I went to prison. Just an empty threat I made a long time ago in another life. Who cares? Not me.

I took a long look around the cabin. So long good life. So long warm showers. So long heated towels, so long maid service, clean sheets every day. I pulled down my suitcase, threw it on the bed, opened the dresser and tossed everything inside. Zipping up that side, I flipped the bag over, went into the bathroom and scooped up my toilet articles and dumped them into the bag and closed it up. Packed. I had the impulse to just walk out, get in the car and leave, let Scolari clean up after me. But another night on clean sheets and a hot breakfast wouldn't hurt any. I opened up my plane ticket and fished out a piece of paper. Sitting up on the bed, I dialed a long-distance number.

"Yeah," was followed by a belch.

"Is 'The Kurgen' there?"

"Who wants to know?"

"Tell him it's Leo Haggerty. Slag told me to call." Slag was at the top of the prison food chain. He had no natural predators but time.

"Hold on."

I heard feet shuffle in the background, then someone picked up the phone.

"Yo, so you're out. Where are you?"

"Mexico."

"That's too bad. You coming up this way?"

"Looks like it. That job still open?"

"Yeah. There's a couple guys out here think it should be theirs, but if you're everything Slag says you are you'll have no trouble convincing them otherwise."

"I got some business to clean up here first. You should see me in a couple of days."

"Alright. We'll party first, then we'll talk."

"Sounds good."

I went to the mini-bar, poured myself a gin and tonic, and turned on the TV. I muted the sound and just stared at the screen. I stared and I sipped, then closed my eyes and got very still. Five years ago I could play a spider's web like a harp without anybody knowing I was there. At least I thought that, right up to "we the jury."

I was on another web now and I could feel it vibrate under my feet. Somebody was moving out there and it wasn't me. I played back everything that had happened since Scolari first called me, rethinking every slip, every stumble as a feint.

I went back to the bedroom and dialed the switchboard.

"I'd like the phone number for Kiki Davenport."

"I'm sorry. We can't give out crew member's numbers."

"Can I leave a message?"

"I'll connect you with her voice mail."

"Hi, this is Kiki. I'm not available to take your call. At the tone, please leave your name and number and a brief message. I'll get back to you."

"Kiki, this is Leo Haggerty. I need your help. It's kind of an emergency. Call when you get in no matter what the time."

I hung up and waited.

Around 1:30 I put down my drink and then my head. At 8:30 I heard a pounding on the door.

"Leo, are you okay?"

I stumbled across the room and opened the door. She didn't come in. "I didn't check my messages until this morning. Are you okay?"

"Yeah, yeah. I'm okay. Come on in. I need to talk to you."

She slipped inside.

"Does this have anything to do with Derek Marshall?"

"Yeah. How'd you know?"

"Everybody got briefed on it by Tom Munson. If you're anywhere near Marshall, he's to be called."

"That's why I need your help because I can't go near him. I think he's being set up for a hit."

"If what you said is true, why do you care?"

"I'm not sure I do. What I do care about is being hustled out of the way so somebody can get a clean shot at him. I wanted him to pay for Gina Dalesandro. I don't think this has anything to do with her. I don't like the idea that somebody thinks I'll just bow out so murder can be done or that I'm too stupid to know what's going on. Besides, I'm still not convinced that the woman that's with him isn't in danger, also."

"Why don't you tell the captain? Let him take care of it?"

"Because I have nothing but hunches, and my hunches have nothing but questions dangling from them."

Kiki sat down on the sofa. "What do you want me to do?"

"Hear me out. I used to be pretty smart. These days I don't trust myself. But if this sounds plausible to you there may be something to it.

"When Derek Marshall blew my cover, he didn't recognize me at first. He said, 'I told them I'd make the . . .' He didn't finish his sentence. Then he recognized me. He was surprised that someone was there. He thought some 'they' had sent me and it was because he hadn't *made* something for them. Made what? Made it good? Made payments?

"He was reading some book on moneyless investing. Scolari said he'd ruined some of his investments, cost him and some other people a lot of money. Maybe more than he told me.

"If Marshall needs money, she could be a potential victim. If Marshall's a target, they may not care who goes with him. Especially if Scolari's not behind this."

"Why do you think Scolari is not behind this?"

"Let's look at what Scolari did. He hears I'm blown so he fires me. Okay so far. He shows no interest in how Marshall might disappear. *That's* why I'm suppose to be out here, so he can't escape Scolari's scrutiny. I tell him I'll brief my replacement; he says don't bother. He shows no concern for this girl until I raise it. Why? Because the 'them' Marshall thought sent me out here are going to whack him. So Scolari doesn't have to worry about him getting away, or the girl being harmed by him. He just pulls me out of here so there's nobody watching, nobody in the way. That gives them the go ahead. Hell, I have no idea if Marshall's even in the wrong with these people."

"That's it?"

"Yeah."

"I can see why you didn't go to the captain. I can think of half a dozen other explanations that this guy Scolari didn't want to share with you."

"So can I, but this is the one that worries me."

"Okay, what do you want me to do?"

"Find out what you can about the girl. If you can get into the cabin while they're out, look in her purse, get a name, address, whatever. I need to know where she fits in. The other thing is to try to get to Marshall. See if he'll agree to meet me somewhere public. Away from the ship. I ought to warn him that he's a target and it isn't me who's after him. After that, he's on his own."

"All right. I'll go over to his cabin and try to talk to him or the girl, whoever's there. Where will you be?"

"I've got to check out. I'll go down the road towards town, sit in the first gas station I come to and wait for him there. If he comes. If he doesn't, I'll take the car back to Tucson. Then I've got a plane ticket to wherever."

"You going to Fresno?"

"I don't know. The job's still there."

"You called?"

"Yeah."

Kiki shook her head.

"When should I tell him to meet you?"

"I have to be off the ship by eleven. Say ten after."

"I'll call you here as soon as I get in touch with him."

"Okay."

She got up off the sofa and walked to the door. I went to open it for her. She turned in the space between me and the door, reached up to pat my chest and straighten out my collar. I looked down into her green eyes, at the little tug at the corner of her mouth where a smile was struggling to be, and felt an enormous ache in my chest as a huge bubble of longing moved in my blood like a case of the bends.

Kiki kissed my cheek, spun under my arm and out the door.

At nine thirty she called back. "I talked to the woman. Marshall was in the spa getting a fitness evaluation from Joey. He's the personal trainer. She said she'd give him the message. I also got a quick peek into her purse. She was putting on her makeup when I got there. Her name is Leslie Bowen. She lives at 931 Euclid Avenue in San Francisco."

"Great. Thanks."

At ten my phone rang again. It was Scolari.

"Mr. Haggerty. I've got that information you wanted. The woman with him is named Leila Kurland, she's from San Diego. Two priors for prostitution. Not a likely target for a man like him, wouldn't you say?"

"No, not the Derek Marshall we all know and love. I feel a lot better knowing she's okay. I'll be checking out at eleven, then I'll take the car back to Tucson. I have to stop and gas it up before I turn it in."

"Then what?"

"I don't know. See how far this ticket will take me I guess."

"Well, good luck Mr. Haggerty."

"Yeah, thanks."

I grabbed my bag, checked out, went to the car, threw it in the back seat and drove out of the lot. A couple of hundred yards up the road was a driveway that meandered up into the hills to a house that sat up above the Saguaro. I pulled into it and waited.

At 10:45 a white Camry nosed out of the dock's entrance. Leslie/Leila was behind the wheel. A moment of truth. The car turned east towards the mountains and flashed past me. I sat and watched it pull away.

She told Kiki she'd give Marshall the message. She's driving the other way. She didn't give him the message. She's in it with them. Or she did give him the message and he blew her off. Fuck them. It's their problem, not mine. They've been warned.

I pulled out and headed north towards America. I'd be in Fresno tonight. I turned on the radio, looking for something fast, loud and stupid. Look out bottom, here I come. You never bounce back as far as you fall. That's a law of nature. Doesn't matter if it's a basketball, a rock or a man. So why bother?

That worked for about five miles, but a cowlick of doubt kept popping up no matter how hard I tried to slick it down with bitterness or cynicism or self-pity. It just wouldn't go away. Once it came up with Kiki's face. That was easy to dismiss. No future there. Do it for yourself. Then it came back with a question. What would you have done five years ago? Would you drive away and let murder be done? What's different now?

"I am," I said to no one.

"Only if you let yourself be," was the reply.

If you never bounce back as far as you fall, then maybe you shouldn't fall any farther than you have to.

All important journeys begin with a U-turn, so I made one. I pushed the needle past ninety and held it there until I caught sight of Derek's car. I confirmed the tag number and then fell behind.

She was doing a steady seventy going rapidly into the desert, but not so fast that anyone would notice. I looked ahead at oncoming traffic for an opportunity to pull along side and force them over. Dust devils swirled off to either side of the road.

Almost immediately she turned south at an unmarked crossroads. I followed. We were still on paved road, but now there was no traffic at all. Then we had company. I kept flicking my eyes from the road to the mirror. The Camry hadn't changed speed, but the Jeep kept expanding in my mirror. I saw its turn signal flash as it moved to pass me. Smoked glass hid the occupants. I looked for the tag number. There was none. I went to slam on the brakes and let them shoot past me when the jeep hit me broadside and I flew off the road. The car slammed up and down as it bounced across the desert like a brahma bull. I gritted my teeth and strangled the wheel trying to keep control. A giant saguaro stood in front of me, his lone arm up and extended towards me like a traffic cop. I threw myself sideways on the seat as I slammed into it. The giant green cop came crashing down on the roof, and everything went black.

I came to with a throbbing headache. The rest of me checked in as a battered presence. I was on my back and immediately tried to move my toes and hands. That was good. I flexed my limbs and felt their entirety. I opened my eyes and saw that the roof was gone. A bright light made me squint.

"Where am I?" I asked.

Surprisingly, a deep voice said, "You're in the hospital, Mr. Haggerty."

I turned toward the voice. I saw a badge on his chest, the word *policia*, the black string tie, and the long black hair swept back over his ears, like a cutaway jacket behind a holster. His mouth was hidden behind a cookie duster.

"You're a lucky man. That Saguaro you hit must have weighed five tons. Crushed your car flat. You're damn lucky we found you. We weren't even looking for you."

I swallowed. My throat felt creased and raw.

"Water."

He handed me a glass with a straw. I sucked long and hard.

"Thanks. Who were you looking for?"

"Guy named Derek Marshall, a guest on the ship. He missed the boat when it departed. Captain called me because of some trouble with you. We got a call about a vulture dance in the desert so I figured we ought to go check it out. Might be a cow, might be Marshall. We found you on the way there. Which brings me to my next question. What were you doing out there?"

You never tell the law the truth. Because there is no truth. Only your lies and somebody else's.

"I got lost. I wanted to go out into the desert, see it up close for myself, so I left the main road to do a little exploring."

"And what happened?"

"Some kind of pig ran across the road. I swerved to avoid hitting it. Next thing I know, I'm aimed at the Saguaro."

I asked for more water. "You find Marshall?"

"Yeah, we found him, or what was left of him. Between the sun and the vultures, he looked like a half-eaten piece of beef jerky when we got to him."

"How'd he die?"

"Stupidity, I'd say. We have no idea what he was doing out there. He was alone. No one knew where he'd gone. He had no water with him, although he did have a bottle of wine. We found that on the way to his body. Alcohol's the worst thing to drink in the desert. It just accelerates the dehydration. His car was just stopped. It had run out of gas. We guess he thought he could walk out, got disoriented, wandered deeper into the desert, got thirsty, drank the wine he had with him, got dehydrated, then sunstroke. Somewhere along the way he fell into a jumping cholla. His face and hands were covered in spines. Eventually he sat down and died. That's how we found him. Sitting up against a rock with his hands in his lap. They were covered in spines. He had spines in his eyelids, his lips. He was a mess.

"You're lucky we found you. You'd never have gotten out of that car by yourself. We needed a winch to get the Saguaro off you, then we had to use metal cutters to pry you out. Another day and you'd have been as dead as Marshall."

The cop got up to leave, then he turned back towards me.

"You see, that's the only reason I'm not arresting you. You couldn't have killed Marshall, and you wouldn't have staged that as an accident because nobody called us about you. You'd have died for sure. So I'm ignoring all the captain's stuff about you harassing Marshall, or the amazing coincidence of two accidents on that road at the same time. No evidence of foul play, but lots of stupidity, so we're gonna close it up as death by misadventure, unless you've got something you want to tell me?"

"No, I know justice when I see it."

The cop nodded goodbye and left. The door was swinging closed when Kiki pushed through.

She sat down in the chair, threw one leg over the other and clasped her hands around her knees. Her sandaled foot tapped away to silent music. "How are you doing?"

"I guess I'm okay. I've got this drip in me, but nothing seems to be broken."

"That's what the doctor said. You were pinned but not crushed. He thinks you can leave tomorrow."

"That's good. I don't know how I'll pay this bill, so the sooner I get out of here the better."

Her sunglasses were pushed up into her hair and she was nodding though I hadn't said a word.

"Oh, I've got your suitcase and your plane ticket. They gave me your belongings when they cut your clothes off."

"Thanks."

"Yeah, they weren't going to at first, but I told them you had been staying with me. Otherwise, they were going to hold onto everything, and I figured you wouldn't want a policeman holding your ticket out of here, so I told him that and they gave it to me. I hope that was okay."

Her brow wrinkled like a raised blind.

"Yeah, that was good thinking."

"Well, I'll go get your stuff."

"Kiki, thanks for coming. How will you get back to the ship?"

"I've got the company's jeep. I told the cruise director we were old friends, so he let me stay behind to make sure you were okay. I promised him I'd catch up at the next port of call."

"Where is that?"

"We're headed around Baja back to Ensenada. I'll probably get there before the ship does."

"So you wouldn't have to leave right away?"

"No, I wouldn't have to."

"You know, if you were here tomorrow, you could have company for that trip back."

"Really? What would I want with company?"

"I don't know. I hear your compass doesn't work so well. A girl could get lost like that."

"Oh? And you don't get lost?"

"Oh, I get lost, too. That's why you should have me along. That's how I learned what it takes to get found."

# The Wind & Mary

## PIET TEIGELER

**"Y**esss! . . ."

Mary Willoughby shook her chestnut mane and clenched her little fists in triumph. While the croupier pushed the chips in her direction, her eyes met Mikey's. The steward smiled back at her and there they were again: the butterflies. The same electric feeling she experienced when she first saw him standing by the companionway. That was three days ago, in Southampton, and they had been lovers before the cruise ship left port.

As he cleaned the glass ashtrays with a damp cloth, Mikey mused that this one was going to be easy. Tomorrow they would be in Antwerp for twenty-four hours, plenty of time to pluck this little bird, the third of the season. Sweet Mary might prove to be a prize catch and, in the meantime, bedding her was not an unpleasant pastime. Placing a clean ashtray in front of a blue-haired matron, Mikey turned his head and saw Mary cash in her chips and walk out of the casino. The little lilt in her step made his mouth go slack, and holding the cleaning rag in front of his belly, he self-consciously avoided the older woman's knowing eyes.

In the elevator to A deck, Mary pensively pulled at her lower lip. Should she be ashamed of herself? Such a sweet man and she was using him! Not only as a boy toy, but also as an unpaid courier and, if the deal should go sour, possibly as a patsy. Tomorrow, in Antwerp, sweet-talking Mikey, steward on the Northern Queen, would wave to the Belgian custom officers, like he had done every week this summer. The men in their aviator blue uniforms would grin and wave back and Mikey would walk ashore, as he always did on his day off. Only this time he would be carrying the diamond that Mary would have slipped in the left pocket of his jacket, while her tongue slowly traced the contour of his upper lip. The thought of Mikey's lips and the silken tickle of his blonde moustache, sent a delicious shiver down her spine. As soon as the sliding doors opened with their subdued *ping*, she whirled around and walked to her cabin, humming a tune of elevator Muzak.

At 9 p.m. Mikey went off duty. His white waiter's jacket in itself was enough to grant him undisputed entry to the passengers' decks, but Mikey liked to do things in style. He found himself a tray on which he carried a chilled bottle of Moët & Chandon and two glasses. With a white napkin draped over his left forearm, he started walking down the long corridor. H-112 was a modest standard cabin, but Mary had it all to herself and therefore she had paid one and a half times the going rate for shared occupancy. She was a fat catch indeed!

A tired-looking cabin steward gave Mikey a lewd wink, and he smiled smugly, taking his shipmate's complicity for granted. He had learned long ago that if there was such a thing as male solidarity it consisted mainly of helping each other to get laid. Passing the mirrored wall, around the aft staircase, he gave himself an appreciative nod: at twenty-eight Mikhail Karokin was on his way up. By some miracle, he had come back in one piece from the Chechen campaign. After that, he had vowed not to get drafted into anything ever again. Except the *Organisatsya*, of course, but as a native of Avlabar, the *blotnoi*-neighborhood of Tbilisi, Georgia, he had been born into that one. As a matter of fact, the local godfather had helped him to find his way to the West. One day, wherever he was, somebody would contact him and he would know that the *vory v zakone* wished to call in their marker. But that was later! As for now, Mikey balanced the tray on his left hand and gave his moustache a quick pat with his right, before knocking on the stateroom door.

Mary Willoughby looked at her wristwatch and smiled. Her boyfriend was right on schedule, but she took her time and finished brushing her hair, before answering the door. She had worked her way through college entertaining gentlemen and even if she really liked this one, she knew better than to seem eager. Moments later, when she saw him standing there with his pathetic bottle of champagne, brashly hiding his nervousness, she knew she was in love. But she would not give her game away. She would not blow this chance. She had learned to control herself, even when they were making love her thoughts trailed off toward the diamond and the future she had planned for herself. Mikey was a skilled lover though, and after a while Mary contemplated, with a contented sigh, including him in her plans.

"Did you know," Mikey said one night after they had made love, "that Antwerp is the world capital of the diamond trade?"

"What?" It took a conscious effort not to jump out of bed and stare at him. Could he have guessed what she came here to do?

"Almost 70 percent of the world's production passes through Antwerp and half of it remains there to be cut. The finest diamond cutters in the world live in the old city by the river Scheldt. Even if cheap labor countries like India are slowly taking over the handling of second choice stones for the mass markets, the real gems are cut in Antwerp."

Mary lay motionless, waiting. What was this leading up to? It was just not possible that Mikey knew. The little folded piece of paper had contained the seven small diamonds that she had sold in New York over a year ago, plus the big one. Nobody knew about the stones except Mary herself and the Canadian guy who lost them. Rend or Roger or whatever his name was, had never informed his insurance company about the possibility that he might have dropped the little folded paper in her apartment. He was certainly not going to brag about having been one of her johns—how she hated that word!

"You know," said Mikey, "I have a friend who lives over there. On Pelican Street, right in the middle of the diamond district. He is a fine craftsman himself. If you want to, I could . . ."

She almost laughed out loud. The poor darling! He was trying to sell *her* some stones! And in Antwerp, the very place she had come, not to buy a diamond, but to get rid of one. One that would doubtlessly be on every bona fide jeweler's hot list. She needed a crooked diamond dealer and a diamond market so big that even an exceptional gem would gain some degree of anonymity in it. This lovely lover of hers handed her both on a silver platter!

Mary snuggled up to Mikey's neck and bit his earlobe.

"I love you," she said. "I just love you!"

\* \* \*

"EXCAVATIONS HAVE shown," droned the guide, "that there was certainly habitation as long ago as the Gallo-Roman period, and Antwerp became a walled city as early as the eleventh century."

They were standing on the *Grote Markt* with its magnificent Renaissance Town Hall and its impressive guild houses. Mary had recently graduated, with medieval history as a major. Apart from a small fortune in ill-gotten gains, she had expected the seven days of her carefully chosen "Arts & Culture Cruise" to bring her lots of intellectual gratification. She really looked forward to seeing the work and maybe even the ancient townhouses of such world-famous painters as Rubens, Brueghel, or Van Dijk. But first things first, she thought, looking over her shoulder to make sure that she had been overtaken by the platoon of camera-clicking tourists.

Mikey sipped his coffee and nonchalantly leaned back in his padded deck chair. From the terrace of the Antwerp Hilton, he had an unobstructed view of the Cathedral of Our Lady and the statue of Rubens. Next to the church, across the square, was the narrow street the locals called *The Blowhole*, so dubbed because the sheer height of the Gothic cathedral caused it to be drafty even on windless days like this one. Mikey grinned and turned his chair a bit to the right. The walking party from the *Northern Queen* should arrive here anytime now. No doubt some of the elder ladies would arrive flustered from trying to defend their modesty against some unexpected gust of wind. Funny, here they were in a city full of breathtaking works of art, but the one place most of them would always remember seeing was The Blowhole.

Mary, walking well behind the group, didn't even try to hold her skirt down, and the wind from the centuries-old church, took its time to fondle her flawless figure. Mikey followed her with a hungry gaze, but remained seated until he saw her reach the steps towards the subterranean tram, before hurrying across the square. Even if the passengers from the cruise ship were fully absorbed by the guide's explanations, he would not accept the risk of being seen meeting in public. Carefully making sure that there were only unknown faces about, he waited until a tramcar numbered "two" entered the station. Then he took Mary's arm and, while feeding their tickets to the punching device, pressed himself against her hip. She turned and kissed him full on the lips, her arms sneaking around his neck and waist.

People bumped into them and a young ruffian pushed his way past them, rather roughly. But there were no rude remarks. The whole world, Mary thought, took love for granted.

While the tram sped through its tunnel, she used her little finger to wipe a trace of lipstick from Mikey's mouth and smiled lovingly. So far so good. During their impromptu embrace, she had retrieved her diamond and, once Mikey had introduced her to his friend, she would find a way to be alone with him.

Mikey had his right arm around Mary; with his left he held on to a stainless steel bar. There were some free seats in the back of the car, but they only had a few stops to go and they were comfortable like this, close together, almost like a young couple on their honeymoon. Mikey sighed sadly. He wished this one could have been different, for Mary was an exceptional girl. But business was business and Shlomo had set everything up in the usual way. The little gem he was going to sell to Mary would be real enough and so would the bargain price. But Shlomo would then copy Mary's credit card with a handy machine that he kept hidden under his counter, and next time she needed credit, she would find out that the bargain-priced diamond wasn't such a bargain after all.

"Tough shit!" Mikey said to himself, savoring the American idiom, happy that his English was rapidly improving.

"Look!" pointed Mary. "This must be it!"

Large signs in the tram station said 'Diamant.' Once they had surfaced in Pelican Street, they saw dozens of jewelry shops. Many of them were tucked away under the massive railway bridge. Shlomo's was in the middle of the row, a few hundred feet from the magnificent Art Deco railway station.

"Wow!" said Mary. "Look at that!"

"Central Station!" said Mikey. "You want to visit first?"

Mary shook her head no and they walked hand-in-hand to the jewelry shop, where Mikey briefly introduced Mary to his old friend Shlomo before excusing himself for a feigned errand.

"Little errand!" he said. "I'll be back before you know it. Promise!"

He stayed away twenty-three minutes. He had been waiting across the street for half that time. Then Shlomo put the usual sign in the window and Mikey returned, brandishing a box of chocolates.

"From Del Rey," he said, "handmade on the premises. This little treat is to Belgian chocolates what a Cadillac is to motor cars!"

Mary beamed and Shlomo nodded his head. The chocolate gimmick worked every time. Women were suckers for romance, even tough little bitches like Miss Willoughby. She had laid it out for Shlomo without beating around the bush: I've got a hot diamond I want to get rid of. If you sell it for me, you can carve yourself a handsome slice of the profits. I'll buy a small jewel and you can give Mikey his percentage on that. He doesn't have to know about our other little deal.

In Tbilisi, his hometown, Shlomo had been a small-time fence. In the late eighties he got caught one time too many. The local police gave him two choices. The first one, which involved Siberia, made the second one seem very attractive: remember his roots and take advantage of Article Five, which granted Jews the right to emigrate from the Soviet Union. Antwerp, with its large community of Jews from Eastern Europe and its diamond industry, was an obvious choice, and Shlomo had not only remained a small-time fence but had also become a legitimate gem dealer. The fact that the *Organisatsya* had also chosen Antwerp as one of its European bridgeheads, only cost him a few thousand in protection money each week. And they sent him clients too. Like Mikey, the dumb stud from the *Northern Queen*, who kept bringing him naïve little chicks, begging to get stripped to the buff.

Only this one was not so naïve after all.

"Uhuh!" she had chuckled, "that's an old one you're trying to pull, Shlomo! My credit cards are only handled above the counter!"

While he was examining her diamond—five carat, blue-white, flaw-less—she had been standing next to him, watching his every move. And after he had agreed to write a certificate for the stone, she had pocketed it and coolly dictated her terms. He would find a client by tonight or tomorrow at the latest. If necessary, she would spend the night in Antwerp and catch an intercity train for the short ride to Rotterdam, the cruise ship's next port of call. She would bring the diamond if and when these requirements were met.

"Call me!" Shlomo said in Russian.

He was not looking at Mikey. Trying to make his message sound like some exotic goodbye, he was smiling from ear to ear and pinching Mary's cheek, while herding the couple out of his shop.

On the way back to the ship, Mary wanted to have coffee in one of the sidewalk cafés. There Mikey used the public phone in the men's room to call Shlomo. When he came back Mary looked up at him through hooded eyes.

"I feel guilty!" she said.

Mikey's heart missed a beat or two. Was she going to confide in him after all? He had only to wait a second for his answer. But later Mikey would often wonder if he would have asked her to marry him if she had come clean right then and there on that sunny terrace in Antwerp.

But all she did was laugh gaily and confess that she had opened the box of chocolates and eaten some of them. Seven hours later, therefore, Mikey was picking the lock to her stateroom, while Mary was in the main dining room having a T-bone steak and fries. By the time he was fourteen Mikey had mastered the skill of lockpicking, and since the cabin locks were of the easy-to-pick doorknob type, it only took him a couple of minutes to open the door. He routinely hid his tools behind a fire extinguisher in the corridor—stupid to have them on you, if you should get caught—and started his search of the stateroom. He found the diamond right away, inside its suede pouch, taped to the frame of the bed. But he could not find the certificate Shlomo wrote; she probably had it in her purse.

Mikey sat on one of the narrow beds, brooding about how to get at the paper before Mary found out that the diamond had disappeared. He could not take her to his cabin because he was sharing with another steward, and he could not rendezvous with her here because she was sure to check her brainless little hiding place, right away.

Seconds later, his dilemma was unexpectedly solved. Mikey heard the scratching of a key in the lock and barely managed to get to his feet before the door opened and his lovely girlfriend entered, slamming the door shut behind her.

"You slime!" she hissed, her gaze registering the disorder of the bed and the shifty look in the eyes of her stunned lover. She threw herself at him, clawing at his face and screaming like a banshee.

"Give me my diamond back!" she shouted. Exactly what happened during the next few minutes Mikey would never be able to recall. All he ever knew for sure was that he was standing there, breathing heavily, his teeth bared in a savage grin, the knife in his right hand, and Mary was lying on the floor—motionless.

After a while, Mikey closed the switchblade, took Shlomo's certificate from Mary's little rhinestone-studded purse, and pocketed it. He retrieved his burglar's tools and rode the elevator up to the deserted sports deck without meeting anyone. There, one by one, he threw the miniature Allen wrench and the minuscule screwdriver into the river. He took the knife, which he had carried ever since Chechenia, and looked at it before throwing it overboard. There was blood on it, but not much. Maybe Mary was not seriously hurt!

By the time Mikey had taken a hot shower and drunk half a bottle of Stolichnya, he was hoping that things could be as they always were when he woke up in the morning.

Mary, for her part, realized that she was never going to wake up again. She had left her dying body before it hit the deck. From somewhere not very high up, but clearly above the cabin ceiling, she had seen herself lying on the deck motionless while Mikey took the certificate from her purse. But then a bright, intoxicating light distracted her from the scene below and as she turned to it she heard the faint sound of heavenly music. She felt herself drifting off into a kind of high, a high that was infinitely more delicious than any earthly drug could ever promise.

Suddenly she found herself screaming, "No!"

A jolt of concentrated energy surged through her spirit, a sensation much akin to the adrenaline rush that human bodies sometimes experience.

No, Mikey Karokin, that dirty rat, was not going to get away with this. Not as long as she, Mary Willoughby, wielded any power over the lower spheres!

THE NEXT DAY was bright and sunny. For once, even the obnoxious fumes from the petrochemical plants on the river Scheldt's left bank managed to escape into the stratosphere before poisoning the city. But chief inspector, Leo Dewit, was not able to enjoy the brackish flavor of the morning. The body in H-112 had been discovered a mere two hours ago, but by then Mary Willoughby, American Caucasian female, age twenty-four, green eyes, chestnut hair, had been dead for at least twelve hours. The forensic team was doing its best and Dewit would handle the investigation by the book, but basically it was a no-win situation.

An American stiff on a British ship with eighteen hundred people aboard, which would have sailed long before even the diplomatic implications could be solved . . . Dewit sighed. He moistened the tip of his forefinger and flipped through his notes. Mary had boarded the *Northern Queen* in Southampton and was due to disembark there, after the full roundtrip of seven days. She had booked First Sitting at dinner and she shared her table with three English couples and a Norwegian bachelor, who was obviously gay. None of her seven fellow diners ever met her outside the main dining room. Yesterday the deceased had left the table before the main course was served. She just excused herself and left without any explanation. Nadine Reed, of Chicago, Illinois, a retired schoolteacher, had been on several land trips with Miss Willoughby, and she described her as a very intelligent and cultured girl, who liked to keep very much to herself. Nobody knew about any associates and apart from Miss Reed and Mary's dining partners, none of the passengers had even heard of her. A croupier recognized her photograph, but all he could say was that she played roulette for modest stakes and with an air of confidence, as though she had played before. Zilch in aerobics class and sauna; nada in both nightclubs. Her cabin steward knew only that H-112 rose early and went to bed even earlier. No, to his knowledge, no one ever visited her in her stateroom. Dewit had scratched his head upon taking that statement, but if the steward were lying, he did so like a pro and there was nothing the chief inspector could do.

At ten minutes to eleven, two orderlies disembarked Miss Willoughby's remains. Dewit witnessed the maneuver from the navigation deck, where he had gone to interview the captain. Seven decks below, the stretcher with the body bag, was half-carried, half-wheeled ashore over the crew's gangway.

Leaving by the service entrance, thought the chief inspector. All of a sudden, the sound of the carillon of Our Lady's cathedral seemed to double in volume and a current of air ruffled Dewit's sandy hair. The policeman searched the sky, but there were no clouds. There was no reason for any wind to even be there, let alone blow from the unusual inshore direction. The chief inspector craned his neck to look at the decks above him. High up, on sports deck, he saw the backlit shape of a man, standing erect, apparently fascinated by the body bag and the waiting hearse.

"At least someone to see her off," murmured the policeman.

He turned and pulled at the door to the bridge, but a sudden gust tore it out of his hand. Dewit turned in surprise and again stuck his neck over the railing. The man on the highest deck made an incoherent gesture, but was too late to catch his hat. A very uncharacteristic whirlwind took hold of it, tossed it around some and smashed it down and inward. As it landed at his feet, Dewit saw that it was a seaman's cap. He bent over and picked it up. Tucked under the sweatband was a piece of paper. Without thinking, the policeman took it out and unfolded it. It was a certificate of appraisal for a five-carat diamond. The name "Mary Willoughby" was printed in capitals on the first dotted line.

The chief inspector looked up. The backlit human shape on sports deck had not moved. It seemed that its head was hanging down though. While Dewit heard more bells join the chorus of Our Lady's carillon, the third unexpected squall of that windless morning hissed something akin to "Yesss! . . ."

# The Theft of the Bingo Card

EDWARD D. HOCH

Some of the most pleasant hours of Nick Velvet's life had been spent sailing with Gloria on Long Island Sound, and that was why he finally agreed to her suggestion that they escape the bitter February cold with a week-long cruise in the Caribbean. The giant cruise ships that traveled the southern routes were nothing like the small yacht he guided through the waters of the Sound, but he thought it was the sort of vacation he could be comfortable with.

"We'll have fun," Gloria said. "And you'll be away from the telephone for once. I won't have to worry about our plans being disrupted by some client wanting you to steal the wig off a mannequin or—"

"That didn't disrupt any of our plans," Nick reminded her. "You're beginning to sound like a wife."

"Don't I have a right, after all these years?"

"We'll go to the Caribbean," he agreed. "I'll leave the travel arrangements to you."

THEY FLEW to Fort Lauderdale early on a Saturday morning, leaving behind the snow-dusted expressways of New York and Connecticut. The temperature was seventy-nine when they landed and Nick could feel the warmth begin to thaw out his bones. Their first view of the cruise ship *Antilles* was impressive, and Nick began to understand how someone aboard such a ship could relax and forget the everyday world.

When they were allowed aboard, they found that their luggage had already been delivered to their stateroom. They were on the upper promenade deck, the only one with an outside deck running all the way around the ship. Already, through their stateroom windows, they could see passengers exploring the ship, strolling back and forth as a small band played appropriate music for the sailing.

"How many passengers are on board, Nicky?" Gloria asked as she started to unpack, frowning when she saw his kit of special tools.

"More than twelve hundred, and another five hundred crew members. It's a big ship."

"And we don't know a single one of them. Nothing for you to steal."

"I hope not," Nick said with a laugh. "I didn't come here to meet old friends, Gloria, or to work. Those tools are just force of habit."

The cruise ship had barely left the dock when the loudspeaker blared an announcement that a mandatory lifeboat drill would be held at 5:30 that afternoon. The lifeboat stations were on their deck, and Nick and Gloria helped each other into the bright-orange life jackets that made them bulge incongruously before joining the others at their boat station, number seven.

The boat deck was just above the upper promenade deck, and the oversized lifeboats and ship's tenders hung there on sturdy ropes, waiting to be lowered. Some of the deck stewards called the roll to make certain all passengers were present, then went among them checking and tightening their life jackets. An Englishwoman standing next to Nick made a face as the steward reached around her to retie the jacket.

"What a waste of time!" she told Nick. "I doubt if we'll hit an iceberg in the Caribbean."

She was a slender, good-looking woman in her thirties who managed to wear the unflattering life jacket with a certain style. "Is this your first cruise?" Nick asked her.

"My first for pleasure. We came over on the *QE II* once because Herbert hates to fly. This is my husband, Herbert Black. I'm Marnie Black."

"Nick Velvet. Pleased to meet you." The two men shook hands awkwardly. Black was a grim-faced man, obviously resigned to letting his wife do most of the talking. He was a bit older, probably into his mid-forties, with a stocky build. "I do fly now," he clarified with the sort of deep

British accent Nick had always admired. "I decided if I were to be ill, five hours was preferable to five days."

"Do you get seasick?"

"Not any more. The medication they have now is truly—"

He was interrupted by a booming voice over the loudspeakers announcing that several of the lifeboats would be lowered to give the passengers an understanding of them. "All lifeboats and tenders are motor-driven, and equipped with signal flares, radios, bottled water, bingo cards—"

At Nick's side, Marnie Black laughed. "Can you imagine bobbing about in the middle of the Atlantic playing bingo?"

"It's probably meant to keep people calm," Gloria suggested.

"Well, I wouldn't stay calm for long in an open boat. At least the tenders are closed in."

The lifeboat drill came to an end and the passengers scattered. A ship's photographer was busily taking pictures of groups in their awkward attire, and Nick was certain the pictures would be on sale soon, along with those taken when they'd boarded the ship. "I hope we don't need to wear those again," he grumbled as he stowed the jackets away in the closet. "What's next on the agenda?"

"We're in the second seating for dinner," Gloria told him. "That's at eight-fifteen. That leaves us plenty of time to look around the ship."

NICK WAS GETTING used to the slight vibration of the engines. They'd be at sea for forty-eight hours until the ship docked late Monday afternoon in Puerto Rico. It wasn't the same as cruising on his yacht, but he was beginning to like it. He and Gloria went down the hall from their state-room to a cocktail lounge that overlooked a dance floor and stage on the deck below. A pre-dinner party was in progress for a group of fifty or so men and women, apparently sales representatives for a computer firm. Nick and Gloria stood at the railing for a few moments looking down at the group. Suddenly she tugged on his sleeve. *"What's that?"*

Her attention had been attracted by a slim man with dark hat and a moustache who had appeared suddenly on the stage in front of the audience. He took two or three steps forward and then collapsed. There was a knife buried deep in the center of his back. A few people in the crowd screamed when they saw him. "Get the ship's doctor!" someone shouted, and a man immediately came forward to examine the body.

"He's dead," he announced in a voice that was a little too loud.

Nick began to doubt what he was seeing. "I think it's a game," he told Gloria. "One of these mystery-party things where the guests try to solve a murder."

"But that knife—"

"There's blood all over the back of his shirt, but the stain isn't spreading. It looks more as if it was painted on. Let's go down and see."

They hurried down the stairs to the promenade deck, just in time to intercept the doctor as he was leaving. "Are you really the ship's doctor?" Nick asked.

"Oh, yes—Dr. William Kites from Omaha," the man said with a slight smile.

"And was that a real murder?"

The smile became a chuckle, "No, no. These people are top sales reps from all over the country. They're being rewarded with this cruise, and the company threw in a mystery game for them to solve. It adds to the fun."

"Who's the man with the knife in his back?"

"Well, that depends. To the group he's an industrial spy from a rival company. In actuality, he's a fellow named Simon Franz, one of the dancers in our nightly cabaret."

"You're not going to help solve the mystery?" Nick asked Kites as some husky crewmen carried off the victim.

"No, they just wanted me to examine the corpse and declare him dead. I was glad to do that."

"We've got an hour before dinner," Nick said. "Would you care to join us for a drink?"

Kites smiled. "I wouldn't mind that."

They found a lounge decorated with a large white statue of King Neptune and ordered cocktails. "Is this a permanent job for you?" Gloria asked the doctor.

"No, I'm on board only for three weeks. That's three round-trip cruises to the islands. Then someone else takes over. It's good duty, though. Most of the time it's simply a vacation, with little call for my services unless the seas get rough."

He was a jovial, friendly man and they spent an enjoyable time with him before dinner. Finally, when the steward's ringing of the chimes signaled them, they went down to the dining room. Their tables weren't far apart and Nick and Gloria were facing the one where the doctor sat with some other ship's officers.

"And there's the couple we met on deck," Gloria said. "The Blacks."

Nick half turned in his chair to see them seated at a large table toward the center of the vast dining room. Their own table was only for four, and the other couple were an older man and woman from Seattle who informed Nick and Gloria they'd been given the trip as a forty-fifth anniversary present from their three children. While Nick was glancing about the room, he saw one of the dinner captains stride quickly to Dr. Kites's side and whisper something to him. Kites was on his feet at once, following the man. "Excuse me," Nick told Gloria, "I'll be right back."

There was no reason to suppose that Dr. Kites's sudden errand concerned him in any way, but Nick had always had an innate curiosity that sometimes got him into trouble. This time it led him to the cramped backstage area away from where he'd seen the men lug the body of the murder-game victim. There he found three or four crew members standing around, looking glum. Nick hesitated, and almost at once Dr. Kites reappeared through a doorway with the ship's officer. The group spoke in low voices and then Kites headed back toward the dining room.

"What happened?" Nick asked, falling in step beside him.

"It's that man, Simon Franz—the one who was the murder victim in the game earlier. He's dead."

"*Dead?* What killed him?"

"I'm not exactly certain. There are needle marks on his arm. It could have been a drug overdose. We'll want to keep this quiet, of course. Please don't tell any of the other passengers . . ."

Nick wasn't a detective, and the death of Simon Franz meant little to him. When he told Gloria about it later, she speculated about whether one of the mystery-game players had taken the role of murderer seriously.

"Did anyone see Franz alive after they carried him out this afternoon?" she asked.

"Apparently not. If an injection killed him, I suppose it might have been administered while he was being carried out, or later. Or maybe it was an accidental drug overdose. Things like that happen."

"I'd hate to think the crew is high on drugs."

"The crew is mainly Indonesian and Filipino. Franz was a dancer with the troupe hired to do the shows. He had no connection with the crew."

"I don't know," Gloria said as she climbed into bed. "It still makes me uneasy. I don't think I'll sleep a wink."

Nick was surprised at how well they slept, lulled by the gentle movement of the ship. In the morning they took a few turns around the deck before breakfast and spent the rest of the morning relaxing around the pool.

At the buffet lunch, Nick found himself in line behind Marnie Black, who turned to him with a conspiratorial whisper and asked, "Did you hear that someone was killed on the ship last night? One of the performers in the lounge show."

"Really?"

"They say the police will be meeting the ship in San Juan tomorrow."

Word of the death was obviously spreading. As Nick told Gloria about his exchange with Marnie Black, she said, "There's a woman watching you from that table to your left. One of your many admirers, I suppose."

He waited a moment and then casually glanced in that direction. The woman was dark-haired and a bit overweight, with an attractive face. Nick's eye was caught by the glitter of diamonds on her fingers and an expensive-looking bracelet watch on her left wrist. "I have no idea who she is," he told Gloria.

But he was soon to find out. She approached him as they were leaving the dining room and asked, "Aren't you Nick Velvet?"

"Yes, I am."

"You helped a friend of mine once. I wonder if I could speak with you privately."

"I'm—"

"I want to hire you." She spoke intently, lowering her voice.

"I'm on vacation," he told her, watching Gloria's back as she kept on walking. Down the hall a bit, she stopped to study the photographs of the passengers that had been taken the previous day.

"What's your usual fee?" the woman asked.

"Thirty thousand," Nick told her, raising it by five thousand because he didn't want the job.

"I'll pay you forty." Other people were coming out of the dining room behind them and she was forced to cut their conversation short. "Meet me at the bingo game this afternoon."

She hurried away and Nick walked on to join Gloria. "Have you found our picture?"

"Right here. It's terrible of me."

"No, it isn't. Let's order one."

"Who was your girl friend?"

Nick grinned. "Jealous?"

"I told you she was watching you while we ate. What did she want?"

"To hire me."

"Nicky, we're on vacation!"

"I told her that."

"Good! What are we going to do this afternoon?"

"How about some bingo?" Nick suggested.

On the way to the lounge where the bingo game was held each afternoon, Nick and Gloria encountered Dr. Kites again. Nick took him aside and asked, "Have you determined anything about that death last evening? Rumors are spreading that he was murdered."

Kites looked uncomfortable. "As near as I can tell, death was caused by an overdose of cocaine. Whether self-administered or not, I have no way of knowing."

"I thought cocaine was inhaled."

"Usually it is, but some addicts prefer to inject it." He broke off the conversation and moved away. "Good to see you again, Mr. Velvet."

Nick rejoined Gloria and they continued into the lounge where the bingo game was about to begin. He bought just one card for each of them because he didn't intend to stay long. The cards had slides across each number, which could be moved with the finger as that number was called. "That's neat," Gloria decided, working the slides. "You don't need those old plastic markers."

"When's the last time you played bingo?" Nick asked her.

"About twenty-five years ago, when I was in high school."

Herbert and Marnie Black were at one of the tables and motioned for Gloria and Nick to join them. The British couple had three cards each and obviously took their bingo seriously. "They have a game called the snowball," Marnie explained enthusiastically. "You win a big prize if you cover all your numbers. If nobody gets it, the prize is added to the following day's jackpot."

Nick covered his free-play square in the center of the card and waited for the first number to be called.

"G-49," a voice called out over the loudspeaker. The game had begun.

Almost at once Nick spotted the dark-haired woman who had accosted him earlier. She was standing near the windows, seemingly more intent on the sea outside than on the bingo game. He excused himself, passing his card to Gloria to play.

"I'm glad you decided to come, Mr. Velvet," the woman said, turning from the window.

"I didn't catch your name earlier."

"Dolores Franz."

Nick frowned. "Wasn't Franz the name—?"

"Simon Franz was my husband, but that needn't concern you. I will pay you forty thousand dollars in cash to steal a bingo card."

Nick let his gaze take in the room. "One of those?"

"Just like those, but it's in one of the lifeboats at the moment."

"Oh? Which one?"

"Sorry, I don't know. As you may have noticed, the bingo cards are numbered in the upper left-hand corner. I want card number 253."

"How do I get in the lifeboats?"

"That's what I'm paying you for. I need the card by Wednesday evening, when we leave St. Thomas."

"I'll need ten thousand as a down payment."

"It will be delivered to your room this evening."

"You're serious about this, aren't you?"

"I certainly am."

From across the lounge came the triumphant cry of "*Bingo!*" There were groans from the other players as a white-haired woman hurried forward with her card to claim the prize, "The word is your husband died from a cocaine overdose," Nick said.

"Simon didn't do drugs. He was murdered."

"Who by?"

"Someone who wanted to keep him from getting that bingo card."

"What makes it so valuable?"

"Just find it," she said, "and deliver it to me."

That night when he and Gloria returned to their stateroom after dinner, there was a small parcel wrapped in coarse brown paper resting on the bed. Nick carefully opened one end and counted out the ten thousand dollars in fifty-dollar bills.

WHILE GLORIA RELAXED by the ship's pool, Nick spent part of Monday afternoon strolling the upper promenade deck, trying to come up with a plan for locating the bingo card. There were fourteen lifeboats in all, counting the ship's tenders—larger enclosed craft used to ferry passengers to the dock when shallow waters kept the ship anchored out in the harbor. The lifeboats were secured to mooring posts on the boat deck and were lowered when needed. The only way to gain access would be to lower each of them in turn until they were level with the upper promenade deck and could be boarded. Surely that was an impossibility. Nick was certain an alarm would sound somewhere as soon as the first boat was lowered, and the odds were only one in fourteen that the first boat would be the one he wanted.

"Getting your daily workout?" someone asked.

Nick saw it was the ship's doctor, who'd come up beside him. "I was just looking at the lifeboats, Dr. Kites. Is it true they keep a set of bingo cards on each boat?"

"The ships on this line do. If you have a hundred panicky people in a lifeboat in the middle of the Atlantic Ocean, you need to keep them occupied with something until help arrives. These days, it would likely only be a matter of hours, but lives can be lost in a matter of minutes."

"Still, the idea *is* a bit bizarre."

William Kites lowered his voice. "Here comes Mr. Perkins, the organizer of the murder game."

Perkins was a bright-looking man around fifty, with eyeglasses and a receding hairline. Nick remembered seeing him the previous night during the beginning of the murder game, when Simon Franz had been playing the victim he was soon to become in reality. "Dr. Kites," Perkins said.

"Hello, Mr. Perkins. How's the mystery game going?"

"Fine, just fine. But I've been hearing stories that the chap who played our victim is really dead. Can that be true?"

"Mr. Franz did pass away, but I can assure you it wasn't related to your game."

"Was he—murdered?"

"No, it seems to have been a natural death. But the authorities in San Juan will perform an autopsy."

"In my brief dealing with him, he was most friendly and cooperative. I'm sorry to hear of his death."

Perkins nodded slightly to Nick and continued on his way around the deck. "What about Franz?" Nick asked the doctor. "Did he have any family on board? A wife, perhaps?"

Kites shot him a questioning glance. "Not that I've heard. He was with a troupe of dancers hired out of Miami."

"Has there been any trouble with drugs aboard ship?"

"No, we have to be very careful of that. When we return to Florida, the Customs agents go over everything. What are you, a detective or something?"

"Hardly," Nick answered with a laugh.

When the ship docked in San Juan later that afternoon, he went ashore with Gloria, taking one of the tour buses with Herbert and Marnie Black. It wound its way through the city and then followed a road up to El Morro Castle, the harbor's brooding guardian they'd seen from the ship. They spent an hour touring the old fortress, posing for pictures by stacks of cannonballs that had once been the city's defense against pirates and invaders.

At one point, as Nick trudged up one of the castle's ramps with Herbert Black, the Englishman asked, "Did you see them removing the coffin as we docked?"

"No—I missed that."

"I didn't point it out to Marnie. She's upset enough already about the rumors we've been hearing."

"What rumors are those?"

"That there's a killer loose on the ship."

The women rejoined them and the conversation shifted abruptly. "Isn't this a fantastic view?" Marnie asked, pointing out toward a string of small islands that were catching the last rays of the setting sun.

"Beautiful," Gloria agreed.

Nick returned to the ship still wondering how he would manage to steal the bingo card from a lifeboat. . . .

On Tuesday they were anchored off Tortola in the British Virgin Islands, using the ship's tenders for the shore excursions. Seating and storage on the tenders was quite different from the slightly smaller open lifeboats. Nick assumed they had a full stock of bingo cards on board, but he had no opportunity to check, with other passengers and crew members always present.

As they waited on the dock for their tour bus—a small vehicle with open sides that held about fifteen people—he noticed Dolores Franz standing by herself, away from the other passengers. "Hello again," he said, tipping the peaked cap he'd worn against the tropic sun.

"Good afternoon, Mr. Velvet." She smiled slightly, then asked, "What luck have you had?"

"None, so far."

"You only have until tomorrow night."

"How was your husband going to do it?"

"Climb into the lifeboat and get it."

"He knew where it was?"

"He said he did."

"Where did that card number come from?"

"It was sent to him in a telegram just before we sailed."

"What else did the message say?"

"Nothing else," she insisted. "I saw it. There was only the number."

"Had he done this before, with the bingo card?"

"I don't know. I guess so."

"Was the card always hidden in the same lifeboat?"

"I don't—No, it was in different boats. I remember him saying this one wouldn't be too difficult."

"Nicky," Gloria called, "our tour bus is here!"

"I'll have it tomorrow night," Nick assured Dolores Franz.

They took a winding mountainous road that crossed the island to a lovely sandy beach on the opposite side. Gloria went wading in the gentle surf while Nick watched from a distance, then they sat and relaxed with a couple of beers on the shady terrace of a little cafe.

"It's a good life," Gloria decided. "I could stay here forever."

"You could, but I couldn't. I have a job to do aboard the *Antilles* tonight."

"Be careful. Don't do anything foolish at your age."

"My mother told me the same thing when I was fifteen . . ."

* * *

Nick left their stateroom just after midnight and made his way to the boat deck above them. He was dressed in black slacks and sweater to protect against being seen and also to add a layer of warmth against the strong nighttime breeze. The door to the railed balcony by lifeboat ten was kept locked, but opening it presented no difficulty. Getting to the boat itself was another matter. It could be lowered from where he stood, but it was still a good six feet over to the boat itself. Simon Franz had been a younger man than Nick by a couple of decades, and perhaps that distance had presented no obstacle. Nick opened his kit of special tools.

He took two heavy-duty suction cups from the kit and attached them to the palms of his hands. Then he began climbing up one of the metal mooring posts that held the lifeboat in place. Each was shaped like an inverted "J" and with the help of the suction cups he was able to clamber up the left one with ease. Then he swung himself down into the boat, which was uncovered, relying on a drainage hose to remove any rainwater.

Once in the boat, it took Nick only a minute to locate the supply chest with its hundred or so bingo cards. He hoped his hunch about the boat number had been correct.

He missed it the first time through, and cursed his luck. Then he looked more carefully and spotted it, right near the top.

Card number 253.

He slipped it under his sweater and returned the other cards to the supply chest. He climbed back to the deck the same way he'd come, deciding he was still in pretty good shape.

When he reached his own deck, he stopped to examine his prize for a moment before returning to the stateroom. It looked pretty much like all the others he'd seen:

### Card 253

| B | I | N | G | O |
|---|---|---|---|---|
| 3 | 17 | 22 | 47 | 63 |
| 6 | 20 | 31 | 50 | 66 |
| 9 | 23 | W | 52 | 67 |
| 11 | 25 | 75 | 55 | 70 |
| 14 | 27 | 45 | 58 | 71 |

"Is that you, Velvet?" a voice called to him. He turned to see Herbert Black coming toward him. "Fierce breeze tonight."

"It is," Nick agreed.

"What's that you've got?"

"One of the bingo cards from inside. I forgot to turn it in after the game."

"I didn't know they played at night. Marnie and I have been at the casino ourselves. Slip won twenty dollars at blackjack."

"Good for her." Nick showed him the bingo card. "You two are familiar with the game. Do you notice anything odd about this card?"

"No, not really."

"It has a W in the center space instead of the words Free Play."

"You're right—it's a British bingo card. We use a W for Win. But why would one of the bingo cards be British?"

Nick shrugged. "Beats me. A mistake, I suppose. I won't worry about it."

Black fell into stride with him. "I enjoy walking the deck just before bedtime. Marnie's always dead tired, but this makes me sleep better."

"I expect to sleep well tonight," Nick told him. "I've had an invigorating day."

WEDNESDAY, on St. Thomas, Nick and Gloria strolled through the crowded streets of Charlotte Amalie, the little portside town filled with jewelry and linen shops. There were passengers off a half dozen cruise ships, many already carrying bags of expensive purchases. "I might see something I like," Gloria decided after looking in a few shop windows.

"Why don't you look around for an hour or so?" Nick suggested. "I'll meet you back at the dock at one-thirty." He'd telephoned Dolores Franz's stateroom before they left the ship, arranging to meet her in front of the Charlotte Amalie post office at one o'clock. The bingo card was inside his shirt, and he planned to deliver it in return for the balance of the money.

"Let's have a quick lunch first," Gloria suggested. "I'm spoiled by that big buffet on the ship every day."

They found a place in one of the narrow shop-lined alleyways. Over a sandwich, Nick asked, "Have you noticed any British people on board besides the Blacks?"

She thought about it. "There's a woman in that group of sales reps— I think her name is Elizabeth something. Elizabeth Armstrong. She seems quite nice. I met her when I was lounging in a deck chair yesterday. Why do you ask?"

"I may want to speak with her."

They parted after lunch and Nick headed along the main shopping street toward the post office indicated on his map across from an unimposing two-story building called the Grand Hotel just around the corner from a small park with a statue of some local hero. He saw Dolores at once, leaning unsteadily against the post-office building as crowds of tourists hurried by.

He hurried up to her. "What's wrong?"

"I—" Her eyes glazed as she tried to focus on him. "My arm—"

He slid up the sleeve of her white blouse and saw the mark of the needle. "Dolores, who did this?"

She was sinking to the pavement and he could no longer hold her up. "She's ill," he told a man who stopped to help. "Call an ambulance!"

He waited with her while a crowd collected around them until the ambulance came. As she was being lifted onto the stretcher, he told one of the white-coated attendants, "She's a passenger on my ship, the *Antilles*. How does it look?"

The grim-faced attendant shook his head. "Drug overdose. I've seen 'em before."

"Stay here," the ambulance driver said. "We'll want your name."

But Nick preferred to fade into the crowd. He knew his money was probably in Dolores Franz's purse but there was no way he could take it now. Instead, he walked back to the dock and met Gloria.

On their way back to the ship, he told her what had happened. Once they were back in their stateroom, she asked him, "What are you going to do with the bingo card?"

"I don't know. It was valuable to Simon Franz and to his wife. I suspect it's valuable to the person that killed them both, but I don't know who that is."

He took out the card and studied it. "I think I'll go looking for Mr. Perkins," he said.

Nick found the short man with the receding hairline in one of the cocktail lounges, enjoying a pre-dinner drink. "I'm looking for a British lady named Elizabeth Armstrong, Mr. Perkins. I understand she's with your group."

"Certainly. We all dine together and we usually drink together, too. She's right over at that table there."

Elizabeth Armstrong proved to be a stout woman with an infectious laugh. Nick had noticed her earlier without being aware of her name. "Someone looking for me?" she asked. "As long as it's a man!"

The people at her table joined in the laughter as Nick drew her aside. "I want to ask you a question, Mrs. Armstrong."

"It's Miss Armstrong, and the answer is yes!"

Nick laughed, showing he could go along with the joke. "It'll only take a minute," he told her.

She rose and followed him away from the table.

He asked his question and she answered it. Somehow it was the answer he'd been expecting. "Thank you, Miss Armstrong," he said fervently.

He left the lounge amidst more laughter and went out to one of the ship's bulletin boards, near the the front office. It was one of several places where a map of the Caribbean was posted, with a red line showing the ship's daily progress. It was on its way back now, heading west northwest toward the Bahamas and Nassau. Next to the map, the exact locations at various times of the day were duly noted.

He read them and nodded, knowing at last what he had to do.

THURSDAY WAS SPENT at sea, a bit roughly, sailing toward the ship's next landfall. Nick spent the day making certain preparations, which involved a ship-to-shore telephone call and a meeting with the ship's captain and chief security officer. Nick wasn't in the habit of working with authorities of any kind, but this time seemed different. When Dolores Franz had died virtually in his arms, something had changed.

Much later, past midnight, as the *Antilles* was cruising through the Ragged Island Range and beginning to turn north northwest toward Nassau, there was some unusual activity on B deck, where passengers usually disembarked for the ship's tenders. The door in the side of the ship had been opened by one of the cabin stewards and one of the ship's bulky inflatable life rafts was being pushed out into the night sea.

At that moment, Nick stepped into view. "There will be some delay in your delivery," he told the taller of the two men. "The United States Coast Guard has a cruiser out there."

Herbert Black turned from his task. "I should have killed you along with the woman." He started for Nick, and something glistened in his hand, but now the corridor was filled with ship's officers and armed Coast Guardsmen.

"Be careful!" Nick shouted as they moved in. "He has a needle!"

Black dropped the hypodermic to the floor and ground it underfoot as they moved in to take him.

NICK SAT in the deserted main deck lounge with the ship's captain, a Coast Guard officer, and a man from the Drug Enforcement Agency, trying to explain at two in the morning how he'd known exactly where fifty pounds of uncut cocaine was to be dropped from the *Antilles* into the Atlantic Ocean.

"It was the bingo card," he told them, passing it around for their examination. "The drug dealers who were receiving the shipment had a virtually foolproof method of arranging delivery. The cocaine was delivered to the ship with ordinary supplies at one of our ports of call. The crew member assisting Simon Franz hid it somewhere below deck. Meanwhile, the drug dealers had hidden a bingo card on board with delivery instructions. Franz was sent the number of that bingo card and nothing more. If he had been arrested or the message intercepted, nothing would have happened. Again, if the bingo card was discovered without knowing the plan, its message would have been unreadable."

"Why was Franz killed?" the DEA man asked.

"Because Herbert Black heard about the scheme and decided he'd take it over. He killed Franz and waited for his wife Dolores to lead him to the hidden bingo card. Unfortunately for her, she hired me to steal it. I ran into Black with the card in my hand and asked him to look at it. Once he'd seen it, he didn't need Dolores Franz alive any more. He injected her with an overdose of cocaine, just as he'd done her husband."

"This card does look a bit strange," the captain commented.

"Of course it does, in two ways. First, there's the W in the center free space, and, second, the four numbers in that N line are 22-31-75-45. Any bingo player will tell you that the numbers are listed consecutively on the cards, so they're easy to locate quickly, and the N row always contains numbers from 31 through 45. On that card, the numbers 22 and 75 are misplaced."

"I'll be damned!"

"The entire middle row is a careful paste-up job. My misfortune in showing the card to Black solved the mystery, even though it also led to Dolores Franz's death. Anyone who'd played bingo like Black did would have spotted those wrong numbers at once when I asked him if there was anything wrong with the card. And when I asked him specifically about the letter W in the middle, he said it stood for Win on British bingo cards. I've been to England a couple of times and I didn't think this was true, but I sought out a British lady and asked her, just to be certain. She told me British bingo cards have no free-play space at all. There are twenty-five numbers on every card. So Black had lied about that."

"But what do the numbers mean?" the DEA man asked. The others didn't have to ask. "And how did you know where to find this particular card?"

"I'll answer the last question first. If the message to Franz contained only the number 253 and that told him not only the number of the bingo card but in which of fourteen lifeboats it was hidden, there could only be one explanation. I added the three digits of 253 together and came up with lifeboat number ten. You may want to check the other lifeboats for similar cards that could be used on future voyages."

"And the numbers?"

"Obviously it was the center, or N, row that was gimmicked. What do we have there? N-22-31-W-75-45. What else could it be but latitude and longitude? Latitude 22 degrees, 31 minutes north, longitude 75 degrees, 45 minutes west. Our exact location, as the crew member could verify to Black, when the cocaine was to be dumped."

The Coast Guard officer said, "We have the yacht that was waiting for the pickup. They had other cocaine on board."

"You'll want to question the crew member," Nick suggested. "He was probably the one who first tipped off Herbert Black." He yawned and got to his feet.

"Where are you going?"

"It's been a long night and my wife will be looking for me," Nick said. "I'm going to try and get some sleep."

* * *

FRIDAY MORNING, as the ship docked in Nassau, Gloria finished hearing about the night's activities. "I'm glad you were working with the law for once," she told him. "Are you giving up that other life?"

"This was special," Nick said. "I owed it to Dolores Franz."

"And you didn't take any money for it."

"Well, I still have my down payment. Come on—" he took her hand "—I'll buy you something at the straw market."

# Mutiny of the Bounty Hunter

## RALPH MCINERNY

**W**atching the spangled wake of the ship slide away in the moonlight, Lucy felt that she had sailed right out of her old life. This cruise was self-contained. She had been born when she boarded and her biography would include only the two days since they had left Fort Lauderdale. She did not pursue the analogy to the point where the *Anastasia* would return to its Florida port. That docking could not loom like imminent death, not the way Henry had been pursuing her.

Lucy had thought of asking a girlfriend to sign on to the cruise with her, for companionship, as a hedge against disappointment, but, as when she considered placing an ad in the Personals on a local television station, she had decided to strike out on her own. Henry would never guess the connection between her thinking about that ad and their being together on this cruise. They had met in the offices of the travel agency.

"But I'm from Minneapolis too!" he cried.

"*Are* you?"

"Of course, it's been years since I lived there."

Lucy felt that she had lived there a lifetime; actually it had only been three years. They were three years in which nothing had happened in her life. Nothing. But meeting Henry and spending these days with him aboard the *Anastasia* had changed everything.

"I feel I've known you all my life," Henry sighed the first time he kissed her. "I feel as if I've never known another woman."

"Have there been others?"

"Let's not talk about others."

Lucy agreed, as if she were closing the book on dozens of previous conquests. Would Henry believe how long it had been since a man kissed her? She felt dizzy in his arms, not quite able to believe the wonder of it all.

"I'm not married," he said the second day.

"Good." Her laugh sounded squeaky and unreal.

"Are you?"

"No."

They were on the sports deck where spectator benches provided an excellent opportunity for them to behave like teen-agers. Imagine, necking at ten in the morning on a sun-filled deck with the shouts of bathers and badminton players as background music.

"Marry me," Henry whispered.

"I don't know you. . . ." She choked back the words as they emerged. *Not know him?* She felt as close to him as she did to herself. The night before, they sat on deck until two, just talking. About what? It didn't matter. Words were only a musical accompaniment, an audible means to bring their heads more closely together, to touch temples and then to turn their heads ever so slowly until her lips met his.

"There should be a song about you," he breathed.

"Oh Henry."

"Or a poem."

"There is. 'A violet by a mossy stone, half hidden . . .'" She stopped. Wordsworth's poem would have been figured into her personal ad. Henry seemed not to have heard her. After a moment, he said, "There's 'You Picked a Fine Time to Leave Me, Lucille.'"

"I hate that song."

"Who sang it?"

"Kenny Rogers."

"Don't you like Kenny Rogers?"

*How odd.* Just a couple of weeks ago when she had been talking to the man at the television station about placing a personal ad, he had confided in her that at one time he too had considered placing an ad. When she asked him how he would describe himself, he said, "I don't know. . . . Sometimes people tell me I look kind of like Kenny Rogers."

*Henry did resemble the singer.*

It had taken some time before she conquered her reluctance and called the station. She watched the program with fascination as message followed message on her television screen—women looking for men, men looking for women. At first she was appalled. It took a while to decipher the codes—DWF, DPF, SHCF—and to appreciate the jocular half-serious nature of the messages. It seemed shameless for a woman to announce on television that she wanted a man, however anonymously it was done. A respondent had to call the studio and use an identifying number, but at some point someone had to know the real name of the one running the ad. Her first gingerly step had been to call the station and ask how she could be sure no one would know her identity.

"It will be between you and God," the man on the other end of the line assured her.

"And you?"

"If I couldn't be trusted, I wouldn't have this job."

She gave him her mother's maiden name, Manzoni, and they talked a bit about the procedure. He was very nice, and they worked out a tasteful message, but even so she felt weird about it all.

"Manzoni," he repeated. "Lucille Manzoni."

"I thought that was a secret."

"Between you and me."

The next time she called, a woman answered and Lucy hung up. She wanted to talk to the man again, to go on from before, but she didn't even know his name. Thank God for her hesitation. A week later, before her ad was scheduled to run, she met Henry, an answer to her prayers. With a certainty that surprised her, she called the station and canceled.

Henry had been at the travel agency when she inquired about cruises. It had been meant to be an alternative to the television ad. At thirty-one, she intended to take fate into her own hands. If nothing happened on the cruise, then she would resort to the ad. She was desperate to meet someone.

"Have you ever been on one of these things?"

She looked up into Henry's quizzical frown. On her lap was the open brochure she had been studying. It all looked like such carefree fun. Henry might have been looking at her in one of the photographs in the brochure.

"This would be my first."

"*Would be*? Haven't you made up your mind?"

"The question is, *why*?"

He came and sat beside her. It was possible to imagine that they were planning the cruise together.

"Flaherty," she said when he asked her name. "Lucille Flaherty."

He pulled back. "You don't look Irish."

"I'm half Italian."

He was Henry Hazlitt. He had just sold his business with the stipulation that he would stay out of software for two years.

"Not that I'll have to work again." He grinned boyishly. He couldn't be much older than she was.

"My girlfriend isn't able to go. . . ."

"Hey, cruises are for singles."

That seemed to answer her question. They made plans together, got cabins on the same deck, and had their first date the following night. Lucy was not really surprised when, on the second night aboard, Henry asked her to marry him.

LIFE IS A series of coincidences. When the woman on the phone said her name was Manzoni, Henry was just about to ask if she was a descendant of the great Italian novelist when a little bell went off in his head. He made a note of the number from which she called and then erased from the computer all the information she had given him for her ad. After a little research that night at the library he was assured that his hunch was well founded. He drove out Cicero and stopped at the Palermo Club and talked with Tony Purcell, a nightclub owner whose grandfather had been ripped off by a courier named Manzoni.

"You writing a *book?*" Tony pronounced the word plosively and Henry got a whiff of garlic.

"It's just a hobby of mine."

"What is?"

"Chicago lore. The good old days."

"These are the good old days."

"You may be right."

On their second date, after he spent an hour complaining about what a nuisance it was to manage his money, she told him of her strange inheritance.

"It's a Swiss account."

Telling her he was rich had removed any qualms she might have had about divulging this secret. But it turned out that she had never even been to Geneva to find out what she had been left by her uncle.

"Actually, it was left to my mother. She kept the information about it in a safe deposit box that she asked me to clean out before she died."

"Sounds mysterious."

"It probably amounts to nothing anyway."

"Flaherty . . ." he said, giving it some thought. "I wonder how he would have made his money?"

"Oh, this is my mother's side of the family."

He didn't press it. By then he knew that she had not picked Manzoni out of a hat when she called the station to ask about personal ads. Hadn't her mother ever told her about her uncle's betrayal? The money he had absconded with had never been recovered. Manzoni himself just disappeared, and apparently the money had been sitting all these years in Geneva, the title to it passed first to a sister and then to a niece. By now it must have been written off as an unrecoverable loss. Of course, the police could not have been asked to help recover it. What would Tony Purcell do if he learned about Lucille? Henry dismissed this. Purcell lacked the imagination to pursue such a matter.

Henry felt that years of apparently pointless studying and endless gathering of trivia were about to pay off dramatically. He had researched lost treasures; he had sought to discover what had happened to the great fortunes that were made before predatory taxes made amassing money difficult; he had read with envious fascination of the fortunes being made in computers. But it was the tainted money, the fortunes made beyond the law and fought over ruthlessly, that gripped his imagination. That was how he had learned of the Manzoni betrayal.

Leonardo Manzoni had disappeared on a routine courier run, within the city limits of Miami. He left point A and never arrived at point B. Fifteen million dollars in untraceable cash disappeared with him. A gang war ensued, the assumption being that he had been kidnapped by a rival mob. Perhaps he had been. When the blood stopped flowing, none of the survivors had firsthand knowledge of what the war had been about. Henry first came upon the story in a book by an FBI informant that contained the teasing suggestion that somewhere the money lay unclaimed.

They would have looked for Manzoni in Palermo, Henry figured, assuming he might have fled to retirement there. Lucy said the Flahertys came from Cork, and Henry had already learned that her mother had visited Ireland often, at least once a year. Henry thought he knew where Leonardo Manzoni had lived out his life.

Seen through the lens of fifteen million dollars, Lucy was not a bad looking woman, though it was no mystery why she had never married. The overbite canceled out a vague prettiness—she cut every smile short, as if remembering something, and when she closed her mouth she appeared to be sucking her teeth. But she had the figure of Venus and a yielding, feminine manner that was irresistible.

From time to time, he left Lucy alone on deck, telling her he had to keep in touch with the mainland and his brokers.

"Just *having* money is more of a bother than running a company."

She laughed. "Put it in a Swiss bank."

"I could use your account."

She giggled as he held her close. High in the sky above them, the Caribbean sun burned brightly. Far off in a Swiss vault lay the millions that would be his reward for treating poor Lucy as if she were a beauty queen.


IT WAS HIS Kenny Rogers remark that first set Lucy's mind going. It was too much of a coincidence. Now she could half believe that she had suspected it when Henry spoke to her in the travel office. Far from being put off by his subterfuge, she found it exciting, even romantic. He must have taken calls from hundreds of women inquiring about an ad. It wasn't opportunity he had lacked. *Had he come to the travel agency to see without being seen?* Of course, he had mentioned the cruise, said he was going, and maybe she ought to try it. But at the travel agency, he had not identified himself as the man who answered the phone at the television station. Now that she had guessed, she could close her eyes and verify that his voice was indeed the voice on the phone. *And wasn't it cute the way he pretended to be a wealthy man?*

"My mother wasted her life away, dreaming of it," she said, when Henry kidded about the account, and then asked exactly where it was. "Did she ever . . ."

"Go to Switzerland? My uncle would have killed her. You see, the money was only hers if he died."

"Ah."

"But he was much older, and she was certain . . . ." Lucy shook her head sadly. "When news came of his death, Mom already had cancer."

"Did you ever go to Ireland?"

"Ireland? Why?"

He was momentarily flustered. Then he grinned. "For the pot of gold at the end of the rainbow."

"It's funny you should mention Ireland."

"Why?"

"I own a little farm there, in the west."

"You're kidding."

"It came to me through the Flahertys."

"What's it like?"

"I've never been there."

"We'll go together."

They spent that night in his cabin. He had a single, and she didn't care what the two old ladies in her cabin thought of her absence. The ordinary rules no longer applied. After breakfast she sat looking at him as he studied the financial report the ship provided daily. What if he really was a wealthy man, retired at his age? That seemed as plausible as him being the man who had taken her call at the station.

"Maybe you're right, Lucy," he said, laying aside the report.

"About what?"

"Putting everything in a Swiss bank and forgetting about it."

"It wouldn't gain any interest that way."

"Tell me how it works."

She laughed. "As if I understand it all. Whatever I know I got from my mother, and she was about as practical as I am. . . . No, that's not true. She spent her life dreaming about one day being rich."

Henry shook his head. "If she had ever become rich she would have seen how few problems it solves."

"I am not going to be governed by a little row of figures."

"The number of the account?"

She got out her purse, and from a buttoned-down pocket of her wallet produced the little plastic encased slip. There must have been ten numbers carefully written out in her mother's hand.

"What bank?"

She turned the card over. She didn't try to pronounce it. Neither did Henry. He nodded and, after she had put the slip away and closed her purse, held her silently.

"Well, you can forget all about it, Lucy. We will live on my money."

NUMBERS ARE numbers, but there are an endless number of them and they can be arranged in an infinite number of ways. The carefully formed numerals on the slip Lucy had taken from her purse were only useful in that exact order. Scramble them, and they were meaningless. But as written, they spelled wealth. For *him*. As for Lucy . . . well, she had already played her role. Now that he had the number of the account and the name of the bank, he would leave the cruise at St. Thomas and fly to Switzerland before she suspected what had happened.

Her innocence almost frightened him. *Imagine showing him that slip.* Anyone with those numbers could gain entrée to that account in Geneva. Henry shut his eyes and read the numbers on his closed lids. At a glance, his memory had photographed the slip. He had confidence in his memory. Nonetheless, as a precaution, he wrote down the numbers as they appeared in his mind, and put them in his wallet.

Now that he had what he wanted, Henry felt a strange letdown. The truth was that he never really thought he would succeed. It is the pursuit of treasure that excites; achieving it is anticlimactic. Imagine opening a chest and running your fingers through all those Spanish doubloons. *Who was the crazy guy stranded on Treasure Island who popped up like a ghost when Jim and the Squire and Long John Silver arrived?* Henry already felt a bit like him, out of his wits with luck.

That night, Lucy shook her head when he asked her to come to his cabin. Suddenly, he was filled with tenderness for her. She had trusted him, taken him at his word. She was convinced that love had struck and nothing but happiness lay before her. For the first time, he imagined how she would react after she realized she had been betrayed. She would look for him and not find him, and then learn he had left the ship. *My God.*

He took her impulsively in his arms, and her resistance fled. But now he did not want to spend the night with her. He did not want to take further advantage of her. He looked into her eyes, moist with tears of joy, and saw his future wife. *Had Lucy been the treasure all along?*

* * *

IN HER OWN cabin, lying awake while sounds of sleep came from the other bunks, Lucy told herself she was a fool. Stripped of moonlight and shipboard romance, it was a sordid little story. Somehow Henry had known all along of that Swiss account. Giving the name *Manzoni* must have done it, although all of that had been such a long time ago. Her mother had not needed to tell her that the money in Switzerland had not been come by honestly.

"Is taking from thieves stealing?" she had asked, sitting at the kitchen table in a tufted gown and a scarf wrapped around her dyed hair.

If her mother was right about that, Henry had as much claim to the money as she did. *Well, he could have it.* She had seen him jot down the numbers after she showed him the slip from her wallet. He was concentrating so, he looked like he was almost in a trance. *Could he really remember all those numbers after only a glance?* She felt like handing over the slip and giving him his freedom. *He would want to be on his way to Switzerland as soon as possible.*

Lucy squeezed her eyes shut and told herself that Henry's only interest in her had been the bank account in Switzerland. But she could not bring herself to believe it. He had been so tender and gentle, and just tonight he embraced her almost desperately before she finally went off to her own cabin. *How could anyone pretend so convincingly?*

Was he sincere, or a consummate actor? All she had to do was wait in order to find out. But *that* she refused to do. She would leave the ship and fly home, and hope the wound would heal. Tomorrow the *Anastasia* would stop at St. Thomas. That would be her chance to go, and she was going to take it.

THE GANGWAY was down, and passengers were streaming ashore to shop and gawk, but Henry could find Lucy nowhere. To go down to the B deck where their cabins were was to run the risk of missing her if she came up by elevator. Besides, no one answered the phone in her cabin. Henry now realized that his pursuit of Lucy was what the cruise was all about. If she were penniless, he would still love her.

He was standing at the rail when he saw Tony Purcell come up the gangway against the flow of passengers. Tony's eyes were on Henry, as if he had spotted him from the dock. Henry felt an impulse to run, but the expression on Tony's face indicated he would follow him to the ends of the earth. Behind that expressionless face, two and two had added up to four, and Henry knew Tony was on the trail of those missing millions. Henry leaned against the rail, a fixed smile on his lips.

"Mr. Purcell," he said brightly when Tony stood before him, blotting out the sun. "Joining the cruise?"

Tony took his arm, and Henry found himself being hustled away to the deserted lounge. He was hurled onto a leather couch. Tony stared menacingly down at him.

"Where's that money?"

"You'll have to be more specific."

Tony kicked him painfully in the ribs.

"The money Manzoni stole. You found it. Where is it?"

"You're wrong. I have not found it."

"Yeah. You can afford a cruise?"

Henry noticed a figure standing in the entrance of the lounge. It was Lucy. The last thing he wanted was for Tony to connect the Manzoni money with her. He rolled onto one thigh and extracted his wallet. From it, he took the slip on which he had written the numbers Lucy had shown him. The name of the bank was also on the slip.

"It's in Geneva. I'll expect a percentage."

Tony frowned at the slip. *How long would it take him to grasp what he held?* He looked narrowly at Henry.

"If this is phony, you're dead."

LUCY STEPPED OUT of sight when the huge man left. He still held the slip of paper Henry had given him. She was trying to understand what this meant. Obviously the man was not a confederate of Henry's. She stepped forward and was nearly bowled over by Henry, who was dashing from the lounge.

"Lucy!" he cried, taking her in his arms.

"Who was that man?"

"It's a long story."

"I want to know."

"And you shall. First, get your luggage. We're going ashore."

Her luggage was already packed. She had been waiting for the crowd to subside before she asked a porter to bring her baggage up.

"Henry . . ."

"There'll be a priest there. We'll get married and then go to Ireland for our honeymoon."

"What did you give that man?"

"I got rid of the last obstacle to our love."

"Oh, Henry."

SOME WEEKS LATER, Mr. and Mrs. Hazlitt were in residence in the little house on the Flaherty property in western Ireland. Henry had brought home from the pub an American paper, several days old, that a tourist left behind. He showed Lucy the story.

"Isn't that the man who met the boat at Saint Thomas?"

Tony had been arrested in Geneva for assaulting a bank officer and threatening several others when his request for withdrawal of funds from "his account" at the bank had been refused. The bank had no such account number.

Lucy looked at Henry. Henry looked at Lucy.

"Could I have copied them wrong?"

"Would my uncle have played such a trick on his sister?"

"Well, at least this farm is real. And he bought it in her name."

Lucy realized that neither of them lamented the loss of the money. *Was it just honeymoon talk that they would just stay on here at the farm?* Henry did have some savings: twenty-five thousand dollars. That could carry them for a long time in the Irish economy. When that began to run out, they could decide about the future.

And so they walked the country lanes and spent hours in the local pubs. They assured the local priest that they had been validly married on a Caribbean isle. They soon became accepted by the neighbors. It was weeks later, when Lucy was struck by the nesting impulse and insisted they clean the house from top to bottom, that they found the trap door in the floor of the room where Uncle Leonardo had died.

In it was an old pigskin suitcase with buckled straps. Henry lifted it out and put it on the bed. Lucy had trouble unbuckling a strap, but Henry helped her after he had loosened the other. Their eyes met before he lifted the cover. Whatever the suitcase contained, it did not really matter to their love.

Even so, they squealed with delight when he pulled back the cover and revealed the neatly packed bundles of money as green as Ireland.

# The Mermaid

## JACOB VIS

**K**atrien Welling came on board in Port Said, among a group of new passengers: Dutchmen, Britons, Germans, Americans, Frenchmen, even Arabs accompanied by veiled women in long, black robes. I hardly noticed Katrien at first, as she was hidden behind her uncle, Robert Klaassen, a noisy, red-faced, fat-bellied, estate manager of Belanda Negri. Klaassen is the prototype of the old-fashioned Deli-tobacco planter: stern as a vicar, rigid as a Calvinist, a rude bastard to his assistants and a ruthless son of a bitch to his *koelies*.[1] I intend to be his successor at Belanda Negri when he becomes head administrator of the Deli-Batavia company, God forbid, not on my behalf, of course, but for all the guys who already run an estate of the company.

I tried to find the right words for the greeting—polite, without kissing his ass, the up-and-coming colleague who knows his place in the Deli-world. But he slapped my back and pumped my hand as if I were his long-lost son and barked, "Hello Sanders. Fucked the Whities, hey? And now back to the Blackies for another six-pack?" The ship rang with his laughter.

I grinned sheepishly, not knowing what to say at this unexpected outburst of geniality. Back there in the East we keep an iron hierarchy, and an estate manager being on equal terms with an assistant, even if that assistant is nominated to be an estate manager, is almost unthinkable. But we were not yet in Deli. We were on our way back, halfway there after a

---

1. *koelie* - workman.

half year's leave. Maybe even Klaassen would become human after six months in civilization.

He turned, pushed the young woman forward and said, "This is my niece, Katrien Welling. Going to meet her brand-new husband."

We shook hands. Katrien was a tall, slender young woman, maybe twenty years old. She had a round, pretty little face with a big mouth, blue eyes and long hair put up on her perfect little head. A beauty. Unbelievable that a troll like Klaassen could be related to a delicate little creature like this Katrien Welling. She was taller than me, at least an inch. I am built like her uncle—short, broad, down to the earth—the way survivors in Deli are built.

Rudolf stood behind me. He is my youngest brother and although you can see some resemblance in our faces, we are very different. Rudolf is the aristocrat in the family—tall, slender, well built. They shook hands and for an instant they looked deep into each other's eyes. Two thoroughbred yearlings sniffing at each other's noses. Katrien cast down her eyes and said, "Nice to meet you, Mr. Sanders. Where are you going?"

"To Deli," he said, blushing like a schoolboy.

"I am going to Atjeh," she said cheerfully. A cloud came over her face and she went on, "They say it is dangerous there."

"It *was* dangerous," Klaassen said. "But we control that area now. If not, I would never allow you to go. Whether married to an officer or not."

"You are naughty, Uncle Robert," she said smiling and patted his sunburned arm. "You know Rudolf will protect me with his life."

"Oh yes!" Rudolf said.

She smiled. "My husband. Rudolf van Waveren. He is a lieutenant in the Royal Dutch Colonial Army. We are going to live in the south of Atjeh."

"He has only one life," Klaassen said. "And there are too many Brownies." He looked sharply at my brother and asked: "Who is this *sinkeh,*[2] Sanders?"

"My brother, Rudolf," I said hastily. "Mr. Klaassen is the oldest estate manager of our company."

Rudolf raised his hand, but Klaassen nodded without taking his hand and asked, "*Sinkeh,* hey? Where will you start?"

"At Tandem, sir, I hope."

---

2. *sinkeh* - newcomer.

"I hope not," Klaassen said brusquely. "I hope they will send you into the bush, making your own *kebon*,[3] nothing around but trees and monkeys and have your *koelies* cut the trees on the right spot." He spat on deck and I saw a shadow of shame on Katrien's face. "All these *sinkehs* coming in and having it so easy. They must work!" He pushed a big, hairy finger at my brother's chest and barked, "You hear that? Work! Nothing better than the smell of your own sweat mixed with that of burning wood on the place of your own *kebon*, understood?"

"Yessir."

"Good. If I am in charge you will start in the bush. Now go and amuse my niece. Come on, Sanders let's have a beer. You're buying."

He turned and walked to the bar. I grinned at the youngsters who stared with bewilderment at his back as they walked behind the *toean besar*.[4]

Katrien giggled. "He is not bad, Uncle Robert," she said.

"I suppose not," Rudolf said dryly. He looked in her eyes and went on. "So your husband's name is also Rudolf. How coincidental!"

"Is it?"

"Yes, it is. It is a sign from heaven. Now your uncle has ordered me to amuse you. It is the sweetest duty I will have in my whole life. How do you want to be amused?"

"I want to see the city."

"Then you will see the city. And the city will see you." He smiled. "She will be impressed."


DO YOU KNOW Port Said? Nowadays it has some sort of an administration—traffic rules and so on—but at that time, late spring 1906, it was in complete chaos. Fortunately, traffic consisted mainly of thin, hollow-eyed creatures with muscular legs—a donkey, a woman, a camel, or a man—who carried almost unbearable loads. All these creatures ran through unbelievably narrow streets, shouting, yelling, whistling, barking, making noise fit to raise the dead. How did Rudolf manage to get a guide and a small carriage and show Katrien Welling around in this cacophony? He never told me. Katrien loved it. When they returned to

---

3. *kebon* - enterprise.
4. *toean besar* - big boss.

the ship hours later and found us in the bar, she said it was the most exciting experience of her life.

Klaassen, already drunk, called her his "little pigeon" and tried to kiss her, which she deftly evaded. Klaassen's drunken state diminished his perception. But I saw it. The inevitable had happened. Rudolph and Katrien were in love. Inevitable? How could we be so stupid as to let them go alone? From the very first moment, anyone could see that they were deeply attracted to one another. Klaassen and I had to put them at opposite ends of the ship and keep them there until we debarked in Medan. But we fell for the curse of the Delian: we drank beer and got drunk. In the beginning we had the normal talk of Deli-planters: the *koelies*, the prices, and the prosperities of the harvest. Klaassen suddenly poked his finger at my chest and grumbled, "Won't make it there, your brother. Neither will she. Why did you bring him?"

"He wanted to come," I said.

"Her too," he said gloomily. "I warned her parents. And her, of course. Won't listen to an old tigerhunter. Fell in love with this fellow, what's his name. Van Waveren. Good family. Good young officer too. Brave little bastard. Gets the Willemscross, young as he is." He shook his head. "Poor girl. Will be a widow soon."

"We have peace in Atjeh," I said.

"There is never peace in Atjeh," he said. "There are periods when the KNIL stays in her casemates and the prickhunters stay in the bush. They keep a pretense of peace. But as soon as one of our boys sticks his nose out of the gate, they cut his prick off and put it back in his mouth. We saw the pictures. Then they go out and have their expedition. Her husband will lead one and will die. The brave ones always die. Only the cowards survive." His eyes were bloodshot and he looked a bit woozy but his voice was stern. "You'd survive, Sanders. You're a coward, like me. We are ruthless bastards and our way to the top is paved with cripples and corpses. You *must* be a ruthless bastard to reach the top in Deli, you know that? If you don't kill, you will be killed. If not by a *koelie* who gets *mata gelap*[5] then by yellow fever or one of those sneaky whores who puts a snake under your *klamboe*.[6]"

---

5. *mata gelap* - mad.
6. *klamboe* - mosquito netting.

He fell silent. I didn't dare interrupt. After a while he poured a new beer into his glass and said, "Your brother won't survive in Deli. Good breed, good looks, good eyes. But he does not fit into our world. He will die for an idea." He shook his head and looked me right in the eyes. "But you won't, Sanders. Never. You will die for money, as we all do." He laughed. "I dare to let my niece go into the city in his company. He will protect her with his life. You wouldn't. And I would not. We would find an excuse to stay aboard." He laughed again, amused, not bitter. "You would sell your children at the *pasar*[7] if they brought a good price."

"Why can't Katrien survive in Atjeh? Even if she becomes a widow?"

"She has been three years in Davos."

Davos! The place where the rich recover from tuberculosis. The *Kurort* for the happy few. "Is she completely cured?" I asked.

"She can breathe."

"But . . ."

"But the worst place for a young woman who has been cured in Davos is Sumatra. It is a rotten place, Sanders, and we know it."

"Didn't you tell her parents?"

"Of course I did! Who the hell do you think I am? I told them all about the rotten climate and the rotten diseases and believe me, I spoke convincingly."

I believed him. "They ought to believe you," I said. "You are *toean basar*."

"In Deli, yes. In Holland I am Robert Klaassen. Uncle Robert!" He grinned. "Come on, buy Uncle Robert another beer."

He sipped his beer and got very drunk. Although we both became *toean basar basar*, the biggest bosses of the company with expensive cars and well-dressed drivers and other *toean basars* kissed our asses, he never mentioned that conversation again. Never.

KATRIEN AND RUDOLF talked. All day long, day after day. After breakfast they would meet on deck two and greet one another as if it were pure coincidence. They never touched each other. They walked side by side along the railing, sat in the deck chairs or leaned against the wall of the cabins. Katrien loved the shade, so Rudolf always found a place in the

---

7. *pasar* - market.

shadow. Klaassen guarded her, but not as closely as a chaperone should have, and at 4:30 each afternoon he entered the bar and left her alone.

I told Rudolf to quit, but he tried to persuade me that it was only friendship.

"She is *married*," I said. "If her husband finds out you fancy his wife, he'll kill you."

"I amuse her. Go and ask her. There is nothing that can't be seen."

"It can be smelled, Rudolf. The bittersweet smell of temptation. So stop it! That is an order!"

"I can't," he said in a soft tone. "But I promise you, Dirk, I will not touch her."

"What the hell are you two always talking about? You have been talking for days!"

"We talk about life."

"Life!" I gave him a sharp look. "Your life for the next six years is work. Work, work, and more work. Klaassen is right. You will start in the bush."

"How did you start?"

"The same."

"What's it like, really?"

"It is hell. Bloodsuckers, mosquitoes, snakes, poisoned water and mud wherever you go. Trees like cathedrals that have to be cut and burned. You have to dig up the stumps and burn them too. You must hurry, because it must be done before the rains come and spoil the earth you just gained. It is a thin layer, you know. Spoil it and there will never be anything but *lalang*.[8]"

"Will you help me?"

"No. I have my own job."

"But how will I know what to do?"

"I'll give you a good guide. The best I have. Listen to him, do exactly as he tells you and you'll survive."

"Am I supposed to be his boss?"

"Of course. But in the bush other things count more than Western knowledge. How to make a fire when it rains. How to kill a snake before it kills you. How to avoid bloodsuckers which drink more blood than you drink water."

---

8. *lalang* - high grass.

He gave me a strange look. "You never told me."

I shrugged. "You never asked."

"Well . . ."

"Nobody knew. We all had to find out." I saw Katrien leaning over the railing of the upper deck. "There she is. Now go tell her, you're through."

"Must I?"

I looked at his young, noble face. How would it look after six years?

"All right. Talk about life. But behave yourself!"

"I will." It seemed as if he wanted to say something more, but he suddenly turned and went to the stairs. Katrien waved and I waved back. What would I have done if she had fancied me? I grinned to myself. *I would have touched her. In all the forbidden places.*

AFTER THE Gulf of Aden a small group of about seven dolphins accompanied the ship. We stood at the starboard railing and watched the graceful animals tumbling around the ship. Katrien was excited.

"Look!" She took Rudolf's arm and for an instant leaned against him. "Oh look! How marvelous. They look like mermaids!"

"Every dolphin has a human soul," Klaassen said. He seemed to be serious as she looked in astonishment and he went on, "The soul of a drowned sailor."

"How about the females?" she asked.

"Drowned women become mermaids."

She smiled. "You're kidding."

He shrugged. "It is just a story."

"But a lovely one," she said in the special tone she kept for her uncle. "Tell us more about the mermaids, Uncle Robert."

So he told her the stories everybody knows, but it was her first trip and she hung on his words. The dolphins disappeared, but as we walked along the portside Katrien cried, "Here they are again!"

"The cook cleaned the kitchen," Klaassen said dryly.

"No," she said. "They eat fish. Fresh fish. How can you suggest that these beautiful creatures eat the cook's waste."

"Look." He pointed down. Somewhere in the deep a porthole opened and two enormous arms chucked a tub into the sea. The dolphins reacted like sea lions in the zoo.

"Oh no!" Katrien said.

"Even the beautiful must eat," Klaassen said. "That reminds me. We'll have dinner at the captain's table tonight. Come on, Sanders, time for a drink."

THE DAY WE passed the equator was too hot for a party, but the captain ordered the traditional Equator party. For a few hours the ship stopped exactly at zero degrees latitude. The sea was calm and now that the ship was not moving the heat was almost unbearable. But everybody came, dressed as coolly as they could. Mrs. Vinken, a huge matron, appeared in gauze veils over which she wore a heavy pearl necklace. Faux, of course, but impressive nonetheless. Her husband, an old rubber planter and Russian clown, wore a tie on his bare chest. Rudolf and I were dressed as Arabian princes, the short one and the tall one. There was no question who looked better.

Everything was prepared. In the middle of deck one stood a big round bath filled to the rim. In front of the bath was a throne decorated with shells and dried seaweed. Near the throne was the captain's chair, less majestic but much more comfortable. These were the only seats.

All passengers shuffled in a wide circle around the bath.

"Where is she?" Rudolf said, looking around like a hawk in the mountains.

"Here I am," Mrs. Vinken said cheerfully.

"Oh, hello Mrs. Vinken. You look beautiful."

"You too," she cooed. She pulled a veil a little closer around the soft mountains in front and asked, "Are you alone?"

"Just the two of us, Mrs. Vinken," I said hastily. One woman in love was more than enough. But she stayed close as if I had invited her to join us.

"You will have to go there," she said to Rudolf. "There" was the bath where Neptune would baptize everyone who passed the equator for the first time. Fourteen newcomers stood in a row near the throne, but Rudolf still hesitated joining them. Again he looked about for Katrien. Mrs. Vinken gave me a glance and said, "There they are."

I froze. Neptune strode to the throne. The captain rose and bent his head in a gesture which had an unmistakable undertone of mockery. And by God, he was right! Klaassen looked more like a troll than ever, despite his trident, the mussels in his fogey and the green swimsuit. But almost no one noticed the captain's gesture. Everyone looked at the mermaid. Rudolf took a deep breath. "Isn't she beautiful?" he whispered.

"She is," I said. "Come on. Maybe you will get a chance to kiss her."

He took his place in the row near the bath. Neptune sat on his throne. Blushing, Katrien sat near the throne on a small cushion, erect, her tail in a graceful curve. She called the names in a clear voice and one by one the newcomers came forward. They got down on their knees, swore the oath to the trident, and said what they wanted us to believe to be their most secret wish. Neptune made fun of the man in front, everybody laughed and two sailors lifted the poor fellow and threw him into the tub amid loud cheers from the audience.

Rudolf was last. He stood in front of the throne, close to mermaid Katrien who looked at him with big blue eyes. He sank to his knees.

Neptune pointed his trident at Rudolf's chest and barked, "Swear the oath."

Rudolf said the same stupid words we already had heard fourteen times.

"Kiss it!" Neptune hissed.

Rudolf kissed the central tooth of the trident.

"All three of them!"

He did. Then Neptune made a gesture that he could stand and grumbled, "Well, *sinkeh*, what is your wish?"

"I want to kiss the mermaid."

Neptune's terrible face turned red. He leaned in toward Rudolf and said, "You want what?"

"I want to kiss the mermaid," Rudolf repeated in a stern voice.

For a moment I thought that Neptune would drop down, but he pointed the trident at Rudolf's chest and said, "All right. You may kiss the mermaid. But you will be baptized my way. You will dive from the ship on starboard and rise at port. You may kiss her after that."

"No!" Katrien cried. "No, Uncle Robert, no!"

"All right. No dive, no kiss."

She looked at Rudolf and shook her head. The sailors took my brother's arms and prepared to throw him in the tub, but he tore himself loose and said, "I will do as you say, Neptune."

"You will not," I said. "It is a foolish wish and a commission that can not be carried out. Jump in that tub!"

"Wait," the captain said. "Are you serious, young man?"

"I am, sir."

"You want to dive from my ship, swim under it and rise at the other side?"

"Yes sir."

"Are you aware that we have a draught of nine meters and a width of more than twenty-four meters?"

"I did not know the exact figures, sir, but I know it is a large ship."

"You bet it is. In the early days they were a lot smaller and one seldom survived a keelhaul."

"I'll do it all by myself, sir. And I am a good swimmer."

"Just good is not enough. You must be excellent."

"I am."

The captain gave him a searching look. "I want you to sign a paper that you take full responsibility for this attempt."

"Of course, sir."

The captain wrote in his booklet. Rudolf read his note and signed it.

"Good," the captain said. "Prepare yourself. Good luck."

Rudolf went to starboard and pulled off his clothes. The passengers and the sailors crowded around him, patting his shoulders, laughing, shouting, wishing him luck. Mrs. Vinken took off her necklace. "Take this. It will help you dive fast."

He hesitated. "I must also rise, Mrs. Vinken."

She smiled. "Then drop it. Let them go where they came from."

Katrien who had stayed near the throne hobbled to the railing and said in a desperate tone, "Please Rudolf, don't!"

But he jumped. He reached the water near the dolphins and they all disappeared in a wink. Katrien looked at me in despair. "Why didn't you stop him?" she cried. "He is your brother!"

"He will come back," I said weakly.

She turned and looked at her uncle. Her eyes were almost black. "Uncle Robert, you are a beast."

A minute passed. The longest minute I can remember and surely the longest minute in Katrien's life. We all stood side by side at the railing and stared at the sea. Nobody spoke. I imagined my brother under the ship, wrestling to reach the surface, desperately trying to keep the air in his lungs.

"There he is!" the boatswain shouted at the other side of the ship.

We all ran to port and there he was, amidst the seven dolphins, a pale little spot in the sea, waving and smiling.

"Thank God!" Katrien said.

The ladder went out and he climbed up. I ran to him, hugged and asked, "How did you do it so fast? It took less than a minute!"

He smiled. "The dolphins helped me."

He waited for Katrien and then told us the story. He dived straight down, surrounded by the dolphins until he reached the keel. As he was about to drop the necklace one of the dolphins dove for it. Instinctively, Rudolf grabbed its fin. They went deep down and then up at dazzling speed, and at the instant his lungs would have burst, he reached the surface.

"What a marvellous story," Mrs. Vinken sighed. "You are a hero, Rudolf." And we all applauded and cheered.

A few minutes later he stood in front of Neptune's throne. Katrien looked at him with shining eyes. She sat near the throne as she had done before, straight up, her tail in an elegant bow. Rudolf smiled at her and said, "Neptune, I come for my reward."

Neptune looked at him with a hard, pale face and grumbled, "How did you manage to do it so fast?"

"The dolphins helped me, sir."

Neptune's eyes narrowed. "So you did not do it all by yourself?"

"No sir. Without their help I would have drowned."

"Well, then you have had your reward already."

Rudolf's smile disappeared. "What reward, sir?"

"Your life! It is a reward from God. Now jump in that tub!"

"Do you mean that you won't keep your promise?" Rudolf asked in a soft, low tone.

"*You* did not keep your promise," Neptune barked. "You cheated."

Rudolf stared at him, utterly astonished. For a moment I thought he would hit Neptune, but he turned without saying a word.

No one spoke. The captain made a gesture to get him back, but Neptune sat motionless on his throne.

Katrien rose. Neptune tried to hold her back, but she freed herself and hobbled behind the man who had risked his life on her behalf.

"Rudolf!"

He turned. For a moment they looked deep into each other's eyes.

Then she pulled her arms around his neck and kissed him.

"Oh yes!" Mrs. Vinken said in a soft tone.

It was a deep, tender, loving kiss. The most erotic kiss I have ever seen in my life. The man and the mermaid became one creature. After a moment they let go of each other. Rudolf bent his head and Katrien made a little bow. Then she returned to her place near the throne.

Rudolf bowed to her. He greeted the captain who answered his greeting with a courteous gesture. Then he turned, ignoring Neptune.


THAT NIGHT Rudolph disappeared. He never explained his absence and I did not want to ask. The next morning we had breakfast together as usual. He asked the cook to feed the dolphins fresh food every day. I forbad him to throw his money into the ocean, but he said smiling that he owed them his life. Mrs. Vinken, who heard the story from one of the cooks, organized an "our young hero" collection and collected enough money to feed the animals for the rest of the journey.

Katrien became ill. The doctor said it was an infection, nothing serious, but three days later she had an extremely high temperature. Nobody except the doctor and the nurse were allowed to go in her cabin. At the end of the fourth day the doctor came out with a pale, solemn face. We stood outside.

"Is it over?" Rudolf whispered.

"Yes. I am sorry."

Rudolf turned white as a corpse. The doctor looked at him without saying a word. Rudolf started to tremble and the doctor said, "Take care of your brother, Mr. Sanders."

Rudolf staggered. The man who had survived a voluntary keelhaul fainted like a young girl. The doctor loosened his collar and patted his cheek.

"Wake up, Mr. Sanders."

Rudolf raised his eyes. He took the doctor's hand and said something without making a sound.

"Yes, she spoke about you," the doctor said. "At the end she could not speak anymore."

Rudolf rose laboriously, as if he were an old man.

"I don't know what to say," I said.

"Then say nothing," the doctor said. "Again, take care of your brother. He is going to have a bad time."

That was an understatement. The next morning we all stood on deck one, gathered around the small bundle near the railing. Rudolf stood beside me, holding my hand like a child, his face pale as a corpse.

The captain said the prayers. We all mumbled the words as he spoke the "Our Father." Then came the final words:

"One, two, three, in God's name."

A splash was followed by a deep cry of sorrow from my brother. And down she went. One instant we saw the little bundle, the next moment she disappeared out of sight. So did the dolphins.


IT WAS IMPOSSIBLE to comfort my brother.

"Leave me alone, please," he said in an unrecognizable voice. I did as he asked. But in the evening when he returned from his place at the stern of the ship, he gave me a fright. Can people alter so fast? Could a firm, young face become the face of a ghost in a few hours?

Without saying a word we walked along the starboard railing. The dolphins were back. Rudolf looked intently at the animals. Suddenly he took my arm and said, "Look!"

"Look what?" I asked.

"Don't you see! She's back! She's back!"

"Rudolf, what the hell are you are talking about?"

"Look Dirk, there she is! She is waiting for me!" His voice cut through my soul, but I still did not understand him. He pointed at the dolphins. "Look! There are eight of them now. She joined them. O God, Katrien, my love!"

I patted his shoulder and said useless words of comfort. One of the dolphins raised its head and made a loud, smacking noise.

"Yes, I'm coming! I'm coming!" he said hastily and started to undress.

"Stop, you idiot! Stop!" I shouted, but he looked at me in a strange way and said, "She is calling me, Dirk. Don't you hear that? I have to go."

Before I could prevent it he stood naked. Again the dolphin made the sound.

He jumped.

"Man overboard!" I shouted in my loudest voice. "Stop the engines!

Man overboard!" Like a madman I started to throw lifebelts in the ocean. Others took over. "Man overboard!" And after a long, long time the ship fell silent and two lifeboats were lowered. We searched until dawn, but we only found empty red and white lifebelts floating on the long swell of the Indian Ocean.

SIX YEARS LATER, I spent the last week of my leave in Paris. The next morning I was to go by train to Marseille and go aboard the ship there. I walked through Paris, feeling a little sad and decided to treat myself to a dinner at the Ritz. It was raining, so the porters went up and down with umbrellas. When I came in, a young American couple with a little boy left for a waiting taxi. Their faces were covered by umbrellas as they hastily descended the stairs, but I glimpsed the woman's face. I froze. For one endless moment we stared at each other. Then she called the boy. "Come Rudolf!"

I stood in the rain and looked after the cab, unable to move. A porter came but I sent him away. A thousand thoughts tumbled through my head: Klaassen's awkwardness after her death, Katrien's cabin that stayed closed for the rest of the journey, the doctor who did not want to speak about her illness.

I was furious. I wanted to vent my rage, run after the cab, drag her out and scream at her that she had killed my brother, but I did nothing. I just stood there near the Ritz in the pouring rain. Finally, I went in. I could ask Klaassen. After six years he might be willing to talk. And even if not, at least he would know that I knew.

It must have cost him a fortune.

# Chess on Board

## ERIK AMDRUP

Albert is a primitive soul, but a shrewd businessman and stinking rich. I had successfully embellished his wife with a breast-lift, tummy-tuck—things of that sort. His invitation for me to join a one-week autumn cruise in the Baltic was in appreciation of my efforts.

"Martin Ask, MD, plastic-aesthetic surgery" is what's written on my business card. While my field of expertise may not live up to the idealistic dreams of my youth, it is lucrative. My wife, Cora, is an attorney who legally guides wealthy women through a "satisfactory" divorce. Yes, we both serve those who are able to pay.

When I boarded the yacht in Copenhagen harbor around seven p.m., I was received by a humbly apologizing steward. "I'm so sorry, the director is delayed. Our chief and his other friends will board in Stockholm!" He smiled, subservient in a way that I'm used to and secretly despise. "The yacht is entirely at your disposal! Just call me for whatever you want!"

My cabin was rather small, but absolutely comfortable. I strolled 'round and inspected the yacht. It seemed only to have awaited my arrival before it was on its way out of the harbor. I leaned over the rail and enjoyed the lights glimmering from both coasts of Oresund. However, the evening became more and more chilly, and I went to the bar.

The bartender bowed his head and rapidly turned his back to me. I recognized him, however, at once: Gösta, my best companion throughout our college years and the first part of our professional studies. I'm well padded now, but he had grown thin. Most of his curly blonde hair was gone and his face was pallid and heavily lined like a longtime prisoner's. I turned my back towards him, sipped my whiskey, and considered the situation.

His academic career ended in an odd way, and I came to hate him, but for other reasons. But once, in our youth, we spent a lot of time together, talking until late hours, drinking beer, enjoying music, and playing chess. *Why didn't we forget that our friendship had ended?*

"Don't you recognize me, Gösta?" I asked.

"Of course, I do. Mainly because I knew you were coming," he answered without enthusiasm.

Gösta had developed a habit of looking away, thus you couldn't catch his eye. I suddenly felt a nostalgic melancholy. He had been so brilliant, admittedly more than a match for me in every way.

"How is it? Do you still play chess?"

"I don't have a partner."

"What a pity. You were extremely good. I have joined a club and play regularly. Perhaps not at a high professional level, but I find it quite amusing. I'm sorry you have given it up."

"Did I say so? Newspapers and periodicals publish chess problems, and you can fight a computer program or even yourself!"

"So that's what you do? I wish we could take a game now just as in the good old days."

He gave me a quick glance. "Do you really want that?"

"Certainly. It would be a pleasure."

He shrugged. "Well, I was told that the entire ship is at your disposal, so why not? I close the bar at ten and will come directly to your cabin with a board and pieces. You may order drinks from the steward."

He turned away and I left. The Scandinavian September night was bright with a multitude of stars, and the sea quiet as the ship proceeded at full speed. The steward served an absolutely delicious dinner in the mahogany saloon, and upon returning to my cabin I called my wife.

"Incidentally, I met an old friend here, and we are going to have a game of chess!" I said as I ended the conversation.

"It's not Gösta, is it?"

"Why? Do you know him?"

"Of course I *did*. But I was just a young student then, and you two only had eyes for Inge!

*Did she also know Inge? Why did she remind me of her?* I had planned a nice game with Gösta, talking about our mutual time at college, breaking the ice but avoiding dangerous themes. Now the sad events from the past returned.

NEITHER GÖSTA NOR I was a particularly good student in college. However, when Gösta began studying law he quickly rose to the top of his class, while I was a mediocre medical student. He was the ideal Scandinavian youngster: long, slender, blue-eyed, with blonde curly hair, and over-whelming charm. I must admit that I admired as well as envied him, as did most of his contemporaries.

Through college we continued our regular contact, including playing chess. Girls? Yes, of course. And we had the agreement that whenever one of us pointed one out and said "Madame," the other did not try to compete.

It was at a bottle party that I met Inge. She was invited by Gösta, who knew her from the tennis court, but he became absorbed in another girl and left Inge disappointed and alone. It was out of pity that I approached her. Inge was nineteen, not especially beautiful or bright, but a nice, natural girl, preferring sports like riding, swimming and tennis to reading, let alone studying. We danced, and I liked her and Gösta didn't protest to my "Madame" announcement.

That was the beginning of what I recognized as a close, however pla-tonic, friendship. In fact, Inge and I spent more and more of our spare time together, and I grew terribly fond of her.

GÖSTA ARRIVED at ten sharp dressed in a worn blazer, white shirt with a blue tie, and grey trousers that hid his knobby knees. He hesitated but finally agreed to a small glass of red wine. I was lucky enough to get the white chess pieces, thus being the first draw, and rewarded myself with a stiff whiskey. The game started and I soon realized that Gösta had devel-oped into a very slow player, probably because he wasn't used to consid-ering an opponent. He bowed silently over the board, thus I had only his naked crown to admire.

"Are you married?" I couldn't keep from asking.

"Not at all!"

His answer wasn't commented further, and this made my question nearly improper. I tried to compensate by talking about Cora and our two teenage children. He didn't show any interest, and the game continued in silence.

INGE WAS BORN into a wealthy family. Her mother died when she was a young child and her father was always extremely busy. She could do whatever she wanted, had her own car, etc. I was very well received as her friend and a probable future partner, and accepted the situation without much reflection. I didn't want to marry as a student—but when I had passed my final examination, why not? I felt quite confident and didn't really think about what Inge might want.

"Chess!" Gösta interrupted my reflections. I had allowed myself to become too distracted and paid for it by having to exchange my castle for his knight, a damned reduction in power. He didn't comment or move, he just sat silently with his eyes fixed on the board.

Naturally, Inge met Gösta again, this time on the tennis court. They were both able tennis players and enjoyed a good match. I have never been the sporty type and had to remain an onlooker, but it didn't matter. No, that wasn't the reason for the disaster.

Damn, now Gösta threaten my only remaining castle and I had to abandon a pawn to rescue it. Well, it wasn't a large loss, but it increased Gösta's superiority. I decided to concentrate, to pull myself together.

We sat comfortably in my nice cabin with wine and liquors at hand, while the ship plowed its way through the small waves. A rich milieu, a good deal more showy than Inge's, but her father's holiday house was quite impressive to a student. Inge invited Gösta and me to a weekend there, and we certainly enjoyed everything. After a superb dinner on Saturday evening, we strolled lazily to the beach and further out to the end of the long bathing jetty.

"Let's take a swim!" Gösta suggested, and began to undress.

I shook my head and Inge admitted laughingly that she was naked under her dress. Gösta jumped into the sea, shouted with joy, and swam energetically back to the jetty.

"Why, my sweet, are you afraid of water?" he cried. Grabbing Inge, he swung her around, threw her out into the sea, and followed headlong.

Inge was the first to return. The thin dress stuck to her body and I guess this was the first time I realized how pretty she was. She sent me an odd, apologizing glance and went back in the direction of the house.

When Gösta began to follow, I grabbed his arm. "She is shocked! How could you? You behaved like a bloody brute!"

"What a fucking fool you are!" he snarled. "Poor Inge has needed a *real* man for months. No girl will ever feel satisfied by your virginal politeness, stupid! Your 'Madame' has no value any more. It's my turn now!"

It was late. I couldn't find them and finally had to return to my room; but I wasn't able to sleep. All I could think of was finding Inge and apologizing for my friend. However, the hours passed and it was she who came to me, nervous and upset, face flushed.

"Martin, I have to speak to you!"

She turned toward the window. With her back to me she stammered in a hushed tone, "I spent the night with Gösta. Martin, I'm sorry, I'm in love with him. I thought it should be us, but . . . well, you never said, and . . ."

It was then that I realized how much she meant to me—*her*, not the wealth and power of her family. I tried to explain, but it was all too late. We both wept and Inge fled. I never saw her again.


CHESS! I WOKE up and saved my king, but again had to offer a pawn. My hatred for him blazed up as he sat there, motionless and silent, not for his ability to play chess but for his stealing the only girl I ever really loved. And yet . . . how reduced he was, so shabby and pitiable. How could it be that he had ended like that, the brilliant charmer, the star student?

I didn't learn anything for some weeks after it all happened. When I left the holiday house I hid in my room, buried myself among my books, and spent all my time studying. This led to some splendid results I didn't really enjoy. It was some months later that a colleague spoke of Gösta. "Why, didn't you hear? Gösta broke into the university administration office and copied the papers for the coming examinations. He confessed and naturally he was expelled."

I didn't hear a word and asked, timidly, if he knew Inge. My colleague eyed me suspiciously. "Tell me, have you been sick or abroad? She is dead! Suicide. She drove her car into the harbor."

I returned to my studies and tried to forget. I passed the final examination with one of the top scores and decided on plastic surgery as the most profitable speciality. My life might not be happy, but it would definitely be comfortable. I'm sure Cora shared this view and selected me for financial reasons, certainly not for my expertise as a lover.

"It's your turn!" said Gösta, the first sentence he uttered. My mind drifted far away and I tried to concentrate on a speedy analysis. Well, I couldn't win . . . or had Gösta really overlooked that possibility? If my bishop made this move, his queen would be in severe danger. Yes! "Madame," I warned smiling.

Surprisingly, he didn't touch his queen but moved a pawn. I didn't hesitate to snatch the black lady.

"Mate!" Gösta's bishop terminated the game. I had again been too quick and hasty.

"You haven't improved your chess," he concluded while collecting the pieces. "But of course you are doing well in all other respects?"

"Fine!" I assured him, not wanting to tell him how boring I found my career or about my domestic troubles, our spoiled children's unfairness, Cora's perpetual adultery. "Just fine!" I repeated.

"I'm glad to hear it!" He smiled equivocally, emptying his glass and filling it up with whiskey. "So, you have forgotten everything from the past? Even Inge?"

"I honor her memory," I answered with dignity.

"Absolutely appropriate! Do you know that she died because of you?" Our eyes met for the first time and I could see that his hatred was even deeper than mine.

"Spare me that damned nonsense! She left me because you seduced her!"

"I did!" He sipped his whiskey and shook his head. "At first I was just out for a good time. Besides, it was sickening to watch the romantic crush the two of you had on each other. However . . . well, I don't think you ever comprehended Inge's qualities. But I did. She was a very special girl with an unusual gift for caring, for loving. She bewitched me. I became mad about her, yes, I'm sorry to have to admit I fell in love, deeply so."

"But you had her! Or did she leave you? Was it because of that affair . . . ? Well, the papers for the examinations . . ."

"The *affair*? He aped the word. "Why not call it the 'theft'? Okay, that could have ended in a better way. My pieces turned out to be in the wrong position and the same happened with my marriage. After a few weeks she began crying because she had deceived the wonderful Martin."

"Why didn't she come back to me, then? I would have been pleased!"

"Pleased! Christ, your gamut of emotions is certainly limited. I was in despair. I humiliated myself before her, even wept and begged her to stay. And at last . . ."

"But why . . . I mean, why did she kill herself? If it was like you say, it might have been your solution. But hers?"

"She sent me a farewell letter describing the nice time she was going to have with you."

"I don't understand. She didn't come, I never saw her again after that bloody weekend!"

I felt thirsty and grasped the bottle. I had to hurry as long as there was some whiskey left. Gösta seemed to like it. "And this . . . this 'theft' as you call it?"

"It wasn't me who copied the damned papers, but it was arranged that if it went wrong I was the one who would be suspected. In the beginning I thought it was you."

"Me? Why the hell should I! I would never do a thing like that!"

"No, your fantasy is too limited. It was revenge, however. A girl I screwed when I met Inge. I feel sure it was her. An intelligent and ambitious young student. Incidentally, you know her."

"But how could they . . . you were the star student, they couldn't possibly think . . ."

"I confessed!" He smiled that ugly smile again. "You wondered why Inge didn't come back to you. It was because I didn't want her to. Don't you get it? Inge wasn't the driver when her car ended in the harbor. She sat beside me, sleeping heavily from a drugged drink. This is confidential, of course."

"You're trying to fool me, Gösta. You are lying!"

"Not at all, silly. It's the truth, the whole truth and nothing . . ." He laughed and saluted with his glass. I felt sick, cold and sweaty at the same time.

"I've been looking forward to telling you all this!" he continued. "So you can go home to your bourgeois little family and have a nice time with your memories."

"You are the most disgusting devil I've ever . . . why didn't they arrest you? Inge was young, healthy, rich. Why should she want to die?"

"As I told you, she wrote me a letter. Poor girl, signed it herself, the most stupid thing one can do. It ended like something like, 'Gösta, you have to realize, that this is goodbye. I can't take any more. Forgive me!' In general, the police accepted it. But one of them, an intelligent fellow, sensed foul play and came back to question me again and again. Then I had to confess!"

"Confess the murder?"

"God no! Confess that stupid theft at the faculty! It happened to have occurred the same night and it gave me a steady alibi." He rose and went to the door, but before it closed behind him he stopped and looked back. "Well, I was expelled because of that, but still it rescued me from something worse. Best regards to Cora. I'm sure she remembers me!"

I messed up my bed so that it looked as if I had been sleeping and stayed in my cabin until Albert and his friends boarded. *Sorry I had to leave, but the good doctor had to return to one of his patients*, I explained in a note. I booked a room at a fashionable hotel in Stockholm. It was well heated but not warm enough to thaw out a frozen heart. I didn't know which way to turn, only that I would never ever board a ship again.

# A Cruise to Forget

## BARBARA COLLINS
## MAX ALLAN COLLINS

**B**efore he signed on as medical officer aboard the Carnival Fun Ship *Fantasy*, Dr. Tom Swayze had interned at Cook County Hospital. At first, the excitement of working in the notorious Chicago emergency room exhilarated him, made him feel indispensable and important; but, in time, the incessant array of blood and pain, torn tissue and red tape, began to chip away at him, and one day the thirty-one-year-old bachelor woke up feeling that if he didn't get out of that Dante's Inferno of an E.R. soon, he would be the next patient admitted, strapped to a gurney and shuttled off to the nearest psychiatric unit.

When a former colleague approached him to work for the Carnival line, Tom eagerly "jumped ship" and turned in his hospital resignation. The idea of sun and snorkeling and shipboard romances was irresistibly seductive—fun, even glamorous activities he'd never had time for in his current life.

But after four years of sun and snorkeling and shipboard romances, Dr. Tom Swayze—his hair sun-lightened to the color of a sandy tropical beach, his boyish, round-as-a-coconut face handsomely tanned—woke up one day feeling that if he didn't get off this ship soon, they'd be wheeling him down the gangway, strapped to a gurney and shuttled off to the nearest psychiatric unit.

Shipboard life, he found, was incredibly boring, and this latest cruise was no exception. The *Fantasy* was about to leave Port Canaveral, Florida, for a four-day trip to Nassau, and out of two thousand passengers only three had bothered to look him up in his office adjacent to the infirmary on the main deck. Two were a husband and wife, Anthony and Margaret Vane, who the doctor found seated in his outer office after coming back from the pharmacy.

The husband looked to be in his early fifties, suavely handsome, already deeply tanned, with dark, slicked-back hair in the time-honored Valentino fashion, and dark, deep-set eyes hooded with apparent concern. He was wearing tailored tan linen slacks and a silk cream-colored shirt, open at the neck, his black chest hair curling out. His left hand sported an expensive gold watch and a gold ring with a diamond that was no larger than the knuckle it rode.

Seated next to the aptly named Mr. Vane, the wife was a bundle of twitches and tics. Perhaps fifteen or even twenty years older than her husband, she had been beautiful once, but her face had been ravaged by one too many lifts. She, also, was expensively dressed, wearing a white pants suit with gaudy silver rhinestones and too much jewelry.

"Margaret, I'm afraid, has misplaced her medication," Anthony Vane said, after introducing his wife and himself to the doctor. There was mild irritation in his tone, but Vane seemed, for the most part, anxious, genuinely worried for his companion's welfare.

"I'm so sorry, dear," she said to him, her body moving in a jerky, bird-like fashion. "I'm afraid I'm getting forgetful in my old age."

Vane slipped his hand in hers. "You? Never. . . . But it was hectic at the hotel—we stayed overnight at Cape Canaveral, and I blame myself, really. When she's feeling good, my wife tends to put her medication out of her mind. . . ."

"That's understandable," the doctor said.

Vane smiled tenderly at his elderly bride. "I just don't want anything to spoil this trip for you, dear."

Her smile in response was more a twitch than a smile.

"I'm sure we can remedy the situation," Swayze told them, in his practiced, calm tone. It was what he said to everyone who came to see him, to put them at ease. He gestured toward his inner office.

Once inside, with the couple seated in front of him, Swayze sat behind his desk as Vane handed the doctor a folded sheet of paper.

"It's a letter from our doctor," the man explained. "Just in case something like this might happen. You can give him a call if you like."

Swayze read the note regarding the woman's medication, which was written on stationery from a Fifth Avenue doctor in New York. Fifth Avenue doctors didn't seem to have any better penmanship than anyone else in the medical fraternity.

"This will be fine," Swayze told them. "I'll just make a photocopy and return it to you." He looked at the wife, fidgeting in her chair. "And I'll need to ask you a few questions . . ." He consulted the letter again. ". . . uh, Margaret?"

Her reply was a mouse-like squeak: "Yes."

He gave her his best, bland, meaningless physician's smile. "How long have you been taking this anti-depressant, Margaret?"

The woman peered sideways at her husband as if asking permission to answer. He nodded reassuringly.

"About a year now."

"And you feel it's helping your depression?"

Again she looked at her husband, who again nodded.

"I think it is," she said.

Swayze didn't. He thought this bundle of nerves needed something a whole lot stronger, and soon. But it wasn't his job aboard ship to fix a gaping wound, just slap a Band-Aid on it.

He wrote on his prescription pad. "This should be sufficient to carry you through the cruise. . . . Then you'll need to see your own physician as soon as you get back, understand?"

The woman smiled, relieved. "I will, and thank you, Doctor."

"Don't hesitate to come see me again if you have any more trouble," he told them, as he told everyone when they left.

The *third* person who came to see him the morning the ship sailed for Nassau required a bit more of his time; but he didn't mind—he had plenty of it to spare. And besides, she was attractive, and (he soon discovered) single.

Wearing navy slacks and a red top decorated with little gold anchors, the thirty-something blonde with shoulder-length hair sat across from his desk, her poise undermined by hazel eyes that hinted that not all was well, and in fact carried a look of controlled hysteria.

"Thank you for your time, doctor," she said. Her voice was a melodic alto. "You're probably very busy."

Swayze half-smiled, saying, "Whatever your problem is, I'm sure we can remedy it," then wondered if he'd sounded too openly flirtatious.

She shifted in her seat. "I wish you could," she said sadly, "but I don't think you'll be able to . . . I don't think anyone would be."

He frowned.

"My name is Jennifer Kafer," she explained. "I'm on the cruise with my mother, Cora Hazen, and I have reason to believe she's in the early stages of Alzheimer's."

Swayze leaned forward in his chair. "I am sorry," he said. "You haven't seen a doctor at home, then?"

"No, this is a problem that has accelerated rather rapidly, I'm afraid," Jennifer said, and went on to explain. "After my father died last year, I had Mother move in with me and my six-year old daughter, Lisa, who's staying with her father while Mother and I take this trip. . . . We've been divorced for several years."

He managed not to smile at this good news, keeping a professionally concerned expression in place; and he *was* concerned, even if his musings about this pretty passenger were somewhat less than professional.

"Anyway," Jennifer Kafer, continued, "Mother seems fine most of the time—I would have canceled the trip, if she weren't—but every now and then, more and more often, Mother just isn't herself. She's almost like a child. Last week, I came home and found her playing with my daughter's Barbie dolls. . . . She looked at me like she didn't know who I was. But then, a few hours later, she was back to her old self again."

Swayze leaned on his elbows and made a tent with his hands. "Has your mother shown any violent tendencies?"

Jennifer shook her head. "No, she's always quite cheerful." She paused, then added, "I guess I should be thankful for that. My girlfriend, Susan, her mother has Alzheimer's . . . and Susan's mother has turned *very* mean. Last year, when Susan bought a new television, her mother smashed it with a baseball bat and cursed her for buying a TV that played commercials. She became so abusive she finally had to be institutionalized."

Swayze sat back in his chair and heaved a sympathetic sigh. "It's quite typical, people suffering with Alzheimer's venting their anger and frustration on family members. But if your mother remains cheerful, and content, as the disease progresses, you will indeed be lucky . . . at least as lucky as a caretaker of a loved one with Alzheimer's could ever hope to be."

Jennifer nodded in agreement, then dug into her purse. "I'd like to give you this picture of her," she said. "Even though I'll be with her every moment on the ship, well . . . sometimes small children can wander away, if you know what I mean." She placed the photo on his desk. "It could be helpful in finding her."

Swayze looked at the photo. "Is this a recent photo?"

"Just a year ago, before any signs had become apparent."

Cora Hazen was a vibrant older woman with short red hair, a dazzling smile and intelligent bright eyes that in time, he knew, would be dimmed by the insidious disease, robbing the poor woman, and her family, of the last years of her life.

"I could arrange to sit at your table during meals," the doctor offered.

Jennifer's face lighted up like fireworks off the starboard bow. "Oh, that's very generous, doctor!"

And it was a generous offer, but then, the lovely woman seated in front of him would be enjoyable company, and he'd grown tired of eating at the staff table.

"That is," he said, "if you think my observations might help, or at least give you some peace of mind."

"Oh they would, and I hope I can find some way to repay you, doctor," she said, her expression radiant.

He said, "No thanks are necessary," thinking that he hoped she would find a way, adding, "And of course don't hesitate to come see me again if you have any more trouble."

When the woman had gone, Dr. Swayze put the picture of Cora Hazen aside, filed away his thoughts for a promising shipboard romance, and settled back in his chair for yet another uneventful cruise.


THE SHIP'S ENORMOUS Celebration dining room, located in the middle of the Atlantic deck, was decorated as if every night were a party: carpet like colorful confetti, tables aglow with candles, streamers hanging from the ceiling, and everyone dressed to the nines; the whole place looked like a big birthday cake with all its candles glowing, ready for a wish.

Anthony wished he was on the boat with one of his several current, younger love interests, and not his stupid older wife. But, then, the three women he was having affairs with did not have Margaret's money.

Margaret had Margaret's money—and for him to have access to that tidy fortune, he had to put up with having Margaret.

It was the first evening meal of the cruise, and they were dining near the center of the room at one of the round, white-linen-sheathed tables that seated eight. He didn't know the others at his table (nor did he want to); they were just strangers thrown uncomfortably together for a few days. But by the end of the cruise, Margaret would know all of them intimately and add the whole boring bunch to their Christmas card list.

He looked at his wife, chattering away giddily, endlessly, to anyone who would listen, about their quiet country life in South Hampton alternating with travel like this "scrumptious cruise." Social situations like this gave her a means of channeling her nervous energy. He concentrated on his Beef Wellington and did his best not to show how he felt, or what he was thinking.

Earlier, when he first arrived in the dining room, he'd spotted Dr. Swayze several tables away, seated between a shapely thirty-ish blond and an older attractive redhead—the lucky bastard. Either woman would have suited Anthony just fine—they both looked like they had money—but if he had his choice he'd pick the redhead; it wasn't so much that he had a penchant for older woman as they seemed to have a penchant for him.

It never occurred to him that perhaps younger women saw through his dated technique.

After being seated, however, Anthony never looked their way again, other than to make sure the doctor didn't notice him perfidiously keeping his wife's wine glass filled. Alcohol, in combination with her medication, made Mrs. Vane grow quiet . . . and depressed.

Thinking back, Anthony wasn't exactly sure when he first decided to do away with Margaret. At some point, the scales had tipped: living with a neurotic woman, and having anything her money could buy, seemed far less attractive than just having anything her money could buy.

In the beginning, it was a daydream, a fantasy; but he had returned to the thought again and again, until it hardened into reality. . . .

He had met Margaret just over ten years ago in Central Park, when he was in his early forties and insolvent, having run through the meager inheritance left him by his previous wife, who had been in her seventies and whose estate had largely gone to her grown children. Margaret was younger than the previous Mrs. Vane—she'd just turned sixty—and was the childless widow of a Manhattan real estate tycoon, who'd made his mint long before Donald Trump came on the scene.

At first, the future Mrs. Vane had been cautious about sharing her wealth with him, and even spoke of a prenuptial agreement; but soon Anthony's talk of love and trust, plus his considerable sexual prowess, convinced her that there was more to life than money.

"Is anything the matter, dear?" he asked his wife sweetly. "You seem so quiet."

Morosely, she shook her head.

Voices from the doctor's table drifted to him, and Anthony caught snatches of conversation. It seemed the two women dining with the physician were mother and daughter—the mother widowed, the daughter divorced. He wondered idly if they might be interested in a threesome? *Menage* with a mother and daughter was on the short list of sexual adventures life had as yet denied him.

But it was the mother's youthful voice and musical laughter that made the front of his black tux pants tingle. He wanted to look the redhead's way, to catch a glimpse of her enticing smile, but instead he adjusted his linen napkin in his lap and forced himself to carry on a conversation with the stodgy banker from Boston seated next to him.

After the main course plates had been cleared, Anthony leaned toward his wife and said, "You don't look at all well, my dear—you seem rather peaked. Why don't we go for a stroll on deck?"

She peered at him, blue eyes touched by a filigree of red. "I don't care to. Dessert is coming."

He gave her a little smile. "Just thought you might like to catch a little air, sweetheart."

The others at the table had stopped their conversation and were looking the couple's way, but Margaret didn't seem to notice.

Anthony leaned toward her and, giving her an affectionate peck on the cheek, asked, "Then you won't mind if I stretch my legs for a while?"

What to the other passengers might seem an innocent question to Margaret was a veiled threat. She knew, as well as her husband, that there were any number of lonely women on board the *Fantasy*, eager to meet a handsome stranger.

"I've changed my mind," she said abruptly, placing her napkin on the table. "I'll get some air with you."

Their fellow diners had noticed his wife's dramatic mood swing—from belle of the ball to sullen wallflower—and this suited Anthony's plans ideally.

As they exited the dining room, Anthony put a comforting arm around his wife, as if she were ailing. And when they passed the doctor's table, Anthony maintained his concerned expression, his eyes fixed only upon his dearly beloved.

On the upper deck, he opened the heavy wood door inset with oval cut-glass and the burst of weather from the outside was almost enough to make Margaret turn back; the wind was strong, the night black, and a slight drizzle spat insolently in their faces.

"My hair!" she wailed, both hands flying to the sides of her head. She had spent two hours in the ship's beauty shop that afternoon, a waste of time and money in her husband's opinion; her looks were gone, like his patience with her.

He ignored her plea, ushering her out on the narrow platform and over to the steel rail. The deck was deserted; everyone else was still in the dining room, gorging themselves on pastries and pies, and even the non-gluttons had been warded off by the weather.

Mr. Vane had planned on taking Mrs. Vane in his arms and kissing her one last time—he really was a romantic, and once had felt something akin to love for her, when she was still attractive. One last kiss, remembering some of the good times . . . But since nothing came to mind, he gathered her in his arms, like a bride about to be ushered over the threshold, and—her eyes wide, her mouth open, as she tried desperately to make this a romantic gesture—he hurled her unceremoniously over the rail.

He was surprised at how light she'd seemed in his arms, and how quickly she disappeared into the ocean, the black, white-capped waves reaching upward as if to catch her, then pulling her down and under.

She'd been too surprised to scream; or had she simply accepted her fate, and would rather be dead than unloved by him? Anthony would never know, and would also never ponder the answer again.

He lingered only a second or two before turning toward the outer deck door to leave. The door was being partially held open by someone.

Hell!

It was the red-haired woman, the attractive older widow, who had stepped out onto the deck—her daughter was nowhere to be seen. How long she'd been there, Anthony didn't know; but her expression of shock told him what she'd seen.

Everything.

He froze, horrified, not knowing what to do. And as voices trailed out to him from the open door, telling him others were on their way to the deck, he realized there wasn't time for the woman named Cora Hazen to join his wife under the choppy sea.

"I . . . I . . . ." He could only stammer as he took a few tentative steps toward her, his suave facade dropping like pants whose suspenders had snapped.

Cora Hazen let go of the door and plastered herself against the wall of the deck.

"Please keep quiet," he said, gathering the shreds of his dignity about him. "I have money . . . A great deal of money."

Her eyes seemed oddly blank, then came alive. "Money? Let me see!"

He quickly dug into his pants pocket and brought out a wad of cash that had been meant for the casino, later that night, and thrust it toward her.

"This is all I have on me . . . but I can get you more, much more. . . ."

Her eyes were as wide as Margaret's going over the side; but her face had taken on a child-like glee.

"I *like* money!" she said and snatched the cash from his hand.

He leaned an arm against the deck wall, pinning her there. "We're alike, you and I."

She gazed up at him girlishly. "You like money, too?"

What a tease!

"Oh yes," he said. She was riffling through the money as if she were counting it, but not really keeping track, taunting him, the clever bitch.

So, the eyewitness to his crime was as greedy as he was, it seemed; this would be costly, but with Margaret's fortune, he could control it. He could turn this around. . . .

Then the deck door opened again, and the woman's daughter emerged. Cora quickly thrust the wad of bills behind her back.

"Mother," the pretty woman said anxiously, "I've been looking all over for you." The daughter seemed oddly distraught.

"Dear," the mother said, "I've been talking to this nice gentleman." She leaned toward her daughter and added in a loud whisper, "He has a lot of m-o-n-e-y."

Damn her, needling him like this.

Fortunately, the daughter merely looked at him with embarrassment. "I'm sorry about this, Mr. . . . ?"

"Vane," he said with slight bow of his head. "Anthony Vane. It's so nice to meet you and your delightful mother."

"And you, too," the daughter said distractedly, then turned to the older woman. "Mother, it's time we get back to our stateroom."

"Yes, and I must try to find my wife," Anthony said. "I seem to have misplaced her." He laughed a little, sneaking a look at the mother. No reaction. Her lovely face remained cheerfully placid.

A cool customer, this one. Had he finally found the woman who was his equal?

"I hope you ladies have a pleasant evening," he said, bowing to the women. "Perhaps I'll be seeing you later."

The mother giggled. "If you're lucky."

Damn, if she wasn't a beguiling creature! He watched the pair go back inside, standing there with his heart pounding as if trying to burst from his rib cage. Funny—he'd been calm as he tossed Margaret overboard; only now was his pulse racing, fear and excitement coursing through him.

He leaned at the rail and breathed deeply of the cold night air. It was time to put the rest of his plan in motion—he would go to the casino for a few hours, then when he returned to his room and found his wife not there, he would search the ship (making sure his efforts were witnessed) and finally report that she was missing.

The cloak that was his suaveness gathered about him again, self-composed once more, he headed for Club 21 on the promenade deck, wondering what he should do about Cora—kill her, or make love to her.

Or both—in reverse order, of course. He wasn't sick, after all.

IT WAS ONLY when the dessert dishes were being cleared that Jennifer realized how long her mother had been away on her trip to the ladies' room, and began to panic. She had been engrossed in conversation with the doctor (Tom was single, she discovered, with a fascinating history as an ER doctor) when her mother had said she'd be right back.

But "right back" turned into fifteen minutes and Jennifer stopped listening to what the doctor was saying and began looking anxiously around the vast dining room.

"I'm sure she'll be along soon," Tom said, doing his best to put her at ease. "She seems fine tonight."

"It's so easy to forget," Jennifer said. "When she's behaving like herself, it's easy to treat her like the adult I knew."

"There's nothing to worry about—really."

Jennifer was shaking her head. "I shouldn't have let her go by herself. Even *I* can get lost on this big ship. . . . And you just don't know how quickly she can *change*." She stood, pushing back her chair.

"Why don't I go with you," the doctor offered, putting his napkin down. "We both can search."

Jennifer put a hand on his shoulder. "No. Let me look first, and if I can't find her, I'll come back and get you."

"You're sure? Because it's no trouble . . ."

"I need to learn to handle situations like this," she told him, firmly but not unkindly, "myself."

Jennifer first checked the restrooms just outside the dining room near the elevators, then moved on to the pavilion with its smaller restrooms, and finally descended the grand staircase in the center of the ship to the lower floor. As she hurried along she was reminded of the time she'd lost her own daughter in a big department store, and all kinds of terrible images had rampaged through her mind, until the child was at last found in the toy department, playing happily away with Barbie dolls.

Perhaps the Galleria Shops had caught her mother's attention; they were located back on the same deck as the dining room. She was taking a short cut past the galley when she spotted her mother's red hair through the oval window of a deck door; her mother was standing on the windy deck, talking to a handsome middle-aged man.

When Jennifer went through the door into the cold, spitting sea air, she knew in an instant that her mother was not herself; she could tell by the animated way her mother was talking to the man, who upon closer look had the slick, archaic appearance of a Noel Coward-era gigolo. She remembered noticing him a few tables away, with a dejected-looking older woman seated at his side.

Jennifer got her mother away from the man as gracefully as she could—he seemed to be misinterpreting her infantile behavior as coquettishness, thankfully—and, back in their stateroom, called and left word for the doctor that she had found her mother and that they were in for the night.

As Jennifer undressed, she wondered if the two of them were going to survive the trip; in a very short time her mother had gotten so much worse.

Their (so-called) stateroom on the empress deck had two twin beds and an ocean view. It was a little cramped, but nice enough, the decor a soothing mauve and turquoise, with a TV high in one corner, a writing table with fresh flowers against one wall, and a lovely pastel picture of a tropical beach on another.

"I think we should get some sleep," Jennifer said to her mother. "It's been a very long day."

"But I'm not sleepy yet," her mother responded. She was sitting on one of the beds, bouncing ever so slightly.

"We're going to have an even longer, busier day tomorrow, Mother. We'll be docking in Nassau in the morning."

Her mother wrinkled her nose, as if smelling something icky.

"Why don't you get into your new nightgown," Jennifer cajoled. "I've put your things in the closet."

Her mother got up from the bed and went to the closet, but instead of retrieving her nightgown, she brought out a small pink suitcase, which she took back to the bed and opened.

Jennifer sighed. "Mother, please don't get into that. It's late."

Her mother ignored her plea, rifling through the pink child-size suit-case—which had once belonged to Jennifer's daughter—filled with old and new Barbie dolls, accessories and tiny clothes.

Jennifer stared at her mother, who in her heyday had been one of the movers and shakers of the fashion world, designing and launching her own workout clothes, long before any other designer had. Now she was stripped of any remaining talent, still somehow connected to fashion in the withering recesses of her mind, reduced to playing with doll clothes, drawn to them, perhaps not even knowing why.

Mother looked up at daughter anxiously. "Where's Nibbles? I can't find Nibbles."

"We talked about that before we left, Mother," Jennifer said slowly, trying to stay calm but feeling exasperation begin to overwhelm her. "I told you we couldn't bring everything. Don't you remember?"

But, then, that was the whole problem, wasn't it?

"But I need Nibbles! You know Barbie will want to ride her horsey." She held up one of the dolls; its blonde hair was a mess, giving it a crazed look.

Jennifer closed her eyes, gathering all the strength she could. Then she went over and sat on her mother's bed and slipped an arm gently around the woman's shoulders.

"Look, Mom," she said tactfully, "you be a good girl and get to bed, and tomorrow we'll find another horsey in Nassau." It was a fib, of course, or close to one: Jennifer doubted any store on the island carried Barbie toys.

"But what if they don't have it? What then?" her mother sniffed, holding back tears.

"Then we'll buy something else, just as nice."

"Nicer!"

"Nicer."

"Like My Very Own Vanity for fifty-nine dollars and ninety-five cents? Or the Cruisin' Car convertible for thirty-four dollars and ninety-five cents?"

"That's right. One of those."

Her mother shifted on the bed, barely able to contain her enthusiasm. "Or the Malibu Beach House for ninety-nine dollars and ninety-five cents?"

"We'll see."

"I have my very own money, you know," her mother said, with a smile that was lovely if you didn't study it.

"Yes. Yes." Before the trip Jennifer had given her mother twenty dollars to carry; she dare not trust her with anything more. "But you have to get to bed, first."

"Goodie, goodie, goodie! G'night . . . what's your name again, dear?"

"Jennifer, Mother. It's Jennifer."

"You're my daughter." Her mother seemed proud of this observation.

"Yes. Yes I am."

Five minutes later, with the lights out and the ship rolling gently over and through the waves, steaming its way to Nassau, Jennifer lay in her bed staring up at the cabin ceiling.

How could her mother remember every single Barbie toy and exactly what it cost and not remember her own daughter's name? Such was the way of this maniacal disease.

Maybe someday, she thought, I'll laugh at the absurdity of it all.

But not tonight.

Jennifer waited until she heard her mother softly snoring before turning her head into the pillow and sobbing.

IT WAS A VERY distraught Anthony Vane who banged on Dr. Swayze's cabin door, well after four in the morning, waking him from a sound sleep.

"I just don't understand it," Anthony said, tightening his forehead as if in concern, working exasperation into his voice, words tumbling out. "I don't know where my wife could be. I took her back to our stateroom after dinner, then went off to the casino and stayed till closing."

The casino closed at three a.m.

"And when I returned shortly thereafter," Anthony continued, "she wasn't there."

"Now, just take it easy, Mr. Vane." The doctor put his hand on Anthony's shoulder. "Most likely you're just missing each other—she probably went to the casino to look for you, and—"

"No! No, I went back and checked, I've been all over this damn ship, searching, and no one's seen her!" He paused. "And the bed hadn't been slept in. . . . Doctor, I'm worried that . . . that something has happened to her."

"That something has happened to her? Or is it that she may have . . ."

Anthony covered his mouth with a hand, spoke through his splayed fingers. "I don't even want to think it."

Swayze frowned. "She did seem a little blue at dinner. I was seated a few tables away from you."

"Doctor, I'm afraid . . . she was drinking."

Alarm flared in the doctor's eyes. "Mixing alcohol with her medication?"

"Just wine. I didn't say anything to her about it, because I know it relaxes her . . . oh, hell, I blame myself for this."

Swayze sighed. "Mr. Vane, there's not much you can do right now, other than return to your room, and try to remain calm."

"That's easily said. . . ."

"In the meantime, I'll contact ship's security. Just try not to worry. She isn't the first person to get lost on this ship. I'm sure she'll turn up."

Keeping a dejected expression going, should he be seen, Anthony strolled along the deck, making his way to his stateroom. It was nearly five in the morning and he paused at the rail, not far from where he'd pitched his wife into the sea; he took in the first purple-pink rays of a magnificent sunrise appearing on the ocean's horizon as the *Fantasy* slowly cruised into Nassau Harbor, heading for Prince George Wharf.

In the stateroom, Anthony got out of his evening clothes, put on a pair of silk pajamas, climbed into the king-size bed and fell fast asleep, dreaming of wealth, no story really, just lots of pretty women and nice things and so very much money.

Around nine, the phone by his bedside rang him awake.

Startled, as if a long-dormant conscience had stirred, he sat up, rubbed his face with the heels of his hands and grabbed the phone before it could ring for a fourth irritating time.

"Hello," he answered thickly.

"Mr. Vane?" a husky voice said.

"Yes."

"This is Jake Lausen." The voice had a Brooklyn tinge. "Chief of ship's security."

"I'm relieved to hear from you, Mr. Lausen—you've found my wife?"

"I'm afraid she hasn't turned up." The voice paused. "Could you come to my office?"

"Certainly. Where and when, sir?"

"On the veranda deck. Would now be convenient?"

"I'll be there in half an hour, if that's all right," Vane told him. "I've been up all night with worry."

"I could see that. Half an hour, Mr. Vane." The phone clicked dead.

In the shower, Anthony mentally rehearsed. He shouldn't appear too distraught—overplaying could raise suspicion; but he had to appear distressed enough, as underplaying could make him seem cold. This needed to be a suicide, otherwise he was the chief suspect—really, the only suspect. He toweled off, blow-dried his hair and applied gel, shaved and splashed on Polo cologne, trying on various faces of concern and sorrow in the mirror. When he stepped from his stateroom, dressed in Armani head to toe, he felt confident he could strike the right tone.

The security office, located next to the radio room on the veranda deck, was tiny and messy, files and papers littering the small desk. That put him instantly at ease; nothing about this cubbyhole looked very official.

Except for the chief of security, Jake Lausen. The man gave Anthony a bit of a start: short and stocky, balding, thickly mustached, the man's facial features seemed benignly bland, even babyish. But his eyes belonged to a grown-up: under mini-mustache slashes of eyebrow, they were cobalt blue and ball-bearing hard.

What if this Lausen character had been one of New York's finest who'd gotten his fill of big city crime and moved to this cushy job? The man could be a real threat, a slumbering beast awakened by the wrong word or gesture, if Anthony didn't watch his step.

Lausen had opened the door for him and was now gesturing toward a gray steel folding chair across from the cluttered desk. "Have a seat, Mr. Vane, would you?"

"Thank you."

"I've already spoken to Dr. Swayze," Lausen said. He perched on the edge of his desk, looking down at Anthony like a huge stone gargoyle from a church rooftop. "And he filled me in, as regards to your wife's depression. If you don't mind my asking, was this cruise meant to cheer her up, that sort of thing?"

Anthony, shifting in the uncomfortable metal folding chair (was that on purpose?), nodded. "Yes, precisely. And earlier in the evening, she seemed fine, conversing with the other passengers seated with us for dinner. But then, as has been the case of late, her mood shifted, and she simply didn't seem herself. So we took a brief walk on the deck, and then I escorted her back to our room."

"What was her mood?"

"Withdrawn. Quiet. She and I frequently gamble together, but last night she sent me to the casino by myself. The last thing she said to me was . . . 'Enjoy yourself, sweetheart.'"

Anthony swallowed; touched the thumb and forefinger of one hand to the bridge of his nose, then drew a breath and composed himself. A nicely acted piece of business, he thought to himself. "When I returned around three in the morning," Anthony continued, "she wasn't there, and the bed hadn't been slept in."

"Not a good sign," Lausen said, looking thoughtful for a moment. "Is there anything else you can tell me?"

Anthony swallowed. "Well," he began hesitantly. "There is something else."

The security man gazed at him with his ball-bearing eyes.

"Last year we took this very same cruise, and . . . Margaret threatened to jump overboard." The first part was true, the second a lie.

"Why?"

" . . . Why?"

A non-smile twitched under Lausen's mustache. "When people threaten to kill themselves, there's usually a reason. What reason did your wife give you, Mr. Vane?"

"I feel . . . awkward discussing this, Mr. Lausen. As if I might be . . . betraying my wife's confidence."

"This situation is a little beyond social niceties, Mr. Vane. Why did your wife threaten to kill herself last year?"

Anthony heaved a sigh. "She was once a very beautiful woman, Mr. Lausen. She still is . . . to me. But she was very unhappy with the way her last cosmetic surgery came out, and as you may have suspected, there's something of an age difference between us. . . . At any rate, her seventieth birthday was fast approaching, and she became . . . despondent."

All of this was true, more or less—except for the threat of suicide. Margaret had been depressed about her fading beauty—and her husband's roving eye.

"Did you get your wife any help?"

"Of course. She's been seeing a psychiatrist, and has been on anti-depressant medication for almost a year. Well, but then, you know that already, from Dr. Swayze. . . ."

"Yeah. She ever threaten to kill herself again?"

"No. Never."

"Not even last night?"

"No. But . . . I shouldn't say."

"By all means, Mr. Vane, 'say' away."

Another sigh. "I thought perhaps that this cruise . . . being as we'd taken it before, and she'd made that threat, walking on the very deck where we strolled last night . . . this cruise had brought all that unpleasantness back to mind."

The small room fell silent, with Lausen staring down at Anthony from his perch. Then the security chief stood up and went around behind the desk and sat.

"Well, your wife isn't on the ship, Mr. Vane. We've done a cabin-to-cabin canvas, and she didn't disembark in Nassau this morning." He paused. "That leaves only one other place she *could* be."

Anthony hung his head. "Oh, my God," he said softly. His hands were shaking; he hoped Lausen would see that as sorrow, and not the unexpected nervousness Lausen's hard gaze had engendered in him.

"There's a procedure we follow when a passenger turns up missing, Mr. Vane. I'll have to ask you to remain on board today. I'll want to talk to you again later, and sign some missing person's papers."

Anthony nodded solemnly. "I understand."

"I hope I'm wrong," Lausen said. "And that she turns up. Otherwise . . . sorry for your loss, sir."

But he didn't sound very sorry.

"Thank you," Anthony said, as if the expression of condolence had been sincere. "Should you need me, I'll be in our stateroom."

Anthony hated the thought of that—missing the Nassau stop, losing out on a sumptuous meal at Greycliff, the only five-star restaurant in the Bahamas, and a fun-filled evening in the casinos on Paradise Island. But it was a sacrifice he could live with; after all, with Margaret's money he could come back any time he wanted.

He strolled down the narrow corridor, away from the security office, wondering if Lausen harbored any major suspicions about him. Perhaps that sour demeanor, that terminal cynicism, simply went with the job.

But so what if Lausen did suspect him? That insignificant little bastard couldn't prove anything. There was only one person on earth—one person on this ship—who could.

He went in search of her.

He was beginning to think she'd gotten off the boat already and gone into Nassau for the day, when he spotted her flaming red hair. Cora and her daughter were up on the sun deck. They were in casual attire, the mother in a knit turquoise pants suit, her daughter in a sunny floral-print sundress, next to each other in deck chairs, big straw hats on their heads, big straw handbags at their feet; their slender, shapely figures were identical. When the daughter saw him, her face lighted up and she called out to him.

"Oh, Mr. Vane!" she motioned with one hand. "Could you come here?"

"Good morning, ladies," he said as he approached them, rather surprised by this greeting from the younger woman, who'd barely seemed to notice him last night. "Isn't this sun lovely, after that cold wet evening?"

"Could you do me a tremendous favor?" the pretty blonde woman asked.

"Anything."

"You remember my mother—Cora?"

"How could I forget?"

Cora, that minx, looked up at him with a blank expression, as if he were a stranger. The daughter said, "Would you please keep her company while I run to the gift shop? I need to pick up some suntan lotion before we head into town."

He beamed at her. "I'd be delighted. Simply delighted." Then he smiled at the mother, who looked back at him with an expression as blank as a doll's.

"I'll be only a minute or so," the daughter said, leaving the two behind.

"Take all the time you need, my dear," he responded.

Anthony settled into the vacated deck chair next to Cora, who was staring out at the magnificent view of Nassau which lay before them, a tourist's dream come true.

He leaned toward her. "And how are you today, my love?"

She turned to him. "Do I know you?" she asked.

He half-smiled at her. She was good; so very good. "You don't have to pretend, now. We don't have to be strangers."

The woman shrugged and looked back at the view.

"What are you going to do with the money?"

She looked at him and blinked. "What money?"

He laughed out loud. "Oh, so *that's* how you're going to play it? I told you last night . . . if you agree to keep our little secret, there will be plenty more where that came from. The question is, Cora—will we be business partners, or could we explore a more pleasant option?"

She didn't respond to that, which unnerved him a little. He'd better find out how much her silence was going to cost him.

"What do you want from me, Cora?" he asked quietly. Gently, he placed a hand on her thigh. "There's so much more than money that I can give you. . . ."

Cora turned back to him and her placid face came suddenly alive. "I want My Very Own Vanity!" she said.

Such poetry in her speech—her own vanity, indeed. She had that ability so many vixens had, to seem at once a woman and yet child-like in her energy, and her greed.

And he found that beguiling; something about her told him she was a kindred spirit, and he hoped they would not be adversaries.

"What specifically can I give you, my love?"

"I want a Cruisin' Car Convertible."

Now *that* was specific. Wanting a car was more along the lines he'd expected, but a convertible? She was a remarkable lady; young, at any age.

"And what else?" He was almost afraid to ask.

"A Malibu Beach House. I *really* want that."

The back of his neck tingled. "Do you have any idea what a house in Malibu costs these days?"

"Ninety-nine ninety-five."

He laughed hollowly. "Maybe when you were in bloomers, a beach house went for ninety-nine thousand. Now it's more like nine million . . . but maybe that wouldn't be out of the question, my love, if we could share it. . . ."

She frowned. "I don't *like* to share my toys."

"I'm back, you two!"

Anthony looked up from his deck chair at Cora's daughter, whose smile upended into a frown. "Is everything all right, Mr. Vane? You look . . . strange. I hope Mother behaved herself."

"She does like to get her way," he said pleasantly, standing.

"Yes she does," the daughter admitted.

"But she's certainly charming company," he said with a smile, nodding at Cora, who was looking off to the right, as if the children splashing in the ship's pool were particularly fascinating.

"I'm glad you're getting along so famously," said the daughter. "Perhaps we'll see you again, Mr. Vane, when we get back to the ship. Come, Mother, it's time to go."

He watched the pair leave, then wandered back to his room, where he sat on the edge of his bed. This Cora was a shrewd one, black-mailing, scheming bitch that she was; there was much to admire in the woman.

What a team they could make. He could love a woman like that; but could he ever trust her?

And could he ever hope to outsmart the likes of her?

* * *

IN HIS STATEROOM, Anthony basked in self-pity; everyone else was off roaming the bustling, native-filled streets of Nassau, enjoying the beautiful day, eating traditional Bahamian conch fritters and grouper fingers from colorful vendor carts.

The phone rang beside the bed.

"Mr. Vane," the Brooklyn-tinged voice said, "Jake Lausen again."

"Any news, Mr. Lausen?"

"Afraid not. Need you to stop by my office at four this afternoon."

"All right."

"Listen, you don't have to hang around till then. If you want to get off the ship, go into Nassau, take your mind off things, go ahead."

"Well, that's kind of you, Mr. Lausen. I am getting a little stir-crazy. Walking around town might help calm my nerves; Margaret's disappearance has me at wit's end."

"No problem. Just be back by four."

As he disembarked onto Woodes Rogers Walk, Anthony tried not to seem too happy as he strolled along the harbor where sponge boats were docked, bobbing in the water. Now and then a Bahamian woman tried to get him to buy a straw hat or shell, but he ignored them. He passed over the fresh conch, too, because he had a place in mind for lunch.

Nowhere in the world had he ever had a finer meal than those he'd enjoyed, over the years, at Greycliff. Once the summer home of Lady and Lord Dunmore, the elegant but unpretentious restaurant catered to the well-off from royalty to rock stars, from CEOs to drug dealers. All of their food was magnificent, but his favorite was the well-cooked goose.

Crossing Bay Street, crowded by mid-afternoon with its horse-drawn surreys carrying well-heeled tourists, he quickened his step as he thought about the culinary delights which awaited him just a few blocks away, up steep Blue Hill Road. As he passed Rawson's Square, where tuckered-out travelers sat on quaint wooden benches, he stopped short. Sitting in the shade of a palm tree, with their backs to him, but their identity unmistakable, were Jennifer and Cora.

The daughter seemed somewhat worked up, saying impatiently to her mother, "All right, I'll go back to the store and buy it, even though it's not the right one. . . . But you have to promise me not to move from this bench."

He couldn't hear what the mother said, but saw her nod her head, yes. Then Jennifer stood up, and hurried across the plaza.

He approached Cora, whipping off his Ray-Bans dramatically. "Well, hello, my love," he said, looming over her. "We meet again."

She ignored him, continuing to mutter to herself.

"What's wrong?" he asked. "Not having a good time?"

"No," she said, scrunching up her face, like a kid talking back to a parent. This coy act was starting to get to him; she was attractive, but playing cute simply wasn't cute, at her age.

"What's the matter, my love?"

"We couldn't find him."

"Who?"

"Nibbles."

"Nibbles?"

"The right horse."

He couldn't imagine why she was looking for a horse.

"Well, I'm sure he's around somewhere." After all, there were plenty of horses pulling carriages in downtown Nassau. Then he asked, "Where did your lovely daughter go?"

Cora looked at him oddly. "I don't have a daughter."

"Oh, I see," he smiled. "Have a fight, did you?"

She looked away, pouting.

And he made a decision; sudden, but necessary. This woman was too unpredictable, too cunning. Right now he didn't want a lover or need a partner, and he certainly didn't need some blackmailing bitch, however clever and attractive, in his life.

"Have you been up the Queen's Staircase yet?" he asked, working some enthusiasm into his voice. The last thing he wanted to do right now was trudge up some cliff-side stairway. But if it was the last thing Cora did, it would be worth the effort. . . .

"No."

"It's just a short distance from here. And at the top of the stairs is a fort with all the armaments; it's like stepping into the past. Very romantic."

She considered that. "You mean, like My Very Own Castle?"

"Our very own castle," he said, and touched her thigh.

"Oh, take me there. Take me there now!"

Just off East Street, steep steps had been carved into a limestone hill leading to Fort Fincastle. Shaped like a paddle-wheel steamer, the small fortress was built to protect the town from any enemy who landed. Heavy cast-iron cannons pointed out to sea, guns that had never been fired.

Cora climbed briskly, with an enthusiasm and energy a young girl might have envied. What a handful she was! What a pity she had to go. . . .

Halfway up the steps Anthony halted. "Let me rest," he said, wiping sweat from his brow, "catch my breath a second." He couldn't believe that the older woman wasn't even breathing hard.

"Well, okay, but not for long." She was standing one step ahead of him. "I want to see the castle."

Two teenagers, most likely brother and sister, squeezed around them on the steps, raced each other to the top, soon disappearing from view.

Then they were alone on the stairs.

He felt a pang of regret; what a beautiful relationship he might have had with such a beautiful, vibrant and oh so cagey a woman. . . .

"Okay, I'm ready," he said and they continued the climb, with her in the lead and him just behind. As they neared the top, he reached out and gave her arm a quick vicious tug, side-stepping as she fell backward past him, cascading down the limestones steps, leaving red impressions as she went.

He didn't stick around to watch her tumble all the way down, but turned, wanting to remove himself from the scene and let someone else discover the body, and bolted to the top.

And bumped into a man beginning to descend.

A baby-faced, mustached man named Jake Lausen.


"WELL, MR. VANE," Lausen said, "it doesn't look like you're having a very relaxing cruise, now, does it?"

Lausen was again perched on the edge of his desk, with Anthony seated before him in the hard, cold folding chair. "Disaster seems to follow you, Mr. Vane, wherever you go."

Anthony avoided the security chief's glare. "I've told you a dozen times, it was an accident," he said. "I was taking Cora—Mrs. Hazen—to see the fort and she lost her footing, and slipped on the stairs."

"Problem with that story," Lausen said, "is I saw you give the gal a yank, to help her along."

Anthony said nothing.

Lausen sighed. "Of course, I'm just a little ol' eyewitness. I'm sure the victim herself will have her own opinion of exactly what happened."

Anthony looked at him sharply.

"That's right," Lausen smiled nastily, "she's got some broken bones, some bumps, some scratches, a concussion. But she's a tough old gal. Dr. Swayze will be bringing her here in a few minutes to give a statement."

Anthony sat forward, gesturing frantically. "It was an accident, I tell you. I mean, maybe it was me who slipped on the steps, and I grabbed her to catch my balance. . . ."

"Again, let's see what Mrs. Hazen thinks—and I'm hoping she'll have some idea of what your motive might've been. After all, I can understand why you tossed your rich wife over the rail . . ."

"That was uncalled for."

"It sure as hell was."

Anthony scowled at the smug son of a bitch. "What were you doing there, anyway, Lausen?"

"When I saw you head up the stairs, I couldn't follow, since I was in a car," Lausen said flatly. "I took the drive up to the top . . . see, my men and me have been keeping you in our sights ever since you reported your wife missing, and saw you hookin' up with this Hazen woman. It's gonna be real interesting findin' how she's involved—but I'm sure she'll be willing to fill us in, now that you've just tried to kill her."

There was a sharp knock at the door, and Lausen said, "Come on in."

The door opened and Cora Hazen came slowly in, on crutches, one arm in a cast, a bandage wrapped around her head as if she had a big toothache. Dr. Swayze followed right behind her.

Anthony groaned at the sight of her and lowered his gaze and shook his head.

"Mrs. Hazen," Lausen said gently, "how are you feeling?"

"Awful!" she snapped. "Just awful. Somebody pushed me down some stairs."

"All right, all right," Anthony blurted, "I waive my rights. I pushed her. I pushed the silly bitch!"

"And your wife?" Lausen asked.

"Ask Cora Hazen—she was there. She saw me throw Margaret over the side. She . . . she saw it all."

Lausen smiled, gesturing to Anthony. "Mrs. Hazen, is there anything you'd like to tell us about this man?"

Cora looked sideways at the doctor, then at Lausen, and finally at Vane. "I've never seen him before in my life!" she said. "But he is a nice-looking gentleman."

"Thank you, Mrs. Hazen," Lausen said. "That'll be all for now."

And when they'd gone, Lausen explained everything to Anthony.

"Alzheimer's?" Anthony mumbled.

And Anthony began to laugh, laughter that turned to tears as he buried his face in hands, wishing he could forget.


THAT NIGHT, on deck, standing at the rail, Jennifer Kafer and Dr. Thomas Swayze looked out at the gently rolling ocean painted ivory by moonlight.

"You've been wonderful about Mother," she said to him. She wore a blue evening gown and he wore his dress uniform. Her arm was hooked in the crook of his.

"Keeping her in the infirmary, under constant watch," he said, "is a precaution I felt needed taking."

"I hate to say this, but it is nice to have some time away from her, alone . . . I mean, I love her, and as you said, I feel lucky that this disease has taken only her memory, not turned her mean or ugly."

"You can still have many wonderful moments with your mother . . . worth remembering."

"Even if she can't," Jennifer said, with a sad, wry smile.

"You know what you need?"

"What do you prescribe, Doctor?"

"You need some memories of your own. . . ."

And he kissed her, and she kissed back; it was just a shipboard romance, of course, but it would be fun for both of them to remember in their old age.

# Havanightmare

## JOSÉ LATOUR

**D**arkness was in full flight to the east when Megan Olwin rested her forearms on the teak rail enclosing the liner's floodlit upper deck. She took a deep breath and let her gaze sweep over the little puffs of water that danced on the choppy sea ahead before peering at the black horizon and overcast sky. Enjoying the wind's playful fondling of her shoulder-length brown hair and the misty brine dampening her face, the woman wondered how the ship could remain so steady in the swell caused by what she judged to be an advancing cold front. Megan Olwin had no idea that the *New Galaxy* was equipped with fin stabilizers protruding from its sides below the water to reduce the roll. In fact, she ignored everything about the design and construction of luxury ocean liners. She didn't know she was standing on the covering of the captain's bridge deck; that the tall, elongated white structure behind her hid sophisticated navigational and communication systems, and that precisely at 07:09 on February 9, 1997, the vessel was plowing ahead at twenty-three knots.

MEGAN OLWIN was on her fourth Caribbean holiday. One snowy January evening, the thirty-four-year-old biochemist, who was born, raised, and presently living in Vermont, had found in her day's mail a brochure from her travel agent. On her three previous tours she had gotten smug satisfaction out of fancying her friends shoveling snow from their doorsteps as she—bikini-clad in dark sunglasses—basked in the sun along the strand of emeralds known as the Lesser Antilles, sometimes on a sandy beach close to a port of call, more frequently by the ship's pool. From Grenada to the Virgin Islands, she had observed with interest the differences among small multiracial communities with African, Spanish, French, and English ancestries.

This time she had signed up for a cruise starting in Puerto Plata that would take her to Havana, Cancún, and Santiago de Cuba before returning to the Dominican Republic. As she began limbering up for her usual early morning jog, Megan was about to admit a serious error of judgement in her choice of attire. Sailing by Cuba's northern coast, she was much closer than she originally realized to the huge masses of frigid air.

Not wanting to return to her cabin for warmer clothing, she sighed in resignation, turned left, and started to trot. She wore a crimson crew-neck pullover, black satin skating shorts, and well-worn sneakers. The port course took her by the children's playground, past the pool, sun decks, tennis court, and funnel. She rounded the deck's stern section by the starboard walkway, reached her starting point, and began a second lap.

She was hoping for a gorgeous sunny day, but it seemed a bleak prospect by the time she slowed down to a walk thirty minutes later. To port, a low rocky coastline could be guesswork behind the fine mist that was created by the smashing waves that climbed geyser-like to impressive heights. To starboard, the cold front seemed more menacing under the weak sunlight that was filtered by low-hung clouds. Gripping the rosewood banister of a beautiful, wide stairway, Megan Olwin returned to the cozy ambience of the ship's passageways and felt glad for it. A few moments later she unlocked the door of her first-class cabin, went in, closed it, and, just as she was headed for the shower, came face to face with a tall, swarthy man pointing a gun at her.

"Sorry lady," the man said with a heavy Spanish accent. "Next three days you do as I say or die."

FIVE HOURS LATER a perplexed Megan realized she wouldn't be able to hold out for another five minutes and wondered if some sort of plastic covering protected the mattress. Still in her jogging outfit, arms alongside her torso, wrists and ankles tied to the legs of the bed, her head was propped on a pillow to favor the observation of a seventeen-inch TV set tuned to CNN. Her lips were sealed with a three-inch-wide strip of adhesive tape that had a dime-size hole at center to allow breathing, should her nose get stuffed. Unable to control her bladder any longer, Megan felt the warm urine dampening her buttocks up to her waist.

She knew the *New Galaxy* was moored to the port of Havana's passenger pier. The cruise program said they would arrive at the Cuban capital around 9 a.m. and, according to the news channel, it was 11:25. Besides, she recognized the berthing maneuver from previous trips. As she lay on her bed, she kept her eyes closed, hoping to impress on the kidnapper her scorn. When she felt the ship slowing down, she visualized the launch detaching itself from a larger vessel to bring the pilot on board. As the *New Galaxy* positioned itself by the pier, she conjured up ropes being thrown, imagined hearing the air-operated ladder hiss along the liner's side, and envisioned sweaty, half-naked natives dancing to some local tune to appropriately welcome those bringing much-needed greenbacks.

What she couldn't picture was the present whereabouts of her kidnapper. Megan had no way of knowing that the man had gone ashore donning a white plastic cap, sunglasses, an outmoded, light-green long-sleeved shirt, a shoulder bag, tight tan slacks, and brown lace-up shoes— an attire which singled him out among the flock of tourists in garish shirts, Bermuda shorts, and assorted headgear. But when a mere three blocks from the pier he lagged behind the group pacing off Old Havana's Plaza de Armas, turned onto San Ignacio Street, and joined the locals hurrying along narrow sidewalks and stone-paved streets, the kidnapper became one more fish in the shoal. Walking briskly and oblivious of the surroundings, he covered the distance between the House of Africa and a bank of public phones on San Rafael Street in less than twenty minutes. From a hip pocket, the man produced a few Cuban coins, dropped one in the slot and dialed a number.

For close to ten minutes, he talked in whispers, his lips brushing the mouthpiece, his face a study in mood swings. Dropping a five-cent coin every three minutes, he alternately looked depressed, hopeful, and overjoyed. One moment he was begging; the next ordering. For a while he reasoned, listened to the other party, and then argued intensely before coming out on top. Before hanging up, a broad smile lit up his face, and nodding contentedly he returned the handset to its hook.

The kidnapper sighed deeply, took off his sunglasses and, suppressing a smile, looked around as if he just now realized where he was. Leisurely he strolled around what fifty years before had been Havana's downtown, now a mishmash of well-provisioned state shops where only dollar-bearing customers were admitted, and old department stores sparsely stocked with low-quality products sold for pesos. But the man didn't seem to mind dilapidated façades, the litter on the asphalt, or the drizzle that began to fall. He looked enraptured by something that had nothing to do with the neighborhood, though for a passerby he would have seemed engrossed in the widely varying architectural styles all around him.

Precisely at that same moment back on the ship, Megan was recalling that the kidnapper had groaned, "I'll be back in a few hours," before grabbing the DO NOT DISTURB sign from the coffee table, opening the main door, slipping the sign on the passageway side of the handle, and leaving the cabin. Megan had no idea what a "few hours" meant to the kidnapper. The *New Galaxy* would leave Havana at midnight, so she still might have to wait twelve hours before seeing the motherfucker again. Or longer. Suppose the spic shacked up with some broad, or got coked-out or drunk somewhere? And she was very hungry. A tendency to chubbiness had made Megan a standard card-bearer for Weight Watchers since her teens, and her supper had consisted of Norwegian salmon poached in tarragon sauce, three celery sticks, and half a bottle of Calistoga. She had asked for and got a glass of water a little after eight a.m. and fear had kept her stomach quiet, but now it rumbled demandingly.

The asshole had pledged not to harm her without volunteering explanations. After tying her up in bed—at which point Megan was absolutely certain she would be raped—the creep sat on a deep chair, wiped the sweat from his face with a perfumed handkerchief, and heaved a sigh of relief. "I give you my word nothing's gonna happen to you if you do as I say," he stated. Megan was considerably mollified, not so much by the promise as by some undercurrent of sincerity in his voice.

"Why are you doing this to me?" she asked.

The man shook his head several times and forced a smile the way adults do when dodging a too-complicated answer that would satisfy a child's curiosity. Then he said, "Where's your passport and boarding pass?"

Megan fixed her gaze to the cabin's teak-paneled bulkhead directly ahead to exercise her only possible rebellion: silence. Then Megan had made the mistake of crying out "help" at the top of her lungs. With a panther-like leap, the man pried open her mouth and shoved a perfumed, moistened handkerchief inside. Then he produced from a shopping bag a roll of adhesive tape and surgical scissors, and set about doing what had been undeniably planned beforehand.

Megan Olwin realized the severity of what was happening to her after she listened to the two o'clock news summary: three so-called anti-terrorism experts discussed the Japanese ambassador's residence in Lima, Peru. Basically, they stated that some acts of terrorism are not defensible. Sometimes terrorists win. *Who was this guy? What did he want? I might die at the hands of this nut,* Megan reasoned, *or have a fear-induced heart attack, or starve to death before some cabin boy starts wondering about the number of days that that particular sign has been on that particular doorknob.*

What had she accomplished in life? She hadn't unlocked some transcendental effect or structure or mechanism or protein or hormone, had never published a paper in the *Journal of Biological Chemistry*, had failed in her marriage, had no children, few friends, was estranged from her parents, and the guy she was dating didn't seem to know that women have a clitoris. Tears rolled down her temples, and when her nose got blocked she almost admired the kidnapper's foresight. Drowning in self-pity, her sobs gradually slowed to regular breathing and she fell asleep.

By late afternoon the kidnapper was enjoying a leisurely stroll along the Prado promenade in the company of a nice-looking white woman in her early thirties. She donned a white linen shawl-collar blouse, a neutral-colored, ankle-length split skirt, and ill-fitting sandals. Her accessories included a Panama hat, dark sunglasses, gold studs in her earlobes, and a stainless wristwatch with an art deco dial. She held a purse with both hands as if it contained something extremely valuable. Only her underwear wasn't Megan's.

The couple walked among a crowd getting ready for the evening's carnival. Small kiosks served all sorts of snack foods and beverages, dancers and musicians, dressed alike for the *comparsas*, hurried to their meeting places, early birds swilled beer from huge waxed paper glasses, and many youngsters weaved through slow-paced or stationary spectators. The smell of food overcame the perfumes emanating from people in their Sunday best, and the temperature had dropped to a comfortable seventy degrees.

Even tourists remained unnoticed, but the woman sauntering along with the kidnapper seemed jittery. Occasionally he would say something to her, and she would quickly nod or shake her head without uttering a single word.

At Central Park they turned left to cross a wide, stone-paved space that had obviously been a street in the past, and entered the Floridita, a favorite watering hole for visiting foreigners. Huddled together, exchanging whispers and smiles like reunited lovers, they each had two daiquiris.

In moments of silence they glanced at the mural—flanked by two beautiful bronze lamps—depicting the port of Havana in the eighteenth century. The man ordered a ham and cheese sandwich to go before asking for the check. On her way out the woman pulled up the slingback straps on her sandals.

Night had fallen. The couple turned onto Obispo Street and shuffled by the display windows of the stores. Young and lean police officers kept hookers and peddlers of "genuine" Havana cigars at bay. Trying to improve his tourist impersonation, at each block the man pointed to some odd element as if seeing it for the first time: a bush flourishing on a two-hundred-year-old tile roof, beams propping up a crumbling façade, an art gallery. Relaxed by the drinks, the woman smiled fleetingly at some of his remarks.

When they reached the waterfront promenade known as Malecón, the woman tensed. Keeping their pace slow and casual like typical passengers of a pleasure cruise, the kidnapper did all the talking in primitive English. When they approached the entrance of the pier, the woman unclasped her purse, and with trembling hands, showed Megan's boarding pass and passport to the two security guards blocking the way. One of them searched for the name in the alphabetically-arranged nine-page list on his clipboard before checking it off. The other compared the passport's photo with the passenger and seemed satisfied. She got waved in. The kidnapper also showed his documents and gained admittance. The woman wavered and cupped her hand over her eyes. The kidnapper held her by the right arm and guided her along. Both sentries frowned. The kidnapper rolled his neck and smiled.

"One drink too many," he said to the watchmen in English. Met with ignorant stares, the kidnapper mimicked drinking from a bottle. The guards laughed and turned their backs as the couple hotfooted it onto the *New Galaxy*.

\* \* \*

MEGAN OLWIN was trying to concentrate on Larry King's suspenders when she heard a rustle. Turning her head she saw the kidnapper enter the cabin. The man threw the latch, dropped a small paper bag on the couch, and approached his victim with a few strides. He jerked the adhesive tape from her mouth, and just as Megan was about to let out a cascade of selected profanities, the man dropped to his knees and started kissing her forehead and cheeks and chin and temples. *Oh boy*, Megan thought in horror when the rum in his breath reached her nostrils, *now the drunk bastard feels like pussy.* But with the same suddenness the kidnapper paused, sniffed, and looked around embarrassed.

"Sorry, Megan," he said. "I didn't . . ."

At a loss for words, the man began untying a very confused Megan. In a few seconds, she had gone from lame resignation to a raving mad, frightened person frustrated by her inability to figure out what was going on.

Massaging her wrists, she started for the bathroom.

"I stand in door," the man announced blocking her path. "Don't hurry—an hour maybe—but don't close door and don't scream."

Thirty-five minutes later, after scarfing down the Floridita sandwich, Megan Olwin sat in a deep chair facing her kidnapper. She rubbed lotion on her wrists and ankles. The man had been decent enough to turn the vinyl-covered mattress upside down, substitute the soiled sheets with the bedspread, and hand her the fresh underwear, oversized black T-shirt, and jeans she had asked for from behind the shower curtain. Sitting on the couch across from Megan, the stubble and sheen of grease on his face revealed that he hadn't taken a shower before changing into the white slacks, light-blue Oxford shirt, and navy-blue blazer he wore. Dark circles under his eyes added a touch of exhaustion to his unkempt appearance, but the man looked alert, and the gun by his side was a good dissuader.

Beneath her anger, fear, and frustration, Megan's curiosity pulsed. Her rational mind and scientific training demanded an explanation, although she realized the futility of asking for it. She suspected this was no run-of-the-mill criminal or commonplace crime. The man hadn't even asked for her money, traveler's checks, or credit cards, and as far as she could surmise, they had remained untouched. And the nonsensical kissing spree on his return, as though he was exulting over some incredible achievement. Megan replaced the lid on the bottle of lotion and turned her eyes to the double window near the bed, where she saw a beam of light from a lighthouse move across a pitch black sky.

Maybe he'd fall asleep on the couch, Megan speculated. It would be her chance to slip out. Except there was a strong possibility the schmuck would tie her down again should he feel sleepy. She knew she should pretend to sleep, make him feel confident, but after close to twelve hours lying on her back the idea did not appeal to her. They sat in silence for a few more minutes before Megan remembered the *Vanity Fair* she hadn't had time to read.

"I have a magazine somewhere in that chest of drawers," she said, pointing to the piece of furniture. "Can I get it? Read a while?"

Grabbing the gun, the kidnapper stood up, found the publication, and handed it to Megan. She appeared absorbed in a long piece on the Middle East peace process. As eleven o'clock approached, the ship started droning a little louder, pulling the man out of his state of reverie. He got up and walked to the windows, and gazed out intently. He seemed so deeply engrossed in contemplation that Megan started getting up very slowly. Halfway through the motion, the man turned and stared Megan down—literally. She returned her attention to the magazine.

At midnight, as the *New Galaxy* set out from the pier, the kidnapper chuckled. People could be heard laughing and talking loudly in the passageway. As the ship sailed away, the lighthouse beam disrupted the soft illumination inside the cabin. About half an hour later, the engines slowed down. Megan closed the magazine and imagined the pilot returning to his launch. Two or three minutes later the ship registered an almost imperceptible vibration when, freed from all tutelage, it rode ahead hugging the shore. The exhausted-looking man returned to the couch and plopped down. From the inner breast pocket of his blazer, he pulled out a sheaf of papers which he unfolded.

"Three pages," he said looking Megan right in the eye. "I can't speak English well. Understand? Yes. Talk myself? No. So I sit and write this. Library, bilingual dictionary, I sit down, take time, I make sense. Tonight, I read to you first page. Okay?"

Megan nodded.

The man lowered his gaze to the page and read:

> *"Doing to you what I did was the only way to rescue my wife.*
> *My wife is now on board. She is in my cabin. She does not know*

*what I did to you. I have no quarrel with you and I have no inten-*
*tion of harming you. But I cannot let you free yet. You would*
*denounce me to the shipmaster, to the officers. I would be charged*
*with kidnaping and sent back to Cuba with my wife. I will be shot*
*or sentenced to thirty years in prison. My wife will go to prison too.*
*That is why I cannot let you free yet. You will be free a couple of*
*hours after we disembark in Cancun. I give you my word. Before*
*I say goodbye I will read you the other two pages. Now, please, lay*
*down. I have to tie you up again. I will sleep here too, so no gag.*
*Do not scream. If you need anything call me. Thank you."*

The man folded the pages and returned them to his pocket. Megan was
staring at him open-mouthed. The kidnapper let out a prodigious yawn.

"I can't believe this is happening to me," she said.

"Oh yes," the man said. "Believe, yes, believe."

FOR MEGAN OLWIN, the next thirty-nine hours crawled along like a
caterpillar on crutches. Resigned to her fate, she read and watched reruns
on the TV, taking comfort from the fact that the sky remained cloudy
and frequent squalls sent rivulets trickling down the windowpanes.
Nobody would be swimming in the pool or sunning on the sun deck.

Boredom set in because she believed the kidnapper. *Cuba* had been
a household word when she was growing up. Her parents, like many couples, got carried away during the October 1962 missile crisis, and she
belonged to the scores of babies born between thirty-six and forty-two
weeks later. After learning this in her early teens, Megan had always been
interested in the island, and knew about the one-way human flow, split
families, and trading embargo that stubbornly remained one of the thorns
in America's side. The story the man told was probably true, Megan concluded. She just happened to be the woman on board with the right age
and physical appearance. There was a high probability she wouldn't be
shot or harmed if she behaved.

The kidnapper quickly established a routine. Each time he left the
cabin, he first bound her hands and feet, and sealed her mouth with a
new strip of adhesive tape. When he slept on the couch there was no gag.
If he was just sitting around, which was most of the time, Megan was free
to move about the cabin as she wished, save for closing the bathroom
door from the inside.

Cabin stewards posed the biggest dilemma to the kidnapper and were Megan's permanent hope. The man realized that ignoring the polite knocks would arouse suspicion and had opened the cabin door twice, just a crack, to accept fresh linens and the replenishment of toiletries. He had declined offers to tidy up with substantial tips, conspiratorial winks, and charming smiles, intimating that recent acquaintances had become love-birds and wished to be left alone.

What neither he nor Megan knew was that that same afternoon two different stewards, one assigned to first-class and another caring for sec-ond-class passengers, had made odd reports to the chief steward about travelers that apparently never left their quarters. One steward described a Spanish-speaking lady who ordered triple breakfasts, lunches, and suppers from a cabin that was supposed to be occupied by a lone gentleman. The other report was of a first-class cabin which was supposed to be occupied by an American from which a tall, dark-hued man had twice sent back the cleaning girl and never ordered food.

The ship's security chief was both prudent and knowledgeable. He had been with the *New Galaxy* for six years and had witnessed more cabin swaps than stars on cloudless nights. He knew that part of the fare the ship's passengers paid bought discretion, and he was also convinced that 99.9 percent of what looks remarkable, strange, or suspicious turns out to have very simple and innocent explanations. But he was also well aware he should make sure nothing was really wrong.

To play it by the book, at 15:52 hours on February 11, a Tuesday, when the *New Galaxy* was one hour away from its Mexican port of des-tination, he took up the matter with the captain. Sitting comfortably in the posh suite assigned to Number One, the two men in white starched uniforms with black-and-gold braided insignia of rank, sipped tea and discussed the awkward situation. The captain. remembered the shapely American who boarded his ship in Puerto Plata; now that she had been brought to his attention, he found it strange that he had not seen her since. His subordinate reported that the man who had answered the phone in cabin 111 said that Ms. Olwin was taking a nap, didn't want to be disturbed, and would the caller leave his name and cabin number? The security officer added that nobody answered the phone in cabin 224, in spite of the fact that two hours earlier a Latin lady had admitted an attendant delivering three substantial meals. The decision was made to keep a discreet observation on both compartments and to take a peek as soon as the dwellers went ashore.

Forty-five minutes later, just as a Mexican pilot gained admittance onto the ship's bridge, the buoyant kidnapper sitting on the couch of cabin 111 unfolded the two pages he had just taken out and started reading to his victim, resignedly sitting in the same deep chair.

> "Now I will try to win your forgiveness, and your complicity too. Everything I will tell you is true, every word. My father was a fisherman, he owned a twenty-foot launch and I started going out to sea with him when I was seven. I learned to love the sea. When my time came to fulfill my military service I chose the Cuban Coast Guard. I stayed after completing my tour of duty, studied hard, became the skipper of a fourteen-foot patrol boat eight years later. I was a young Communist, I looked forward to becoming a Party militant. We were supposed to watch out for the Miami pirates that would sail to Cuba to open fire against our people, but all I saw were drug smugglers, fishing parties and rafters trying to reach the Florida Keys. Our orders were to pick up rafters and take them back. I must have picked up two thousand rafters. Men were sent to prison, women and children almost always were sent home. I started wondering, conversed with my only friend on board, the boat engineer. One day I lost my patience when the political officer was giving me a lecture and I asked to him 'What is wrong with what we are doing? Why so many poor people risk their lives to get out of here?' It was a mistake. Three weeks later a stolen tug carrying sixty people was sunk by three other tugs. Forty persons drowned; twenty were children.
>
> "I said to myself "I do not want to be party to this." My engineer and I talked things over. One late evening we took our boat out. A scheduled maintenance had been completed and we were supposed to make a test, check if everything was okay. We set out to Key West and asked for political asylum.
>
> "I could not take my wife with me. There was no way to get her on board, but I planned to send for her as soon as possible. I know the Cuban government hears Miami radio stations and reads Miami press, so I did not give interviews because I figured maybe if I said the truth, brag about our defection, they would not grant her permission to leave Cuba. I kept my mouth shut. A year ago she got a visa from the American embassy in Havana. I sent her the money for all that was needed: birth certificate, marriage

> certificate, medical examinations, passport, everything. But she
> was refused permission to leave. An immigration official told her
> that if I had been man enough to steal a patrol boat, I should be
> man enough to return to Cuba and smuggle her out because she
> would never be given permission to leave.
>
> "I was left no choice. I am a man. I love my wife. I owed it to
> her. So I conceived this plan. I am sorry for you. But even if you
> forgive me now I have to tie you up again. . . ."

"No, listen up," Megan said as she uncoiled from the deep chair.

"Shut up, sit down," the kidnapper snapped. "Let me finish." And for
the second time he stared Megan down.

He resumed reading:

> "I have to tie you up again because I cannot run the risk of
> being deceived by you. There is too much at stake. I promise that
> we will leave Cancun in less than an hour after disembarking, but
> before leaving I shall phone the police and tell them that you are
> here, tied and gagged.
>
> "I said I wanted your complicity because besides wanting you
> to understand why I did this to you, I ask you not to tell to the
> Mexican authorities what I just told you. Not to tell about my wife,
> not to say that I am a Cuban and to delay reporting your lost pass-
> port for a few hours. If you do this, you will make it easier for us
> to get away. If you do not, I will understand. Now, please, lay
> down on the bed, please."

ON THE UPPER DECK of the New Galaxy, a security guard in civilian clothes
drew the walkie-talkie to his mouth and pressed the send key.

"The man in the blue blazer and the woman in the white blouse are
going down the ladder. Over."

The security officer and the chief steward slipped a master key in the
lock of cabin 111 and opened the door. Without a word they gently
stepped inside the small living area and looked around, footsteps muted
by the thick, plush carpet. Behind the partition they found Megan in
bed. Both men rushed forward. The chief steward carefully removed the
adhesive tape as the security officer began untying what he recognized as
fishermen's bends.

"Are you all right?" the steward asked Megan.

"I guess so," she said feeling her hands.

"Untie her legs," the security officer instructed. "I'm gonna get the son of a bitch."

"No, wait!" Megan shouted.

Paying no heed, the security officer picked up the radio from the rug and left the cabin. Once in the passageway he broke into a run.

Free at last, Megan rushed out, leaving the slack-jawed chief steward behind. She stopped in the passageway to get her bearings, looked both ways and chose the stairway to the upper deck. From there she saw the security officer going down the ladder two steps at a time. A hundred yards away her kidnapper, holding a woman by the elbow, was reaching the end of the pier. On the other side of a tall chain-link fence stood a building that housed Mexican immigration and customs. The security officer hit the ground and sprinted after the couple.

"Nooo!" Megan cried at the top of her lungs.

The wind blew in the right direction, and the swarthy man turned his head for an instant. He pushed the woman in the white blouse forward, pulled out a gun and turned to face his pursuer. Passengers around him scattered in all directions. The security officer stopped dead in his tracks and lay down on the concrete. To Megan's left, a man in civilian clothes was excitedly babbling into a walkie-talkie.

The woman in the white blouse crossed the fence after looking back several times, and a hand pulled her inside the Mexican compound. The swarthy man turned away from the ship and approached the fence. Two Mexican security guards with guns drawn came out the building shouting something that Megan couldn't hear. Holding his gun at waist level, the swarthy man seemed frozen for an instant, as if considering something. Megan saw three flashes and heard three pops. The swarthy man fell and after a few spasmodic kicks lay still.

Megan's vision blurred and she felt two trickles warming her cheeks.

# Miscalculation

### JAN BURKE

"All set?" Ada asked. "Of course you are. There isn't a Girl Scout in the world who took 'be prepared' as seriously as you did, Sarah."

"From the size of that trunk I saw poor Mr. Parsons carrying out of here, I'd say you're the one who's over-prepared," Sarah Milington replied. "Really, Grandmother, we're only staying on the *Queen Mary* overnight."

"I'm sure you're right," her adoptive grandmother said, embracing her as she reached her. "And it's likely I still haven't brought half of what I really need. You're the one who's best at details. If you would come to live with me again—"

"Grandmother . . ." Sarah warned.

"Never mind, I won't pester you about that now. I just think a trunk makes it seem so much more like a real cruise—Oh, here's Robert," she said, seeming so pleased that Sarah had to tamp down an annoying little flair of jealousy. More irritating, she was fairly sure Robert Parsons had noted her discomposure.

Although he was always polite to her, Sarah had yet to feel completely at ease around Parsons. Some of this unease was undoubtedly due to her grandmother's delight in surrounding both Parsons's background and his position in her household with an air of intrigue, but Sarah knew this only part of why she felt self-conscious when Parsons was near.

For all his own quietness, his presence in this house caused a great deal of talk. He was the inspiration for plenty of local gossip—gossip that undoubtedly pleased Ada Milington. Robert Parsons—good-looking, broad-shouldered and not more than thirty years old—had been part of Ada's household for nearly a year now.

At first, Sarah had believed that the rest of the staff, all much older than Parsons and notoriously protective of her grandmother, would rebel against his presence. In this she was mistaken. Parsons, she now reflected—recalling that he had just carried the largest trunk she had ever seen out to the van—was undoubtedly a godsend to the aging servants. He seemed more than willing to do heavy lifting and to take on any task, no matter how arduous. And, she was forced to admit, he gave every sign of being sincerely devoted to her grandmother.

Sarah knew she had no real personal complaint to make of him. Long ago accustomed to her grandmother's love of outrageous behavior, she decided that it was not her place to interfere. Ada had survived four husbands, and if she now wanted to have a fling with a man almost fifty years her junior, Sarah would not be the one to object.

Ada turned to the rest of the staff, which had gathered in the entry. "We're off on our cruise!" she announced grandly, waving a kiss at them. Amid tossed confetti and their boisterous cheers of "Bon voyage," and "Many happy returns!" she took Parsons's arm and allowed him to lead the way to the van.

He hadn't loaded the luggage very efficiently, Sarah thought with a frown, seeing that he had strapped the huge trunk to the long rack on the van's roof. By simply removing a seat, he could have fit it inside. The wind resistance would have been lower, and she would have obtained better gas mileage. She was considering this problem when Parsons, after gently helping Ada into the front passenger seat, surprised Sarah by opening the sliding door to the side of the van and seating himself in the back.

*No wonder he had left the seat in place!* She felt herself blush at the thought of her grandmother marching up the *Queen Mary's* gangplank with this virile-looking male in tow. And if Robert Parsons was sharing a room with Ada—but then, she quickly reminded herself, *that* was none of her business.

Ada's smile told her that her grandmother was waiting for a challenge, but Sarah merely started the van and began the drive to Long Beach.

She couldn't help but feel herself an injured party, though. She had wanted to talk privately to her grandmother, perhaps even to confide in her about the dream she had had last night—a recurring, claustrophobic dream from her childhood, of being locked in a closet. That was certainly not possible now. She could picture Robert Parsons's amusement over that.

"A little ridiculous to have Bella and the others throwing confetti," she said aloud. "It isn't really a cruise, after all."

"I'm pretending it is," Ada answered. "It's the closest I can come to a cruise. You know I get seasick."

"I know nothing of the sort. You've been on real cruises."

"And got sick on the last one. Never again. I do love the ocean, I just don't want to be feeling it pitch and roll as I blow out my candles. So this will be my cruise—perhaps my last one."

"It's not a cruise," Sarah repeated obstinately.

"Technically, no."

She might have left it at that, but when she glanced at the rearview mirror, she saw that Parsons was smiling. Smugly, she thought.

"Technically, it isn't even a ship," she added.

"No?" Ada said, turning to wink back at him.

Sarah felt her fingers tighten on the steering wheel. "No. It's officially classified as a building now, not a ship. It's permanently moored at that pier. It doesn't move. It doesn't go anywhere."

"You don't say," Ada replied.

"It's afloat," Robert said. "It moves with the tide."

Sarah fell silent.

After a moment, Ada said wistfully, "I saw her sail once, long ago. Back in the days when she did sail, when she was definitely a ship."

"You saw your first husband off to war," Robert said.

He sounded bitter, Sarah thought. Was he jealous of Ada's previous husbands? It seemed absurd. Perhaps it was only this first husband, she thought. Elliot. She was fairly sure he had been the first. Or was it Arthur?

Sarah knew little about any of Ada's husbands. Ada was someone who lived, by and large, in the present day, seldom discussing her past. And by the time Sarah had come to live with Ada, the last of Ada's four spouses had been dead for more than twenty years.

Sarah tried to remember the little she had been told. There had been an Elliot, an Arthur, a Charles, and finally John Milington Sr. Yes, that was the order. She remembered that Ada had married the first one when she was eighteen, and that he had died in World War II.

Bella had once let it slip that Ada had a son from that marriage, a son who so disliked Ada's third husband, mother and son had become estranged. Sarah frowned. *Or was it a son by the second husband who disliked the third?* Sarah couldn't remember. She couldn't even recall Ada's eldest boy's name. She did recall Bella's warning never to mention this son to Ada. Not wanting to cause Ada pain, or to make trouble for the old housekeeper, Sarah had kept her silence.

She glanced at Ada, and saw that her grandmother was frowning. It was then that another implication of Robert's remark came home to her.

"If you said good-bye to your first husband that day, he must have sailed on the *Queen Mary* when she was used as a troop ship, during the war."

Ada nodded. "I never saw him again."

"But being on the ship again—won't it be sad for you?"

Ada smiled and shook her head. "No, Sarah dear. Not at all. I was never actually aboard the ship, of course. We said good-bye at the dock. And the ship doesn't even look the same on the outside now. She was painted a dull gray then, and her portholes were blackened. She was called the *Grey Ghost* during the war."

"I read about that period of the ship's history," Sarah said. "The *Queen Mary* was able to cross the Atlantic in four or five days, which made her the fastest ship on the sea—capable of outrunning German submarines, if need be. She was even faster than German torpedoes." She paused, frowned, and added, "Faster than the ones used at the beginning of the war. There was a bounty on her. Hitler promised he would give a quarter of a million dollars and Germany's highest honors to the submarine captain who sank her."

"My, you have read up on her," Robert Parsons said.

Sarah responded as she always did under stress. She turned to numbers. "Yes. The ship made a great contribution to the Allied efforts. During the war, the *Queen Mary* carried over 765,000 military personnel over half a million nautical miles."

She saw that Parsons was smiling again, until Ada said, "One of those three-quarters of a million was mine."

"Yes, of course," Sarah said. "I'm sorry."

Robert reached forward and took Ada's hand.

Ada, never one to brood, soon changed the subject. She began to recite the guest list for the party. Sarah stayed silent, only half-attending as local dignitaries and old friends were named. While a woman of Ada's wealth and influence would never have trouble finding guests for her parties, her reputation for holding lively, out-of-the-ordinary celebrations made her invitations much sought after.

At last the *Queen Mary* came into sight. Sarah, seeing the long, sleek giant before her, its trio of mammoth red stacks cuffed in black towering above them, quickly realized that all the reading she had done about this historic vessel could never do it justice.

"A building?" she heard Robert Parsons ask.

"No," Sarah said quietly. "A ship, a beautiful, beautiful ship."

"Nothing like her in the world," he agreed. "Wait until you're aboard."

"You've been on the *Queen Mary* before?" she asked, surprised.

"A few times," he said, but Ada began directing her to the hotel entrance before Sarah could ask more.

AS THEY WERE welcomed by the staff at the registration desk, Sarah's eyes roved over the Art Deco lines of the ship's interior, the etched glass and shining brass, the rich exotic woods that surrounded her—crafted into curving, sumptuous, smooth surfaces, and marquetry unlike any she had ever seen.

She was recalled from her admiration by Ada's voice. "The small bag to Mr. Parsons's suite, please. The trunk and the rest of this group to mine, all except those two very serviceable but dowdy bags, which I'm sorry to say, belong to my granddaughter."

Sarah followed mutely as they were shown to their rooms, noting that like Ada, Robert was staying in one of the royalty suites. Each suite, Sarah knew, featured a large sitting area separated from a spacious bedroom, a private bath and additional small bedroom with a single twin bed in it—servant's quarters. In the ship's glory years, the luxurious suites had been occupied by the wealthiest of first class passengers, who paid the equivalent of an average Englishman's annual wages for round-trip passage—a large sum, even with the servant's fare and all meals included.

Robert's suite was near Ada's, but not adjoining it. Having braced herself for the likelihood that Ada would make the most of such a romantic setting, Sarah was surprised by this arrangement. He had been given a room that certainly placed his status well above that of hired help, but an adjoining room would have made assignations much easier.

Ada had offered a suite to Sarah, but Sarah had opted for one of the staterooms. Not as grand as the suites, it was nevertheless spacious, and like the suites, had many original furnishings in it. Sarah opened the two thick portholes, which provided a view of the Long Beach shoreline and downtown skyline. Taking a deep breath of cool air, she soon put aside her questions about her grandmother and Parsons. She spent the next half hour exploring her own luxurious room.

Soon her toiletries had been neatly arranged, her clothes hung in one of the closets, and nearly every other item she had carried with her stowed in an orderly fashion. She was just deciding where she would place a pair of books she had brought—about the history of the ship— when the phone rang.

"Sarah? Be a dear and run along to the Observation Bar, will you?" Ada said. "I told Robert I would meet him there, but now I've learned that Captain Dolman will be here any moment."

"Captain Dolman? Is he the ship's captain?" Sarah asked.

"No, no, an old friend. An army captain, retired for years. Now be a dear and don't make Robert wait there alone—some young wench might look at his handsome face and decide to lead him astray. A man like that, drinking alone in the bar—the consequences are not to be thought of."

"I don't —"

"Think you can find it? Of course you can. It's near the bow of the ship, on the promenade deck. Thank you, dear, it's such a relief to know I can depend upon you."

Sarah bore this with her usual good grace. She climbed the stairs to the promenade deck and moved quickly through the ship's shopping gallery to the cocktail lounge. Stepping into the curving, multi-level room, she saw before her a row of tall windows with a view of the main deck and bow, and the harbor beyond; nearer, in the room itself, she saw a nickel-colored railing made up of a mixture of creatures real and mythological. She turned—above the mirrors behind the bar, she saw a painting that, up until now, she had only seen in black-and-white photographs of this room. For several long moments, she forgot all about looking for Robert Parsons.

The painting stretched across the length of the bar, and depicted a street scene. More than two dozen figures were caught in motion. They were people from all walks of life, dancing hand-in-hand: sailors, bakers and men in top hats cavorting with stout matrons, and elegantly clad ladies and women in everyday dress. All were laughing as they circled 'round and 'round in celebration. Pennants fluttered above them; one of the revelers had lost her footing, but this was forever that moment before the others would notice.

"Makes you want to join them, doesn't it?" a voice said from just behind her right ear.

Startled, Sarah turned and found herself nearly nose-to-nose with Parsons. "No, Mr. Parsons—"

"Robert—"

"No, Mr. Parsons," she said, taking a step away from him. "It doesn't. They're all about to stumble over the one who has fallen."

He looked up at the mural and smiled. "They'll help her to her feet and carry on with the dance."

"At best, they'll step over her and continue without her."

He shook his head, but said nothing.

"The banners carry the insignia of St. George," she said quickly, fixing her eyes on the painting.

"In honor of King George V's twenty-fifth year as king," Parsons said, "which is being celebrated by the dancers. The work was painted by A. R. Thomson—and is called 'Royal Jubilee Week, 1935.'"

She turned scarlet.

"Oh, now you're angry with me. I've spoiled your fun. Let me buy you a glass of wine."

"I don't—"

"You can toss it in my face if you like. I'll present myself as a target."

"No, no, I'm sorry. It's a bad habit of mine, spouting off facts and figures nobody cares to hear."

"But you're wrong—I'm very interested in what you have to say, Miss Milington."

"Please, let's go back to 'Sarah' and 'Robert.'"

He smiled. "All right." He motioned to a doorway. "I'm sitting outside, but if you find it too chilly there for you—"

"No, I prefer it," she said truthfully.

She was soon seated at his table, shielded from the afternoon breeze by a row of Plexiglas panels. Belatedly, she remembered to deliver her message.

"It was kind of you to walk all the way here to tell me," he said, "but Ada is so seldom on time, I don't think I would have worried."

"I think she sent me as your chaperone," she admitted.

He laughed. "No, no, I doubt that. Tell me, have you had a chance to see much of the ship yet?"

"No, I've only just unpacked."

"Hmm. Then you must let me show you some of the more interesting sights—"

"I'm not sure—"

"You aren't afraid of me, are you?" he asked. "I promise you won't come to any harm."

Not unaware that this was the longest conversation she had ever had with him, she said, "Oh, no, I'm not afraid. It's just that Grandmother may not like me dominating so much of your time."

"Trust me, she'll be delighted. Besides," he added quietly, "she'll have other demands to make of me later."

Again Sarah felt herself blush.

"You misunderstand—" he began.

"It isn't any of my business," Sarah said quickly, relieved to see Ada approaching, accompanied by two elderly gentlemen, one on each arm. The men seemed to be doing their level best to keep up with her. Sarah, familiar with most of Ada's friends, did not know either of these men. But as they drew closer, she thought one of them did seem familiar.

Ada came to the table with long strides, flamboyantly garbed in a hot pink and turquoise jogging suit, wearing a white turban. *How does she manage*, Sarah wondered, *to wear such silly outfits and still look great?*

"Sarah!" Ada called out, "Meet the congressman!"

"Oh, not yet, not yet!" the taller of the two men exclaimed. "A mere state senator at the moment, but with your grandmother's generous help, I may trade Sacramento for Washington, D.C." He extended a hand. "Archer Hastings, my dear, at your service."

"A pleasure to meet you, Senator," Sarah said, now realizing why he seemed familiar. She was sure she had seen him on the evening news once or twice. He wasn't the senator for their district, but Ada had many political friends, not all of them her own representatives.

When Ada introduced the second man, Gerald Dolman, the retired army captain turned crimson and nodded in Sarah's direction, but did not meet her eyes. He was a thin man with a prominent Adam's apple. It bobbed as he swallowed nervously. She wondered why he was so flustered over meeting her, but soon decided he was merely shy—he would not, in fact, look directly at any of the others, and the blush which had stolen over his neck and face remained throughout the time he sat with them.

Archer Hastings had no such reticence. He gave the others a quick biography of himself, a sort of resume from the time he was a paperboy in the 1930s. He spoke at length about his enlistment in the army, and his service (mostly behind a desk) during World War II. By the time he was telling them about his return to California and his establishment of an accounting firm, the drinks had arrived. *What a pompous ass*, Sarah thought, but Hastings was only warming up.

"Have you had a chance to tour the ship?" Ada was asking him.

"Yes, yes. Wonderful! Wonderful place for this lovely lady to celebrate her birthday," he said to the others. "I'm certainly looking forward to that party tonight. The Grand Salon. Used to be the first class dining room. Largest single public room ever built on a ship. You could fit all three of Christopher Columbus's ships in there and still have space left over. Have you seen it yet, Sarah? No? Oh, you must see it. Probably won't let you in while they're getting ready for the big to-do, but"—he winked conspiratorially—"you have friends in high places. Then of course, you will see it tonight, won't you? Yes, a grand ship."

Captain Dolman was making quick progress through his drink as Hastings went on.

"A symbol of triumph over the Great Depression, that's what it was to the British," the politician said.

"Yes," Robert Parsons said, "she was a symbol of hope."

For reasons Sarah could not understand, this caused Captain Dolman and Ada to look at him sharply. But Hastings was oblivious.

"I've always liked the British," he was saying. "Don't you like them? Sure. Like to do things on a grand scale—just like you, Ada. Say, did you know that if you measure from the *Queen Mary*'s keel to the top of her forward funnel, this ship is one hundred and eighty feet tall? That makes her eighteen feet taller than Niagara Falls! Now, *that's* something, but her length is spectacular. If you could stand this ship on end, it would be taller than the Washington Monument. Taller than the Eiffel Tower, too. In fact, the Empire State Building would only be two hundred feet taller."

"Two hundred and thirty feet," Sarah said without thinking.

Parsons smiled, Ada laughed and Captain Dolman nervously rattled the ice in his glass, which he was studying intently. Archer Hastings seemed taken aback until he noticed Ada's reaction, then burst into hearty guffaws. Sarah felt her own cheeks turning red, and wondered if her complexion now matched Captain Dolman's.

"I warned you, Archer," Ada said. "She's a wonder with numbers. As addicted to facts and figures as you are."

"Really?" Hastings seemed unable to resist the challenge of testing this claim. "I suppose you know about the anchors?"

Sarah hesitated, but seeing Ada's expectant look, answered, "There are two eighteen-foot-long anchors, each weighing sixteen tons. The anchor chains are each nine hundred and ninety feet long. Each link of an anchor chain weighs two hundred and twenty-four pounds."

"Very good, very good," he acknowledged, although Sarah thought he did not seem to be truly pleased. "Your grandmother told me you had an excellent head for figures. Numbers have always been a specialty of mine. Making good use of them, not just dithering around with some theoretical nonsense. Of course, one can't expect a young lady to have an appreciation of statistics; rare enough to find one who has any kind of brain for mathematics in the first place. No wonder your grandmother is so proud of—"

Sarah fixed him with a narrow glare, but it was Robert who interrupted, saying, "Mrs. Milington is proud of her granddaughter for a great many reasons, of course. Her abilities with mathematics and statistics are just one source of that pride."

Hastings seemed finally to become aware Ada was looking at him in a way that seemed to indicate that subtraction—from the amount he was hoping to receive from her for his campaign—seemed the most likely piece of arithmetic to be going on in her mind.

"Oh, Sarah, I apologize," he said quickly. "I behave just like a crotchety old man on some occasions. You are clearly an exceptional young lady! I am astounded at your knowledge of the ship."

"I haven't seen much of it," she confessed in some confusion, still amazed at Robert's defense of her, and uncomfortable with all the praise Hastings had heaped upon her.

"But she's read a great deal," Robert said.

"Ask her anything about it!" Ada said.

Sarah noticed a particular gleam in his eye as Hastings said, "All right. What type of fuel did the *Queen Mary* burn?"

"Bunker C oil," she answered promptly. "The ship averaged thirteen feet to the gallon."

Ada gave a crow of laughter.

"Thirteen miles to the gallon?" Hastings asked.

"No, sir. Feet, not miles."

Hastings, skeptical a moment before, now became fascinated by Sarah's love of data and would not be side-tracked from his game. He asked for statistic after statistic, and Sarah answered accurately every time.

She could not help but feel a glow of pride, and her original appraisal of Hastings mellowed considerably. But just as she was saying that there were over six miles of carpet on the ship, she happened to glance at Robert Parsons. He was frowning at Hastings, and his fists were clenched on the table.

I'm boring him, Sarah thought, all the pleasure suddenly going out of the game. Her voice trailed off, and she stared down at her hands, too humiliated to continue. Robert was obviously wishing that Hastings would stop encouraging her. She probably hadn't amused anyone other than Hastings and her grandmother; Robert and Captain Dolman, she was sure, were wishing Ada had left her at home. She had been an obnoxious, unbridled know-it-all.

She was about to apologize when she heard Robert say, "I have an extra pass for the next guided tour, Sarah. Would you care to go on it?"

She had not thought she could be more deeply mortified, but she was wrong. *So he wanted to send her off on a ship's tour, as if she were a child not ready to share the company of adults.* Well, and why not? She had just behaved as if she were the kid in the class who waves his hand and shouts, "Me! Me! Call on me!"

"Thank you," she managed to say.

"Yes," her grandmother agreed, "an excellent notion."

So even Ada was defecting, she thought, as Robert, ever the gentleman, stood and helped her from her chair. She was a little surprised when he continued at her side, but she said nothing. She crossed the bar and took the exit to her left, and still he followed. As they passed two of the larger shops along the passageway, he said, "These were once the first class passengers' library and drawing room. Winston Churchill was given use of the drawing room when he was aboard the ship during World War II. He and other leaders finalized plans for the invasion of Normandy while on this ship, probably in that room."

Sarah glanced into the rather barren souvenir shop that now occupied the space.

"Don't worry," he said, reading her thoughts. "Not all of her dignity has been lost."

"Where does the tour begin?"

"The port side of this deck," he said.

"I'm sure I can find it," she said.

"Undoubtedly. But I'm going with you."

"But you've been before . . ."

"Yes," he said, "but much of the ship can only be seen on the tour. You don't mind if I join you?"

"Of course not."

THE TOUR (she couldn't prevent herself from counting the group—eighteen sightseers, including the two of them) was lead by a retired naval officer. Parsons stayed at her side, but did not touch or crowd her. She soon relaxed and began to thoroughly enjoy the tour itself, fascinated by the grandeur and history of the ship.

When the tour group reached the cabin class swimming pool, she heard a woman say, "I've heard that it's haunted."

Sarah looked around the room of beige and blue-green terra cotta tiles, the etched wire-and-glass image of an ancient sailing ship behind her, the glimmering mother-of-pearl ceiling above, the empty, sloping depth of the pool itself. There were no windows or portholes, but the room was large enough to prevent her from feeling claustrophobic. Nothing about any of it struck her as particularly scary, nothing sent a chill down her back. But when she turned to make a joke to Robert about ghosts who had turned green from chlorine, she saw that he was pale, and had a strange, intense look on his face.

The guide was making light of the woman's remark. "Do you mean the woman in the mini-skirt or the one in the bathing suit? I'd settle for a glimpse of either one."

"There's more than one ghost?" the woman asked.

"Oh yes, the ship has long been reported to be haunted," the guide said lightly. "If you believe in such reports, this ship is loaded with them. Myself, if I see one, I hope it's one of the young ladies who rove in here."

The group laughed and began to move after the guide as he went on with the tour. Robert, however, remained motionless, and continued to stare into the pool.

"Robert?" Sarah asked. "Are you feeling ill?"

When he seemed not to hear her, she touched his sleeve. "Robert?"

He turned to her with a start. "Oh—I'm sorry, we've fallen behind. We'd better catch up with the others." They were not far from the group, though, and once they reached it Sarah asked again if he was feeling ill.

"No," he said, "I'm fine now, thank you."

She did not believe him, and glanced back at him several times as they made their way to the next area, along a catwalk over one of the cavernous boiler rooms. He was still pale.

By the time the formal tour was finished, though, he seemed himself again, and Sarah happily allowed him to accompany her to the other shipboard exhibits. He seemed to enjoy her enthusiasm as she was able to see the anchor chains and lifeboats and all the other parts of the ship she had read about. She lost her self-consciousness over her study of the ship's statistics and decided her knowledge gave her a better appreciation of what she was seeing now.

Not that her appreciation was limited to the ship's physical power. There was nostalgia, pure and simple, to be relished. She lingered over photos of Winston Churchill, Queen Elizabeth, Clark Gable, Marlene Dietrich, the Duke and Duchess of Windsor, Spencer Tracy, and other famous passengers. She tried to take in every detail of the displays of passenger accommodations and dining rooms.

Robert, cheerful through most of their exploration of the ship, grew solemn when they reached the wartime exhibits on the sun deck. The subject matter deserved solemnity, Sarah thought. His mood, however, seemed to remain grim even after they left the exhibit. She felt much more at ease with him by then, which gave her the courage to ask him what was troubling him.

He hesitated, then said, "Did you see how the soldiers were forced to live aboard this ship?"

Sarah, recalling the photos of thousands of soldiers crammed together on the decks of the ship, shuddered. "Yes, it was very crowded—"

"*Crowded*? You like numbers. The ship was designed to carry about two thousand passengers. On one of its wartime voyages, it carried over sixteen thousand men."

"It carried 16,683," Sarah said. "The largest number of people ever to sail on any ship—a record that still stands."

"Sarah, think of what that meant to each of those sixteen thousand!"

She had seen some of this in the exhibit, of course. Tiers of standee berths—narrow metal frames with a single piece of canvas stretched over them—six and seven bunks high, each only eighteen inches apart. The men slept in three shifts; the beds were never empty. Soldiers were given colored badges to be worn at all times; the badges corresponded with a section of the ship, where the soldiers were required to stay throughout the voyage.

But for Sarah, who had struggled for years with a fear of confined spaces, thinking about what it actually meant to each soldier was nearly unbearable. Suddenly, she felt dizzy, unable to breathe.

In the next moment she heard Robert Parsons saying, "My God, I'm so sorry! I forgot! Let's go outside, onto the sun deck."

She raised no objections, and found herself feeling a mixture of relief that she was once again in the open air and an acute embarrassment that her grandmother had apparently informed Robert Parsons about her problem.

When he tried to apologize again, she said, "I do believe you're much more upset about this than I am. I'll be all right."

"When did it start?" he asked.

"My claustrophobia? Didn't Grandmother tell you that, too?"

"No. She's never said anything about it. I've noticed it before—at her dinner parties. Too many people in the room and you have to go outside. On nights when it's too cold to be outdoors in an evening gown, you step out for a breath of fresh air."

She was quiet for a moment, not sure what to make of his observation of her. Then she said, "I don't know why this memory has been so persistent, but when I was about four, at the orphanage, I was once punished for something by being shut up in a closet. I don't remember what I had done wrong, or even who put me in the closet. I just remember the darkness, the sensation of being confined, the smell of the coats and mothballs. I was terrified. I remember counting, singing a song about numbers to stay calm."

He put an arm around her shoulders, gave her a brief hug. But he seemed to know not to hold on to her—not when she was feeling so close to the memory of that closet. He let her be. As she felt herself grow calmer, she ventured a question of her own. "I've been thinking—the way you responded to the wartime exhibit—do you have problems with claustrophobia, too?"

He shook his head. "No, I don't."

"But it was personal for you somehow, wasn't it? You're too young to have fought in anything other than the Gulf War—"

"My grandfather went to war on this ship."

"Oh! You have something in common with Grandmother then."

He smiled slightly. "Yes. Ada and I have a great deal in common."

Not wanting to pursue that subject, she said, "So your grandfather told you about traveling on this ship?"

"No," Parsons said, looking out over the railing, toward the sea. "He died before I was born. Even before my father was born. My grandfather died aboard the ship."

"Aboard the ship?" she repeated, stunned.

"Yes. He was a young soldier, newly married. His wife was pregnant with their first child, although he didn't know that when he left for war. He was, by all accounts, a bright and talented man with a sense of humor; he used to draw cartoon sketches of his fellow soldiers and mail them home to my grandmother. He went off to war, not willingly parted from her, but willing to fight for his country." He paused, then added bitterly, "He was murdered before he had a chance to reach his first battle."

"*Murdered?!*"

"Yes."

Sarah's own thoughts raced. It was not difficult to see that under the crowded wartime conditions aboard the ship, tempers might easily flare. She suddenly knew without a doubt that his grandfather had been killed near the swimming pool; this, she was sure, accounted for Robert's reaction when they were in that area of the ship.

"I'm sorry, Robert," she said. "What a terrible blow for your grandmother."

"She didn't learn exactly what happened until many years later. She thought he had been killed in action."

"Was the killer punished?"

"No. He got away with it. Listen, I shouldn't be talking to you about this," he said. "You're here for a pleasant occasion and Ada would tan my hide if she knew I was—"

"Ada doesn't entirely rule my life," Sarah said. "I'm glad you told me. Does she know about your grandfather?"

"Oh, yes."

"And she still insisted on bringing you here!"

"Sarah, as I've told you, I've been here before." He smiled. "And not just to lay my family ghosts to rest. I'll admit that was why I made my first visit, but I found I couldn't dislike this ship—she's not to blame for what happened to my grandfather. I suppose I fell in love with her style and elegance. She was built for pleasure—a thing of beauty, not death and destruction. And she's a survivor. Of all the great luxury liners built before the war, the *Queen Mary* is the only survivor."

They resumed their tour of the ship. He had saved the art gallery, one of his favorite rooms on the ship, for last. As they left it, he said, "Ask Ada to tell you what sort of relationship I share with her."

"Why don't you tell me instead?"

"I promised her I would leave that to her."

They soon reached the stateroom. As he was about to leave her at her door, he paused, and said, "Something was troubling you this morning."

Her eyes widened.

He shrugged. "I saw it. In your face, I suppose. Your eyes."

"It was just—just something silly," she said. "Just a dream."

"A nightmare?"

"I dreamed of that closet—the one at the orphanage."

"You're all right now?"

"Yes. I'll be fine."

He started to walk off, then turned and said, "Thank you for taking the tour with me."

"My pleasure," she said softly.

* * *

WHEN SHE HAD finished dressing for the party, Sarah knocked on her grandmother's door. Ada opened it herself, beckoning Sarah in as she returned to her dressing table. To Sarah's surprise, Ada was nearly ready, and she was attired not in one of her wild ensembles, but in a very simple but elegant black dress.

"Are you feeling all right?" Sarah asked.

Ada gave a shout of laughter. "It's best not to let everyone become too sure of what I'll do next. Do you like it?"

"You look fantastic." She gave her a kiss. "Happy birthday, Grandmother."

"Thank you, my dear. How was your afternoon with Robert?"

"Very pleasant. He said I should ask you about your relationship with him."

She raised an eyebrow. "He did, did he?"

"Yes. Now don't tease or put me off, Grandmother."

Ada smiled into the mirror as she fastened an earring. "Do you like him?"

"Grandmother!"

"I'll tell you this much. He's not my employee." She grinned wickedly, then added, "And he is not my lover. Oh, don't try to look innocent, I know what's being said. But he's not. I have no romantic interest in him—none whatsoever."

"But you seem so close—"

"We are very close. But that has nothing to do with the price of eggs, so get off your pretty duff and pursue the man." She turned and gave Sarah a quick kiss. "You were very sweet not to offer your old granny any competition for that young fox."

"Grandmother!"

"You're attracted to him, Sarah. Have been from the day you met him."

"What utter nonsense."

"Is it?"

Sarah opened her mouth to protest, then closed it again.

Ada laughed and turned back to the mirror. "I thought so. Well, my dear, you have my blessing."

THE BIRTHDAY PARTY was wildly successful. Sarah, returning from one of her frequent strolls on one of the upper decks, saw Ada dancing an energetic fox trot with Captain Dolman—an excellent dancer, but he still seemed very nervous. Ada, she noticed, had spent a great deal of time with the captain. Although Sarah had been dreading another encounter with Senator Hastings, she had not seen him since the first hour of the party, when he had been talking to Robert. Surprised that he would pass up an opportunity to work a crowd this wealthy and influential, she was, nevertheless, pleased that she had been spared another round of quizzing.

She hadn't seen much of Robert, either. She had danced with him once, but he had seemed so preoccupied that she had difficulty holding a conversation with him.

"I'm terrible company tonight," he said as the dance ended. "May we try this again, another evening? Just the two of us?"

Telling him she would consider that a promise, she resolved not to make a nuisance of herself to him.

Now, several hours later, she strolled near Ada's table. Although the invitations had said "no gifts," a few of Ada's friends had ignored these instructions. When her Grandmother returned from the dance floor, Sarah offered to take the packages to her room.

"Thank you, Sarah!" she said. "How very thoughtful of you." She gave Sarah the key to the room and turned to accept an offer to waltz with one of her other guests. Captain Dolman offered to help Sarah, but as there were only five boxes, she politely declined his assistance.

As she came down the stairs, her arms full, she was surprised to see Robert leaving his suite, his face set in a forbidding frown. He did not see her, however, and quickly moved off in the opposite direction, toward the elevator. She nearly called to him, to ask what was troubling him, but decided not to delay him, as he was apparently in a hurry.

She managed to open the door to Ada's suite, only to discover that she had entered through the servant's door rather than the main door, which opened into the sitting area. This part of the suite—this small room, and beyond it the bathroom and large bedroom—was closed off from the sitting room, and except for the light from the hallway behind her was in darkness. Sarah tried to reach for the old-fashioned light switch, but couldn't manage it with her arms full of boxes and holding the key. She decided to lay the boxes on the twin bed, but as she stepped inside, the door closed behind her with a loud click. The small room was plunged into nearly total darkness. Panicking, blindly rushing back to the door, Sarah whirled and stumbled over something. The boxes went tumbling from her arms as she fell, and she heard the flutter of papers, and then felt them raining down on her. She scrambled to her knees, ran her hands wildly over the wall, and found the switch.

For a moment, she could only catch her breath and wait for her heartbeat to slow. Gradually, she noticed that she had knocked over an old leather briefcase. It had opened and spilled its contents across the room.

Gathering the gifts first, she was relieved to see that none of them were damaged, and placed them on the bed. She then went to work on collecting the scattered papers.

Most seemed to be old letters, bearing three-cent postage stamps. Among them, she saw an old photograph; the smiling young soldier in it looked familiar to her, she thought, picking it up. The back of the photo bore an inscription in a neat masculine hand. "Give me a kiss goodnight, Ada—I'll return every one with interest when I come back home to you! Love, Elliot."

Her grandmother, Sarah realized, had brought her first husband's photo on this ship, where she had last seen him. Moved by this, she carefully returned the photo to the briefcase. But it was as she gathered the scattered envelopes that she received a shock. The letters, postmarked during 1942, were addressed to Mrs. Elliot Parsons.

*Parsons. Elliot Parsons.*

Robert was related to Ada. He was her grandson. She knew it as surely as she knew anything. Her mind reeled. Robert was Sarah's cousin—her adopted cousin, at any rate. And all this time—all this time!—Ada had made a guessing game out of her grandson's identity. *Why?*

Mechanically, Sarah began putting the letters away. She came across one other item, a drawing. A cartoon. The subject of the cartoon had aged, but he was easily recognized. The Adam's apple was exaggerated, of course, and so was the blush. "Capt. Dolman, our fearless leader," was scrawled at the bottom of one corner of the drawing.

The room seemed to be closing in on her, and she stood up and made her way into the sitting room. She turned the light on, and moving to the portholes, opened one, and took a deep breath of the cold air. She sat down in a nearby chair. She was glancing at the carpet, noting a pair of parallel lines on it. Wheel marks from a dolly or handcart, she thought to herself, just as she heard a key sliding into the lock.

She braced herself for a confrontation with Ada, but it was not Ada who opened the door. Robert Parsons stood before her.

"Sarah? Are you all right?"

"I'm fine."

"Ada's worried about you," he said, closing the door behind him, crossing the room to sit near her. "She's been waiting for you to bring her key back. Are you sure you're okay?" he asked, glancing at the open porthole.

"I'm fine, cousin."

He stiffened. "She told you—and apparently didn't do a very good job of it."

"No, I found out quite by accident. By being clumsy. I knocked over a briefcase full of letters from your grandfather. I didn't mean to snoop, but . . . well, I didn't read the letters."

"Sarah, I've never wanted to hide anything from you. Ada insisted, and I let her talk me into it. I never should have gone along with it."

"Why? Why didn't she want me to know?"

He hesitated, then said, "For two reasons. The first is that she didn't want you to get hurt. She was afraid—after the way the Milingtons treated you—she didn't want you to feel as if I were more important to her than you are. I'm not Sarah—honest to God, I'm not."

When she didn't reply he said, "You've been her granddaughter for years. If you don't want to share her, I'll understand."

"Oh, it's not that!" she said. "It's just—just a lot to take in."

"Yes, it's a lot for me to take in, too, and I've had a year to get used to the idea. She didn't even know I existed. I managed to track her down when I was trying to learn more about what happened to my grandfather—to Elliot Parsons. Ada and my father were estranged."

"Because of his stepfather? Ada's next husband?"

"Yes. So you know about that?"

"Not much."

"When my dad died, I wanted to learn more about his side of the family, and meet this grandmother of mine. I also wanted to know more about my grandfather. At first, I just wanted to find out if my father's story was true, that his father had died aboard the *Queen Mary*, while on the passage to Europe. I learned much more. And I told Ada what I had learned."

"About his murder?"

"Yes."

"What's the second reason she didn't want to tell me?"

But before he could answer, there was a knock at the door of the suite. "Robert? Sarah?" they heard Ada's voice call.

Robert opened to door to admit Ada and Captain Dolman.

"Here's your key, Grandmother," Sarah said.

Ada studied her as she took the key, then rounded on Robert. "You told her!"

"No," Sarah said, and explained how she had learned that Robert was Ada's grandson. "And he is just about to tell me the second reason you didn't want me to know about it."

"Nonsense!" she said firmly. "Now, although the party was wonderful, I'm completely exhausted, so all of you will please leave my room. All except Sarah."

"Ada—" Robert began.

"*Now*," she said, giving him a look that would have sent an emperor running. It was more than enough for Captain Dolman. For several long minutes, it seemed that Robert would refuse to obey.

"I'll be all right," Sarah said. His frustration evident, Robert finally followed Dolman's lead.

But in the meantime, Sarah had given some thoughts to the events of the day, and when the door closed behind Robert, she asked, "Where is Senator Hastings?"

"How should I know?"

"You know. Why did you invite him?"

"He practically invited himself."

"I don't believe that. He's not running in your congressional district; he's not your state senator. And he is certainly not the type of person you would back in either race."

"Whom I invite to my own birthday party—"

"A party on a ship where, according to Robert, your first husband was murdered—"

"Robert will have to learn to keep quiet. Although I daresay you might receive more of his confidences than anyone else would."

"I should hope so. I'm his cousin."

"He doesn't think of you in that way, Sarah. I can guarantee you that much. And that is not to say that he doesn't want to be related to you."

Blushing, Sarah said, "Don't try to change the subject, you wily old woman."

Ada smiled, but didn't reply.

"You invited two men I've never heard you mention before, and you were with both of them before the festivities began. One of them disappeared not long after the party started. The other man hasn't been three feet from your side all night; you have a funny little caricature of him drawn by your late husband."

"What you think you're getting at, I'm sure I don't know," Ada said.

"I think you were getting at something—or rather, someone tonight, Grandmother. Maybe it's too late for justice—legal justice. But you've arranged for revenge, haven't you?"

Ada said nothing. She moved to the porthole, looked out at the harbor.

"Grandmother, you can trust me. I—I may not be family, but I love you as much as—"

"Don't talk nonsense!" Ada said, her voice quavering. "Of course you're family. I don't want you to come to any harm, don't you see? And you wouldn't like this particular brand of revenge."

Sarah took a deep breath, and said, "Have you murdered a state senator, Grandmother?"

Ada turned to look at her. "You think I'm capable of that?"

"No," Sarah answered.

"Thank God for that, at least."

"Well, if you haven't killed him—" She looked around the room, an idea suddenly occurring to her. Horrified, she said, "Grandmother—the trunk! You've locked him in the trunk!"

"Yes," Ada said.

"Where is it? Where's the trunk?"

"Sarah—"

"It's in Robert's room, isn't it? That's why Robert had the other key to your room—you didn't give it to him, he already had it." Her eyes went back to the carpet. "The wheel marks—that's what made them. Oh, Grandmother! It isn't right."

"Where are you going?" Ada asked in alarm as Sarah hurried toward the door.

Sarah didn't answer.

\* \* \*

SHE COULD HEAR the phone in his room ringing, even before she got to the door. It was quiet on the ship now, most of the guests had turned in for the night.

When he answered the door, she said, "I don't care what Grandmother said to you just now—"

"Come inside," he said, glancing up and down the passageway.

Once the door was closed behind her, he said, "She only wants to protect you, Sarah. I'm in too deep now, but you don't have to be involved. It would be better if—"

"Remember that painting?" she interrupted. "The one of the dancers, in the Observation Bar?"

He nodded.

"I don't want to be an outsider, Robert. We're all in this together. Please, Robert—"

"All right," he said, "but Sarah—"

She heard a muffled thumping sound, and pushed past Robert into the bedroom.

The trunk lay near the foot of the bed. She heard the thumping sound again. Her face pale, she turned to Robert and said, "Let him out!"

"In a moment, when your Grandmother and Captain Dolman arrive."

But images from her own nightmares surrounded her, and when she heard the thumping again, she turned to Robert with such a look of horror on her face that he relented, and began unfastening the trunk's latches.

As he lifted the lid, she saw that Hastings was bound and gagged. His face bore an expression that quickly passed from relief to anger.

"Wait in the other room," Robert said. "I'll bring him out."

A few moments later, an irate Archer Hastings was led to a chair in the sitting room.

"You're out of that box thanks to Sarah," Robert said. "But if you raise a ruckus of any kind, you'll go right back into it."

Sarah saw the fear in Hastings eyes.

"The trunk is custom made, isn't it?" she said to Robert. "It's built to be the same size as a soldier's berth on the ship."

"Yes."

There was a knock at the door, and in another moment, Ada and Dolman had joined them.

Hastings glared angrily at Ada.

"You'd like to see me arrested, wouldn't you?" Ada said to him.

He nodded vigorously.

"The feeling is mutual." She turned to her granddaughter. "Do you know how Elliot died?"

Sarah shook her head.

"Tell me, Sarah," she asked, "do you know if the *Queen Mary* was air conditioned?"

"Not all of it—not until later years, after the war."

"And before the war?"

"Not on all decks. It wasn't necessary. The ship was built for travel on the North Atlantic. The electric fireplaces in the first class cabins—"

"Never mind the fireplaces," Ada said. "You just made an important point. The ship was built for North Atlantic crossings."

"You knew that, didn't you Mr. Hastings?" Robert said.

Hastings made an angry sound behind the gag.

"Oh, pardon me. I'll remove the gag, but I'll expect you to keep your voice at a conversational level. If you don't—" he nodded toward Captain Dolman, who held a gun aimed at Hastings. "I'm afraid Captain Dolman, who is an excellent shot, will be allowed to fulfill his fondest wish."

"Now see here," Hastings said as the gag was removed, "I've heard for years about Ada Milington's crazy parties, but this is too much! Let me go now, and we can forget this ever happened."

"As you've forgotten what happened to those men you murdered?" Ada asked.

"I don't know what you're talking about!"

"Sarah," Ada said. "How many standee berths were placed in the cabin class swimming pool?"

"One hundred and ten," she answered promptly. "Was that where Elliot was assigned while on the ship?"

"Yes," Dolman answered. "My unit was sent to that hellhole."

"It was crowded for everybody!" Hastings said. "There was a war on, remember? We needed to get troops to Europe and the Pacific."

"And that was your responsibility," Robert said.

"Yes, of course it was. I made this ship ten times more efficient for the transporting of troops."

"The numbers got bigger and bigger, thanks to you."

"That's right. That's why you didn't grow up speaking German or Japanese, sonny boy."

"I fought against them," Dolman said, "but they were the enemy then, and the war was on. But you weren't supposed to be our enemy, Hastings. Troops weren't supposed to die because of you."

"You're insane! All of you! I worked at a desk job! I didn't kill anybody. Sarah—" he pleaded, turning to the one person who seemed inclined to show him mercy.

But Sarah had been thinking about the questions that had been asked so far. "The ship has no portholes in the pool area," she said, frowning. "The room is completely enclosed. During the war, the pool was drained, but that would mean that the temporary berths were positioned . . ." She looked at Robert.

"Yes, you've guessed it."

"Directly above one of the boilers," she finished, staring at Hastings now.

"We crossed the damned Equator in a ship built to go from Southampton to New York," Dolman said. "The tropics, Hastings. Do you know what it's like to watch men dying of the heat? Suffocating to death? No fresh air, just the stench of people getting sick and sweating and some of them dying. Temperatures over a hundred and ten degrees— and that's on the upper decks. Down where we were, it was a damned oven, Hastings. I say we put you in that trunk and we heat it up until you feel your blood boiling. You should have had to watch men like young Elliot Parsons die. I had to, Hastings, and I'll never forget it!"

"There was no way I could have known—" Hastings pleaded. "We were just trying to do out best to fight the war."

"Until now," Dolman said, "I didn't know who made the decisions about how we were going to be loaded in there. There wasn't any escape for us then, and there shouldn't be any for you now."

"You aren't going to kill me! Not for something that happened so long ago! Not for a simple miscalculation!"

"What do you want from him?" Sarah asked.

"Withdraw from the Congressional race," Ada said.

"What?"

"And resign from office," Robert added.

"You'll never get away with this!"

"People get away with things like this all the time. You've been getting away with murder for over fifty years."

"It wasn't murder, I tell you! We didn't know."

Sarah frowned. "But you must have known."

"What?"

"The voyage Elliot Parsons sailed on—it wasn't the first voyage to cross the Equator." She looked at Hastings. "You didn't miscalculate. You accepted the fact that some men might die on the voyage."

There was a long silence, broken only when Robert said, "Bravo, Sarah."

"We can prove all of this, Hastings," Ada said. "Retire as a state senator, or lose an election in shame."

"Do you think anyone is going to care about what happened then?"

"Put him in the trunk again!" Dolman said. "He'll have just as much room to move around as we did. Let's see him win an election from there."

"No—no! I won't run for office. I swear I won't. Just let me out of here!"

"Don't trust him!" Dolman said.

"There's another alternative," Robert said, opening a drawer in a built-in desk.

"What?" Hastings asked, apprehensively.

Robert didn't answer right away, but when he turned around, he held a syringe.

"What's in there?" Hastings asked.

"Oh, you'll just have to trust me," Robert said, "maybe it will give you a fever—something that will make your blood boil, as Captain Dolman says—or maybe it will just help you to sleep."

WHEN STATE SENATOR Archer Hastings awakened, he was hot, unbearably hot, and thirsty. He was still on the ship, he realized hazily. The damned ship. And, he realized with alarm, he was not in his bed, but in an enclosed space—the trunk. He pushed against the lid—it flew open.

Shaking, he crawled out of it, onto the bed. He was still hot, miserably hot, and the terror of the trunk would not leave him.

He reached for the phone next to his bed, and said thickly, "Help. Send a doctor in to help me. I'm ill."

Not much later, a doctor did arrive. He stepped into the room and said, "Are you chilled?"

"Chilled? Are you mad? I'm burning up!"

"So am I," the physician said, and turned down the thermostat. "Open the portholes and you'll be fine."

"Those damned people!" Hastings exclaimed.

"Which people?" the doctor said, in the tone of one who has encountered a lunatic.

"Mrs. Ada Milington—is she still aboard?"

"Oh no. I'm the last of Ada's party still on the ship. She said you'd had a bit too much to drink last night and asked me to make sure you got off the ship all right. She was in a rush."

"I'll bet she was."

"She asked me to give you a message. She said for you to remember that you have an open invitation to a pool party."

Hastings frowned. "Where's she off to? I need to talk to her."

"Oh, I believe she's well on her way to Glacier Bay by now—one of the Alaskan cruise lines. She said something about her grandchildren getting married at sea. Quite eccentric, Ada," the doctor mused, as he was taking his leave. "Yes, eccentric—but I'd take her seriously, if I were you, sir." He paused before closing the door. "Shall I ask the hotel to send someone to help you with that trunk?"

"No! I don't want the damned thing."

The doctor shrugged and left.

Hastings brooded for a moment, considered the odds of convincing anyone that he had been kidnapped by Ada Milington. He would retire, he decided. There was a sense of relief that came with that decision.

All the same, he continued to feel confined. He hurried to a porthole, opened it and took a deep breath.

For Archer Hastings, it offered no comfort.

\* \* \*

*Author's Note:*
Although Archer Hastings and all other characters in this story are entirely fictional, the *Queen Mary* statistics in this story are real. Under

the control of Allied military personnel, the ship made an enormous contribution to the war effort. However, conditions were extremely crowded, and soldiers did die during voyages into the tropics—most often in the cabin class pool area above the boilers. This story is dedicated to the memory of those young men.

# The Deep Blue Sea

## INA BOUMAN

"*. . . Imagine yourself in a dream world, a world free of worries, a world of adventure and romance, while sailing along the most enchanting coastlines in the world. . . .*" She had never known Herbert to be so lyrical, except maybe the first time he explored the internet. Now he stood holding the *Cruise Travel Magazine* like a libretto in his outstretched arms and sang on: "*You will fly to Singapore where we will welcome you on board for an unforgettable cruise to the Pearls of the Orient: Songkla, exotic Ko Samui . . .*"

"Pardon?"

"They're ports in Thailand. *And from exotic Ko Samui you sail via Laem Chebang to Bangkok and from there fly back to Amsterdam.* Twelve days altogether."

"Not my sort of thing."

"But you're getting this on a plate! Free! Look at this ship! And you can't possibly get bored . . . it says here . . . there's a cinema, a sauna, a swimming pool!"

"A swimming pool at sea?"

"Yes. You don't even have to see the sea if you don't want to."

"I will want to if I'm on a boat."

"You can! And you can relax on a sunbed, or . . . *take an evening stroll on deck or dance in the moonlight. . . .* It says so right here, look."

She turned her head away but he thrust the brochure in her face. She squinted at a full color photograph of an anorexic looking pair of teenagers frozen in a dance movement on the deck of a white streamlined vessel floating on an azure blue sea.

"That's not a ship, that's an iron." He had difficulty controlling his impatience with her.

Melanie wondered why he was making such a fuss.

"Why don't *you* go," she suggested.

"The ticket is strictly personal and non-transferable. Besides, I can't go because of my work."

"That's a flimsy excuse." Melanie went into the kitchen to finish the fish stew. It was an exceptionally laborious recipe, coincidentally of Oriental origin. Herbert followed her.

"You're always moaning about never getting away. Now's your chance . . . go!" She felt his hot breath on the back of her neck.

"And what about your food, if I go away?"

"Surely you could just stick twelve days' worth in the freezer?"


TWO WEEKS LATER Herbert drove her to the airport—destination Singapore. Not that she longed for a cruise, but Herbert had continued to press the matter and the idea of being without him appealed to her. According to Herbert, a chance like that shouldn't be ignored and she had to agree that the prize had fallen into her lap out of nowhere. She never entered competitions, never sent in vouchers or slogans. The only thing she did do was enter her bank account number automatically in a monthly lottery. She had never won a penny, which was why she dared not stop, lest her number should then come up immediately. It was pure chance that Herbert had discovered her win in that extra draw. He obtained all the information and had been amazingly helpful. But it all checked out, the ticket was indeed in her name and all paid for. Strange that it should be a trip for one, usually these things were for two she thought, but it was clear that Herbert was keen for her to go alone. She suspected an ulterior motive, normally he never let her go off on her own. He kept his eye on her at all times. This was easy enough as he ran his so-called business from home. His days were spent surfing on the internet but if she was out longer than an hour he would come after her. He always managed to find her. Terrible scenes. Sometimes he locked her up, treated her like a dog. Of course she had dreamt of escape, but it would mean always looking over her shoulder, Herbert had a large network of so-called colleagues and he would never let the matter rest. The last few years she had been too exhausted to offer any resistance. So she stayed at home and started to invent recipes. Not that she enjoyed cooking, but it stimulated her senses, giving her the feeling of being alive in her isolation. She cooked, he guzzled. When she didn't cook, he didn't eat and became aggressive. The rest of the time he took care of his shady business on the electronic superhighway. Recently he had bought a new toy, a scanner, and insisted on showing it to her, as if she would be interested in some gadget used to transmit visuals on the internet. His demonstration was done with a photograph of her. Don't do that, she had protested. Chuckling, he had torn up the picture.

THE STEWARDESS CAME by with a trolley filled with lunches. Melanie declined and requested a bottle of champagne and some crackers. She didn't like eating. The plane was half empty so she stretched her legs and took up another seat, relaxing a little. On second thought, this trip suited her just fine.

The airplane seemed to hang motionless in the pale blue sky, occasionally a white swirl of cloud passed by. She decided to take a look at the cruise brochure. Her ship was a British vessel called *The Deep Blue Sea*, with a Greek crew and a Swedish captain. It was relatively small, she read, which meant *a very personal service*. There was room for seventy passengers and thirty crew. The brochure promised that she would be *looked after and pampered from the moment of embarkation. Your personal steward is at your disposal to ensure your relaxed enjoyment of the luxurious, tastefully furnished cabin. Dining takes place in the intimate restaurant, where the most refined dishes will be carefully prepared and served.* She'd be surprised if they were more refined than the ten dishes she had left Herbert. They sat in the freezer, neatly packed and clearly labeled: Friday, Saturday, Sunday, and so on.

The plane lurched and the FASTEN SEATBELTS sign came on. Nervously she glanced at the stewardess, who gave her a relaxed smile. She's been trained to do that, thought Melanie; to stay cheerful under all circumstances, even whilst crashing to the ground. The plane regained its stability and the stewardess offered her another drink.

"Whiskey please."

At the baggage claim the bags moved slowly past her. The man beside her took his suitcase clumsily from the moving belt and knocked into her.

"Do excuse me," he said, "may I help you with your luggage?" Melanie turned towards him. He was good-looking—tall, dark, and slim—*just the sort of thing to be looking for*, she chuckled to herself.

"Perhaps we could share a taxi," he continued, "we have the same destination."

"How do you know?"

"*The Deep Blue Sea*. I saw you reading the brochure on the plane."

*I see. The personal service seems to start here*, thought Melanie, slightly irritated. But after a moment's hesitation she agreed to his suggestion. It was the easy option.

He introduced himself as Louis Dankert from Flanders, but didn't stop there, proving himself to be quite a talker. He was in ladies' underwear he joked, that is, a salesman thereof. This was also to be his first cruise, which he felt was the ideal holiday for a single man. Which he was since his divorce. Was she also divorced?

Melanie resolved to avoid the man and his conversation once they were on board.


THE SHIP LOOKED the way a ship ought to look. No aerodynamic streamline and a friendly size. A gangplank with thick ropes along both sides. A handsome steward welcomed her on board. He checked her ticket and took her bag from Louis.

"I'm Dimitri, your personal steward and therefore a happy man." She acknowledged the cliché that rolled off his tongue with such ease. His teeth shone.

"May I show you to your cabin?" She waved to Louis, luckily he was being pampered by another steward, before following Dimitri.

A narrow corridor with a brass rail and threadbare red velvet carpet led them to the door of her cabin, which he flung open in a dramatic gesture.

It didn't look luxurious; rather faded, shabby even. But it had a good bed, a small writing desk, a comfortable leather armchair and a porthole through which she could see the sea. The small en suite bathroom had beautiful old taps.

She thanked Dimitri and sent him on his way, having assured him that she was capable of finding the lounge by herself. The passengers were to gather there for a cocktail before dinner.

She took her time unpacking. She left the crumpled, dated evening dress, which Herbert had insisted she pack for The Captain's Dinner, in her suitcase.

The walnut-paneled lounge was decorated with brass furnishings and a bar leaning towards Art Deco. The room was humming with conversation. As she accepted a cocktail, Melanie was surprised to note there were mainly women. Most were about her age, she estimated, the middle-aged type who look after themselves. An uninspired pianist played a medley of English waltzes on a grand piano. Her eyes met those of a red-faced man who smiled at her in a friendly fashion from under a brown tweed cap. Shyly she turned away to face the buffet table where a spread of delicious canapés was laid out. They made her feel hungry and she reached for a delicate fish appetizer. A tall, slim, sportily dressed woman stood beside her unable to make a choice.

"You could try one of these," said Melanie, "they really aren't that bad."

"No, I'm looking for something more solid, my stomach's turning already and we haven't left the dock yet." She bit into a Thai spring roll and spoke with her mouth full.

"I'm Ann Vandyk from Melbourne."

Melanie introduced herself and made conversation. "Is this your first cruise?"

"Yes, and last." Ann picked up another spring roll. "Turn your back for one second and you find yourself on a boat."

"Really?"

"It's a birthday present from my husband. Every year for twelve years he's managed to forget my birthday until this time. Three weeks ago he remembered all about it."

"He must have had a good reason," smiled Melanie.

"Yes, a young blond reason. But enough of that, how did you get here?"

Melanie's reply was cut short by the entrance of the captain, a slim but well-built man with wavy fair hair and an immaculate uniform. He stood with his cap under his arm, eyes guarded but mouth smiling underneath an impeccably groomed mustache, so impeccable that Melanie wondered if it were real. She disliked him on sight. Was a man like that capable of commanding a ship, she thought unreasonably. He resembled Herbert in his younger days, that was it.

After a short speech, which was as pretentious as his mustache, he wished everyone a pleasant cruise and an unforgettable time.

"I'll decide that for myself," growled Ann who was still standing beside Melanie. On her other side Louis Dankert was applauding.

"Charming man," he said with an approving nod, "don't you think?"

"No," Melanie replied. Louis seemed offended. Ann laughed.

Melanie had returned to her cabin, nervous of all those hungry people around her. She asked Dimitri to bring something light to her cabin. The other passengers had all moved on to the *romantic dining experience*. There were only a few she didn't dislike on sight. She thought of the grey eyes belonging to the man in the tweed cap who later introduced himself as Dick Forster, a Welshman. He was travelling alone, as was Lizzy Melay, a peroxide-blond Californian in a loud flowery trouser suit who latched on to Louis Dankert. Melanie heard her say something about being a "consultant." Louis had transferred some of his attention from her to Lizzy, which suited Melanie just fine.

She thought of Herbert, who by now must have taken his second meal from the freezer. She wondered why he was so keen to see her go. *Was he messing around again?* She thought she'd seen the end of all that when he'd set up business at home and started getting his kicks on the internet from his virtual-reality porn club. She barely touched the tray Dimitri brought her.

The first few days flew by. Melanie spent a lot of time in her cabin, having realized how very tired she was. Dimitri had started to get on her nerves with his bowing and scraping, and on the second day she instructed him to stop his sycophantic behavior. Offended at first, he had behaved like a normal human being since. This evening she had again had dinner in her cabin, preferring to avoid company. Last night she'd visited the bar late in the evening for the first time and had a few drinks with Ann, Lizzy, and Dick, whom she was starting to feel comfortable with. Also present were Carol, a young Englishwoman who taught Greek and looked like a goddess herself in every one of her trendy swimsuits, and Kevin, a huge ginger-haired Scot who always wore some kind of hunting outfit. Kevin ran a driving school and made a point of announcing that he was a widower. And then there was Louis, of course, who seemed to pop up no matter where she was. It no longer bothered her, but it did seem to irritate Lizzy, who tried to gain his attention with ever more fantastic stories and a series of garish outfits and jewelry.

Kevin and Carol seemed quite taken with each other and Ann, Dick, and Melanie had retired to a corner of the lounge. The pianist provided a soporific Cole Porter medley. It was as though he sensed Melanie's contempt for his performance: every time she looked in his direction he was looking straight back at her.

Dick had talked about his work. He bred horses. Not something Melanie was especially interested in, but his voice was pleasant and his eyes stayed friendly. Ann was editor of a magazine she didn't name. Melanie declared herself to be a housewife.

"Married?"

"Uh."

"You're hesitating," said Dick.

"Well, let's just say we've grown apart."

They laughed and strolled onto the deck to enjoy the tropical night. Melanie had to agree that it was indeed beautiful.

The amorous couple who introduced themselves on the first day as Jane-and-Jeffrey-from-London, stood as one silhouette in the moonlight, exactly as they were supposed to. Despite this, Melanie was moved by the sight of them. But for the fact that they were too old, they would have fitted Herbert's brochure perfectly.

"Married, but not to each other," Ann chuckled, "I'm not supposed to tell anyone."

A KNOCK ON her door and Dimitri came in to clear away her dining tray.

"Madam had a little more appetite than on previous days."

"You keep track do you?" she retorted, a little sharper than she meant to. He looked hurt and left in silence.

She felt as though she was being watched. *Was this just personal service?* Whatever it was, he was right, she hadn't felt so good in years. It must be the sea air and being away from Herbert's suffocating presence. It was as if a heavy load dropped from her shoulders and she rediscovered her body. For the first time in ages she felt the need to treat it with a little care and attention.

She decided to take a walk on deck before turning in. In the bar she accepted a malt whiskey from Louis, who had been there quite some time with Lizzy, Dick, Ann, and the clandestine married couple. This time the pianist murdered a gypsy melody. She downed her drink, refused Dick's offer of a second and Ann's offer of a cigarette and left the lounge via the disco to reach part of the deck in the stern which was reserved for first class passengers.

It was deadly quiet. She breathed deeply and gazed up into the endless blackness that seemed to deepen the longer she looked at it. More and more stars appeared. She heard the dash of the waves and felt suddenly weightless. Was this happiness? A feeling so close to a shudder of fear. Her body shook as if awakening from a terrible nightmare. What was happening? She turned and looked around. Nobody in sight. Herbert, she thought. Of course. It was the fear of Herbert which pursued her. And her conscience. She tried to regulate her breathing and calm down. She had to face reality; after fifteen years, at the precise moment that she tasted something akin to a feeling of freedom, something approaching happiness, fear had struck. At once she felt doubt again; *had she made the right decision? Was there really no other way?* This was the fifth day, she could still do something. She took a few steps away from the rail to light a cigarette and saw a movement out of the corner of her eye. She froze. There was no sign of anyone. Herbert. He was inside her, clamping onto her, strangling her. She raised her hand to her throat, ran to the rail and vomited over the side until she had stomach cramps. Beneath her the reassuring murmur of the sea beckoned. If she were to just let herself fall, everything would be over. The ocean would gather her up and rock her, devour her lovingly. . . . She felt hands on her shoulders. She wrenched herself loose and turned to stare straight into Dick's startled face.

"What are you doing? What's the matter?"

"Were you over there on deck just now?" she pointed.

"No, I've come straight from the lounge. Why? What's going on?"

"Nothing."

He took her hand. "Come on, you're upset, come back to the bar. It's quiet there just now. That dreadful pianist has gone."

Ann offered her a malt whiskey but Melanie said she'd been sick and asked for a glass of water instead.

"Seasick," said Dick.

Lizzy giggled. "I thought you had a date with Louis, he left just after you did. Ann even followed to try to catch the two of you."

"Don't pay any attention to her," muttered Ann.

* * *

TWO DAYS LATER, the ship docked in the port of *exotic Ko Samui*. They were to moor there for eight hours. The previous evening, Melanie had finally promised to join the others in going ashore. It seemed a pleasant diversion. She had recovered quickly from her depression or whatever it had been. But she still felt somehow unsafe. Was it just her conscience or was something really happening? Had that threatening presence on deck been real or had she imagined it? And that moment at the rail, when she'd almost fallen. Dick's hands on her shoulders. . . .

However, the anxiety was largely disappearing and she realized she was really starting to enjoy the cruise.

About twenty passengers went ashore as well as a few crew, amongst whom were the pianist and the sheepish magician who sometimes performed his tricks during dinner despite being ignored by everyone present. They landed in the middle of a festive and colorful turmoil of people and decorated stalls and tents filled with clothing, food, and spices. Ko Samui at festival time. Melanie decided to dispense with the company of her fellow passengers. This was her first visit to the Far East and she relished it all the more having just rediscovered her capacity for enjoyment. She wandered through the crowded noisy market, and marvelled at the sheer numbers of coconuts, drank coconut milk, and sniffed the exotic mix of herbs and spices. At a stall where the customers were jostling each other for space she decided to stop and buy some. But she hesitated, the crowds were becoming oppressive. Irritated by a tall woman who wore a green scarf as a veil over her face, she moved her arms to create some space for herself. It was not the first time the woman had got in her way. Melanie joined the throng at the stall to get a better look at what was on offer. Someone pushed her from behind. She moved her shoulder to make room. At that moment she felt an icy pain in her back. She tottered, more surprised than shaken, leaning into the crowd. It wasn't until she groaned and sank to her knees that hands appeared to support her.

THE FIRST THING she saw was Louis's face.

"The doctor's on his way," he said. She turned her face away, realizing she was lying in the street in the middle of a crowd. She tried to recall what happened, as sirens approached and she recognized Dick who knelt beside her and laid a hand on her forehead.

"Who the hell did this? What happened?"

"It was over by that spice stall," said Louis. "I heard the commotion and saw a woman in a green scarf running off into the crowd."

Two men in white coats lifted her onto a stretcher, she felt an injection needle pierce her skin.

AT THE HOSPITAL she was told she was out of danger and discharged. She was free to return to the ship and the care of the ship's doctor. It was a miracle that she hadn't been killed, the weapon was a locally made knife, long and sharp. She had probably survived the stabbing thanks to the crowd, which had hampered the attacker's aim, although it had made escape easier.

Melanie decided not to report the incident as it would mean staying in Ko Samui and that was the last thing she wanted to do. She concluded there was a loony on the loose and she was better off returning to the ship.

SHE RECOVERED QUICKLY and tried to contact Herbert by phone. It rang but there was no reply, *thank god*. That way, she wouldn't have to speak to him. It was the ninth day. She felt nothing, as if the knife had cut out her heart, instead of piercing her back. The woman in the green scarf kept appearing in her mind and she told Dick about her in the bar that evening.

"She was tall you see, stuck out above everyone else, and that green scarf . . ."

"But if you're going to kill someone you want to be inconspicuous."

"It's easy to remove a scarf."

Dick nodded thoughtfully. "Do you think she was following you?"

"No idea."

"I bet she was." Louis had joined them. He was convinced the woman in the sari was the attacker. "I saw her at the stall when it happened, maybe she mistook you for someone else."

"I doubt that," said Dick, "but what were you doing there?"

"I was wondering the same about you. You were there less than a minute after me," Louis replied, irritated. "We were all at the market. I saw Ann and Kevin go to find a policeman, I even saw Jane and Jeffrey pushing their way through the crowd, trying to see what was going on."

"Okay," soothed Dick, "I'm not accusing anyone."

Once Louis left and Melanie was alone with Dick he warned her to take care and not have visitors in her cabin.

"What rubbish, besides I don't anyway, apart from Dimitri."

"I've checked him out," answered Dick, his face grave, "he was on board when it happened."

"Stop worrying," she replied airily.

"Have you forgotten that night on deck?"

How could she tell him about this fear which came from inside her? How could she tell him about Herbert? She put his mind at rest.

"I'll do as you say."

THE CAPTAIN'S DINNER took place that evening. Melanie decided to respect Herbert's wishes for the last time. She would wear the evening dress and take her place at the table in full regalia.

In the mirror she saw how the evening gown hung around her skinny body like a faded tea towel. No wonder. The last time she had worn it was over ten years ago. At that time Herbert had been messing about with shares. She ran her hand over the material, a once fine silk that had lost its shine and texture. Taking it off she put on her bathrobe and rang for Dimitri who materialized almost immediately. He must have been hovering. She handed him the dress for pressing.

"This gown is not dirty," she snapped when she saw him take it rather gingerly, "just neglected."

He nodded earnestly, "Are you feeling better, Madam?"

"Yes, thank you."

"Did you manage to contact your husband?"

"I think he must be away for a few days, on business," she improvised. "I'll see him when I get back."

She decided to lie down for a while and fell asleep. A knock on her door made her jump and she stood up, expecting Dimitri with her evening dress. But instead, it was Ann.

They looked at each other for a moment, suddenly shy. Ann had changed since the incident on deck. Her mocking attitude had disappeared, but with it the growing familiarity between them. She stayed in the doorway.

"Are you going to the dinner?"

"Only because I have an ancient evening dress with me . . . "

A trace of cynicism appeared in Ann's eyes for a moment. "Shall we have a drink beforehand, just the two of us?"

"Okay." Melanie hoped Ann had not noticed her hesitation. They agreed to meet in Ann's cabin.

Melanie returned to her bed and absentmindedly rubbed her back near the itching wound, while going over the conversation and the strange tension she now felt. *Didn't she trust Ann?* Surely, when it came to having enemies, the worst was she herself.

Today, taking the time difference into consideration, Herbert must have eaten the last meal. What did she feel? Nothing really.

SHE FELL INTO a deep dreamless sleep and awoke to shouting and the roar of engines.

Quickly she dressed in slacks and a sweater, ran into the corridor and through to the boat deck where passengers and crew stood about nervously. She heard cries of: "Man overboard!"

"What?"

"Where?"

"He jumped overboard!"

"Who?"

"He fell."

"Forster, it was Forster!"

*He fell?* Melanie's heart thudded in her head. How could anyone fall overboard when there was such a high guard-rail? The ship was stationary now, the captain still shouting commands into a radio. The crew was throwing lifebuoys into the sea and lowering rescue boats into the water.

Ann took her arm. "I was speaking to him just half an hour ago. He was terribly upset, said he'd discovered something."

"That's no reason to jump overboard, is it?"

"No, surely not, I'd have thought the opposite."

"What had he discovered?"

"He didn't say, he wanted to speak to the captain."

They walked to the rail. The sea was flat and calm, but there was no sign of Dick Forster. The lifeboats circled the ship, while the crew stood at the rail ready with ropes and lifebuoys.

"Did anyone see him jump?" shouted the captain.

A passenger raised his hand. "I didn't see him jump but I saw him fall. I was in my cabin and I raised the alarm immediately."

"Has anyone seen or spoken to him in the last hour?"

Ann stepped forward. "He said he wanted to speak to you. He seemed anxious."

A sailor called from one of the lifeboats, he held up a brown tweed cap, "Does anyone recognize this?"

Ann gasped and raised her hands to her face. "He was wearing it. It's Dick Forster's!"

"Well, it doesn't look too good," said the captain grimly.

"Do you think he drowned?" Louis had appeared.

"Do we go on with the search?" cried the sailor.

"Yes, of course." The captain continued to give orders, and apologized for the delay to bewildered passengers.

"He wasn't the type to commit suicide," announced Lizzy loudly, wanting an audience.

"I know all about that. I've done all kinds of therapy and I can take one look at someone and know . . ."

Melanie fled the sound of Lizzy's voice, followed by Ann, Louis, Carol, and Kevin.

"It must have been an accident," Louis concluded. "He fell overboard and drowned, very tragic indeed."

"But he was a strong swimmer," Carol said, "I saw him in the pool."

Melanie shivered. In her mind she saw Dick's friendly grey eyes, and the worry in them. *What had he discovered? Why had he warned her, and who against?*

The search lasted for hours. Spotlights were used after dark. Most of the passengers stayed on deck. The Captain's Dinner turned into a dismal buffet attended by few and to make matters worse, the pianist attempted a version of "Moonlight Sonata" in the lounge. Nobody listened. The captain had called out the Coast Guard and was attempting a reconstruction of the events. Nobody had seen Dick Forster on deck after his conversation with Ann. Had anyone seen them together? Nobody had.

* * *

THEY SAT IN the dining room amongst other passengers' dinner debris, watching the tables being cleared. This was infinitely preferable to being in the lounge where the terrible tinkling on the piano could still be heard. Eventually peace returned as the pianist took a break. There was a feeling of dejection and suspicion in the air.

"Maybe he discovered something which drove him to despair. That's possible isn't it?" suggested Kevin.

"Didn't I tell you . . ." Lizzy began.

Ann interrupted her. "Shut up for a minute. The last few days Dick was *angry* not depressed. And you don't commit suicide out of anger."

"You might out of revenge," said Kevin.

"I think we'd better face it," said Carol, "if what Ann says is true, then Dick had discovered something he wanted to report to the captain. Someone must have stopped him."

Ann nodded. "Could be the same someone who attacked Melanie."

Melanie jumped. Everyone's eyes were on her. Was she really connected to Forster's death?

Eventually Carol opened her mouth. "Do you have any enemies?"

"Maybe Forster was the enemy," Kevin said thoughtfully. "Melanie, do you remember that night on deck in the stern? He was with you. I never did understand exactly what happened."

"We thought you and Dick had a thing for each other," said Jane and Jeffrey. "He always looked at you so sweetly."

Louis screwed up his eyes. "Were you two together again this evening, when Dick fell overboard?"

Melanie was silent. She saw Dick's face in her memory of that moment four or five days ago, when she had hung over the rail, had nearly let herself be swallowed by the waves. She felt dizzy.

Ann stood up. "That's enough. Come on, let's get some fresh air on deck."

"I'll come with you," said Kevin.

On deck it was still busy. Dimitri made a beeline for Melanie. Apparently the captain wanted to see her.

His mustache was out of shape and his behavior more humane. He apologized for having to ask her a few questions. She could tell him nothing new. It was getting light when she finally decided to go to bed even though she felt it was giving up on Dick. She still heard the occasional Coast Guard helicopter flapping overhead but on board ship all hope seemed to have been given up.

Ann and Kevin had stayed by her side all night, like two soldiers who did not quite trust each other. Now she'd had enough, she wanted to be alone. They accompanied her to her cabin telling her over and over to lock the door and let nobody in.

DOZING, SHE WAS besieged by merging images of Dick and Herbert. She awoke several times in a cold sweat, crying Herbert's name, panicky, wondering whether she could still warn him. Maybe there was still time to phone or send a message, maybe he'd missed a meal. She'd calculated the precise dose. He could still do something about it if he did so straight away. . . .

Again she awoke with a start and sat up. She heard a noise. A soft creaking. It was coming from inside the cabin! The door. In the semi-darkness she spotted it. The shiny brass knob was turning very slowly. Her heart pounded, pain shot through her back, but she sat motionless as she heard the click of the lock opening. This must just be one of her nightmares. She closed her eyes in disbelief and opened them again. There was a figure standing in the doorway.

Melanie leaned back against the wall without a sound coming from her constricted throat. She tried to scream but only succeeded in emitting a series of choked yelps. The figure closed the door. It was the woman. The green scarf was still over her head. One of her hands reached under the material of her sari.

At that moment Melanie felt a jolt of adrenaline as it raced through her veins and drove away her fear. She stayed where she was like a predator who waits for the perfect moment . . . then after a feigned movement in one direction she leaped in the other and pushed her way past her attacker into the corridor. She must have screamed because here and there cabin doors were opening. She kept on running until she found Kevin in the bar. He was still dressed in his hunting gear. Breathlessly she told him what had happened.

"What?"

"That woman from the market," she panted, "she's in my cabin!"

Kevin swore. "Stay here!" But she followed him back to her cabin. No one was there. A green scarf lay on the bed along with a sari and a knife.

"I only went to get coffee to stop dozing off," apologized Kevin.

"Be quiet!" Melanie heard footsteps in the corridor. Kevin pulled her arm and stood in front of her. It was Ann who appeared. Same height, was Melanie's first thought.

"Stay where you are!" Kevin commanded.

"Relax," said Ann coolly, "and I'll introduce you to that mysterious veiled woman."

Melanie took a step towards her but Kevin grabbed her arm.

"Watch out."

She yanked her arm free and felt a tremendous relief which she didn't quite understand.

Ann looked a mess, but her eyes shone. Her hair was sticking out all over the place and her blouse was torn.

"Did you have a fight?"

"Hardly," Ann smiled.

"What the hell are you two waiting for, just standing there gawking at one another," cried Kevin. "Where is that woman?"

For a fraction of a second Melanie wondered what on earth he was talking about.

"Come on," said Ann.

Ann, like Kevin, hadn't been to bed because she wanted to keep an eye on Melanie's cabin but now and then she had been distracted by helicopters flying over and the activity on deck. The woman must have seized such an opportunity because suddenly Ann saw Melanie race out of her cabin in Kevin's direction, followed almost immediately by someone fleeing in the opposite direction straight into Ann's open arms.

"I didn't realize I was that strong," Ann grinned with satisfaction.

Kevin shrugged his shoulders. "Well, a woman . . ."

Ann giggled. The cabin door in front of them bore a nameplate which didn't ring any bells with Melanie. Ann unlocked the door and let them in. Although facing the other way, the figure tied to the chair with belts and scarves was instantly recognizable. A nauseating musical medley filled Melanie's head.

"I don't understand," Kevin stammered.

Melanie gazed at Ann in wonder.

Ann blushed. "You thought it was me. . . ."

Melanie nodded. "For a tiny fraction of a second."

She stared at the silent apathetic man trying to make some sense out of the events of the past few days.

Ann searched her face. "Do you know him?"

"Only as the ship's pianist."

"Any idea why he'd want to get at you?"

"Maybe." Melanie attempted to order her thoughts as she watched him try to wriggle free.

"But I've done nothing!" His voice was as sickly as his music.

"Madam! Your cabin door was open!" A bewildered Dimitri rushed in, his eyes widening further on seeing the pianist tied up. "What on earth is going on?"

"Get the captain," ordered Kevin.

"Wait a second," said Melanie. "What do you know about this man? Did you notice anything particular about him?"

"He was always wandering around the ship, I didn't really trust him."

"Did you know him from previous trips?"

"No madam, we had the same pianist for years, a lady who played beautifully, many passengers used to come especially to hear her play. This man is new, nobody listens, he plays the same things over and over very badly."

THE CAPTAIN who had just retired to his cabin following the commotion of Dick Forster's disappearance was less than happy with the unmasking of the pianist.

"We have to be sure of our case, these incidents are bad for our company's image," he said after two burly crew members had carried off the pianist to lock him up.

"But this was a second attempted murder," snapped Ann, "and have you questioned him about Dick Forster's so-called accident?"

"I don't see a connection between the two incidents. Besides, he was working when Mr. Forster fell overboard."

Ann shook her head. "No, he'd stopped playing. I remember it was such a relief."

"It still doesn't mean anything."

"And I remember something else," continued Ann, "he had also just stopped playing when Dick pulled Melanie from the rail on deck that night."

"And he was there when we went ashore," added Kevin. "He bought a bag at the market in Ko Samui and there was definitely something in it. Jane and Jeffrey asked him if he'd bought anything interesting, he didn't reply, just seemed startled."

The captain turned to Melanie. "Do you think this is the man who attacked you in Ko Samui?"

"The disguise was the same and his height. Yes, I think so."

"Do you have any idea of his motive?"

*Oh yes*, she thought, but kept her mouth shut and shrugged her shoulders.

"How did you come to hire him?" Ann inquired.

"He had good references, someone in company personnel recommended him. I think he was hired via the internet. However," the captain twisted his mustache, "I must say that I'm not very pleased with his performance."

"A musician from the internet?" Kevin looked incredulous.

"Why not?" said Ann, "You can get anything on the internet. Even murderers."

At the captain's request they went to the crew common room below deck to question the pianist. His story was simplicity itself. He didn't do very well as a musician, they were always firing him, he complained. He'd started surfing on the internet and hit on the idea of advertising himself there. Sometimes he was offered a temporary musician's position, sometimes he found other kinds of jobs.

"Such as?" demanded the captain.

The pianist hesitated. "Courier services for example . . . videos and such like."

When someone he'd couriered for in the past asked him to keep watch on a woman who had destroyed his life and later to push her overboard, he had hesitated but he believed he was doing the guy a good turn and there was a lot of money involved. Besides it was a simple job. "I'll get you hired on the ship, just watch her. She likes to be alone and one night you can just tip her over the side. Nothing to it," said the guy's e-mail.

"What guy?" said the captain impatiently.

The pianist shrugged his shoulders. "That you'll never know."

"Go on."

"Okay, the first time it didn't work out." He spoke as if he were discussing a missed dinner date, thought Melanie. Without emotion, rather resentful. So anyway, he continued, he had to try it again because he'd spent the advance and he wanted the rest of the money. He thought he might get an opportunity ashore but the woman never left the ship. Until at last in Ko Samui. He had planned a disguise but had failed again.

"This is unbelievable," said Ann. "I think he wants us to feel sorry for him."

"Bastard," snarled Kevin.

Suddenly Melanie felt everyone's eyes on her. She shut them out and looked at the pianist. "And what about Mr. Forster? Why him?"

The captain still twisted his mustache. "I ask the questions."

He turned to the purser. "Take notes will you."

The pianist went on with the story. "He was in my cabin. He had opened my bags . . ."

"And found the disguise no doubt," said Ann.

"He was rummaging through my papers. I was just trying to get the print out back from him."

"And he threatened to expose you to the captain," suggested Ann.

"What print out?" demanded the captain. The pianist was silent.

The purser handed the captain a sheet of paper. "We just found this in his cabin, sir."

Ann stood up and looked over his shoulder. "It's a computer scan of a photograph."

MOST PASSENGERS had gone to sleep after the evening's commotion and were unaware of the latest attack on Melanie. A few had woken up, among them Lizzy and Louis. Melanie wondered if they had shared a bed. Perhaps a romance had blossomed on board after all. And then there were those—herself, Kevin, and Ann amongst them—who had been up all night. In the lounge, attentive waiters served tea and coffee while everyone mourned Dick Forster and speculated about the rumored crime.

The captain was due to make an announcement in an hour.

"Shall we sit in my cabin," suggested Ann. "It's quiet there."

Melanie put her hand on Ann's arm for a moment.

"Thank you, but I'd like to be alone for a while."

It was quiet on the stern deck. Melanie looked out to sea. The water was smooth. Dick was there, somewhere deep and far away. He had wanted to protect her. Tears ran down her cheeks. She wiped them with her silk headscarf which she then held up high in the air and let go. She watched it leave the ship and flap through the air, eventually entering the water a few hundred meters behind them.

"Madam . . . a message for you, madam." She turned around. Dimitri held a telex in his hand. He hesitated, "I must warn you . . ."

"What's the matter?"

"It's about your husband."

She took the sheet of paper and read without emotion.

*. . . cause of death unknown/full inquiry/presence requested . . .*

"I'm sorry, madam. It must be a terrible blow, especially now when you need support."

"Yes."

"Is there anything I can do, madam?"

"Thank you, Dimitri. You're right, it's quite a blow. Please don't speak of this, I'd rather keep it to myself."

"As you wish, madam." He left her.

Herbert. He must have planned it down to the last detail. The cruise, the so-called lottery win. He'd been inventive, but he hadn't quite managed to bring his project to a successful conclusion. She'd always been better than him. In everything. He'd tried to keep her small, to humiliate her, even to eliminate her. She no longer felt hatred, but no remorse either as she gazed at the horizon and saw the dawn glimmer. She breathed deeply, inhaling the smells of the sea. The water was an enchanting deep blue with shining waves and white foam alongside the hull of the ship, which cruised at full speed towards Bangkok.

# Rumpole at Sea

## JOHN MORTIMER

**M**r. Justice Graves. What a contradiction in terms! Mr. "Injustice" Graves, Mr. "Penal" Graves, Mr. "Prejudice" Graves, Mr. "Get into Bed with the Prosecution" Graves—all these titles might be appropriate. But Mr. "Justice" Graves, so far as I'm concerned, can produce nothing but a hollow laugh. From all this you may deduct that the old darling is not my favourite member of the Judiciary. Now he has been promoted, on some sort of puckish whim of the Lord Cancellor's, from Old Bailey judge to a scarlet and ermine justice of the Queen's Bench, his power to do harm has been considerably increased. Those who have followed my legal career will remember the awesome spectacle of the mad Judge Bullingham, with lowered head and bloodshot eyes, charging into the ring in the hope of impaling Rumpole upon a horn. But now we have lost him, I actually miss the old Bull. There was a sort of excitement in the corridas we lived through together and I often emerged with a couple of ears and a tail. A session before Judge Graves has all the excitement and colour of a Wesleyan funeral on a wet day in Wigan. His pale Lordship presides sitting bolt upright as though he had a poker up his backside, his voice is dirge-like and his eyes closed in pain as he is treated with anything less than an obsequious grovel.

This story, which ends with mysterious happenings on the high seas, began in the old Gravestones' Chambers in the Law Courts, where I was making an application one Monday morning.

"Mr. Rumpole"—his Lordship looked pained when I had outlined my request—"do I understand that you are applying to me for bail?" "Yes, my Lord." I don't know if he thought I'd just dropped in for a cosy chat.

"Bail having been refused," he went on in sepulchral tones, "in the Magistrates Court and by my brother judge, Mr. Justice Entwhistle. Is this a frivolous application?"

"Only if it's frivolous to keep the innocent at liberty, my Lord." I liked the phrase myself, but the Judge reminded me that he was not a jury (worse luck, I thought) and that emotional appeals would carry very little weight with him. He then looked down at his papers and said, "When you use the work 'innocent,' I assume you are referring to your client?"

"I am referring to all of us, my Lord." I couldn't resist a speech. "We are all innocent until found guilty by a jury of our peers. Or has that golden thread of British justice become a little tarnished of late?"

"Mr. Rumpole"—the Judge was clearly unmoved—"I see your client's name is Timson."

"So it is, my Lord. But I should use precisely the same argument were it Horace Rumpole. Or even Mr. Justice Graves." At which his Lordship protested, "Mr. Rumpole, this is intolerable!"

"Absolutely intolerable, my Lord," I agreed. "Conditions for prisoners on remand are far worse now than they were a hundred years ago."

"I mean, Mr. Rumpole," the Graveyard explained, with a superhuman effort at patience, as though to a half-wit, "it's intolerable that you should address me in such a manner. I cannot imagine any circumstances in which I should need your so-called eloquence to be exercised on my behalf." You never know, I thought, you never know, old darling. But the mournful voice of judicial authority carried on. "No doubt the Prosecution opposes bail. Do you oppose bail, Mr. Harvey Wimple?"

Thus addressed, the eager, sandy-haired youth from the Crown Prosecution Service, who spoke very fast, as though he wanted to get the whole painful ordeal over as quickly as possible, jabbered, "Oppose it? Oh, yes, my Lord. Absolutely. Utterly and entirely opposed. Utterly." He looked startled when the Judge asked, "On what precise grounds do you oppose bail, Mr. Wimple?" But he managed the quick-fire answer, "Grounds that, if left at liberty, another offence might be committed. Or other offences. By the defendant Timson, my Lord. By him, you see?"

"Do you hear that, Mr. Rumpole?" The Judge re-orchestrated the piece for more solemn music. "If he is set at liberty, your client might commit another offence or, quite possibly, offences."

And then, losing my patience, I said what I had been longing to say on some similar bail application for years. "Of course, he might," I began. "Every man, woman and child in England might commit an offence. Is your Lordship suggesting we keep them all permanently banged up on the off-chance? It's just not on, that's all."

"Mr. Rumpole. What is not 'on,' as you so curiously put it?" The Judge spoke with controlled fury. It was a good speech, but I had picked the wrong audience. "Banging up the innocent, my Lord." I let him have the full might of the Rumpole eloquent outrage. "With a couple of psychopaths and their own chamber-pots. For an indefinite period while the wheels of justice grind to a halt in a traffic jam of cases."

"Do try to control yourself, Mr. Rumpole. Conditions in prisons are a matter for the Home Office."

"Oh, my Lord, I'm so sorry. I forgot they're of no interest to judges who refuse bail and have never spent a single night locked up without the benefit of a water closet."

At which point, Graves decided to terminate the proceedings and, to no one's surprise, he announced that bail was refused and that the unfortunate Tony Timson, who had never committed a violent crime, should languish in Brixton until his trial. I was making for the fresh air and a small and soothing cigar when the Judge called me back with "Just one moment, Mr. Rumpole. I think I should add that I find the way that this matter has been argued before me quite lamentable, and very far from being in the best traditions of the Bar. I may have to report the personal and improper nature of your argument to proper authorities." At which point he smiled in a nauseating manner at the young man from the Crown Prosecution Service and said, "Thank you for *your* able assistance, Mr. Harvey Wimple."

"Had a good day, Rumpole?" She Who Must Be Obeyed asked me on my return to the mansion flat.

"Thank God, Hilda," I told her as I poured a glass of Pommeroy's Very Ordinary, "for your wonderful sense of humour!"

"Rumpole, look at your face!" She appeared to be smiling brightly at my distress.

"I prefer not to. I have no doubt it is marked with tragedy." I raised a glass and tried to drown at least a few of my sorrows.

"Whatever's happened?" She Who Must Be Obeyed was unusually sympathetic, from which I should have guessed that she had formulated some master plan. I refilled my glass and told her:

> "*I could a tale unfold*" Hilda "*whose lightest word*
> *Would harrow up thy soul, freeze thy young blood,*
> *Make thy two eyes, like stars, start from their spheres,*
> *Thy knotted and combined locks to part,*
> *And each particular hair to stand on end,*
> *Like quills upon the fretful porpentine: . . .*"

"Oh come on, I bet it wouldn't." My wife was sceptical. "What you need, Rumpole, is a change!"

"I need a change from Mr. Justice Graves." And then I played into her hands, for she looked exceptionally pleased when I added, "For two pins I'd get on a banana boat and sail away into the sunset."

"Oh, Rumpole! I'm so glad that's what you'd do. For two pins. You know what I've been thinking? We need a second honeymoon."

"The first one was bad enough." You see I was still gloomy.

"It wouldn't've been, Rumpole, if you hadn't thought we could manage two weeks in the South of France on your fees from one short robbery."

"It was all I had about me at the time," I reminded her. "Anyway, you shouldn't've ordered lobster."

"What's the point of a honeymoon," Hilda asked, "if you can't order lobster?"

"Of course, you can *order* it. Nothing to stop you ordering," I conceded. "You just shouldn't complain when we have to leave three days early and sit up all night in the train from Marseilles. With a couple of soldiers asleep on top of us."

"On our second honeymoon I shall order lobster." And then she added the fatal words, "When we're on the cruise."

"On the *what?*" I hoped that I couldn't believe my ears.

"The cruise! There's still a bit of Aunt Tedda's money left." As I have pointed out, Hilda's relations are constantly interfering in our married lives. "I've booked up for it."

"No, Hilda. Absolutely not!" I was firm as only I know how to be. "I know exactly what it'd be like. Bingo on the boat deck!"

"We need to get away, Rumpole. To look at ourselves."

"Do you honestly think that's wise?" It seemed a rash project.

"Moonlight on the Med."

She Who Must became lyrical. "The sound of music across the water. Stars. You and I by the rail. *Finding* each other, after a long time."

"But you can find me quite easily," I pointed out. "You just shout 'Rumpole!' and there I am."

"You said you'd sail away into the sunset. For two pins," she reminded me.

"A figure of speech, Hilda. A pure figure of speech! Let me make this perfectly clear. There is no power on this earth that's going to get me on a cruise."


DURING THE COURSE of a long and memorable career at the Bar, I have fought many doughty opponents and won many famous victories; but I have never, when all the evidence has been heard and the arguments are over, secured a verdict against She Who Must Be Obeyed. It's true that I have, from time to time, been able to mitigate her stricter sentences. I have argued successfully for alternatives to custody or time to pay. But I have never had an outright win against her and, from the moment she suggested we sail away, until the time when I found myself in our cabin on the fairly good ship S.S. *Boadicea,* steaming out from Southampton, I knew, with a sickening certainty, that I was on to a loser. Hilda reviewed her application for a cruise every hour of the days that we were together, and at most hours of the night, until I finally threw in the towel on the grounds that the sooner we put out to sea the sooner we should be back on dry land again.

The *Boadicea* was part of a small cruise line and, instead of flying its passengers to some southern port, it sailed from England to Gibraltar and thence to several Mediterranean destinations before returning home. The result was that some of the first days were to be spent sailing through grey and troubled waters. Picture us then in our cabin as we left harbour. I was looking out of a porthole at a small area of open deck which terminated in a rail and the sea. Hilda, tricked out in white ducks, took a yachting cap out of her hat box and tried it on in front of the mirror. "What on earth did you bring that for?" I asked her. "Are you expecting to steer the thing?"

"I expect to enter into the spirit of life on shipboard, Rumpole," she told me briskly. "And you'd be well-advised to do the same. I'm sure we'll make heaps of friends. Such nice people go on cruises. Haven't you been watching them?"

"Yes." And I turned, not very cheerfully, back to the porthole. As I did so, a terrible vision met my eyes. The stretch of deck was no longer empty. A grey-haired man in a blue blazer was standing by the rail and, as I watched, Mr. Justice Graves turned in my direction and all doubts about our fellow passengers, and all hopes for a carefree cruise, were laid to rest.

"'Angels and ministers of grace defend us!' It can't be. But it *is*!"

"What is, Rumpole? Do pull yourself together."

"If you knew what I'd seen, you wouldn't babble of pulling myself together, Hilda. It's *him*! The ghastly old Gravestone in person." At which I dragged out my suitcase and started to throw my possessions back into it. "He's come on the cruise with us!"

"Courage, Rumpole"—Hilda watched me with a certain contempt—"I remember you telling me, is the first essential in an advocate."

"Courage, yes, but not total lunacy. Not self-destruction. Life at the Bar may have its risks, but no legal duty compels me to spend two weeks shut up in a floating hotel with Mr. Justice Deathshead."

"I don't know what you think you're going to do about it." She was calmly hanging up her clothes whilst I repacked mine. "It's perfectly simple, Hilda," I told her, "I shall abandon ship!"

When I got up on the deck, there was, fortunately, no further sign of Graves, but a ship's officer, whom I later discovered to be the Purser, was standing by the rail and I approached him, doing my best to control my panic.

"I've just discovered," I told him, "I'm allergic to graves. I mean, I'm allergic to boats. It would be quite unsafe for me to travel. A dose of sea-sickness could prove fatal!"

"But, sir," the purser protested. "We're only just out of port."

"I know. So you could let me off, couldn't you? I've just had terrible news."

"You're welcome to telephone, sir."

"No, I'm afraid that wouldn't help."

"And if it's really serious we could fly you back from our next stop." And he added the terrible words, "We'll be at Gibraltar in three days."

Gibraltar in three days! Three days banged up on shipboard with the most unappetizing High Court judge since Jefferies hung up his wig! I lay on my bed in our cabin as the land slid away from us and Hilda read out the treats on offer: "'Daily sweepstake on the ship's position. Constant video entertainment and films twice nightly. Steam-bath, massage and beauty treatment. Exercise rooms and fully equipped gymnasium—I think I'll have a steam-bath, Rumpole—First fancy-dress ball immediately before landfall at Gib. Live it up in an evening of ocean fantasy. Lecture by Howard Swainton, world-famous, best-selling mystery novelist, on "How I Think Up My Plots."'"

"Could he think up one on how to drown a judge?"

"Oh, do cheer up, Rumpole. Don't be so morbid. At five thirty this evening it's Captain Orde's Welcome Aboard Folks cocktail party, followed by a dinner dance at eight forty-five. I can wear my little black dress."

"The Captain's cocktail party?" I was by no means cheered up. "To exchange small talk and Twiglets with Mr. Justice Deathshead. No, thank you very much. I shall lie doggo in the cabin until Gibraltar."

"You can't possibly do that," She told me. "What am I going to tell everyone?"

"Tell them I've gone down with a nasty infection. No, the Judge might take it into his head to visit the sick. He might want to come and gloat over me with grapes. Tell them I'm dead. Or say a last-minute case kept me in England."

"Rumpole, aren't you being just the tiniest bit silly about this?"

But I stuck desperately to my guns. "Remember, Hilda," I begged her, "if anyone asks, say you're here entirely on your own." I had not forgotten that Graves and She had met at the Sam Ballard-Marguerite Plumstead wedding, and if the Judge caught sight of her, he might suspect that where Hilda was could Rumpole be far behind? I was prepared to take every precaution against discovery.

\* \* \*

DURING MANY of the ensuing events I was, as I have said, lying doggo. I therefore have to rely on Mrs. Rumpole's account of many of the matters that transpired on board the good ship *Boadicea,* and I have reconstructed the following pages from her evidence which was, as always, completely reliable. (I wish, sometimes, that She Who Must Be Obeyed would indulge in something as friendly as a lie. As, for instance, "I do think you're marvellous, Rumpole," or "Please don't lose any weight, I like you so much as you are!") Proceedings opened at the Captain's cocktail party when Hilda found herself part of a group consisting of the world-famed mystery writer, Howard Swainton, whom she described vividly as "a rather bouncy and yappy little Yorkshire terrier of a man"; a willowy American named Linda Milsom, whom he modestly referred to as his secretary; a tall, balding, fresh-complexioned, owlish-looking cleric wearing gold-rimmed glasses, a dog-collar and an old tweed suit, who introduced himself as Bill Britwell; and his wife, Mavis, a rotund greyhaired lady with a face which might once have been pretty and was now friendly and cheerful. These people were in the act of getting to know each other when the Reverend Bill made the serious mistake of asking Howard Swainton what he did for a living.

"You mean you don't know what Howard does?" Linda, the secretary, said, as her boss was recovering from shock. "You ought to walk into the gift shop. The shelves are just groaning with his best-sellers. Rows and rows of them, aren't there, Howard?"

"They seem to know what goes with the public," Swainton agreed. "My motto is keep 'em guessing and give 'em a bit of sex and a spot of mayhem every half-dozen pages. I'm here to research a new story about a mysterious disappearance on a cruise. I call it *Absence of Body.* Rather a neat title that, don't you think?"

"Howard's won two Golden Daggers," Linda explained. "And *Time* magazine called him 'The Genius of Evil.'"

"Let's say, I'm a writer with a taste for a mystery." Swainton was ostentatiously modest.

"I suppose"—Bill Britwell beamed round at the company—"that since I've been concerned with the greatest mystery of all, I've lost interest in detective stories. I do apologize."

"Oh, really?" Swainton asked. "And what's the greatest mystery?"

"I think Bill means," his wife explained, "since he's gone in to the Church."

"What I've always wanted," the Reverend Bill told them, "after a lifetime in insurance."

"So you've joined the awkward squad, have you?" Swainton was a fervent supporter of the Conservative Party on television chat shows, and as such regarded the Church of England as a kind of Communist cell.

"I'm sorry?" Bill blinked, looking genuinely puzzled.

"The Archbishop's army of Reverend Pinkos"—Swainton warmed to his subject—"always preaching morality to the Government. I can't think why you chaps can't mind your own business."

"Morality *is* my business now, isn't it?" Bill was still looking irrepressibly cheerful. "Of course, it used to be insurance. I came to all the best things late in life. The Church and Mavis." At which he put an arm round his wife's comfortable shoulder.

"We're on our honeymoon." Hilda said that the elderly Mrs. Britwell sounded quite girlish as she said this.

"Pleasure combined with business," her husband explained. "We're only going as far as Malta, where I've landed a job as padre to the Anglican community."

And then Hilda, intoxicated by a glass of champagne and the prospect of foreign travel, confessed that she was also on a honeymoon, although it was a second one in her case.

"Oh, really?" Swainton asked with a smile which Hilda found patronizing. "And which is your husband, Mrs.—?"

"Rumpole. Hilda Rumpole. My husband is an extremely well-known barrister. You may have read his name in the papers?"

"I don't spend much time reading," Swainton told her. "I'm really too busy writing. And where is your Mr. Rumbold?"

"Oh, well," Hilda had to confess, "he's not here."

"You mean?"—Swainton was smiling and inviting the group to enjoy the joke—"you're having a second honeymoon with a husband who isn't here?"

"No. Well. You see something rather unexpected came up."

"So, now"—and Swainton could barely conceal his mirth—"you're having a second honeymoon on your own?"

But Hilda had to excuse herself and hurry away, as she had seen, through the window of the saloon in which the Captain's cocktail party was taking place, stationed on a small patch of windy and rain-beaten deck, Rumpole signalling urgently for supplies.

What had happened was that, being greatly in need of sustenance and a nerve-cooling drink in my Ducal Class dugout (second only to the real luxury of Sovereign Class), I had rung repeatedly for a steward with absolutely no result. When I telephoned, I was told there would he a considerable delay as the staff were very busy with the Captain's cocktail party. "The Captain's cock up, you mean," I said harshly, and made my way to the outskirts of the port (or perhaps the starboard) deck, where it took me considerable time to attract Hilda's attention through the window. "Make your mind up, Rumpole," She said when she came out. "Are you in hiding or aren't you?" and "Why don't you come in and meet a famous author?"

"Are you mad? *He's* in there." I could see the skeletal figure of Graves in the privileged party around Captain Orde. He was no doubt entertaining them with an account of the Rumpole clientele he had kept under lock and key.

"Really," Hilda protested, "this is no way to spend a honeymoon. Mr. Swainton looked as though he thought I'd done you in or something. Apparently he's doing research on a new book called *Absence of Body*. He says it's all about someone who disappears during a cruise."

"Hilda," I said, "couldn't you do a bit of research on a glass or two of champagne? And on what they've got on those little bits of toast?"

So She Who Must Be Obeyed, who has her tender moments, went off in search of provisions. I watched her go back into the saloon and make for the table where the guzzle and sluice were laid out. As she did so, she passed Mr. Justice Graves. I saw him turn his head to look at her in a stricken fashion, then he muttered some apology to the Captain and was off out of the room with the sudden energy of a young gazelle.

It was then I realized that not only was Rumpole fleeing the Judge, the Judge was fleeing Rumpole.

BACK IN THE CABIN, Hilda put on her dress for the dinner dance and added the finishing touches to her *maquillage*, whilst I, wearing bedroom slippers and smoking a small cigar, paced my confinement like a caged tiger. "And you'll really like the Britwells," She was saying, "He's going to be a parson in Malta. They're quite elderly, but so much in love. Do come up to dinner, Rumpole. Then we could dance together."

"We did that on our first honeymoon!" I reminded her. "And it wasn't an astonishing success, so far as I can remember. Anyway, do you think I want Gravestone to catch me dancing?"

"I don't know why you're so frightened of him, quite honestly. You don't exactly cower in front of him in Court from all you tell me."

"Of course I don't cower!" I explained. "I can treat the old Deathshead with lofty disdain in front of a jury! I can thunder my disapproval at him on a bail application. I have no fear of the man in the exercise of my profession. It's his friendship I dread."

"His friendship?"

"Oh, yes. That is why, Hilda, I have fled Judge Graves down the nights and down the days." And here I gave my wife a heady draught of Francis Thompson:

> "I fled Him, down the arches of the years;
> I fled Him, down the labyrinthine ways
> Of my own mind; and in the mist of tears
> I hid from Him, and under running laughter."

"Well, there's not much running laughter for me"—Hilda was displeased—"going on a second honeymoon without a husband."

When Hilda was made-up, powdered and surrounded with an appropriate fragrance, she left me just as the Britwells were emerging from the cabin opposite. They were also in evening-dress and were apparently so delighted to see my wife that they cordially invited her to inspect the amenities which they enjoyed. As the Britwell berth seemed in every way a carbon copy of that provided for the Rumpoles, Hilda found it a little difficult to keep up an interesting commentary, or show any genuine surprise, at the beauty and convenience of their quarters. At a loss for conversation, she looked at their dressing-table, where, she told me, two large photographs in heavy silver frames had been set up. The first was a recent wedding portrait of the Reverend and Mrs. Britwell standing proudly together, arm-in-arm, outside a village church. The bride was not in white, which would have been surprising at her age, but she wore what Hilda called a "rather ordinary little suit and a hat with a veil." The other was a studio portrait of a pretty, smiling young girl in a sequined evening-gown. She asked if that were Bill's daughter, to which he laughed and said, "Not exactly." Before she could inquire further I whistled to Hilda from our door across the corridor as I had an urgent piece of advice for her.

"For God's sake, if you see the Judge," I warned her through a chink in our doorway, "don't encourage the blighter. Please, don't dream of dancing with him!"

I was not in the least reassured when She answered, "You never know what I might dream of, Rumpole."

HILDA DIDN'T DANCE with the Judge that night. Indeed Mr. Injustice Graves didn't even put in an appearance at the function and was busily engaged in lying as low as Rumpole himself.

Most of the dancing was done by the Britwells, who whirled and twirled and chasséed around the place with the expertise of a couple of ballroom champions. "Aren't they good?" Hilda was playing an enthusiastic gooseberry to Swainton and his secretary, Linda. "Don't you think he dances rather *too* well?" Swainton sat with his head on one side and looked suspiciously at the glittering scene.

"I don't know exactly what you mean?" Hilda was puzzled, but Linda told her, "Howard looks below the surface of life. That's his great talent!"

When the husband and wife team came off the floor, perspiring gently after the tango, Howard Swainton repeated, "We were saying you dance unusually well, Britwell, for a vicar."

"Don't forget I wasn't always a vicar. I spent most of my life in insurance."

"Oh, yes. I remember now. You told us that." Howard Swainton seemed to be making a mental note. Hilda said, "Do men in insurance dance well?"

"Better than vicars!" Mrs. Britwell was laughing. The elderly newly-weds did seem an ideally happy couple.

"I was in insurance and Mavis ran a secretarial agency." Bill was telling the story of his life. "Of course, I married her for her money." He raised his glass of wine to his wife and drank her health.

"And I married him for his dancing!" Mavis was still laughing. "Why don't you let Bill give you a slow foxtrot, Mrs. Rumpole?"

"Oh, that would be very nice"—Hilda had not had a great deal of practice at the foxtrot—"but not this evening, perhaps." She was looking anxiously about the room, a fact which the sleuth Swainton immediately noticed. "Are you looking for someone?" he asked.

"Oh. Oh, well. A judge, actually. I happen to have met him before. I'm sure he was at the Captain's cocktail party but I don't seem to see him here."

"A judge?" Swainton was interested.

"Oh, yes. He used to be just down the Bailey, you know," Hilda told them. "But now he's been put up to the High Court. Scarlet and ermine. A red judge. Sir Gerald Graves."

"Graves?" Howard Swainton was smiling. "That's a rather mournful name." But the Reverend Bill didn't join in the laughter. He made a sudden movement and knocked over his glass of red wine. It spread across the tablecloth, Hilda told me, in words I was to remember, like blood.

> *Swiftly, swiftly flew the ship,*
> *Yet she sailed softly too:*
> *Sweetly, sweetly blew breeze—*
> *On me alone it blew.*

It blew on me alone because I was taking a solitary stroll in the early morning before the waking hour of the most energetic judge. The good ship *Boadicea* clove the grey waters, seagulls chattered and soared in the sky behind us, hoping for scraps, and I trod carefully in the shadows of boats and deck buildings.

> *Like one, who on a lonesome road*
> *Doth walk in fear and dread,*
> *And having once turned round walks on,*
> *And turns no more his head;*
> *Because he knows a frightful judge*
> *Doth close behind him tread.*

Coleridge's memorable lines were beating in my ears as I looked fearfully around me and then, almost too late, spotted an energetic old party in a blue blazer out for a constitutional. I ducked into the doorway of the Ladies Health and Beauty Salon, while Graves stopped and peered furtively into the window of the room where breakfast was being served to the Ducal passengers.

I know that he did this from the account that Hilda gave me later. She was at a table with Swainton and Linda Milsom, getting stuck into the coffee and eggs and bacon, when she saw the judicial features peering in at her. She only had time to say, "Ah. There he is!" before the old darling vanished, and she said, "He's gone!" Bill Britwell joined them with a plate of cornflakes he'd been fetching from a central table. "Who's gone?" he asked.

"Mr. Justice Graves. He must be an early bird." The Reverend Bill sat and ate his breakfast and Swainton asked how Mavis, who was noticeably absent, was that morning.

"Well, not too good, I'm afraid. Mavis isn't quite the ticket."

"The what?" Linda Milsom seemed to be listening to a foreign language.

"Not quite up to snuff." Bill did his best to explain his meaning.

"He means she's sick," Howard Swainton translated for Linda's benefit and his secretary looked deeply sympathetic. "What, on her honeymoon?"

"Do tell her we're all so sorry for her." Swainton was also solicitous, and then he turned his attention to Hilda and asked her, with obvious scepticism, "And how's *your* husband, Mrs. Rumpole? Have you heard from him lately?"

"Oh, yes, I have," Hilda told him.

"Still busy, is he?"

"Well, he's on the move all the time."

"Gee, I hope your wife gets better," Linda was saying to Bill Britwell in a caring sort of way. "I've got these great homeopathic capsules. I could drop them into your cabin."

"That's very kind of you but," Bill told them firmly, "I think she'd like to be left alone for the moment."

"Such a terrible shame!" Hilda was also sympathetic. "And she seemed so full of life last night."

"Yes, that's exactly what I thought." Howard Swainton was looking at the Reverend Bill as though he were an interesting piece of research and he repeated Hilda's words, "So full of life!"

\* \* \*

AFTER FUNKING a meeting with Hilda in the breakfast room, it seemed that Mr. Injustice settled himself down in a deck-chair, with a rug over his knees, in a kind of passage on the upper deck between the side of the gymnasium and a suspended boat into which his Lordship, in time of trouble, ought, I suspected, be ready to jump ahead of the women and children. There he sat, immersed in *Murder Most Foul*, the latest Howard Swainton, when, glancing up after the discovery of the fourth corpse, he saw Hilda standing at the end of the passage. His immediate reaction was to raise the alleged work of literature over his face, but he was too late. My wife gave a glad cry of "Mr. Justice Graves!" And, advancing towards him with indescribable foolhardiness added, "It is Sir Gerald Graves, isn't it? Hilda Rumpole. We met at Sam Ballard's wedding. You remember he got spliced to the ex-matron of the Old Bailey and astonished us all." Whereupon she sat down in one of the empty chairs beside him and seemed prepared for a long chat.

"Mrs. Rumpole"—Hilda, who is always a reliable witness, alleges that the old Deathshead here "smiled quite charmingly"—"of course, I remember. I had no idea you were on the boat." And he added nervously, "Are you here on your own?"

"Well, yes. On my own. In a sort of way."

"Oh, I see. Oh, good!" His Lordship was enormously relieved, but then, Hilda told me, a sort of hunted look came into his eyes as he inquired anxiously, "Your husband isn't about?"

"Not about? No. Well. Definitely not about. Of course, Horace's got a very busy practice," Hilda explained. "I believe you had him before you quite recently. I don't know if you remember?"

"Your husband's appearances before me, Mrs. Rumpole," Graves assured her, "are quite unforgettable."

"How sweet of you to say so." She was gratified.

"In fact, we judges are all agreed," Mr. Justice added, "there's simply no advocate at the Criminal Bar in the least like Horace Rumpole."

"A 'one off.' Is that what you'd say about him?"

"Without doubt, a 'one off.' We're all agreed about that."

"I'm sure you're right. That may be why I married him. He's a bit of a 'one off' as a husband." Hilda began, strangely enough, to treat the old Gravestone as a confidante.

"Forgive me, Mrs. Rumpole"—Graves clearly didn't want to be let into the secrets of the Rumpole marriage—"I have absolutely no idea what Rumpole is like as a husband."

"No. Silly of me!" And here I believe that She laid a friendly hand on the old party's arm. "Of course, you don't know what it's like to go on one honeymoon with him, let alone two."

"No idea at all, I'm delighted to say."

"But I'll tell you all the nice things you've said about him. About him being 'unforgettable' and a 'one off' and so on."

"You'll tell him?" His Lordship's hunted expression returned.

"When I next see him."

"Oh, yes, of course." And he suggested hopefully, "Back in England?"

"Or wherever. It may encourage him to break cover."

"To do *what*, Mrs. Rumpole?" There was a distinct note of panic in the judicial question.

"Well, to come out into the open a little more. Would it surprise you to know, Rumpole's really a very shy and retiring sort of person?"

By this time the shy and retiring Rumpole had outstayed his welcome in the entrance hall of the Ladies Health and Beauty Salon and I began to make my way back to the safety of our cabin, taking cover, from time to time, in such places as the children's play area (where I might have been spotted peering anxiously out from behind a giant cut-out clown) and the deck quoits' storage cupboard. Then, getting near to home, I glanced down a passage between a building and a boat and saw Hilda seated on a deck-chair, her knees covered with a rug. The back of the hanging boat prevented me seeing her companion, until it was far too late. "Hilda!" I called. "Yes, Rumpole. Here I am," came the answer. And then, as I moved towards her, the sight I dreaded most hoved into view. We were forced together and there was no way in which a meeting between old enemies could be avoided. What was remarkable was that the Deathshead greeted me with apparent *bonhomie*.

"Rumpole!" He didn't rise from his seat but otherwise he was cordial. "My dear fellow! This *is* a surprise. Your good lady told me that you weren't about."

"Well," I admitted, "I haven't been about. Up to now."

"What's up, old chap? Not got your sea legs yet? I always thought of you as a bit of a landlubber, I must say. Come along, then. Sit yourself down."

I did so with a good deal of trepidation on the seaward side of She Who Must be Obeyed.

"The Judge has been sweet enough to tell me that your appearances before him were 'unforgettable,'" Hilda said.

"Oh, yes? How terribly sweet of him," I agreed.

"And like no one else."

"And I honestly meant it, my dear old fellow," Graves assured me. "You are absolutely *sui generis*."

"To name but a few?"

"Even if you have so very little Latin. What was the last case you did before me?"

"It was an application for bail." And I added, with heavy irony, "With the greatest respect, my Lord."

"Of course it was!" Graves seemed to recall the incident with delight. "You should have been there, Mrs. Rumpole. We had great fun over that, didn't we, old fellow?"

"Oh, yes," I assured him. "It was a riot. Tony Timson's been laughing so much he could hardly slop out in Brixton."

"He will have his joke, won't he, Mrs. Rumpole?" The Judge's cheerfulness was undiminished. "Your Horace is a great one for his little joke. Well, now I've met you both, there's no reason why we shouldn't have a drink together. After dinner in the Old Salts' bar at, shall we say, five minutes past nine exactly?"

At which point, the Gravestone took up his copy of *Murder Most Foul* and left us to the sound of my, I hope derisory, "If your Lordship pleases." When he had withdrawn, I turned a tragic face to Hilda. "The Old Salts' Bar," I repeated. "At five past nine. *Now* look what you've done!"

"I had to flush you out somehow, Rumpole," She said, unreasonably I felt. "I had to get you to take part in your own honeymoon."

But my mind was on grimmer business. "I told you, it's the awful threat of his friendship. That's what I dread!"

THAT EVENING, in the privacy of our cabin, Hilda read out an account of the delights of the Old Salts' bar from the ship's brochure: "'Tonight and every night after dinner,'" she told me, "'Gloria de la Haye sings her golden oldies. Trip down Memory Lane and sing along with Gloria, or hear her inimitable way of rendering your special requests.'"

"And that's not the only drawback of the Old Salts' bar," I added. "What about 'Stiff sentences I have Passed,' the long-playing record by Mr. Justice Gravestone?"

"Oh, do cheer up, Rumpole. We've got each other."

"Next time you decide to go on a honeymoon, old thing," I warned her, "would you mind leaving him behind?"

"Poor Mavis Britwell getting sick like that!" Hilda's mind flitted to another subject. "She'll be missing all the fun."

"Tonight," I told her, having regard to the rendezvous ahead, "the sick are the lucky ones."

When we left the cabin on our way to dinner, Hilda's mind was still on the misfortunes of Mavis, and she knocked on the door of the cabin opposite with the idea of visiting the invalid. After some delay, the Reverend Bill called from behind the door that he wouldn't be a minute. Then the little man I was to discover to be Howard Swainton, the famous author, came bouncing down the corridor, carrying a bunch of red roses and a glossy paperback of his own writing. "Visiting the sick, are we?" he said. "We all seem to have the same idea."

"Well, yes. This is my husband." Hilda introduced me and Swainton raised his eyebrows higher than I would have believed possible.

"Is it, really?" he said. "I *am* surprised."

"And this is Mr. Howard Swainton, Hilda went on, undeterred, "*the* Howard Swainton."

"How do you do. I'm *the* Horace Rumpole," I told him.

"Your wife says you're a barrister." Swainton seemed to find the notion somewhat absurd, as though I were a conjuror or an undertaker's mute. "I am an Old Bailey hack," I admitted.

"And we've all been wondering when you'd turn up." Swainton was still smiling, and I asked him, "Why? Are you in some sort of trouble?"

Before matters could further deteriorate, the vicar opened his cabin door and Hilda once again performed the introductions. "I'm afraid Mavis is still feeling a little groggy," Bill Britwell told us. "She just wants to rest quietly." Hilda said she understood perfectly, but Howard Swainton, saying, "I come bearing gifts!" and calling out, "Mavis!" invaded the room remorselessly, although Bill protested again, "I'm not sure she feels like visitors."

We followed, somewhat helplessly, in Howard's wake as he forged ahead. The woman whom I took to be Mavis Britwell was lying in the bed further from the door. The clothes were pulled up around her and only the top of her head was visible from where we stood. Howard Swainton continued his advance, saying, "Flowers for the poor invalid and my latest in paperback!" I saw him put his gifts down on the narrow table between the two beds, and, in doing so, he knocked over a glass of water which spilled on to Mavis's bed. She put out an arm automatically to protect herself and I couldn't help seeing what Swainton must also have noticed: the sick Mrs. Britwell had apparently retired to bed fully dressed.

"Oh, dear. How terribly clumsy of me!" Swainton was dabbing at the wet bed with his handkerchief. But Mavis had drawn the covers around her again and still lay with her face turned away from us. "Perhaps you could go now?" her husband said with admirable patience. "Mavis does want to be perfectly quiet." "Yes, of course." Swainton was apologetic. "I *do* understand. Come along, the Rumpoles."

We left the cabin then and Swainton soon parted from us to collect his secretary for dinner.

"She was dressed," Hilda said when we were left alone. "She was wearing her blouse and cardie."

"Perhaps the Reverend Bill fancies her in bed in a cardie."

"Don't be disgusting, Rumpole!" And then Hilda told me something else she had noticed. The two heavy silver framed photographs, which had stood on the dressing-table when she first visited the Britwells' cabin, had disappeared. She Who Must Be Obeyed has a dead eye for detail and would have risen to great heights in the Criminal Investigation Department.

THE OLD SALTS' BAR was liberally decorated with lifebelts, lobster nets, ships in bottles, charts, compasses and waitresses with sailor hats. There was a grand piano at which a small, pink-faced, bespectacled accompanist played as Miss Gloria de la Haye sang her way down Memory Lane. Gloria, a tall woman in a sequined dress, who made great play with a green chiffon handkerchief, must have been in her sixties, and her red curls no doubt owed little to nature. However, she had kept her figure and her long-nosed, wise-mouthed face, although probably never beautiful, was intelligent and humorous. She was singing "Smoke Gets in Your Eyes" and, with dinner over, we were awaiting our assignation with Gravestone in the company of Bill Britwell, Linda Milsom and Howard Swainton— Mrs. Mavis Britwell still being, her husband insisted, unwell and confined to her room. Hilda was giving an account of what she would have it thought of as a happy meeting with Sir Gerald Graves.

"Is he someone you've crossed swords with?" Swainton asked me, "in the Courts?"

"Swords? Nothing so gentlemanly. Let's say, chemical weapons. The old darling's summing up is pure poison gas."

"Oh, go on, Rumpole!" Hilda was having none of this. "He was absolutely charming to you on the boat deck."

"What's the matter with the claret, Hilda? Glued to the table?— That was just part of his diabolical cunning."

"Rumpole, are you sure you haven't had enough?" She was reluctant to pass the bottle.

"Of course, I'm sure. Coping with his lethal Lordship without a drink inside you is like having an operation without an anaesthetic."

At which, dead on time, Mr. Injustice berthed himself at our table, saying, "You're remarkably punctual, Rumpole."

"Oh, Judge! Everyone"—Hilda introduced the old faceache as though she owned him—"this is Sir Gerald Graves. Howard Swainton, *the* Howard Swainton, Linda, his personal assistant, and Bill Britwell, the Reverend Bill. Sir Gerald Graves."

"Five past nine exactly." The Judge had been studying his watch during these preliminaries and I weighed in with "Silence! The Court's in session."

"Well, now. Our second night at sea. I'm sure we're all enjoying it?" Graves's face contorted itself into an unusual and wintry smile.

"Best time we've had since the Luton Axe Killing, my Lord," I told him.

"What was that you said, Rumpole?"

"It's absolutely thrilling, my Lord," I translated, a little more loudly.

"I'm afraid"—the Reverend Bill got up—"you'll have to excuse me."

"Oh. So soon?"

"Can't you relax, Bill? Forget your troubles." Swainton tried to detain him. "Enjoy a drink with a real live judge."

"I must get back to Mavis."

"It's his wife, Judge. She hasn't been well," Howard Swainton said with apparent concern. And as Gloria switched from "Smoke Gets in Your Eyes" to "Thanks for the Memory," Bill agreed, "Well, not quite the ticket."

"I'm sorry to hear it." Graves was sympathetic. "Well, I do hope she's able to join us tomorrow."

"I'm sure she hopes so too." Swainton was smiling as he said it. "Give her all our best wishes. Tell her the Judge is thinking of her."

"Yes. Yes, I will. That's very kind." And Bill Britwell retreated from the Old Salts' bar saying, "Please! Don't let me break up the party." Whereupon Swainton came, like the terrier Hilda had described, bounding and yapping into the conversation with "I say, Judge. Horace Rumpole was just talking about your little scraps in Court."

"Oh, yes? We do have a bit of fun from time to time. Don't we, Rumpole?" Graves smiled contentedly but Swainton started to stir the legal brew with obvious relish. "That, wasn't exactly how Rumpole put it," he said. "Of course, I do understand. Barristers are the natural enemies of judges. Judges and, well, my lot, detective-story writers. We want answers. We want to ferret out the truth. In the end we want to tell the world who's guilty!"

"Well put, if I may say so, Mr. Swainton!" Graves had clearly found a kindred spirit. "In your tales the mysteries are always solved and the criminal pays—"

"Enormous royalties!" I slipped in, "I have no doubt."

"His heavy debt to society!" Graves corrected me and then continued his love affair with the bouncy little novelist. "You always find the answer, Swainton. That's what makes your books such a thumping good read."

Gloria had stopped singing now and was refreshing herself at the bar. Her plump accompanist was going round the tables with a pad and pencil, asking for requests for the singer's next number.

"Thank you, Judge. Most kind of you." Howard Swainton was clearly not above saluting the judicial backside. "But the Horace Rumpoles of this world always want to raise a verbal smokescreen of 'reasonable doubt.' Tactics, you see. They do it so the guilty can slide away to safety."

"*Touché*, Rumpole! Hasn't Mr. Swainton rather got you there?" Graves was clearly delighted by the author's somewhat tormented prose.

"Not *touché* in the least!" I told him. "Anyway, I've heard it so many times before from those who want to convict someone, anyone, and don't care very much who it is. There speaks the voice of the Old Bill."

"But I don't understand. His name's Howard." Miss Linda Milsom, however rapid her shorthand, was not exactly quick on the uptake.

"Detective Inspector Swainton"—I was now in full flood—"distrusts defending counsel and wants all trials to take place in the friendly neighbourhood nick. He's so keen on getting at the truth that, if he can't find it, he'll invent it—like the end of a detective story."

"Is this how he goes on in Court?" Swainton asked with a smile to the Judge, who assured him, "Oh, all the time."

"Then you have my heartfelt sympathy, Judge," Swainton said, and I could scarcely withhold my tears for his poor old Lordship. "Thank you," Graves said. "Tell me, Swainton, are you working on some wonderful new mystery to delight us?"

Then my attention was distracted by the little accompanist, who asked me if I'd care to write down a request for Gloria. I looked across at the tall, sequined woman, apparently downing a large port and lemon, and I was whisked back down the decades to my carefree bachelor days. I was leaving Equity Court, when the Chambers were then run by Hilda's Daddy, C. H. Wystan, for a chop and a pint of stout at the Cock tavern, and decided to give myself a treat by dropping in to the Old Metropolitan music hall, long since defunct, in the Edgware Road. There I might see jugglers and adagio dancers and Max Miller, the "Cheeky Chappie," and . . . At this point I scribbled a song title on the accompanist's pad. He looked at it, I thought with some surprise, and carried it back to Gloria. And then, bringing me painfully back to the present, I heard Swainton tell us the plot of his latest masterpiece.

"In *Absence of Body*," he said, "I am now thinking along these lines. A woman, a middle-aged woman, perfectly ordinary, is on a cruise with her new husband. He's a fellow who has taken the precaution of insuring her life for a tidy sum. He tells everyone she's ill, but in fact she's lying in bed in their cabin"—here Swainton leant forward and put a hand on Graves's knee for emphasis—"fully *dressed*."

"I see!" Graves was delighted with the mystery. "So the plot thickens."

"It's the truth, you understand," Swainton assured him. "It's so much stranger than fiction. Rumpole was a witness to the fact that when we called on Mrs. Mavis Britwell in her cabin, she was lying in bed with her clothes on! I don't know why it is, but I seem to have a talent for attracting mysteries."

"You mean she wanted you to believe she was ill?" Graves asked.

"Or *someone* wanted us to believe she was ill," Swainton told him. "Of course, one doesn't want to make any rash accusations."

"Doesn't one?" I asked. "It sounds as though one was absolutely longing to." But Mr. Justice Graves was clearly having the time of his old life. "Swainton," he said, "I'd very much like to know how your story ends."

"Would you, Judge? I'm afraid we'll all just have to wait and see. No harm, of course, in keeping our eyes open in the meanwhile."

At which moment, the accompanist pounded some rhythmic chords on the piano and Gloria burst into the ditty whose words I could still remember, along with long stretches of *The Oxford Book of English Verse*, better than most of the news I heard yesterday:

> *Who's that kicking up a noise?*
> *My little sister!*
> *Who's that giggling with the boys?*
> *My little sister!*
> *Whose lemonade is laced with gin?*
> *Who taught the vicar how to sin?*
> *Knock on her door and she'll let you in!*
> *My little sister!*
> *Who's always been the teacher's pet?*
> *Who took our puppy to the vet?*
> *That was last night and she's not home yet!*
> *My little sister!*

"What an extraordinary song!" Hilda said when my request performance was over.

"Yes," I told her. "Takes you back, doesn't it? Takes *me* back, anyway."

WHEN THE PARTY in the Old Salts' bar was over, Hilda slipped her arm through mine and led me across the deck to the ship's rail. I feared some romantic demonstration and looked around for help, but the only person about seemed to be Bill Britwell, wrapped in a heavy raincoat, who was standing some way from us. It was somewhat draughty and a fine rain was falling, but there was a moon and the sound of a distant dance band.

Hilda, apparently, drew the greatest encouragement from these facts.

"The sound of music across the water. Stars. You and I by the rail. Finding each other . . . Listen, Rumpole! What do you think the Med. is trying to say to us?"

"It probably wants to tell you it's the Bay of Biscay," I suggested.

"Is there nothing you feel romantic about?"

"Of course there is." I couldn't let that charge go unanswered.

"There you are, you see!" Hilda was clearly pleased. "I always thought so. What exactly?"

"Steak and kidney pudding." I gave her the list. "The jury system, the presumption of innocence."

"Anything else?"

"Oh. Of course. I almost forgot," I reassured her.

"Yes?"

"Wordsworth."

There was a thoughtful silence then and Hilda, like Gloria, went off down Memory Lane. "It doesn't seem so very long ago," she said, "that I was a young girl, and you asked Daddy for my hand in marriage."

"And he gave it to me!" I remembered it well.

"Daddy was always so generous. Tell me, Rumpole. Now we're alone"—Hilda started off. I'm not sure what sort of intimate subject she was about to broach because I had to warn her, "But we're not alone. Look!"

She turned her head and we both saw Bill Britwell standing by the rail, staring down at the sea and apparently involved in his own thoughts. Then, oblivious to our existence, he opened his coat, under which he had concealed two silver-framed photographs, much like those Hilda had seen on the dressing-table on her first visit to his cabin. He looked at them for a moment and dropped them towards the blackness of the passing sea. He turned from the rail then and walked away, not noticing Hilda and me, nor Howard Swainton, who had also come out of the Old Salts' bar a few minutes before and had been watching this mysterious episode with considerable fascination.


TIME, ON A CRUISE SHIP, tends to drag; watching water pass by you slowly is not the most exciting occupation in the world. Hilda spent her time by having her hair done, or her face creamed, or taking steam-baths, or being pounded to some sort of pulp in the massage parlour. I slept a good deal or walked round the deck. I was engaged in this mild exercise when I came within earshot of that indefatigable pair, Graves and Swainton, the Judge and the detective writer, who were sitting on deck-chairs, drinking soup. I loitered behind a boat for a little, catching the drift of their conversation.

"Photographs?" The Judge was puzzled. "In silver frames? and he threw them into the sea?"

"That's what it looked like."

"But why would a man do such a thing?"

"Ask yourself that, Members of the Jury." I emerged and posed the question, "Is the Court in secret session or can anyone join?"

"Ah, Rumpole. There you are." Graves, given a case to try, seemed to be in excellent humour. "Now then, I believe you were also a witness. Why would a man throw photographs into the sea? That is indeed the question we have to ask. And perhaps, with your long experience of the criminal classes, you can suggest a solution?"

"I'm on holiday. What Britwell did with his photographs seems entirely his own affair." But Swainton clearly didn't think so. "I can offer a solution." He gave us one of his plots for nothing. "Suppose the Reverend Bill isn't a Reverend at all. I believe a lot of con men go on these cruises."

"That is an entirely unfounded suggestion by the Prosecution, my Lord." I had the automatic reaction of the life-long defender, at which moment the steward trundled the soup trolley up to me and Graves, by now well in to presiding over the upper-deck Court, said, "Please, Mr. Rumpole! Let Mr. Swainton complete his submission. Your turn will come later."

"Oh, is that soup?" I turned my attention to the steward. "Thank you very much."

"Suppose Bill Britwell wanted to remove all trace of the person in the photographs?" Swainton suggested.

"Two persons," I corrected him. "Hilda told me there were two photographs. One was Bill Britwell and his wife. The other was of a young girl. Are you suggesting he wanted to remove all trace of two people? Is that the prosecution case?"

"Please, Mr. Rumpole, it hasn't come to a prosecution yet," Graves said unconvincingly.

"His wife? This is *very* interesting!" Swainton yelped terrier-like after the information. "One picture was of his wife. Now, why should he throw that into the sea?"

"God knows. Perhaps it didn't do her justice," I suggested, and Swainton looked thoughtful and said, in a deeply meaningful sort of way, "Or was it a symbolic act?"

"A what?" I wasn't following his drift, if indeed he had one. "He got rid of her photograph," Swainton did his best to explain, *"because he means to get rid of her."*

"That is a most serious suggestion." Graves greeted it with obvious relish, whilst I, slurping my soup, said, "Balderdash, my Lord!"

"What?" The little novelist looked hurt.

"The product of a mind addled with detective stories," I suggested.

"All right!" Swainton yapped at me impatiently. "If you know so much, tell us this. Where do you think Mrs. Mavis Britwell is? Still in bed with her clothes on?"

"Why don't you go and have a peep through the keyhole?" I suggested.

"I wasn't thinking of that, exactly. But I was thinking . . ."

"Oh, do try not to," I warned him. "It overexcites his Lordship."

"The steward does up the cabins along our corridor at about this time," Swainton remembered. "If we happened to be passing, we might just see something extremely interesting."

"You mean we might take a view?" The Judge was clearly enthusiastic and I tried to calm him down by saying, "—Of the scene of a crime that hasn't been committed?"

"It's clearly our duty to investigate any sort of irregularity." Graves was at his most self-important.

"And no doubt your delight," I suggested.

"What did you say, Rumpole?" The Judge frowned.

"I said you're perfectly right, my Lord. And no doubt you would wish the Defence to be represented at the scene of any possible crime."

"Have you briefed yourself, Rumpole?" Swainton gave me an unfriendly smile. I took a final gulp of soup and told him, "I certainly have, as there's no one else to do it for me."

When we got down to the corridor outside the cabins, the trolley with clean towels and sheets was outside the Graves residence, where work was being carried out. We loitered around, trying to look casual, and then Bill Britwell greatly helped the Prosecution by emerging from his door, which he shut carefully behind him. He looked at Graves in a startled and troubled sort of way and said, "Oh. It's you! Good morning, Judge."

"My dear Britwell. And how's your wife this morning?" The judge smiled with patent insincerity, as though meaning, We certainly don't hope she's well, as that would be far too boring.

"I'm afraid she's no better," Britwell reassured them. "No better at all. In fact she's got to stay in bed very quietly. No visitors, I'm afraid. Now, if you'll excuse me." He made his way quickly down the corridor and away from us on some errand or other, and Hilda opened the door of our cabin which, you will remember, was dead opposite the berth of the Britwells. "Ah, Mrs. Rumpole." His Lordship was delighted to see her. "Perhaps you'd allow us to be your guests, just for a moment?" and, although I gave Hilda a warning about helping the Prosecution, She eagerly invited the judicial team in, although she asked them to forgive "the terrible mess." "Oh, we can put up with any little inconvenience," the Judge boomed in his most lugubrious courtroom accent, "in our quest for the truth!"

So the search party took refuge in our cabin until the steward pushed his trolley up to the Britwells' door, unlocked it with his pass key and went inside, leaving the door open. Graves waited for a decent interval to elapse and then he led Swainton and me across the corridor and through the door, while the steward was putting towels in the bathroom. There was no one in either of the twin beds, and only one of them seemed to have been slept in. There was no powder, make-up or perfume on the dressing-table and, so far as one quick look could discover, no sign of Mrs. Mavis Britwell at all.

"Can I help you, gentlemen?" The steward came in from the bathroom, surprised by the invasion. "Oh, I'm sorry!" Swainton apologized with total lack of conviction. "We must have got the wrong cabin. They all look so alike. Particularly," he added with deep meaning, "those with only a *single* occupant."

THAT NIGHT, in the Old Salts' bar, Graves and Swainton were seated at the counter, and Gloria was drawing towards the end of her act, when I intruded again on their discussion of the state of the evidence.

"Britwell told us a deliberate lie," the Judge was saying.

"He distinctly said she was in the room," Swainton agreed.

"In my view his evidence has to be accepted with extreme caution," Graves ruled. "On any subject."

"I don't see why." I put my oar in and Swainton gave a little yapping laugh and said, "Here comes the perpetual defender."

"We all tell the odd lie, don't we?" I suggested, and then I ordered a large glass of claret, which I had christened Château Bilgewater, from Alfred, the barman.

"Speak for yourself, Rumpole." Graves looked at me as though I was probably as big a liar as the Reverend Bill. I wasn't going to let him get away with that without a spot of cross-examination, so I put this to his Lordship. "When you met my wife on the deck the other morning, didn't you tell her that you had no idea she was on the boat?"

"I *may* have said that," the Judge conceded.

"And I distinctly saw you at the Captain's cocktail party the night before. You caught sight of Mrs. Hilda Rumpole and went beetling out of the room because you recognized her!"

"Rumpole! That is . . ." The Judge seemed unable to find words to describe my conduct so I supplied them for him. "I know. A grossly improper argument. You may have to report it to the proper authorities."

"Gentlemen!" Swainton was, unusually, acting as a peacemaker. "We may all tell the odd white lie occasionally, but this is a far more serious matter. We have to face the fact that Mrs. Britwell has apparently disappeared."

"In the midst of the words she was trying to say," I suggested:

> *"In the midst of her laughter and glee,*
> *She softly and suddenly vanished away*
> *For the Snark was a Boojum, you see."*

"The question is"—Swainton was in no mood for Lewis Carroll—"what action should we take?"

"But who exactly *is* the Boojum—or the Snark, come to that?" This, I felt, was the important question.

"The circumstances are no doubt very suspicious." Graves had his head on one side, his lips pursed, his brandy glass in his hand, and was doing his best to sound extremely judicial. "Suspicions of what?" I had to put the question. "Is the theory that Bill Britwell pushed his wife overboard for the sake of a little life insurance and then kept quiet about it? What's the point of that?"

"It's possible he may have got rid of her," Swainton persisted, "for whatever reason . . ."

"If you think that, stop the boat," I told them. "Send for helicopters. Organize a rescue operation."

"I'm afraid it's a little late for that." Swainton looked extremely serious. "If he did anything, my feeling is, he did it last night. In some way, I think, the event may have been connected with the photographs that were thrown into the water."

So they sat on their bar stools and thought it over, the Judge and the fiction writer, like an old eagle and a young sparrow on their perches, and then Graves rather lost his bottle. "The circumstances are highly suspicious, of course," he spoke carefully, "but can we say they amount to a certainty?"

"Of course we can't," I told them, and then launched my attack on the learned Judge. "The trouble with the Judiciary is that you see crime in everything. It's the way an entomologist goes out for walks in the countryside and only notices the beetles."

Graves thought this over in silence and then made a cautious pronouncement. "If we were sure, of course, we could inform the police at Gibraltar. It might be a case for Interpol." But Swainton had dreamed up another drama. "I have a suggestion to make, Judge. If you agree. Tomorrow I'm giving my lecture, 'How I Think Up My Plots.' I presume you're all coming?" "Don't bet on it!" I told him. But he went on, undeterred. "I may add something to my text for Britwell's benefit. Keep your eyes on him when I say it." "You mean, observe his demeanour?" The Judge got the point.

Looking down the bar, I saw Gloria talking to Alfred, the barman, while beside me Swainton was babbling with delight at his ingenious plan. "See if he looks guilty," he said. "Do you think that's an idea?"

"Not exactly original," I told him, "Shakespeare used it in *Hamlet*."

"Did he, really?" The little author seemed surprised. "It might be even better in my lecture."

By now I had had about as much as I could take of the Judge and his side-kick, so I excused myself and moved to join Gloria, who was giving some final instructions to the barman. "A bottle of my usual to take away, Alfred," I heard her say. "The old and tawny. Oh, and a couple of glasses, could you let us have? They keep getting broken."

"Miss Gloria de la Haye?" I greeted her, and she gave me a smile of recognition. "Aren't you the gentleman that requested my old song?"

"I haven't heard you sing it for years," I told her. "Music halls don't exist any more, do they?"

"Worse luck!" She pulled a sour face. "It's a drag, this is, having to us a do an act afloat. Turns your stomach when the sea gets choppy, and there's not much life around here, is there?" She looked along the bar. "More like a floating old people's home. I'm prepared to scream if anyone else requests 'Smoke Gets in Your Eyes.' I want to say it soon will, in yours, dear, in the crematorium!"

"I remember going to the Metropolitan in the Edgware Road."

"You went to the old Met.?" Gloria was smiling.

"'Who's that kicking up a noise?'" I intoned the first line of the song and she joined me in a way that made the Judge stare at us with surprise and disapproval:

> *"Who's that giggling with the boys?*
> *My little sister!"*

"That was my act, the long and short of it," Gloria confirmed my recollection. "Betty Dee and Buttercup. I was Buttercup's straight man."

"Wasn't an alleged comic on the same bill?" I asked her. "Happy Harry someone. A man who did a rather embarrassing drunk act, if I remember."

"Was there?" Gloria stopped smiling. "I can't recall, exactly."

"And about Buttercup?" I asked. "Rather a pretty girl, wasn't she? What's happened to her?"

"Can't tell you that, I'm afraid. We haven't kept in touch." And Gloria turned back to the barman. "My old and tawny, Alfred?" She picked up the bottle of port and glasses the barman had put in front of her and went out of the bar. I let her get a start and then I decided to follow her. She went down corridors between cabin doors and down a flight of stairs to a lower deck where a notice on the wall read SECOND-CLASS PASSENGERS. From the bottom of the stairs I watched as she walked down a long corridor, a tall, sequined woman with a muscular back. Then she opened a cabin door and went inside.

IN THE NORMAL course of events, a lecture "How I Think Up My Plots" by Howard Swainton would have commanded my attention somewhat less than an address by Soapy Sam Bollard to the Lawyers As Christians Society on the home-life of the Prophet Amos. However, Swainton's threatened re-enactment of the play scene from *Hamlet* seemed likely to add a certain bizarre interest to an otherwise tedious occasion, so I found myself duly seated in the ship's library alongside Hilda and Judge Graves.

Bill Britwell, whom Swainton had pressed to attend, was a few rows behind us. Dead on the appointed hour, the best-selling author bobbed up behind a podium and, after a polite smattering of applause, told us how difficult plots were to come by and how hard he had to work on their invention in order to feed his vast and eager public's appetite for a constant diet of Swainton. An author's work, he told us, was never done, and although he might seem to be enjoying himself, drinking soup on the deck and assisting at the evening's entertainment in the Old Salts' bar, he was, in fact, hard at work on his latest masterpiece, *Absence of Body*, the story of a mysterious disappearance at sea. This led him to dilate on the question of whether a conviction for murder is possible if the corpse fails to put in an appearance.

"The old idea of the *corpus delicti* as a defence has now been laid, like the presumably missing corpse, to rest." Swainton was in full flow. "The defence is dead and buried, if not the body. Some years ago a steward on an ocean-going liner was tried for the murder of a woman passenger. It was alleged that he'd made love to her, either with or without her consent, and then pushed her through a porthole out into the darkness of the sea. Her body was never recovered. The Defence relied heavily on the theory of the *corpus delicti*. Without a body, the ingenious barrister paid to defend the steward said, there could be no conviction."

At this, Graves couldn't resist turning round in his seat to stare at Bill Britwell, who was in fact, stirring restlessly. "The Judge and the Jury would have none of this," Swainton went on. "The steward was condemned to death, although, luckily for him, the death sentence was then abolished. This case gave me the germ of an idea for the new tale which I am going to introduce to you tonight. Ladies and Gentlemen. You are privileged to be the first audience to whom I shall read chapter one of the brand-new Swainton mystery entitled *Absence of Body*." He produced a wadge of typescript and Linda Milsom gazed up at him adoringly as he started to read: "'When Joe Andrews suggested to this wife that they go on a cruise for their honeymoon, she was delighted. She might not have been so pleased if she had an inkling of the plan that was already forming itself at the back of his mind. . . .'" At which point there was the sound of a gasp and a chair being scraped back behind us. Obediently playing the part of guilty King Claudius, Bill Britwell rose from his seat and fled from the room.

"You saw that, Rumpole," the Judge whispered to me with great satisfaction. "Isn't that evidence of guilt?"

"Either of guilt," I told him, "or terminal boredom."


THE SHIP'S GIFT SHOP, as well as stocking a large selection of Howard Swainton, and others of those authors whose books are most frequently on show at airports, railway stations and supermarket checkouts, sold all sorts of sweets, tobacco, sun oil (not yet needed), ashtrays, table mats and T-shirts embellished with portraits of the late Queen Boadicea, giant pandas and teddy bears, cassettes and other articles of doubtful utility. On the day of the first fancy-dress ball, which was to take place on the evening before our arrival at Gibraltar, the gift shop put on display a selection of hats, false beards, noses, head-dresses and other accoutrements for those who lacked the skill or ingenuity to make their own costumes. In the afternoon the shop was full of passengers in search of disguise in which they could raise a laugh, cut a dash, or realize a childhood longing to be someone quite different from whoever they eventually turned out to be.

"Rumpole," Hilda was kind enough to say, "you look quite romantic." I had put a black patch over one eye and sported a three-cornered hat with a skull and cross-bones on the front. Looking in the shop mirror, I saw Jolly Roger Rumpole or Black Cap'n Rumpole of the Bailey. And then She looked across the shop to where the Reverend Bill was picking over a selection of funny hats. "You wouldn't think he'd have the nerve to dress up this evening, would you?" She said with a disapproving click of her tongue. I left left her and joined Britwell. I spoke to him in confidential but, I hope, cheering tones. "You must be getting tired of it," I said sympathetically.

"Tired of what?"

"People asking 'How's your wife?'"

"They're very kind." If he were putting on an act, he was doing it well. "Extremely considerate."

"It must be spoiling your trip."

"Mavis being ill?" He beamed at me vaguely through his spectacles. "Yes, it is rather."

"Mr. Justice Graves," I began and he looked suddenly nervous and said, "The Judge?" "Yes, the Judge. He seems very worried about your wife."

"Why's he worried?" Britwell asked anxiously.

"About her illness, I suppose. He wants to see her."

"Why should he want that?"

"You know what judges are," I told him. "Always poking their noses into things that don't really concern them. Shall we see your wife tonight at the fancy-dress party?"

"Well. No. I'm afraid not. Mavis won't be up to it. Such a pity. It's the sort of thing she'd love so much if she were only feeling herself." And then Hilda joined us, looking, although I say it myself, superb. She was wearing a helmet and breastplate and carrying a golden trident and a shield emblazoned with the Union Jack. Staring at my wife with undisguised admiration, I could only express myself in song:

> "Rule Britannia!
> Britannia rules the waves, (I warbled)
> Britain never, never shall be . . ."

"Is it going too far?" She asked nervously. But I shook my head and looked at Bill Britwell as I completed the verse:

> "Marri-ed to a mermai-ed,
> At the bottom of the deep blue sea!"

There was a sound of considerable revelry by night and as that old terror of the Spanish Main, Pirate Cap'n Rumpole, made his way in the company of assorted Pierrots, slave girls, pashas, clowns, Neptunes and mermaids towards the big saloon from which the strains of dance music were sounding, I passed an office doorway from which a Chinese mandarin emerged in the company of Captain Orde, who was attending the festivities disguised as a ship's captain. As I passed them I heard Orde say, "The police at Gib have the message, sir. So if he can't produce the lady . . ." "Yes, yes, Captain." The mandarin, who looked only a little less snooty and superior than Mr. Justice Graves in his normal guise, did his best to shut the officer up as he saw this old sea-dog approaching from windward. "Why there you are, Rumpole! Have you had some sort of an accident to your eye? Nothing serious, I hope."

Hilda and I have not danced together since our first honeymoon. As I have already indicated, the exercise was not a startling success and that night, with all the other excitement going on, she seemed content not to repeat the experiment. We sat in front of a bottle of the Bilgewater red, to which I had grown quite attached in an appalling sort of way, and we watched the dancers. Howard Swainton, as an undersized Viking, was steering the lanky Linda Milsom, a slave girl, who towered over him. It might be an exaggeration to say his eye-level was that of the jewel in her navel, but not too much of one. Across the room we could see the Reverend Bill holding a glass and admiring the scene. He was wearing a turban, a scimitar and a lurid beard. "Bluebeard!" Hilda said. "How very appropriate."

"Oh, for heaven's sake!" I told her, "don't *you* start imagining things." And then a familiarly icy voice cut into our conversation. "Mrs. Rumpole," said the ridiculously boring mandarin, "might I ask you to give me the honour of this dance?" She Who Must Be Obeyed, apparently delighted, said, "Of course, Judge, what tremendous fun!" My worst fears were confirmed and they waltzed away together with incomprehensible zest.

In due course, Swainton and his houri came to sit at our table and, looking idly at the throng, we witnessed the entry of two schoolgirls in gym-slips and straw hats. One was tall and thin and clearly Gloria. The other, small and plump, wore a schoolgirl mask to which a pigtailed wig was attached. Swainton immediately guessed that this was Miss de la Haye's little accompanist in disguise. "Betty Dee and Buttercup," I said, only half aloud, as this strange couple crossed the room, and Linda Milsom who was having trouble retaining the liverish-looking glass eye in her navel, said, "Some people sure like to make themselves look ridiculous." A little time passed and then Swainton said, "Well, that beats everything!" "What?" I asked, removing my nose from my glass and shifting the patch so that I had two eyes available.

"An alleged vicar dancing with a bar pianist in drag." It was true.

The Reverend Bill and the small schoolgirl were waltzing expertly. "I think," I said, "I could be about to solve the mystery of the Absent Body."

"I very much doubt it." Swainton was not impressed with my deductive powers.

"Would you like me to try?" And, before he could answer, I asked Linda to cut in and invite Bill Britwell for a dance.

"Oh," she appealed to her boss, "do I have to?" "Why not?" Swainton shrugged his shoulders. "It might be entertaining to watch Counsel for the Defence barking up the wrong tree."

When instructed by the best-selling author, Miss Milsom acted with decision and aplomb. I saw her cross the floor and speak to Bill Britwell. He looked at his partner, who surrendered more or less gracefully and was left alone on the floor. Before the small schoolgirl could regain the table where Gloria was waiting, Cap'n Rumpole had drawn up alongside.

"I'm afraid I'm no dancer," I said. "So shall we go out for a breath of air?" Without waiting for a reply, I took the schoolgirl's arm and steered her towards the doors which led out out to the deck.

So THERE I WAS by the rail of the ship again, in the moonlight with music playing in the background, faced, not by Hilda, but by a small, round figure wearing a schoolgirl mask.

"Betty Dee and Buttercup," I said. "You were Buttercup, weren't you? The little sister, the young girl in the photograph Bill Britwell threw into the sea? Not that there was any need for that. No one really remembered you."

"What do you want?" A small voice voice spoke from behind the mask.

"To set your mind at rest," I promised. "No one knows you've been part of a music-hall act. No one's going to hold that against you. Bill can preach sermons to the Anglicans of Malta and no one's going to care a toss about Betty Dee and Buttercup. It's the other part you were worried about, wasn't it? The part you played down the Old Bailey. A long time ago.

Such a long time. When we were all very young indeed. Oh, so very young. Before I did the Penge Bungalow Murders, which is no longer even recent history. All the same I was at the Bar when it happened. You know, you should've had me to defend you. You really should. It was a touching story. A young girl married to a drunk, a husband who beat her. Who was he? 'Happy' Harry Harman? He even did a drunk act on the stage, didn't he? Drunk acts are never very funny. I read all about it in the *News of the World* because I wanted the brief. He beat you and you stabbed him in the throat with a pair of scissors. You should never have got five years for manslaughter. I'd've got you off with not a dry eye in the jury-box, even though the efficient young Counsel for the Prosecution was a cold fish called Gerald Graves. It's all right. He is not going to remember you."

"Isn't he?" The small voice spoke again.

"Of course not. Lawyers and judges hardly ever remember the faces they've sent to prison."

"Are you sure?"

I was conscious that we were no longer alone on the deck. Bill Britwell had come out of the doors behind us, followed by Graves and Howard Swainton, who must have suspected that the drama they had concocted was reaching a conclusion. "Oh, yes," I said, "you can come out of hiding now."

She must have believed me because she lifted her hands and carefully removed the mask. She was only a little nervous as she stood in the moonlight, smiling at her husband. And the Judge and the mystery writer, for once, had nothing to say.

"Such a pleasure, isn't it?" I asked them, "to have Mrs. Mavis Britwell back with us again."

THE ROCK OF GIBRALTAR looked much as expected, towering over the strange little community which can be looked at as the last outpost of a vanishing Empire or as a tiny section of the Wimbledon of fifty years ago, tacked improbably on to the bottom of Spain. The good ship *Boadicea* was safely docked the next morning and, as the passengers disembarked for a guided tour with a full English tea thrown in, I stood, once more at the rail, this time in the company of Mr. "Miscarriage of Justice" Graves. I had just taken him for a guided tour round the facts of the Britwell case.

"So she decided to vanish?" he asked me.

"Not at all. She went to stay with her old friend, Miss Gloria de la Haye, for a few days." And then I asked him, "She didn't look familiar to you?"

"No. No, I can't say she did. Why?"

"'Old men forget'"—I wasn't about to explain—"'yet all shall be forgot.'"

"What did you say?" His Lordship wasn't following my drift.

"I said, 'What a load of trouble you've got.'"

"Trouble? You're not making yourself clear, Rumpole."

"You as good as accused the Reverend Bill of shoving his dear wife through the porthole." I recited the charges. "You reported the story to the ship's captain, who no doubt wired it to the Gibraltar police. That was clear publication and a pretty good basis for an action for defamation. Wouldn't you say?"

"Defamation?" The Judge repeated the dread word. "Oh, yes," I reminded him, "and juries have been quite absurdly generous with damages lately. Remember my offer to defend you?" My mind went back to a distant bail application. "Please call on my services at any time."

"Rumpole"—the Judicial face peered at me anxiously—"you don't honestly think they'd sue?"

"My dear Judge, I think you're innocent, of course, until you're proved guilty. That's such an important principle to keep in mind on all occasions."

And then I heard a distant cry of "Rumpole!" Hilda was kitted out and ready to call on the Barbary apes.

"Ah, that's my wife. I'd better go. We're on a honeymoon too, you see. Our second. And it may disappoint you to know, we're innocent of any crime whatsoever."

# The Time of His Life

CAROLYN WHEAT

"**N**ot much curb appeal," Margot said, her green eyes peering over the tops of her oversized sunglasses. "But could make someone a nice fixer-upper."

"Margot," the younger woman in the next lounge chair said with a giggle, "you can't talk about him like that. He's a man, not a house." The two basked in the sun on the Lido deck of the *Mayan Princess*, having staked out their spot right next to the Sea Breeze bar, the one with the cutest bartenders.

The object of the women's scrutiny sat in the Jacuzzi, his bald head leaning back over the rim, taking in the sun's blistering rays. He'd be pink as watermelon by the end of the day, and he'd wear his sunburn proudly, tangible evidence that he was having the time of his life.

That was, after all, the motto of the Festival Cruise Lines.

"You'll have the time of your life," the perky honey-blond spokesmodel promised as she danced the macarena with her morning-show co-star on the deck of a Festival ship. "Whether you choose three fun-filled days on the *Mayan Princess* or a three-week scenic adventure on the *Eskimo Princess*, whether you dance to a calypso beat on the *Jamaican Princess* or learn the hula on board the *Hawaiian Princess*, we guarantee you'll never forget your Festival Cruise."

Margot's whisky-deep, cigarette baritone replied, "Sure I can, hon. It's the same principle exactly. When you're young, you want flash, you want to impress people. You get a little older, a little wiser, you'll settle for comfort instead of style. You'll put more work into it, keep it a little longer. Renovate what you've got instead of trading up."

Her companion giggled again. "So who do you see him with?" She pointed a pink-nailed hand in the general direction of the bar. "That fat woman with the umbrella in her drink?"

Margot's answering frown was all in her voice, not on her face. No need to invite wrinkles. "We in the industry prefer the term *zaftig*."

"Oh, is that French for porky?" Sherri ran her manicured hand over the tan flesh of her exposed belly, a belly that sported a neat gold ring in the button, which even the bald man in the hot tub thirty feet away could see was an outie.

"Warning, hon. We don't talk that way about our clients, even when they're not listening. The key to success is respect. R-E-S-P—"

"I know how to spell it," Sherri said with a pout the bald man found extremely sexy. "I heard that old song about a million times. Besides," another sip of the strawberry daiquiri found its way into Sherri's pink-lip-sticked mouth, "she's not our client. She doesn't even know we exist. And neither does he."

"Yet," was Margot's response, which Sherri dutifully echoed.

"Yet."


THE WOMAN AT THE BAR wore sunglasses too—old ones that turned up at the ends like cats' eyes and had little rhinestones at the points and along the sides, the kind teenagers liked to wear when they were goofing on Grandma. But she wasn't wearing them as a hoot, she'd always liked sunglasses like these, and she was going to wear them. Besides, they'd been a present from the only man she'd ever loved, and so what if she'd loved him in the fifties and these were the nineties?

She sipped her piña colada and sat back in her seat with a small sigh of satisfaction. How lovely it was to be on a cruise once again. Something about shipboard life just called out to her, begged her to leave her little condo and take to sea. She loved the organized leisure of it, the decadent pursuit of enjoyment that stretched from the morning breakfast of exotic tropical fruit garnished with flowers to the last after-dinner drink after the last whirl around the ballroom with Pierre, the dancing teacher.

Pierre was such a nice boy. So smooth and sleek and polite. Not like so many men these days, too busy making money to take time with a woman.

Not like her Herb, who had taken her along on all his business trips.

"I FEEL LIKE a matzo ball," the bald man said, but he made no move to step out of the Jacuzzi. Instead, he lay with his head back, lolling in the sun like a big tomcat, except of course that no tomcat worth the name liked getting wet.

He was as hairy as a tomcat; he needn't worry about burning the skin on his arms or chest because the sun was in no position to penetrate the dark mat of hair that covered him like a coat. His head on the other hand would likely look like a pomegranate by evening.

"Yes, isn't it heavenly?" The petite blonde had just immersed herself in the tub, one gorgeous inch after another, in a slow motion ballet he'd found quite entertaining. Good thing her old bag friend was still over on the lounge chair; he had the blonde all to himself.

She lifted a smooth, shapely leg and watched the water drip from it with an air of amused detachment, as though it were a phantom limb belonging to someone else.

"I had the world's worst cramp sitting over there, and I just knew a dip in this tub would make it all better." She rolled her foot in the air; he watched her calf muscles contract and flex. Her toenails were painted a faint shell pink. The color exactly matched her wisp of a bathing suit, which made a nice contrast with her tanned skin.

He was glad the water was steamy hot. He had a sudden vision of himself sucking those toes, one by one, to the music of her delighted giggle-squeals. The heat disguised the resulting blush. *Why would a cute little dish like this let an old fart like him—*

*Well, there you had it. When was the last time you heard anyone call a girl a 'cute little dish'?* Hell, that kind of talk went out with the forties. *It's not like I'm really old enough to talk like that,* he thought; it's just that—well, somehow girls like the little blonde sent him back to childhood, when his older brothers had talked like that, and it had won them girls like her to go to football games with and take to dances and even marry.

Oh, yes, Eddie had married a girl like that. Old Eddie, his second brother, the one with the dimple, had married a cute little blonde with a giggle and the longest, reddest fingernails in Sheepshead Bay. His mother had had a great deal to say, he recalled, on the subject of those nails.

And she hadn't been wrong. While Eddie was fighting for his country, or at least baking for his country—he'd been a pastry chef in the Navy—Cora Jean had gone and had a kid by a Marine on leave. A Marine who looked nothing at all like Eddie, so that the olive-skinned, curly-headed little boy she named Nicky was a constant reminder.

The funny thing was, Eddie didn't seem to mind. He put Nicky on his lap and tickled him and bought him a baseball glove and tossed the ball with him every night just as if it didn't matter. There was never another kid, so Nicky was all he had. Eddie and Cora Jean and Nicky were just about the happiest family he'd ever seen; the brothers who married nice girls who went to Mass every Sunday were miserable, but Eddie was blessed.

"What are you looking at?" The words could have been a challenge, but she asked them with a playful, flirty quality that took the edge off.

"You," he said with a smile. "You remind me of someone."

More flirty glances from under mascaraed eyelashes. "Someone nice, I hope."

"Someone very nice. Someone I think I was a little bit in love with once."

Her face fell. "Just a little bit in love? Not a whole lot in love?"

"She was married to my brother at the time. Still is, actually. I was a kid, and she was my first crush."

"Oh. That's different, then. I remember my first crush like it was yesterday."

"Sweetie, in your case, it probably was yesterday."

His foot jerked; something had touched it unexpectedly. Something touched it again. Something began teasing the hairs on his leg, playing with them, sliding up and down and causing delicious tingles.

Her foot. Her delicate, pink-toed foot was making its way up, up, up his leg.

All the way up. All the way up to his boxer trunks, all the way up to—

Her giggle had nothing on his, once her foot reached its destination.

\* \* \*

MARGOT'S SMILE was not without humor. Rueful humor, to be sure, but humor nonetheless. When she'd first started in the business, it was her job to cozy up to the mark. She was the one with the bikini and the sweet, seductive smile and the active little foot.

There hadn't been that many hot tubs back then. Back then, you sashayed into the cocktail lounge and stood at the bar, waiting for the mark to come over and light your cigarette. Nowadays, he not only wouldn't flip a lighter open for you, he'd tell you in a snarky voice that he was allergic to smoke.

*Chivalry is dead, hon. It died when the Surgeon General put that first warning on the pack.*

Sherri was okay. Bubbly. Guys liked those champagne blondes who went to their heads and made them silly as geese. They liked her petite fragility and the little-girl quality that contrasted so nicely with her healthy appetite for sex. Margot had been more of a Jane Russell type in her day. Big and buxom and brunette and brazen.

Another rueful smile. Mention Jane Russell to Sherri and the most you'd get is, "The bra lady? Isn't she, like, really old?"

Still, Margot reflected, it could be worse. She still had her figure, not like that old gal at the bar, the one with the weirdo glasses and the too-pink skin. She smoothed more suntan lotion on her arms and moved her head ever so slightly to catch more of the conversation in the Jacuzzi.

Sherri was dangling the hook.

The mark was ready to bite.

She had work to do.


WASN'T IT A COINCIDENCE? Not only were Sherri and Stan both dining in the West Wind Dining Room at the first sitting, they were at the very same table. And not only were they both going into Puerto Vallarta the next morning, they had chosen the exact same excursion, the one that cost a bit more but promised authentic Mexican artifacts and the best margaritas in town at a little cantina off the tourist-beaten track.

Some coincidence, Margot thought with a slightly sour air as she made her way to the dining room. She'd paid a handsome price to the young man at the accommodation desk for the last-minute change. She'd always had better luck at the late sitting herself, but Stan was an earlybird, so Sherri would eat her dinner at six and like it, and go into Puerto Vallarta and walk around the dirty little tourist traps in her espadrilles and hang on Stan's arm and laugh at his jokes until she had him eating out of her hand.

And then—

Then came the fun part. The part where money changed hands.

STAN WAS NO FOOL. He knew a cutie like Sherri wasn't making up to him because he'd suddenly turned into Tom Cruise. She figured he had money, and she figured right. But, hell, what good was that money doing him if it couldn't buy him a couple nights of sitting next to a cuddly blonde who giggled at his jokes and slid her tanned legs close to his under the table?

"I'm in cement," he said to the guy across the table. He wished the guy would shut the hell up so he could get to know Sherri better, but the guy was playing the usual social game of 'whose is bigger?' and that was a game Stan sure as hell hated to lose.

"Biggest cement dealer in Southeast Florida," Stan went on. You need something built, you call Stan the Man. And what do you do, Mr.—"

"Actually, it's *Doctor*," the guy said, which figured. He looked like a guy who never actually did a day's work, just made money by knowing things and making people pay for what he knew.

Stan grunted; it was his social duty to ask the next question, to nudge the guy into telling all about his specialty. But Stan really wasn't interested. He didn't want to waste his time with anyone except the cuddly blonde. Hell, he was here for the time of his life, wasn't he?

Well he wasn't going to have *that* listening to some goofus talk about podiatry, or whatever.

Dr. Feigenbaum as it turned out was not a podiatrist; he was a heart specialist. He talked about triple bypasses and heart transplants and artificial hearts until even his wife stopped beaming with pride and started nudging him in the ribs to shut up so someone else could get a word in edgewise.

"My late husband, Herb, died of heart failure," the plump little woman sitting next to Stan said. She pulled an honest-to-God lace hankie out of a straw bag and dabbed at her eyes under her rhinestone glasses.

That shut the doc up at last. Stan turned his full attention to Sherri, who was biting the tails off her shrimp cocktail with such sensuous enjoyment that Stan felt a stirring in his Bermuda shorts.

PUERTO VALLARTA was colorful and noisy. Solid little Mexican women wearing four layers of clothing in ninety-degree temperatures hefted huge armfuls of blankets and displayed them before the tourists with impassive Mayan faces. Sherri clung to Stan's arm with a proprietary air that amused him; overnight they had turned into a couple.

Behind them, a discreet distance away, Margot followed unobtrusively. When Sherri turned to her and glared a warning, she took an immediate and profound interest in a window display of Oaxacan animals, intricately carved and brightly painted.

The plump older woman from the ship stopped also. "What a cute little toothpick holder," she said in a breathless voice. "I wonder why the toothpicks are such a strange color?"

*Because it's not a toothpick holder, you ninny. It's a porcupine and those are its quills.*

She decided the woman would make a good cover in case Stan suspected he was being followed. So she swallowed her annoyance and explained the animal carvings, pointing out that many of them were of mythical animals like the dragon with red-orange flames coming out of its mouth.

When she moved to the next window, the little woman, who introduced herself as Rose, followed with more questions. Why were there so many images of the sun and moon? Why so many snakes? Weren't all the skeletons morbid?

"I've heard they even make candy skulls," Rose said in her breathy voice. "I can't believe any parent would let a child eat candy in the shape of a skull. It doesn't sound nice at all."

*Mexico, my dear ninny, is many things, but nice isn't one of them.*

"The Day of the Dead is very important in Mexico," Margot said. She was aware that she sounded like a tour guide, but what the hell—she might as well play the role so long as Sherri and Stan were still in view up ahead. "Families honor their dead here; they take picnic lunches to the cemetery and have a party among the gravestones."

"Well," Rose replied, drawing herself to her full five-foot height, "all I can say is, we don't do things like that in St. Louis."

* * *

"OH, LOOK, isn't that one cute?" Sherri pointed her pink-nailed finger at one of the Day of the Dead tableaux. They were all three-sided boxes with figures inside. Musicians played instruments and dancers danced and one showed a judge sentencing a prisoner and another showed a couple getting married. And each and every single one of the figures inside the boxes were skeletons, white skeletons with clothes on and big empty eye sockets and death's head grins.

"What a wonderful Halloween present." Sherri picked up one of the boxes and thrust it in Stan's face. "Doesn't this look just like the ship?"

Stan nodded. The artist who'd made this scene might have copied it directly from the Lido deck of the *Mayan Princess*. There was the salt-water pool, where skeleton-children swam in painted blue water. There was the spa, a painted blue circle with two skeletons enjoying the hot water. A twisted bit of cardboard mimicked the water slide; one skeleton with its bony arms and legs outstretched came down the slide while two others waited on the ladder to take the plunge. Paper umbrellas covered tiny plastic tables, and the skeletons in the dollhouse plastic chairs held little tiny tropical drinks in their skeleton hands.

The image struck him as a lot of things: spooky, weird, sicko, off-the-wall, unnerving, and just plain wacky.

It was not cute.

He bought it for her anyway. He'd have bought her the *Mayan Princess* if she'd asked him for it.

And he could have done it, too. With cash.

"You know what would turn me on?" she whispered in his ear between the appetizer and the pasta course at dinner that night. "Making love on the deck. Under the stars." Her hot breath licked his ear.

His Bermuda shorts suddenly felt tight. The vision of him and Sherri on a deck chair roused him in a way that nothing had in a long time.

He'd been busy making money. Too busy to have a good time.

But that was about to change; he was going to go out on that deck as soon as the moon rose and find a secluded place where he and Sherri could—

"More fettuccine, sir?"

He nodded, not really having heard the question. A huge blob of white noodles landed on his plate.

"On the slide," she whispered, and this time more than her breath licked his earlobe.

"What did you—"

"On the water slide. Won't that be exotic? We'll be up on top and then, just when we're ready to well, let's just say we'll come down the slide together."

She put heavy emphasis on the word *come*. He almost did.


THE NEXT MORNING, Margot stepped onto the Lido deck wearing her lime green stretch pants and tank top, a purple straw hat that matched her sandals shading her from the sun. She registered the tiniest of frowns when she saw Sherri sitting alone at the table next to the Sea Breeze bar.

"Where's your escort this morning?" She slipped into the chair next to Sherri but perched on the edge, ready to leave as soon as she spotted Stan's boisterous Hawaiian shirt.

"We were supposed to meet here at nine," Sherri said with more than a hint of pique in her voice. "I've been waiting at least an hour. I hope he hasn't had a heart attack or anything."

Margot's lip turned up slightly. *Had she ever been so young, so innocently self-assured that she believed the only reason a man would miss an opportunity to be with her was that he was dead?*

"Did you think to check with his room steward?" The minute the words left her mouth, Margot realized her mistake. No question that began with the words *did you think* was likely to produce an answer she'd be happy with.

Sherri tossed her blonde curls. "Well, I didn't want to look like some kind of slut. Like I was being too eager or anything. You said yourself that the buyer has to be the one who moves the sale."

"Right. He's on the Riviera deck; I'll just go below and—"

The deckhands had just removed the netting and turned on the water slide when something slid down the chute and hit the water with a loud splash.

It was Stan. Very naked and very dead. Very like the skeleton on the slide in Sherri's Day of the Dead tableau. Very like the way Sherri had suggested they make love the night before.

* * *

THERE WAS A ship's doctor, of course. Dr. Suchat, in due course—with the pool cordoned off and the passengers herded into the Sailors' Rest bar on the promenade deck for an impromptu macarena contest—pronounced Stan dead. He concluded the man was the victim of a massive heart attack, probably brought on by an unseemly display of sexual athletics following a particularly cholesterol-laden dinner at the early sitting.

"He insisted on going to the Grand Buffet last night," a tearful Sherri confessed. "He said he was only going to look at the fancy ice carvings, but I knew he couldn't resist that Death by Chocolate."

Saying the name of the dessert brought on a fresh flood of tears. Margot handed Sherri another tissue from a box she'd found under the bar.

She felt like crying herself. She and Sherri stood to make a nice fat bundle from old Stan, and he'd gone and eaten himself to death before they could capitalize on their investment.

"Will you," Sherri said between gusty sobs, "will you bury him at sea?"

"No, no, do not think about that," Dr. Suchat said in his best bedside manner. "We have a policy in these matters and there is no need for you to—"

"What he means," Margot cut in, "is that they'll pack the poor SOB in ice like a red snapper. I'd order my drinks straight up from now on, hon. You ask for ice, you could be drinking a little piece of Stanley."

Dr. Suchat glared at her. She glared back.

Then a new voice made itself heard.

"I wondered if you might be able to use my help."

"Sir, this area is closed to the passengers at the moment," one of the white-coated stewards said. "If you'll just step this—"

"Dr. Feigenbaum," Sherri said, "thank you so much for coming. I'd feel so much better if you had a look at him."

Dr. Feigenbaum introduced himself to the ship's doctor, whose face wore an expression of mingled relief and pique. On the one hand, it was clear he didn't welcome an outsider looking at his body; on the other, if there was heat to be taken, it would be good to share it with someone else. Dead American passengers, in his experience, meant heat. And an American specialist would carry much more weight with American authorities than a doctor from Thailand.

"I would welcome your professional courtesy, Doctor," Suchat said with as much grace as he could muster.

After ten minutes of poking and prodding, opening orifices and peering inside, Dr. Feigenbaum proclaimed that the deceased had succumbed to—a massive myocardial infarction.

"Oh, thank you, Dr. Feigenbaum," Sherri said, her eyelashes working overtime, "I feel so much better now."

"That is the same thing as a heart attack," Dr. Suchat muttered, as much to himself as to Margot. "The man is agreeing with me. Why can he not just say so?"

Margot was only half-listening. Most of her brain was engaged in speculation. Was it too late, she wondered, for Sherri to turn her attention to the tall, skinny Texan with the bad toupee and the five-million-dollar tire business?

Was he at the early sitting in the West Wind dining room or the late sitting in the East Wind? Was he booked for a sightseeing tour in Ensenada, or was he going snorkeling?

Perhaps Sherri could arrange to sit next to him at the ten-dollar blackjack table. That talented little foot could work its way up his skinny calf, and they might go home winners after all.

But the skinny Texan had heard all about Sherri's pursuit of the late Stanley, and he made it clear he wasn't interested in a trip down the water slide. Neither was the insurance broker from New Jersey or the bowling alley owner from Rhode Island.

"That," Margot said over her third Gibson, "may have been my lowest point in this business. To be turned down by a man whose claim to fame is that he invented the Suds 'N' Strikes combination laundromats and bowling alleys."

"It's not my fault he saw me and Stanley making out on the bus from Puerto Vallarta," Sherri whined.

One more whine and Margot was going to leave her ashore next time, cuddly blonde or no cuddly blonde. She wasn't so old herself that she couldn't pull in a mark if she put her mind to it. In fact, she'd try it right now. She'd get right up this minute and sashay over to the Sea Breeze bar and take out a cigarette and wait for that distinguished-looking man with the blistered nose to light it for her.

"Oh, God, here comes a smoker," the blistered man said in a loud voice to no one in particular. "I'm off to seek refuge in the civilized air of the Jolly Roger. That's the only smoke-free lounge on this tub."

BY THE TIME the ship reached port and was pushed into its berth by a tiny red tugboat that somehow reminded Margot of the little pink woman with the cat's eye glasses, she and Sherri were no longer speaking. They walked down the gangplank separately, moving carefully even in the crush so as to avoid any possible physical contact. They each made for the direction of their luggage, grouped by color according to the deck they'd slept on, without exchanging a word. Margot picked up her imitation leopard-skin cases and marched off toward a waiting taxi she'd arranged before the trip.

*Never again*, she thought as she gave the driver the address—in a much less fashionable section of Los Angeles than she'd led Sherri to believe. Never again would she go to sea with a total neophyte. Never again would she teach the tricks of her trade to an ungrateful little bitch who had no more sense than a Shih Tzu. Never again would she—

Unless, of course, she could reach Joyce. Joyce was a natural. And the *Jamaican Princess* sailed in four days. With good connections, they could meet in Boca and—

She leaned back in the cab with a smile of satisfaction.

SHERRI STOOD at the curbside, her matching pink leather suitcases spread out on the sidewalk. She looked forlorn, as if she'd been abandoned by her only friend. "Is someone picking you up, dear?" A chirpy, breathless voice sounded in her ear. She turned to see the plump lady from the boat, the one with the pointy glasses.

"No," she replied. "I was going to call a cab, but—"

"Oh, don't bother, dear. I can give you a ride as far as the airport. I think I heard you say you had a plane to catch."

Sherri smiled and thanked the lady profusely. As the porters piled their luggage into the roomy trunk, she stepped into the late-model El Dorado with the tinted windows and settled herself into the real leather upholstery with a sigh of relief.

"You did very well, my dear," Rose said as she guided the huge car out of the pier parking area. "I'm extremely pleased with your performance. You are a natural, if I do say so myself."

The breathy quality had left her voice; she sounded very much like a boss lady complimenting a subordinate.

And Sherri sounded every inch the subordinate as she replied, "Coming from you, Mrs. Ballantine, that's a real compliment. Of course," she went on, "it was just sheer luck that Dr. Feigenbaum showed up when he did. I was afraid the police wouldn't listen to that Thai doctor. If they'd held the body for autopsy—"

Rose allowed herself the slightest of deprecating coughs. "Nothing in this business is 'sheer luck,' Sheryl Anne. You should know that by now. Dr. Feigenbaum was a dear friend of my late husband's, even if he wasn't able to save Herb's life with that last bypass."

"You mean you knew Dr. Feigenbaum would be on board?" Sherri laughed. "If I'd known that, I wouldn't have missed two nights' sleep worrying about the doctor finding digitalis in his bloodstream. I was afraid Dr. Suchat would see that puncture wound on his thigh and get suspicious."

"Oh, he saw it, dear. I noticed him frowning when he examined the body."

"Then why didn't he say anything? Don't tell me he's on the payroll too?"

"No. That would become so expensive we'd have no profit from our little enterprise. Dr. Suchat is a man who wants to keep his job. He won't keep it if he tells his superiors they have a murder on board. No, a heart attack after—or perhaps during—a bout of unwise sexual congress is one thing, but murder does tend to discourage tourism."

"During?" Sherri blanched as she realized the little brown doctor had known all along that she'd been present when Stan breathed his last.

The smile on Rose's pleasant face wouldn't have looked out of place on Margot's. "And then, of course, there was that awful woman you were traveling with. Dr. Suchat knew very well what she was up to, and since you were working with her, he assumed that the late unlamented Stanley meant a great deal more to you alive than dead. I was counting on that, of course, when I sent you to her for 'instruction.'"

Another thought struck Sherri. As the brown California hills sped by outside the noiseless white carriage, she said, "I couldn't believe it when I saw that Day of the Dead box with the skeleton coming down the slide. I know you had it made and placed in the shop for me to find, but wasn't it incredibly dangerous? What if someone had made the connection?"

"Ah, my dear," Rose replied, her voice carrying a wealth of nostalgia. "It was your first job, and I wanted you to have a souvenir. Something that will always remind you of your professional debut. I still have my souvenir from that first outing with Herb, and I treasure them still."

She fingered the rhinestone sunglasses and a teary smile spread across her pink lips.

"And now," she said a minute later, all business again, "we must plan your next triumph. I'll give you all the details regarding the target at the airport; I've booked you on the *Jamaican Princess* out of Boca Raton."

# Authors' Biographies

## Agatha Christie

Agatha Christie (1890-1976) rightfully earned the title "the grand dame of mystery" with her detectives Hercule Poirot and Miss Jane Marple crisscrossing the English countryside to solve numerous crimes. Born on the south coast of Devon, she had aspirations of becoming a pianist but could not overcome her extreme shyness. After serving as a volunteer nurse in the Royal Air Corps, she later accompanied her second husband, Max Mallowan, on several archeological digs, functioning as the photographer for the expeditions, all of which served her well in writing her 66 novels and 144 short stories.

## Nancy Pickard

Nancy Pickard is an author who just seems to get busier and busier. Her Jenny Cain mystery series has now reached ten volumes, the latest being *Twilight*. She has also recently turned her hand to editing again, with the anthology *First Lady Murders*, featuring various Presidential wives as detectives. Of course, we've barely mentioned appearances in anthologies such as *Funny Bones*, *Diagnosis: Dead*, and *Cat Crimes at the Holidays*.

### Jeremiah Healy

Jeremiah Healy, a graduate of Rutgers College and Harvard Law School, was a professor at the New England School of Law for eighteen years. He is the creator of John Francis Cuddy, a Boston-based private investigator who has appeared in twelve novels, the most recent being *The Only Good Lawyer*. Currently the North American vice-president of the International Association of Crime Writers, he was also president of the Private Eye Writers of America for two years. A lecturer on mystery writing, he has attended mystery conferences in New York, London, Spain, and Austria.

### Chris Rippen

Chris Rippen was born in Haarlem in the Netherlands in 1940. He studied Dutch Language and Literature at the University of Amsterdam and currently teaches literature and writing in Amsterdam. He has had three crime novels published, as well as a collection of short stories. A winner of the Dutch crime writing award The Golden Noose, he is also the chairman of the Dutch/Flemish branch of the IACW.

### John Lutz

John Lutz is one of the most skilled mystery writers working today with his most recent novels being *The Ex* and *Final Seconds*, co-authored with David August. A winner of the Mystery Writers of America's Edgar award for best short fiction, he has written stories that have appeared in dozens of anthologies and magazines. He lives in Webster Groves, Missouri.

### Richard Deming

Richard Deming (1915-1983) rose to the peak of his form in the post-pulp era of the 1960s. He worked on projects as diverse as novelizations of the television shows *Starsky and Hutch* and *Charlie's Angels* under the pseudonym Max Franklin and police procedurals and novelizations of *The Mod Squad* under his own name. He also wrote non-fiction about such subjects as the metric system and American spies. His considerable contribution to short fiction includes almost 150 stories, of which "Honeymoon Cruise" is one of his best.

## Jacques Toes

Born in 1950 in Hague, the Netherlands, Jac. Toes enjoyed a restless youth that was followed by an even stormier career as a sailor in the Merchant Navy. Later, he graduated at the University of Nijmegen with a degree in literature and linguistics. He has taught secondary education in various colleges, and in 1980 founded the broadcasting station "Radio City." He is the author of several crime novels, including *Twin-Tracks* and *Settling Accounts*, both nominated for the Golden Noose, the Dutch award for best crime novel, and *Fotofinish*, which won the Golden Noose for best crime novel of 1997. He is a full-time novelist who also works as a scriptwriter for various Dutch media.

## Arnaldo Correa

Arnaldo Correa got his start in fiction writing at age sixteen, when a short story of his sold to Cuba's most popular magazine. Deciding to be a writer, he tried to follow Jack London's example and traveled the world as a mucker in the mines of Nevada, a sailor on the Mississippi, a waiter, and an engineer. While biding his time to write about his experiences, he has published five collections of short fiction and one novel. His latest book is about the exploits of Sherlock Holmes's Cuban grandson.

## Benjamin M. Schutz

Benjamin M. Schutz's fiction has appeared in *Deadly Allies*, *Unusual Suspects*, and *The Edgar Award Book*. Recent novels featuring private detective Leo Haggerty include *A Fistful of Empty* and *Mexico Is Forever*. A clinical and forensic psychologist, he lives in Virginia.

## Piet Teigeler

Piet Teigeler found that when he retired from journalism after thirty years, he had more questions than answers. He decided to write ten crime novels to try to answer those questions, and the result includes *Dead Lady on Saint-Anna*, *Elvis Dead in Deurne*, and *Three Dead Masters*. His novels feature the Belgian police officer Commissaris Carpentier and his aide Chief Inspector Dewit, but he claims his antagonists are his real heroes. He lives in Spain.

## Edward D. Hoch

Edward D. Hoch makes his living as a writer in a way that very few other people can attest to—he works almost entirely in short fiction. With hundreds of stories primarily in the mystery and suspense genres, he has created such notable characters as Simon Ark, the 2,000-year-old detective, Nick Velvet, the professional thief who only steals worthless objects, and the calculating Inspector Leopold, whose appearance in the short story "The Oblong Room" won his creator the Edgar award for best short story.

## Ralph McInerny

Ralph McInerny is the Michael P. Grace Professor of Medieval Studies at the Jacques Maritain Center at the University of Notre Dame. He is a past president of the American Metaphysical Society; the American Catholic Philosophical Association; and the Fellowship of Catholic Scholars. In addition to numerous respected academic publications, he is a well-known writer of fiction with more than forty novels to his credit, including the very popular Father Dowling series, which was the basis for the prime-time television series starring Tom Bosley, and is currently airing nationally and internationally in syndication.

## Jacob Vis

Jacob Vis was born in Haarlem, the Netherlands in 1940, and now lives in Kampen, along the border of the Zuiderzee. He is a professional forester and writes during his spare time. He has written several crime novels, either setting them in Holland or his hometown. Two of his books were nominated for the Golden Gallows, the top prize for best novel in the Netherlands. His latest book, *Wetland*, is based on his personal experiences as a forester.

## Erik Amdrup

Erik Amdrup (1923–1998) was an author who lived in Federicia, Denmark. A doctor of medicine and member of the American Collage of Surgeons, he was the chief surgeon at the municipal hospital in Arhus, and also served as a professor of surgery at the University of Arhus. His first novel, *Greetings from Hans*, was published in 1979, and was followed by many other works, including young adult books and short story collections. A two-time winner of The Golden Handcuffs literary crime award, he also received the Palle Rosenkranz award from the Danish Criminal Academy for his novel *Compound Interest*, which was also made into a television movie.

## Max Allan Collins

Max Allan Collins is a two-time winner of the Shamus award for best novel for his historical mysteries *True Detective* and *Stolen Away*, both featuring Chicago private detective Nate Heller. He is also an accomplished editor, having compiled the anthologies *Murder Is My Business*, *Vengeance Is Hers*, and *Private Eyes*, all with Mickey Spillane. He lives with his wife, author Barbara Collins, and their son in Muscatine, Iowa.

## José Latour

José Latour, an avid reader of crime fiction since he was a teenager, has been heavily influenced by American authors. He began writing at night and on weekends in 1987, while working as a financial analyst at the Cuban Ministry of Finance. In 1990, he gave up his government position to become a full-time writer. He is also the AIEP/IACW vice president for Latin America and head of the organization's Cuban branch. His works include, under the pen name of Javier Moran, *Choque de Leyendas*, *Fauna Nocturna*, and *Medianoche Enemiga*.

## Jan Burke

Jan Burke is the author of a mystery series featuring Irene Kelly, a newspaper reporter who, like her creator, lives and works in southern California. Winner of both the *Ellery Queen Mystery Magazine* Readers Award and the Macavity award for her short fiction, she is a former columnist for the *Long Beach Press-Telegram*.

## Ina Bouman

Ina Bouman lives and writes in Amsterdam, the Netherlands. She has written four novels featuring Jos Welling, an inquisitive journalist with a social conscience and an open mind. Her books explore the dark side of the medical field, including drug and organ trafficking, unethical experiments, and genetic manipulation. She also writes poetry and for the stage. Her latest novel is *Body at Risk*.

## John Mortimer

John Mortimer used his background and family life growing up with his barrister father to pursue a career in the law himself, eventually serving as Queen's Counsel in criminal cases. Educated at Dragon School in Oxford, as well as Harrow and Brasenose Colleges, also in Oxford, he is also a famous novelist, playwright, screenwriter, and literary critic. He lives in the Chiltern home where he grew up, along with his wife, Penny. They have two daughters, one of whom is the actress Emily Mortimer.

## Carolyn Wheat

Like many lawyers these days, Carolyn Wheat has put her legal skills, honed by the Brooklyn chapter of the Legal Aid Society, to good use in her novels, which feature Cass Jameson. Recent novels include *Mean Streak* and *Troubled Waters*. She takes a break from the law to examine a different side of crime in "Show Me the Bones." She has taught mystery writing at the New School in New York City and legal writing at the Brooklyn Law School.

# Permissions